CAT on the RUN

IN CUCUMBER MADNESS!

Text and illustrations copyright © 2024 by Aaron Blabey

All rights reserved. Published by Scholastic Inc.,
Publishers since 1920. SCHOLASTIC and associated logos are trademarks and/or registered trademarks of Scholastic Inc. This edition published under license from Scholastic Australia Pty Limited. First published by Scholastic Australia Pty Limited in 2015.

The publisher does not have any control over and does not assume any responsibility for author or third-party websites or their content.

978-1-339-00092-3

10 9 8 7 6 5 4 3 2 1   24 25 26 27 28

Printed in Italy   183
First U.S. printing 2024

AARON BLABEY

CAT on the RUN

IN CUCUMBER MADNESS!

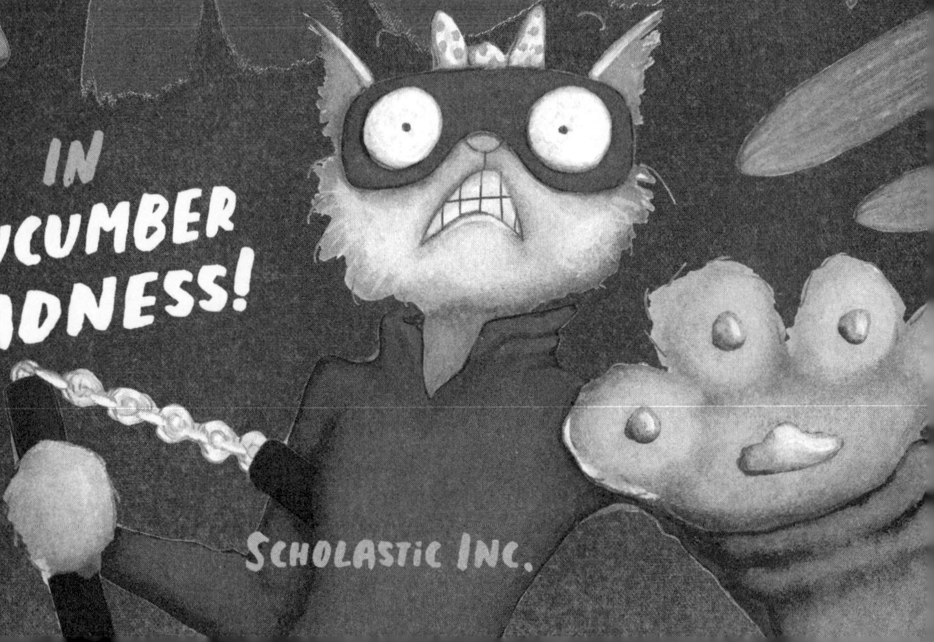

SCHOLASTIC INC.

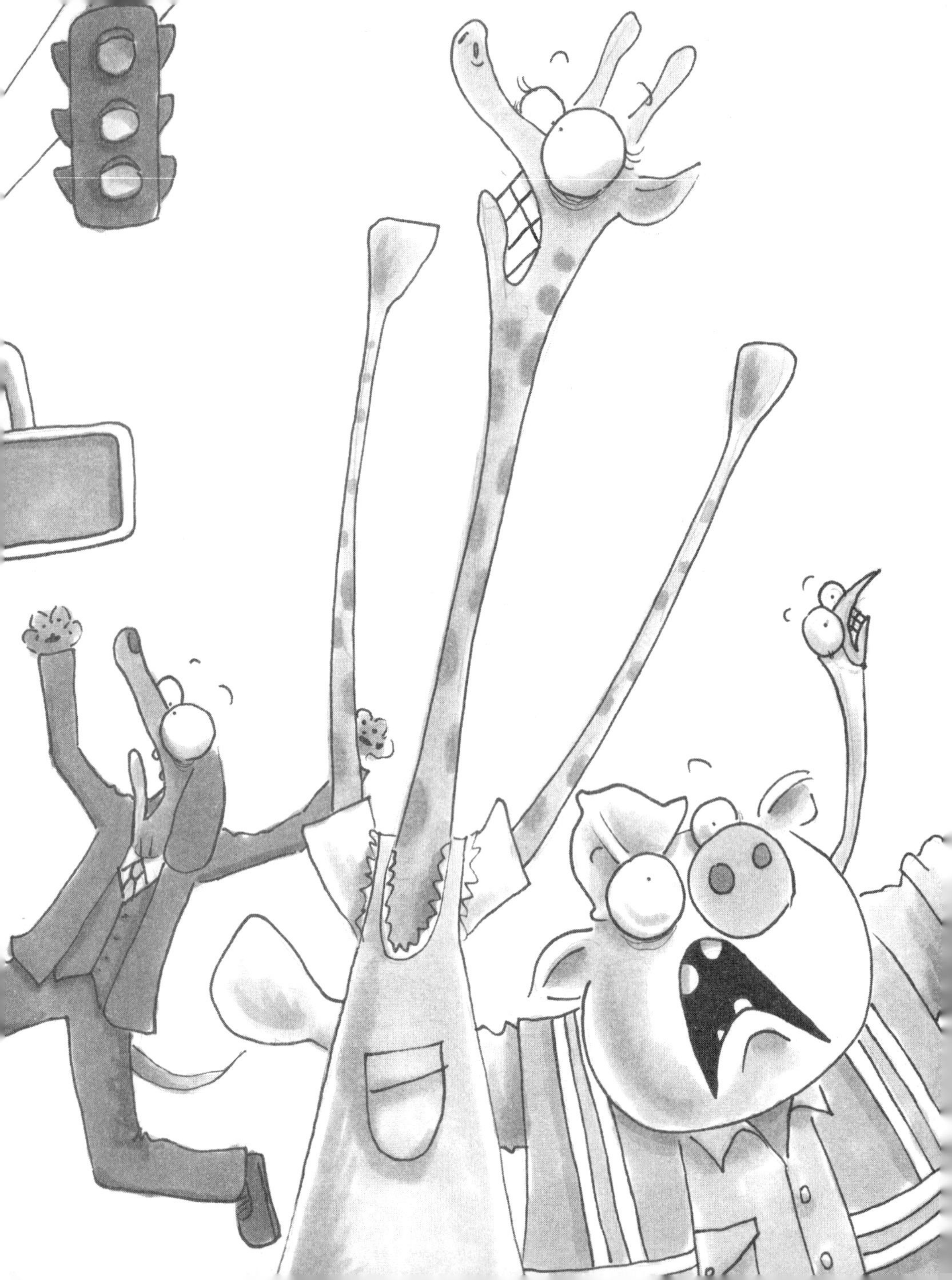

OHMIGOD, SHE'S ON THE LOOSE AND WE'RE ALL GOING TO DIE!

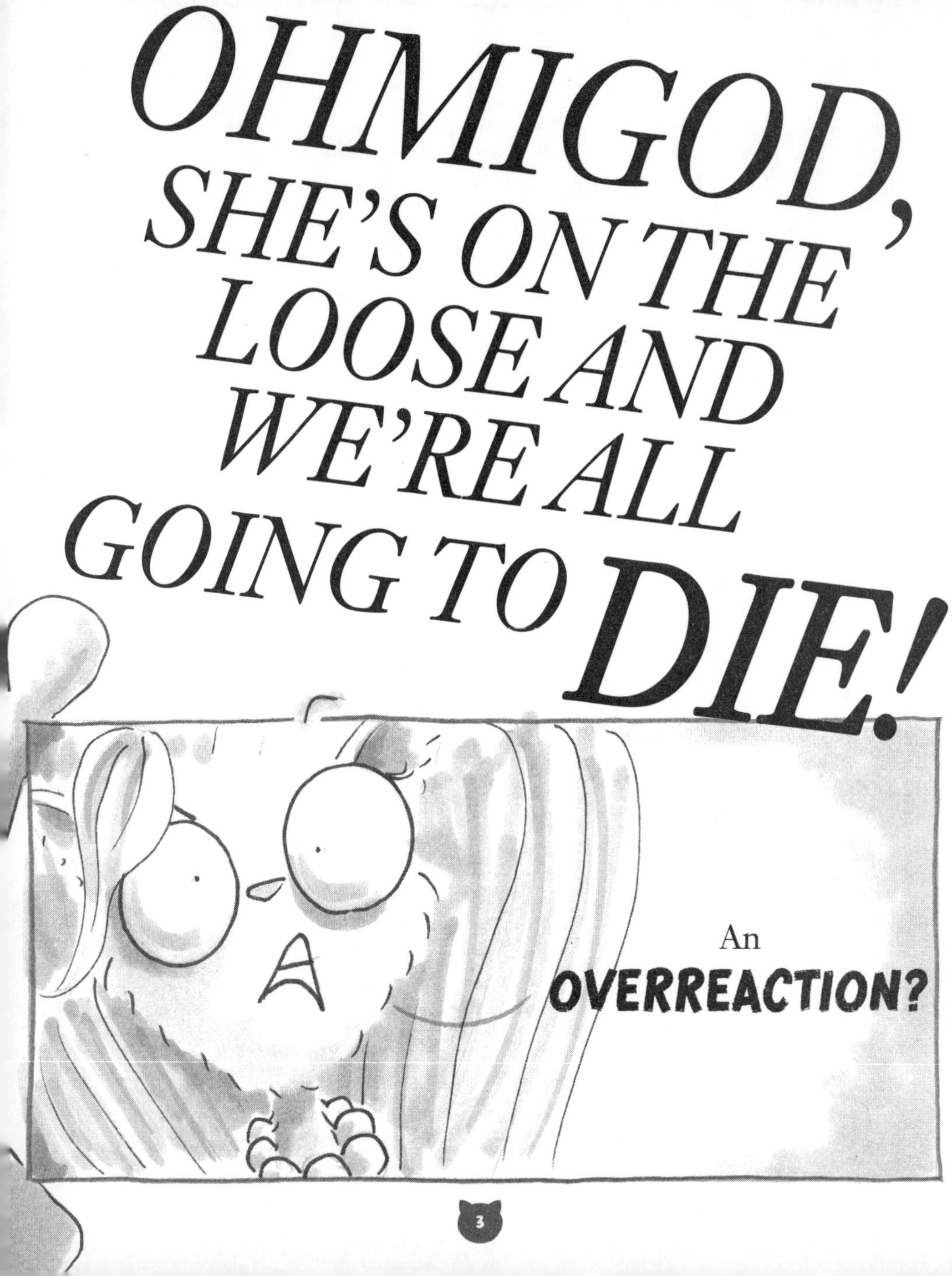
An
OVERREACTION?

NO!

A COLD, HARD FACT.

Just look at this face!

All crazy!

All evil!

All day long!

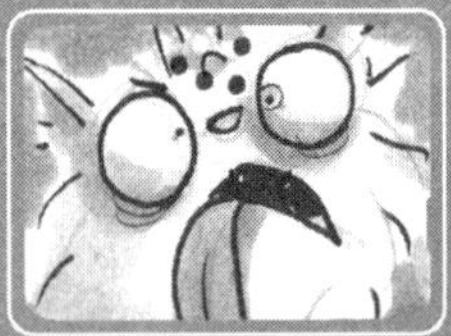

6 NEWS

#FACEOFEVIL

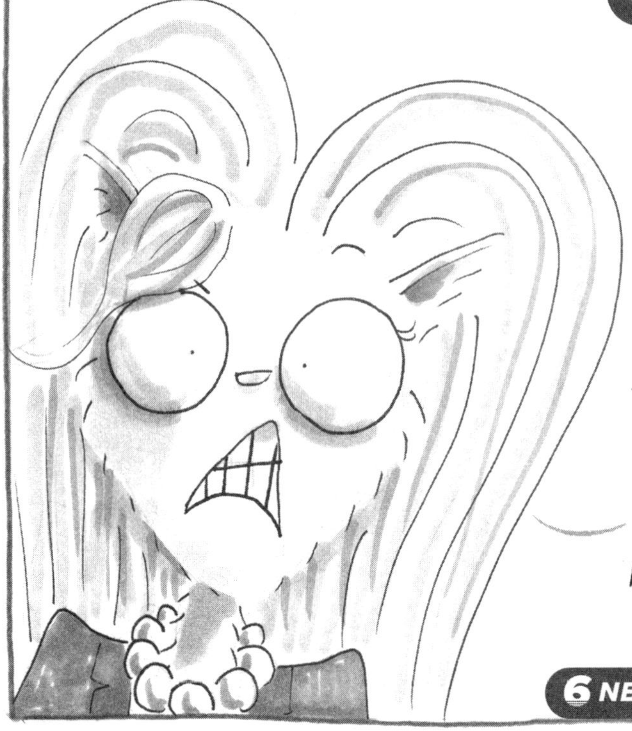

Yes, that's disgraced CAT VIDEO STAR

PRINCESS BEAUTIFUL.

A name that chills you to the bone. I don't like saying it. I just don't.

Who could not see the

MALEVOLENCE

in that face?!

6 NEWS TIFFANY FLUFFIT

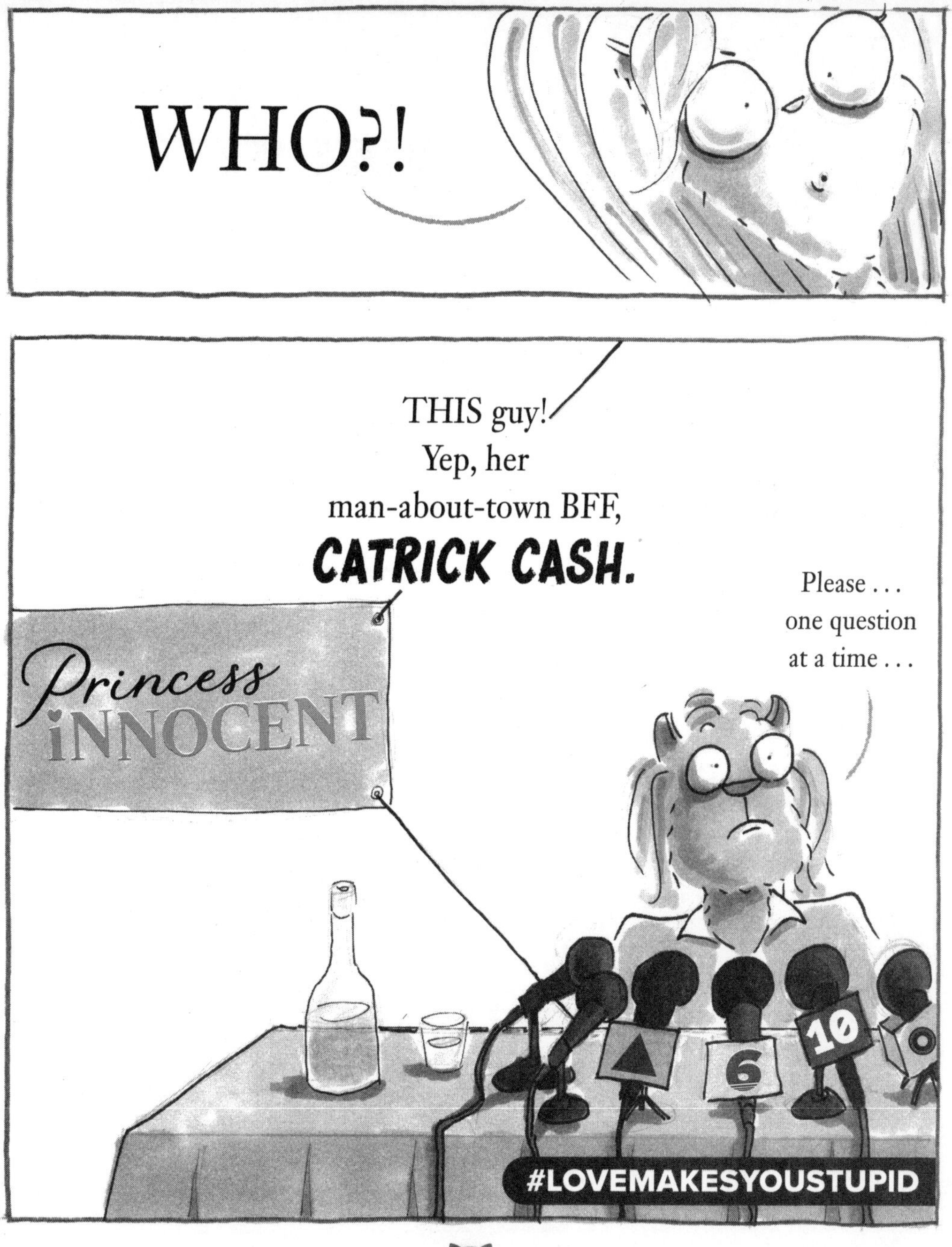
WHO?!
THIS guy!
Yep, her
man-about-town BFF,
CATRICK CASH.
Princess iNNOCENT
Please . . .
one question
at a time . . .
6
10
#LOVEMAKESYOUSTUPID

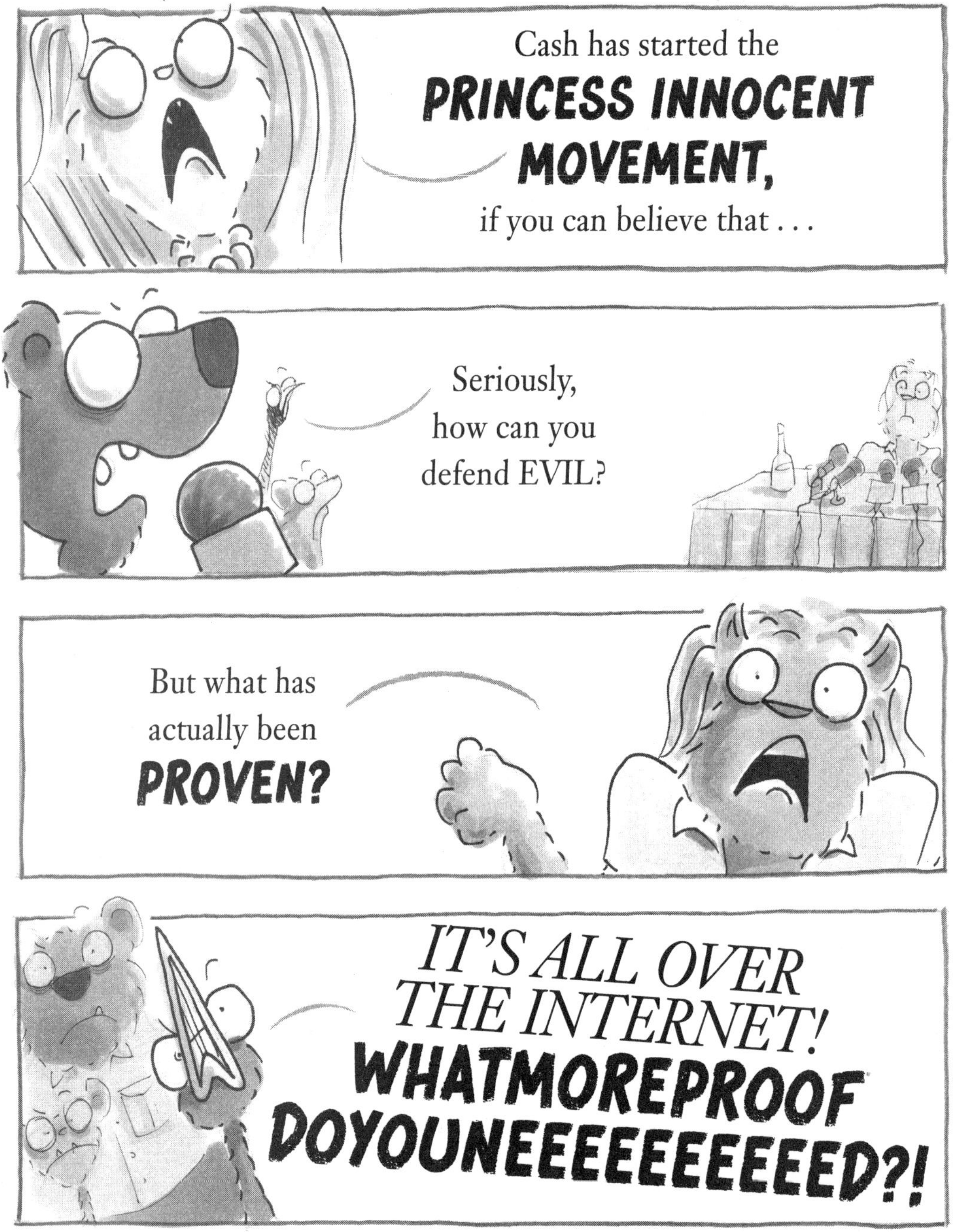
Cash has started the
PRINCESS INNOCENT MOVEMENT,
if you can believe that . . .
Seriously, how can you defend EVIL?
But what has actually been PROVEN?
IT'S ALL OVER THE INTERNET!
WHATMOREPROOF DOYOUNEEEEEEEEEEED?!

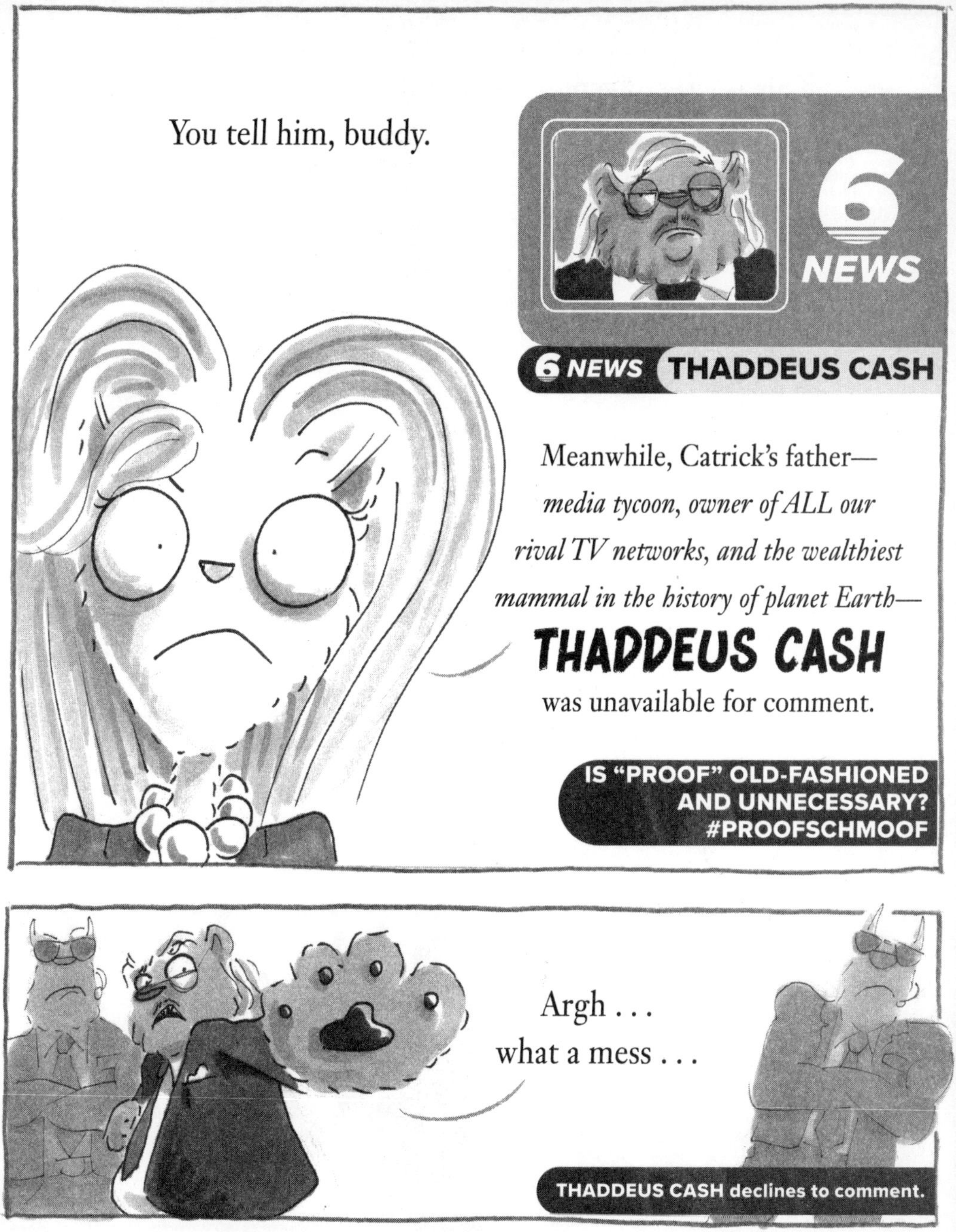
You tell him, buddy.
6 NEWS
6 NEWS THADDEUS CASH
Meanwhile, Catrick's father—
media tycoon, owner of ALL our rival TV networks, and the wealthiest mammal in the history of planet Earth—
THADDEUS CASH
was unavailable for comment.
IS "PROOF" OLD-FASHIONED AND UNNECESSARY? #PROOFSCHMOOF
Argh . . .
what a mess . . .
THADDEUS CASH declines to comment.

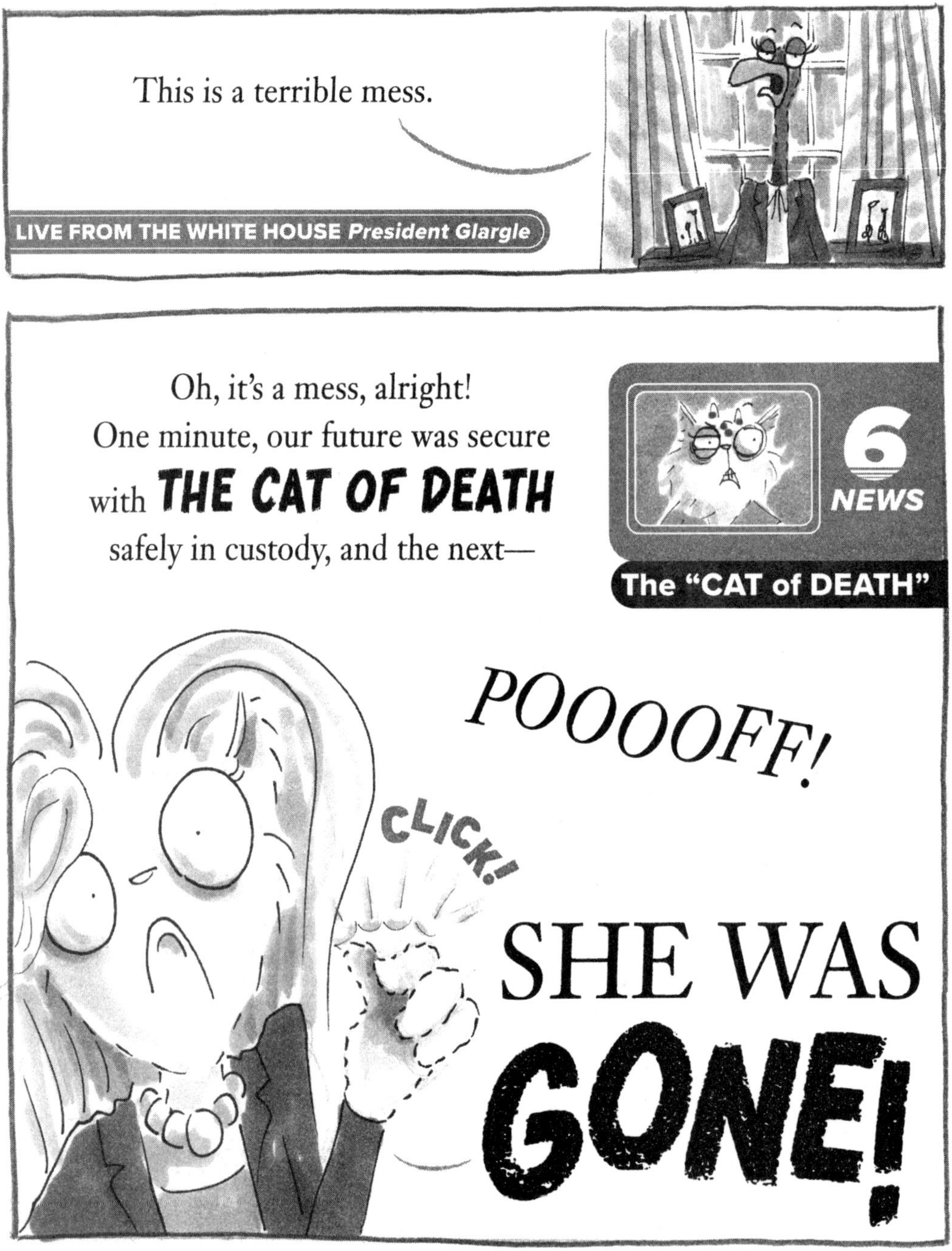
This is a terrible mess.
LIVE FROM THE WHITE HOUSE *President Glargle*
Oh, it's a mess, alright!
One minute, our future was secure
with **THE CAT OF DEATH**
safely in custody, and the next—
6 NEWS
The "CAT of DEATH"
POOOOFF!
CLICK!
SHE WAS
GONE!

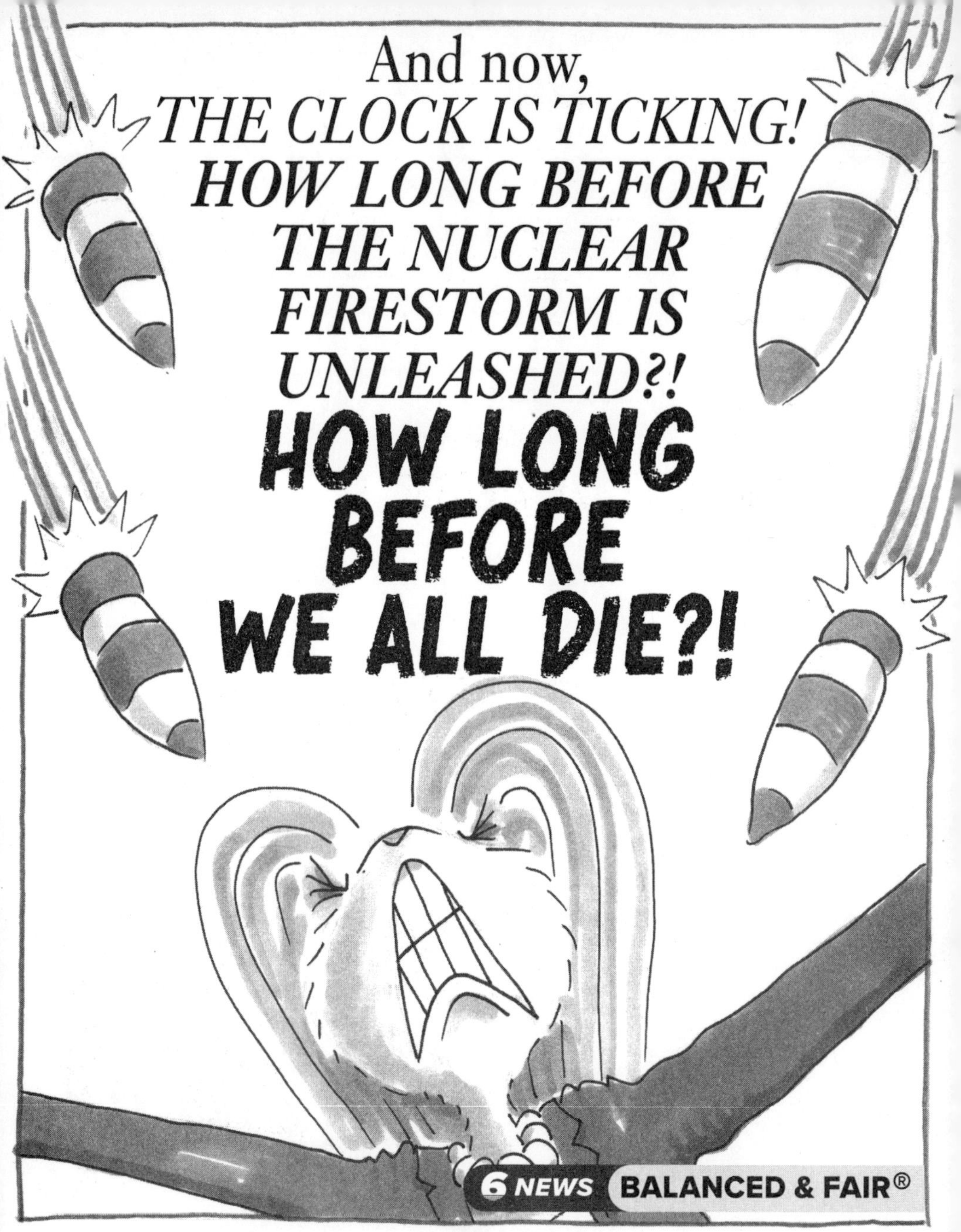
And now,
THE CLOCK IS TICKING!
HOW LONG BEFORE
THE NUCLEAR
FIRESTORM IS
UNLEASHED?!
HOW LONG
BEFORE
WE ALL DIE?!
6 NEWS
BALANCED & FAIR®

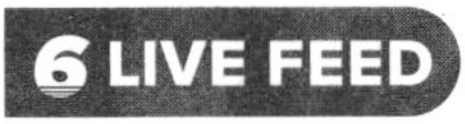

6 LIVE FEED
HAVE YOUR SAY!

- Is anyone else finding this reporter really fear-inducing and manipulative?
- NO, WHAT IS WRONG WITH YOU?!?! TIFFANY TELLS THE TRUTH!!!!!!!!
- Shame on you!
- #TiffanyTruthTeller
- #DontQuestionTHETRUTH
- ITS PEPUL LIK YOO THAT MAK ME SIK!!!!!!!!
- THE WORLD IS ENDING, DON'T YOU GET IT?! TIFFANY IS BRAVE ENOUGH TO CALL IT! AND ALL YOU CAN DO IS THROW SHADE?! OMG.
- #TIFFISBRAVE
- I'm so sorry! I was wrong to question. Thank you for the opportunity to learn from my mistake.
- #JUSTSHUTUP
- Got it. Will do.

*LIFE ON EARTH IS ABOUT TO END!**

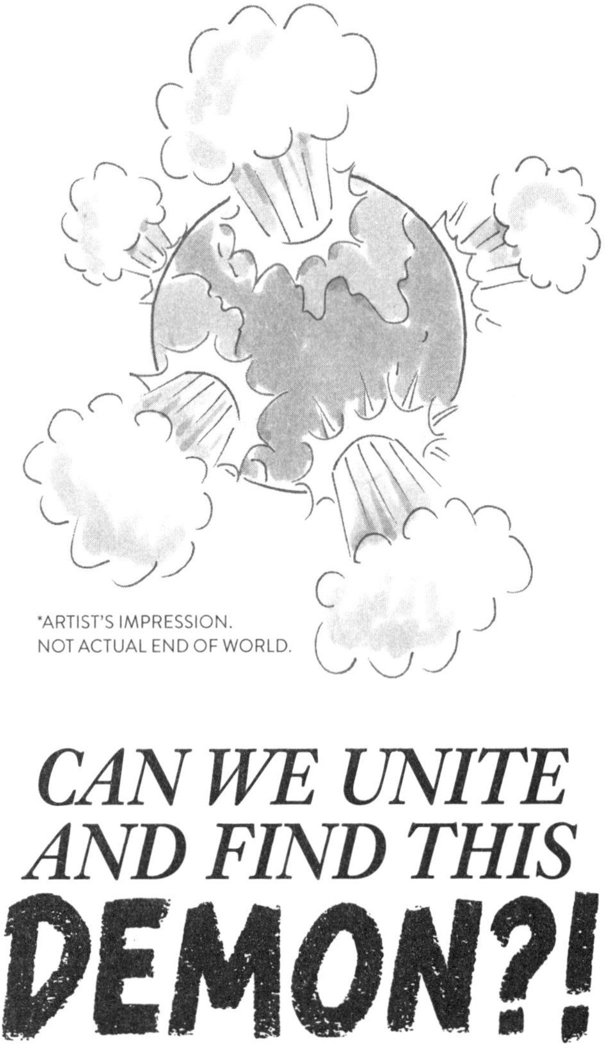

*ARTIST'S IMPRESSION. NOT ACTUAL END OF WORLD.

CAN WE UNITE AND FIND THIS DEMON?!

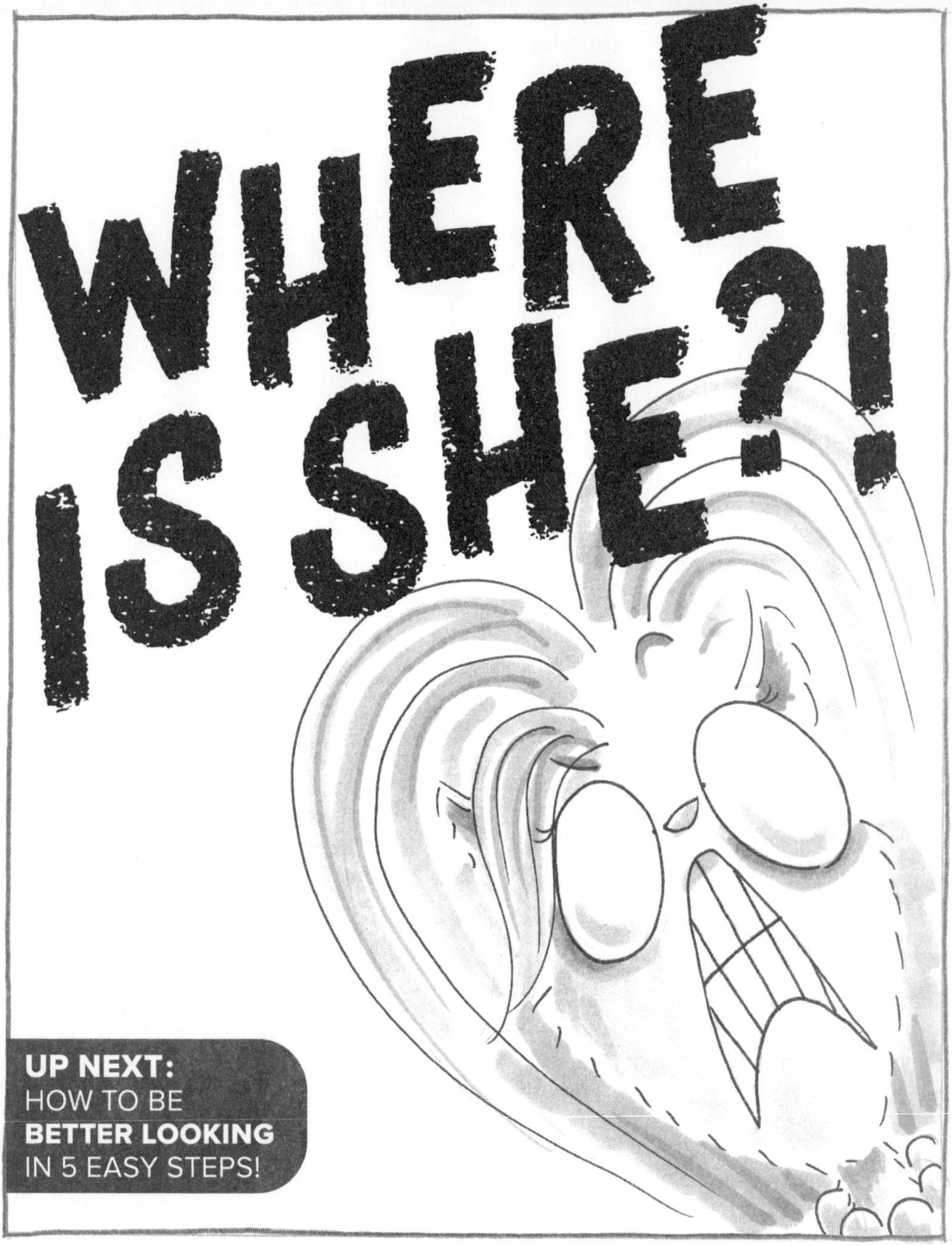
WHERE IS SHE?!
UP NEXT: HOW TO BE BETTER LOOKING IN 5 EASY STEPS!

One
SCAPEGOAT!

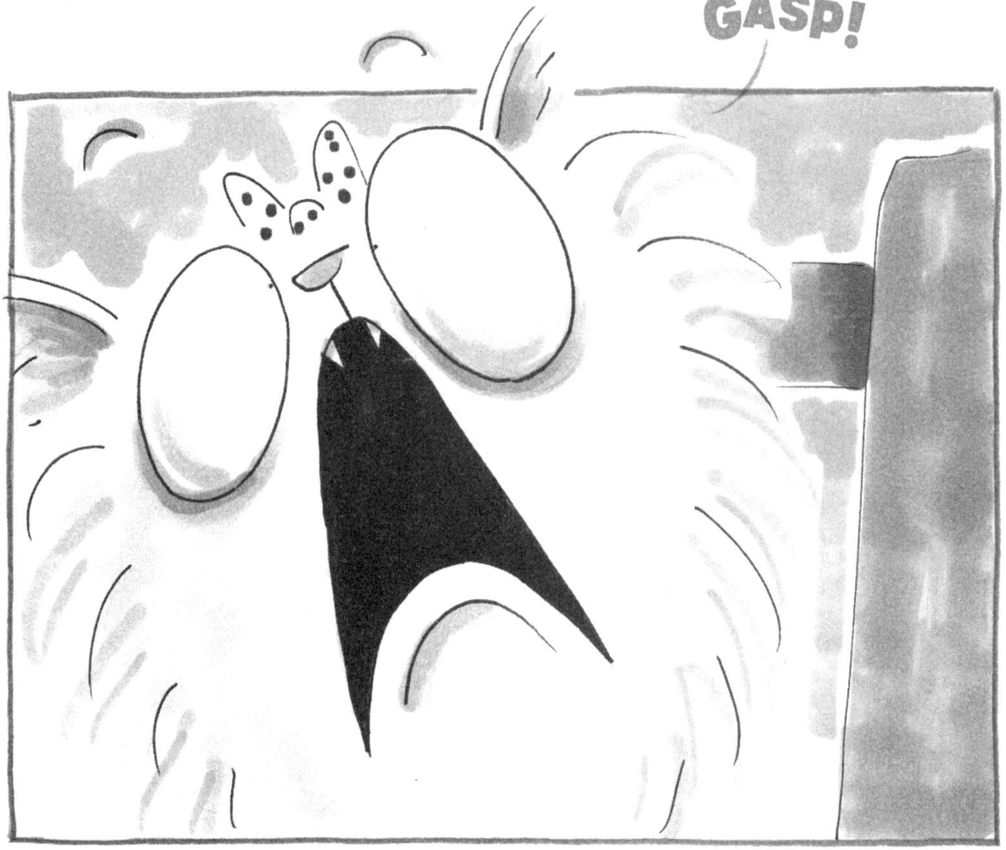
GASP!

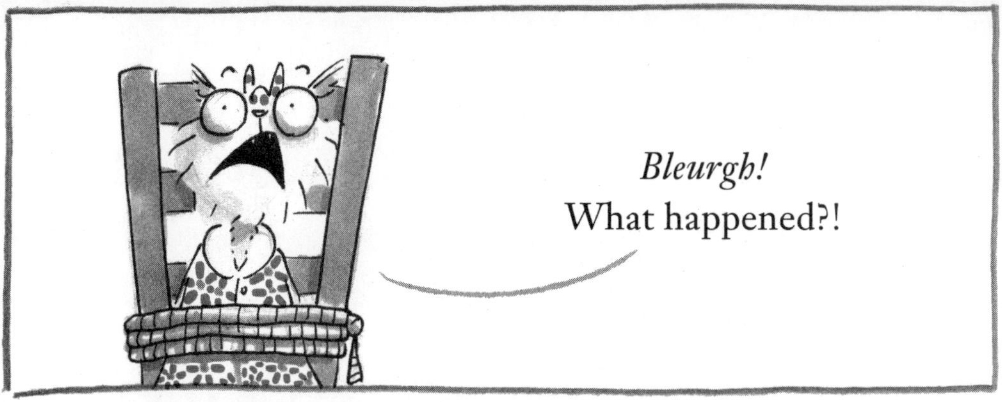
Bleurgh!
What happened?!

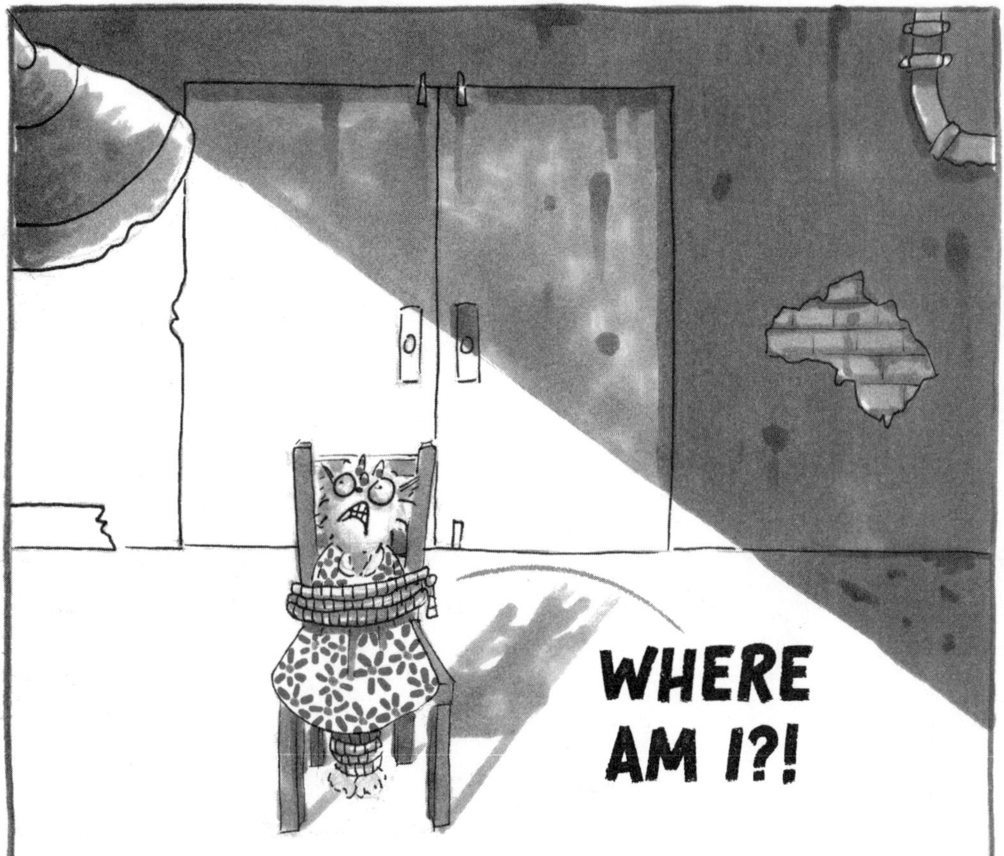
WHERE AM I?!

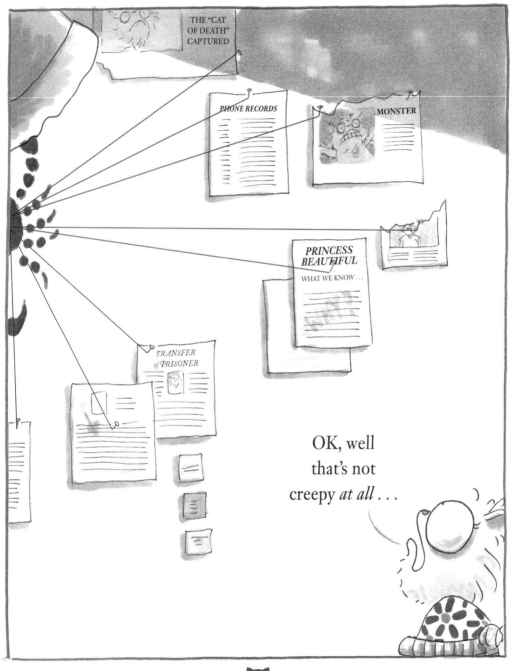

THE "CAT OF DEATH" CAPTURED

PHONE RECORDS

MONSTER

PRINCESS BEAUTIFUL
WHAT WE KNOW . . .

TRANSFER of PRISONER

OK, well that's not creepy *at all* . . .

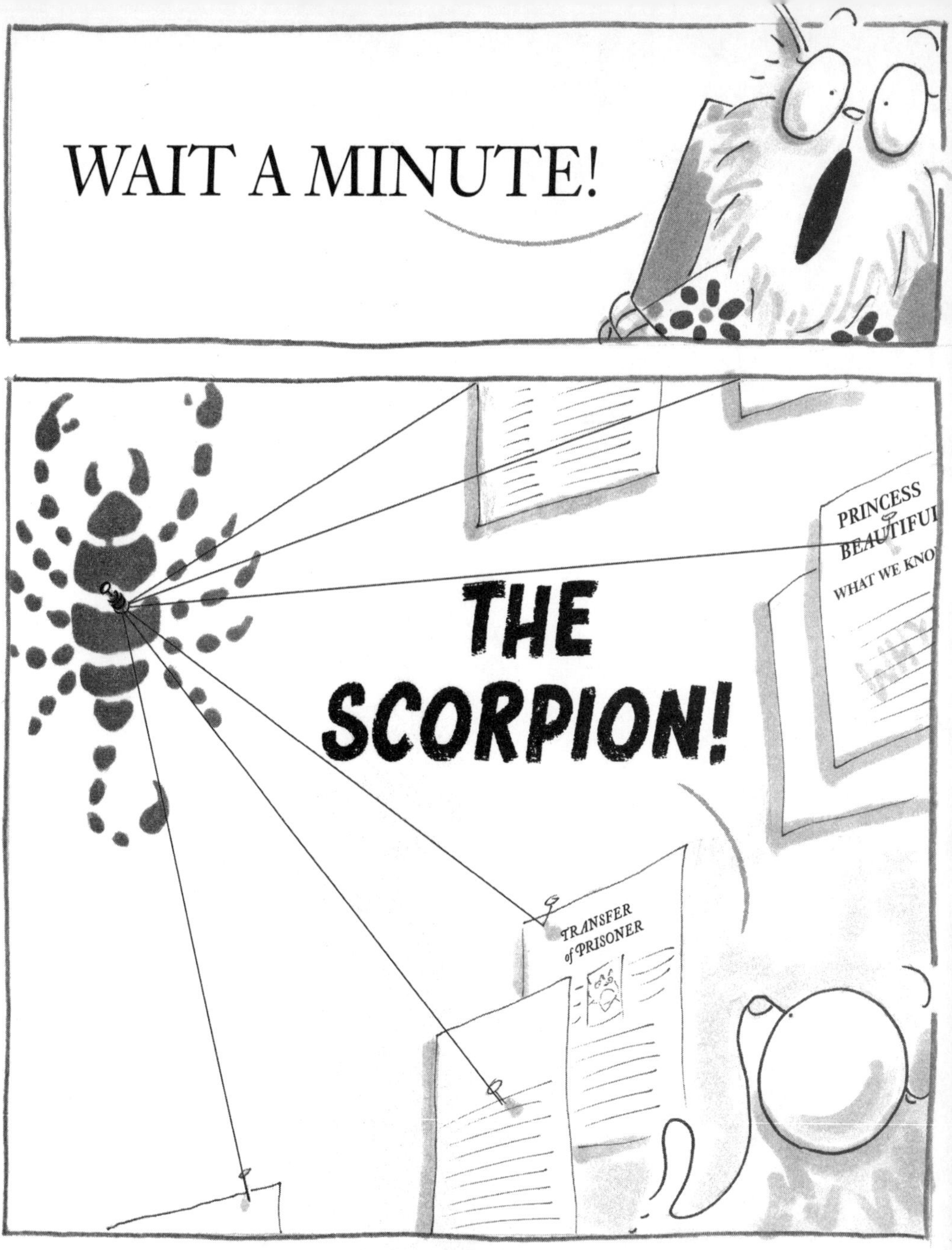
WAIT A MINUTE!
THE SCORPION!
PRINCESS BEAUTIFUL
WHAT WE KNO
TRANSFER of PRISONER

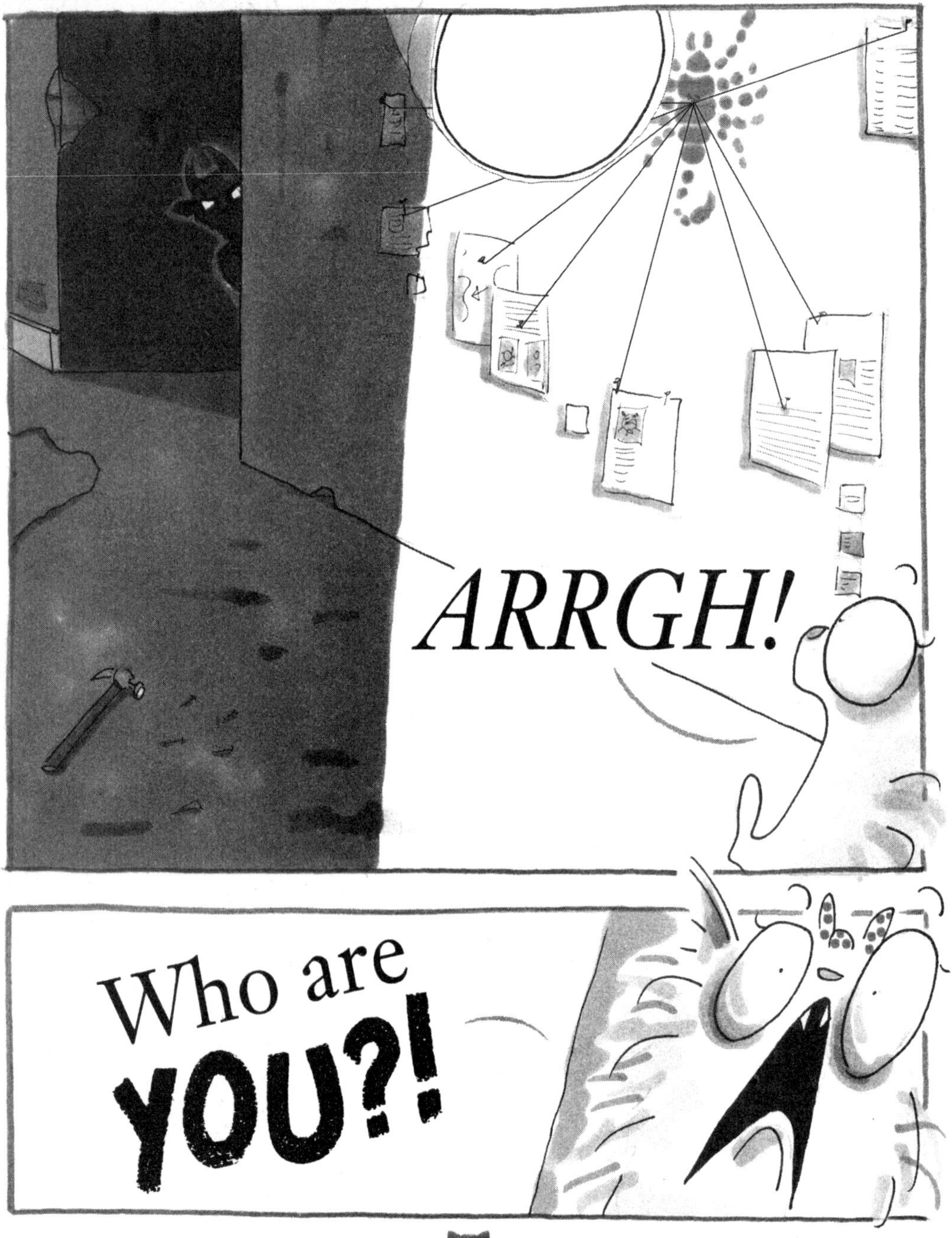
ARRGH!
Who are YOU?!

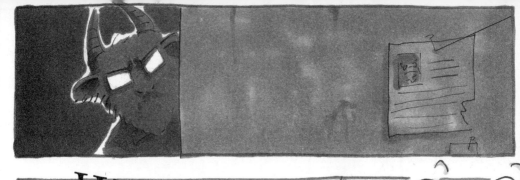

WHERE AM I?!

ANSWER ME!

DID YOU TIE ME UP?
WERE YOU DRIVING
THE VAN WITH
THE SCORPION
PAINTED ON THE BACK?
DID YOU DO THIS TO ME?!
**WHY ARE
YOU DOING
THIS TO ME?!**

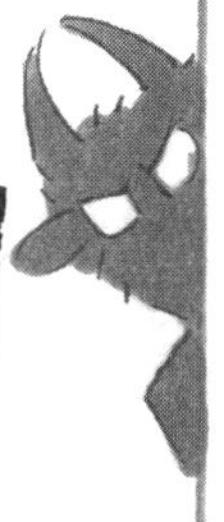

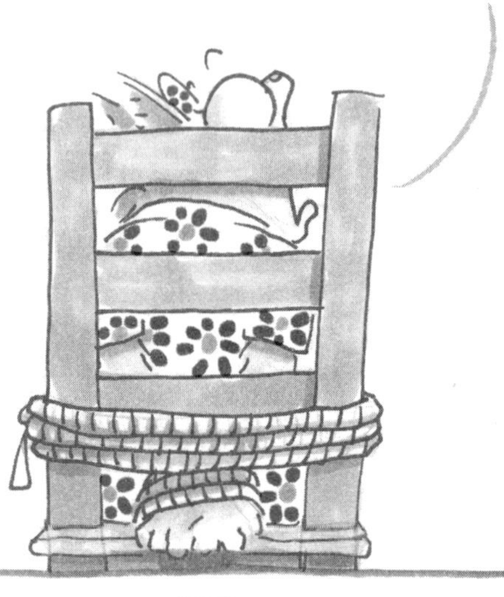

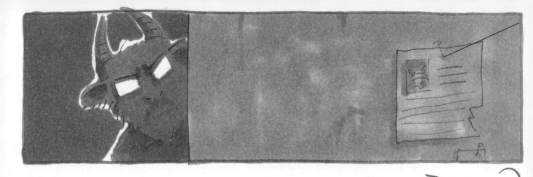

And why does my **BUTT CHEEK** hurt?

Oh . . .

right . . .
sorry about that . . .

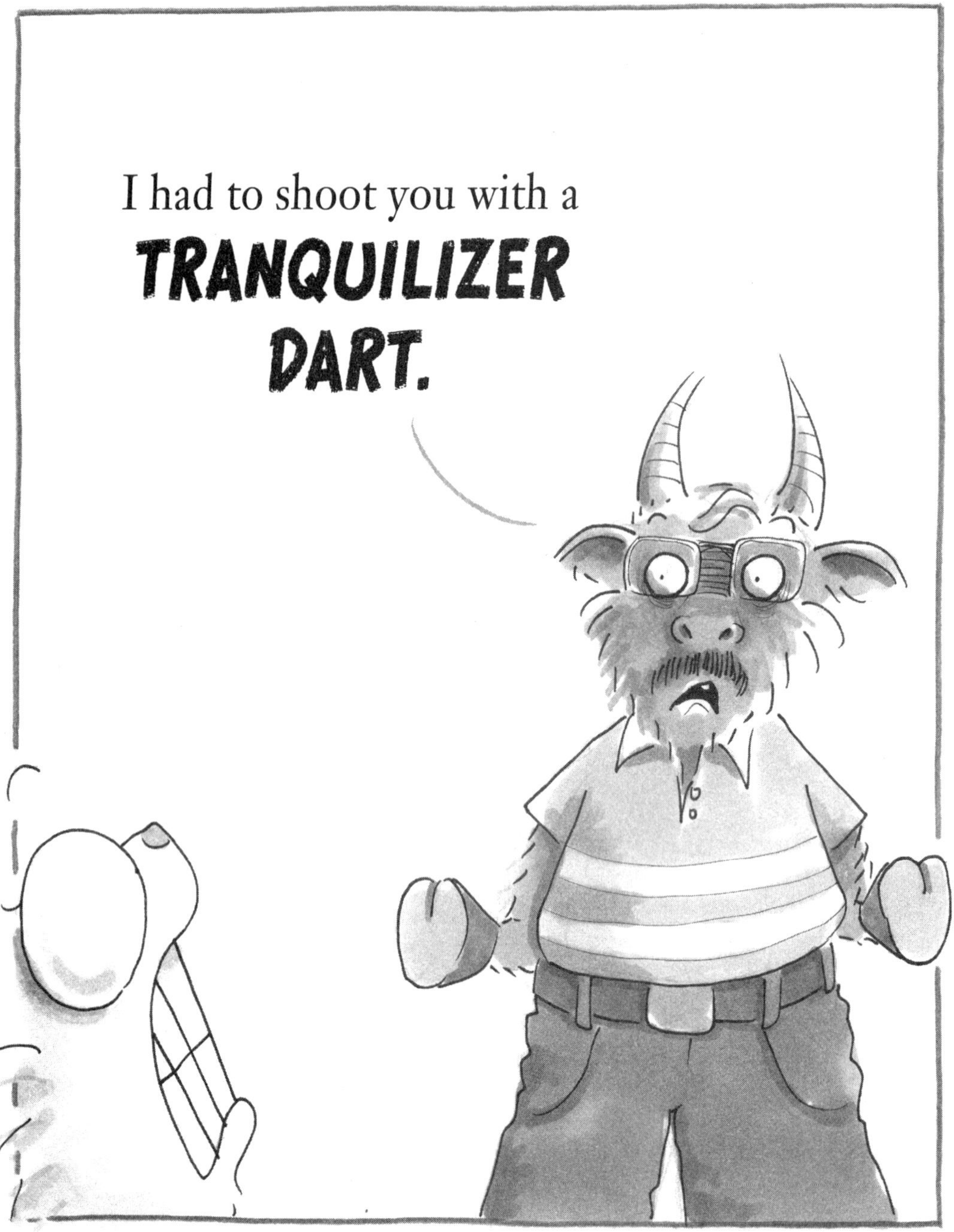
I had to shoot you with a
TRANQUILIZER DART.

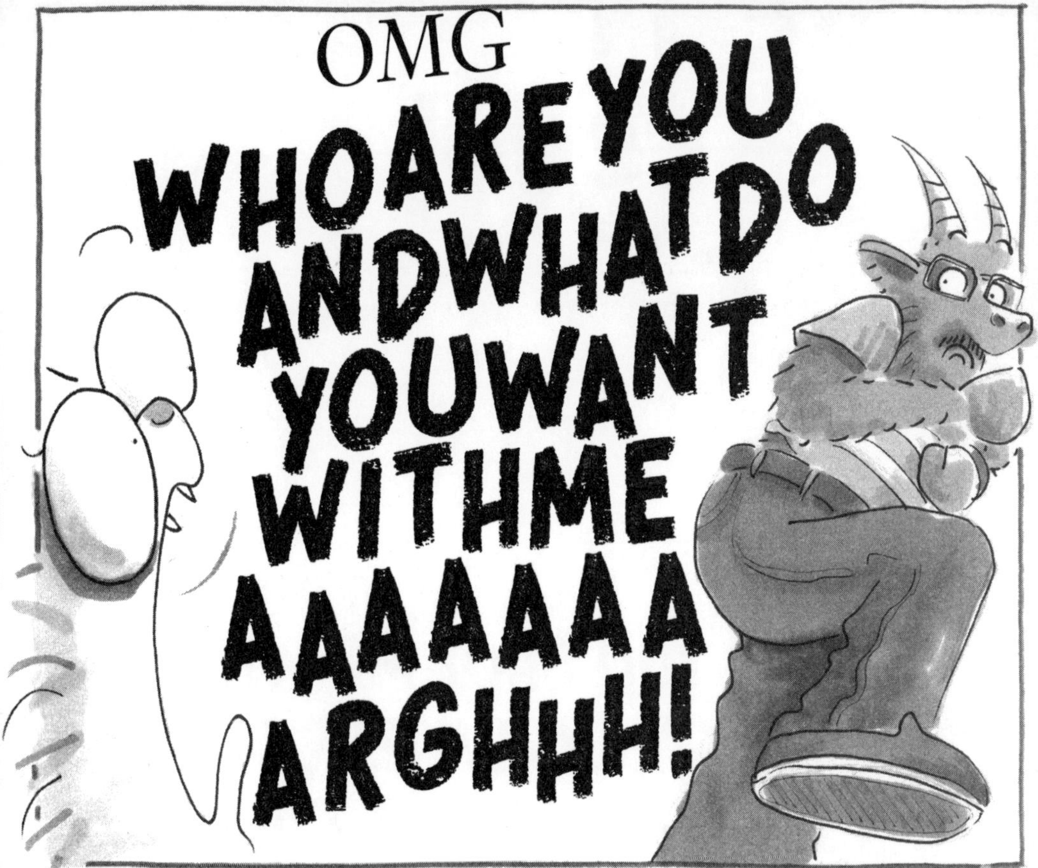
OMG
WHOAREYOU ANDWHATDO YOUWANT WITHME AAAAAAA ARGHHH!

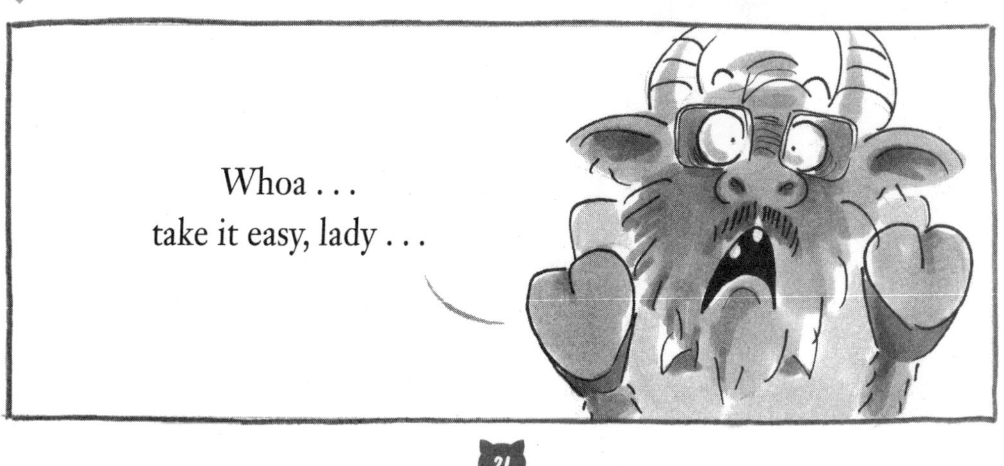
Whoa . . .
take it easy, lady . . .

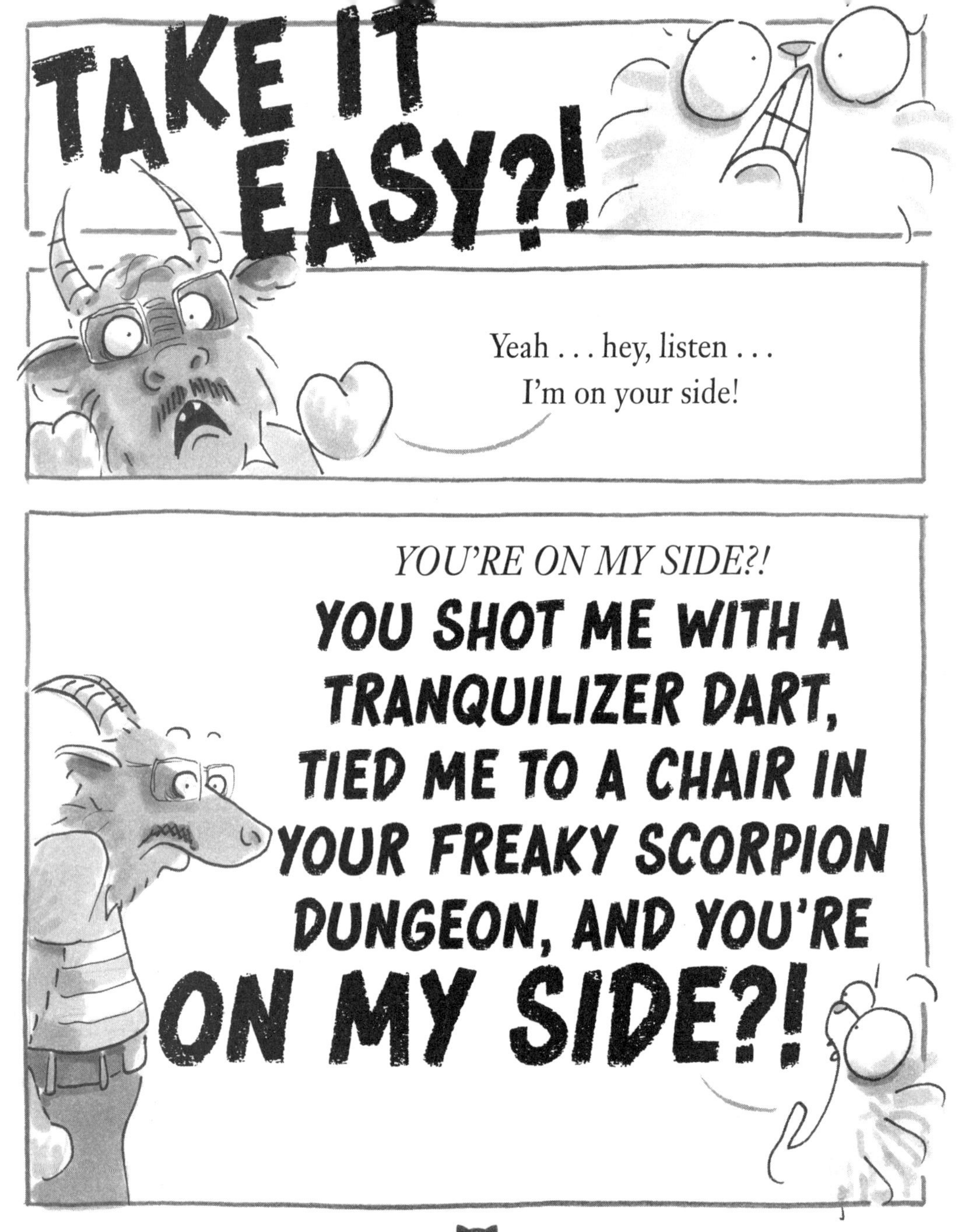
TAKE IT EASY?!
Yeah . . . hey, listen . . . I'm on your side!
YOU'RE ON MY SIDE?!
YOU SHOT ME WITH A TRANQUILIZER DART, TIED ME TO A CHAIR IN YOUR FREAKY SCORPION DUNGEON, AND YOU'RE ON MY SIDE?!

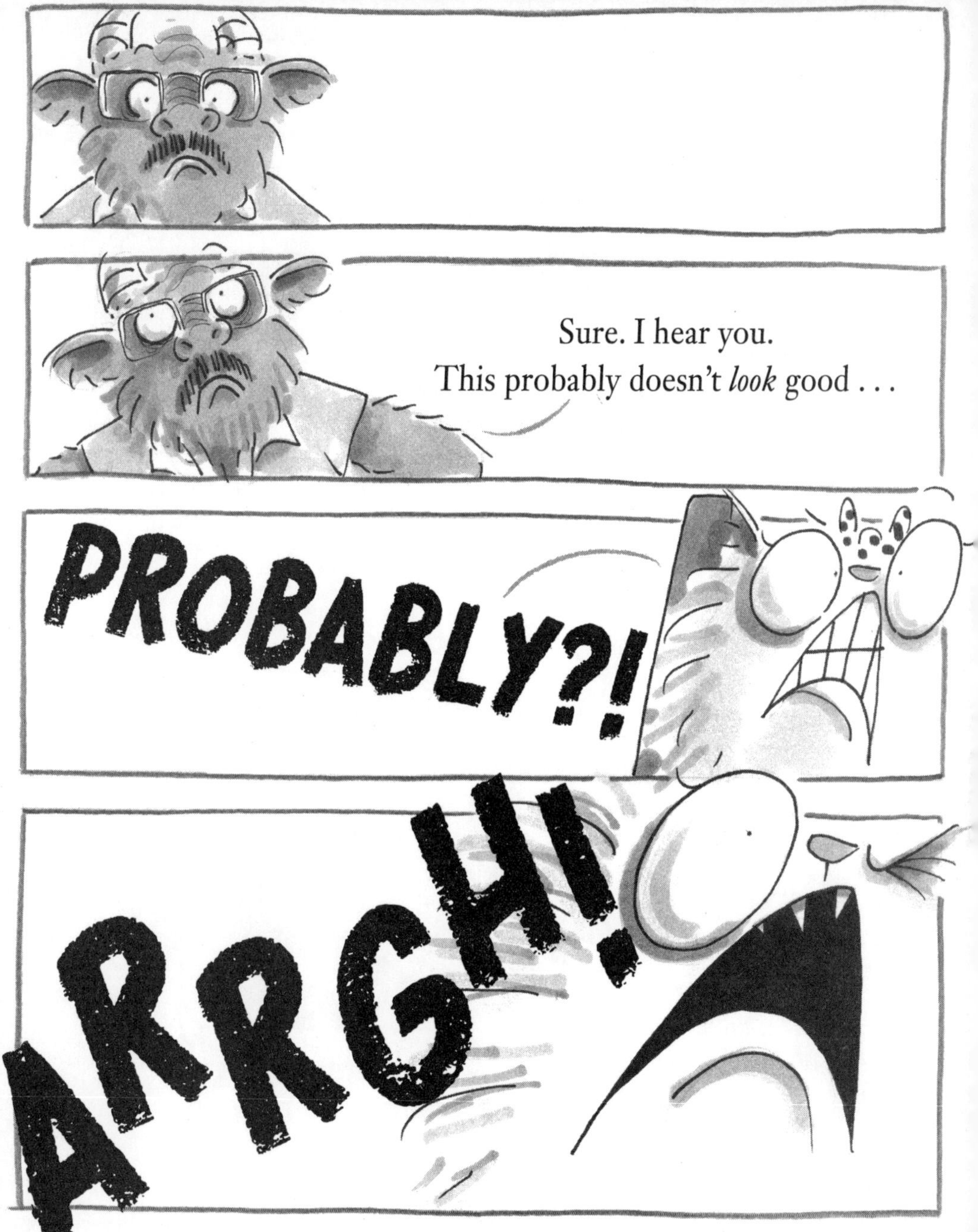

Sure. I hear you.
This probably doesn't *look* good . . .
PROBABLY?!
ARRGH!

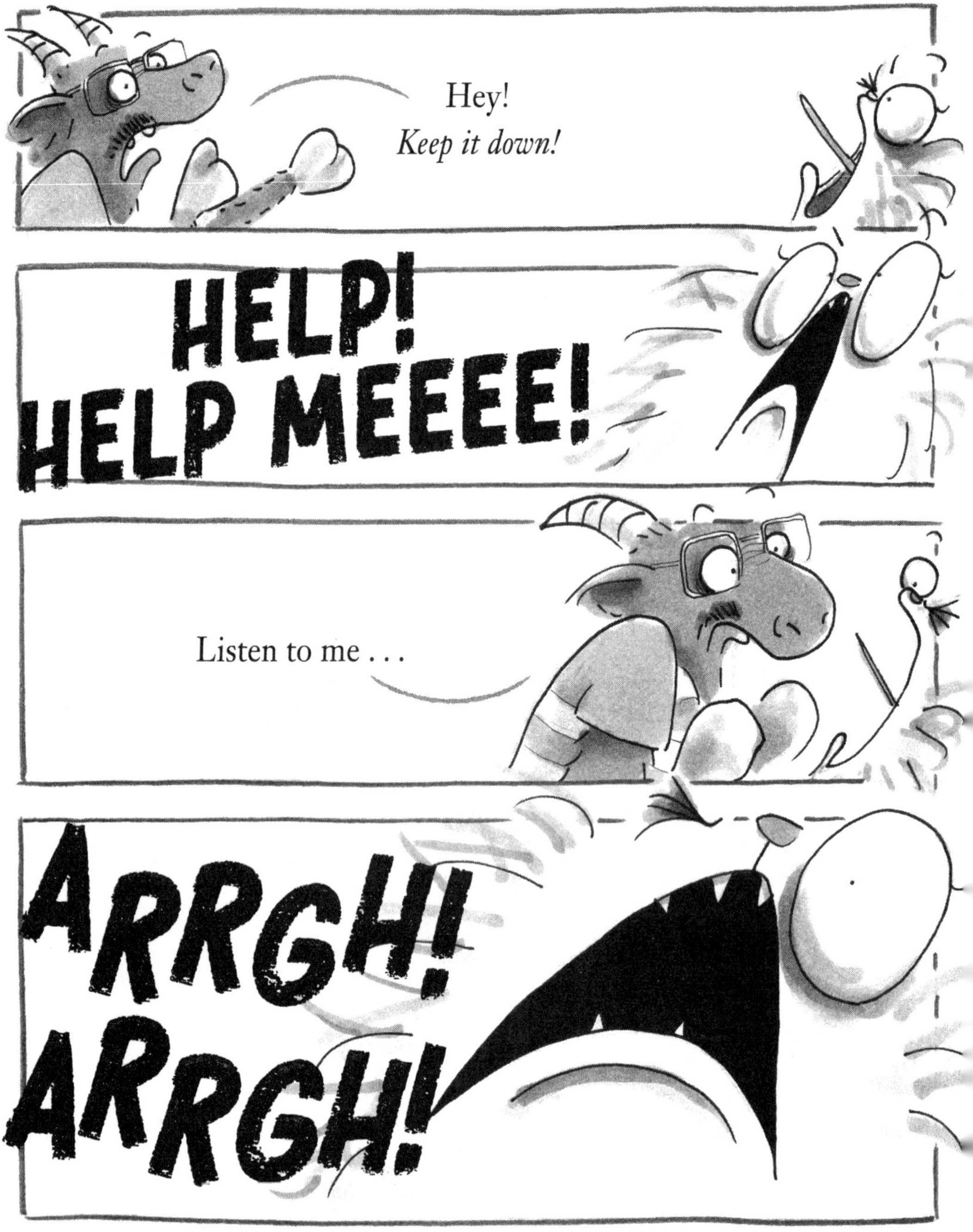
Hey!
Keep it down!
HELP! HELP MEEEE!
Listen to me . . .
ARRGH! ARRGH!

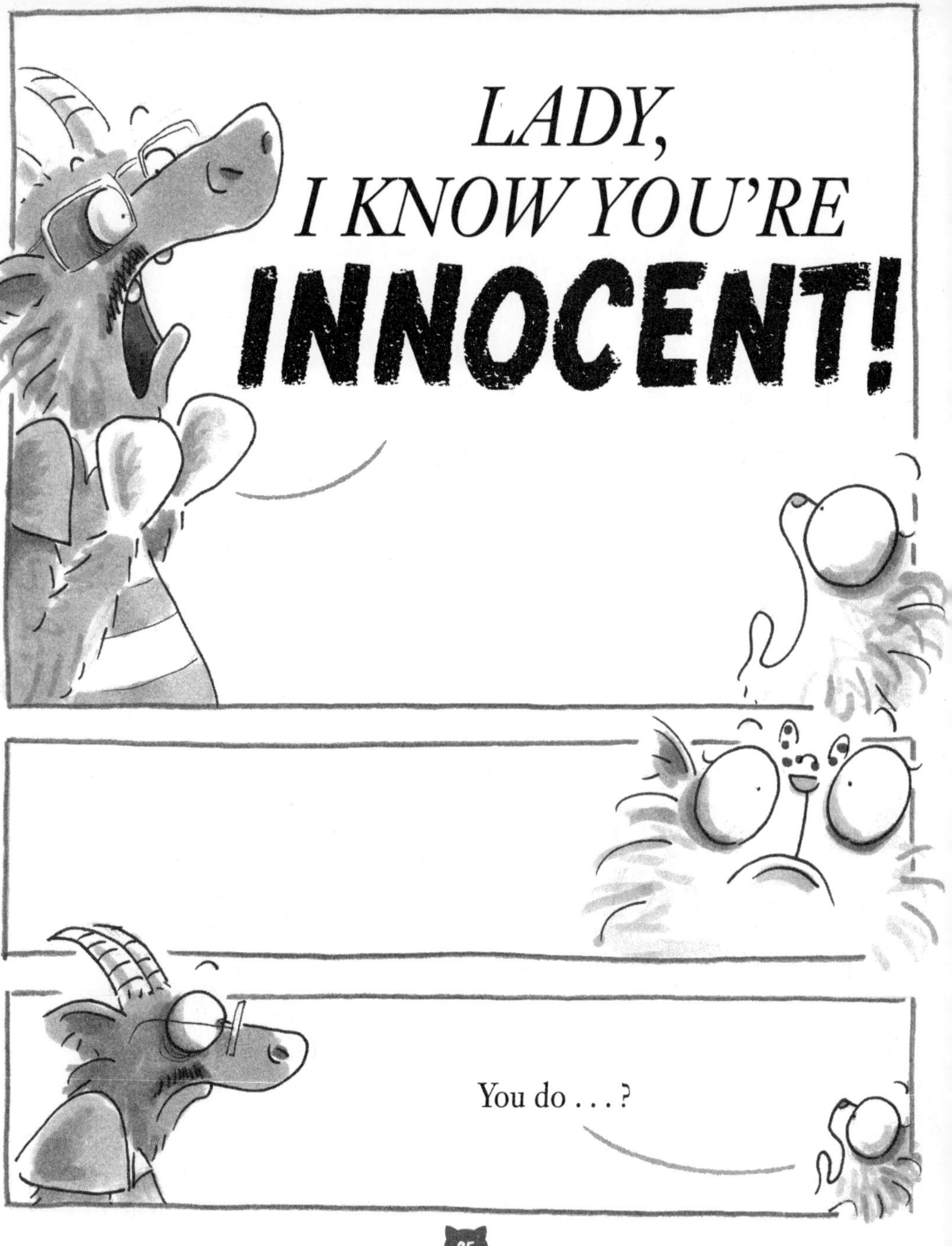
LADY, I KNOW YOU'RE INNOCENT!
You do . . . ?

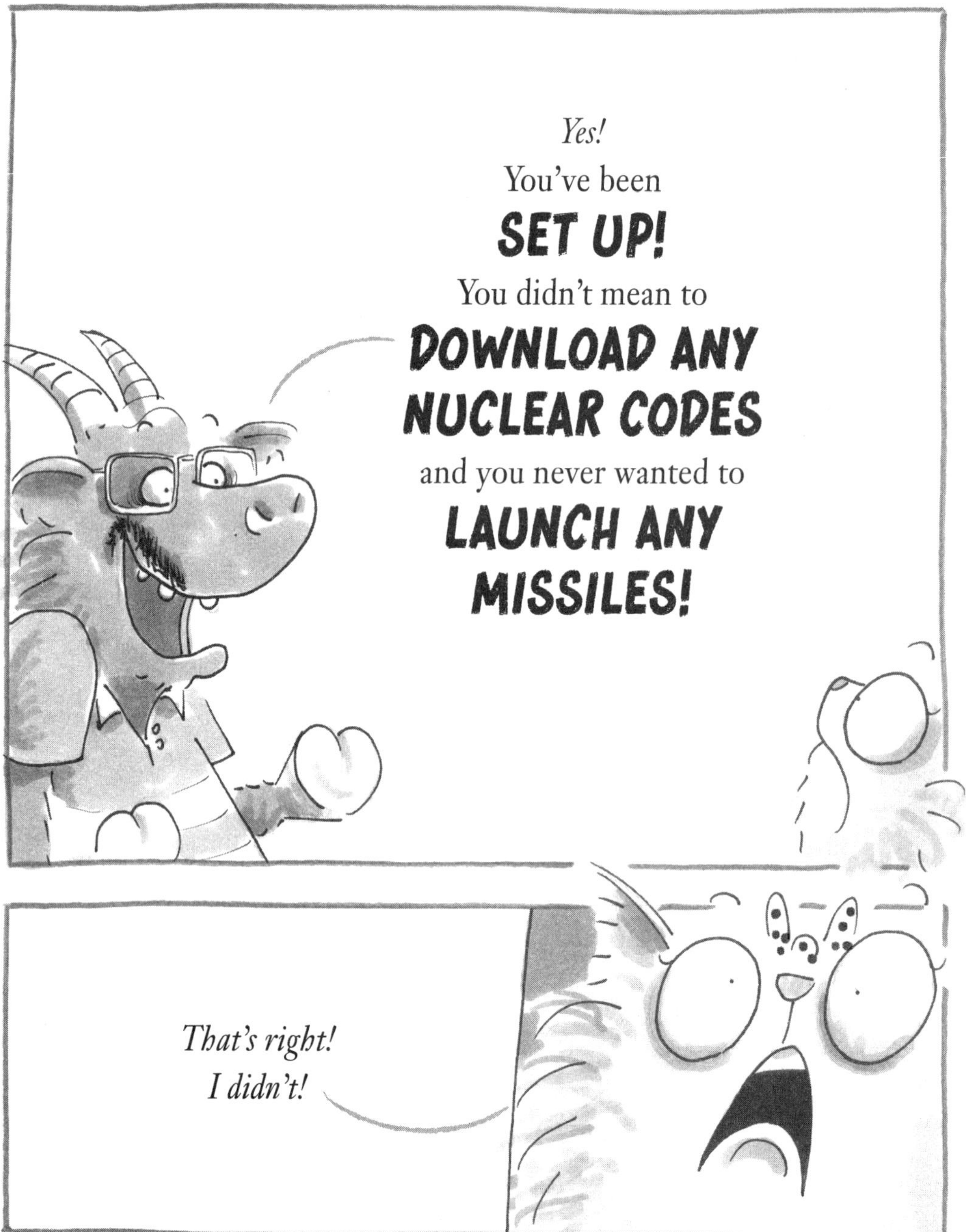

Yes!
You've been
SET UP!
You didn't mean to
DOWNLOAD ANY
NUCLEAR CODES
and you never wanted to
LAUNCH ANY
MISSILES!
That's right!
I didn't!

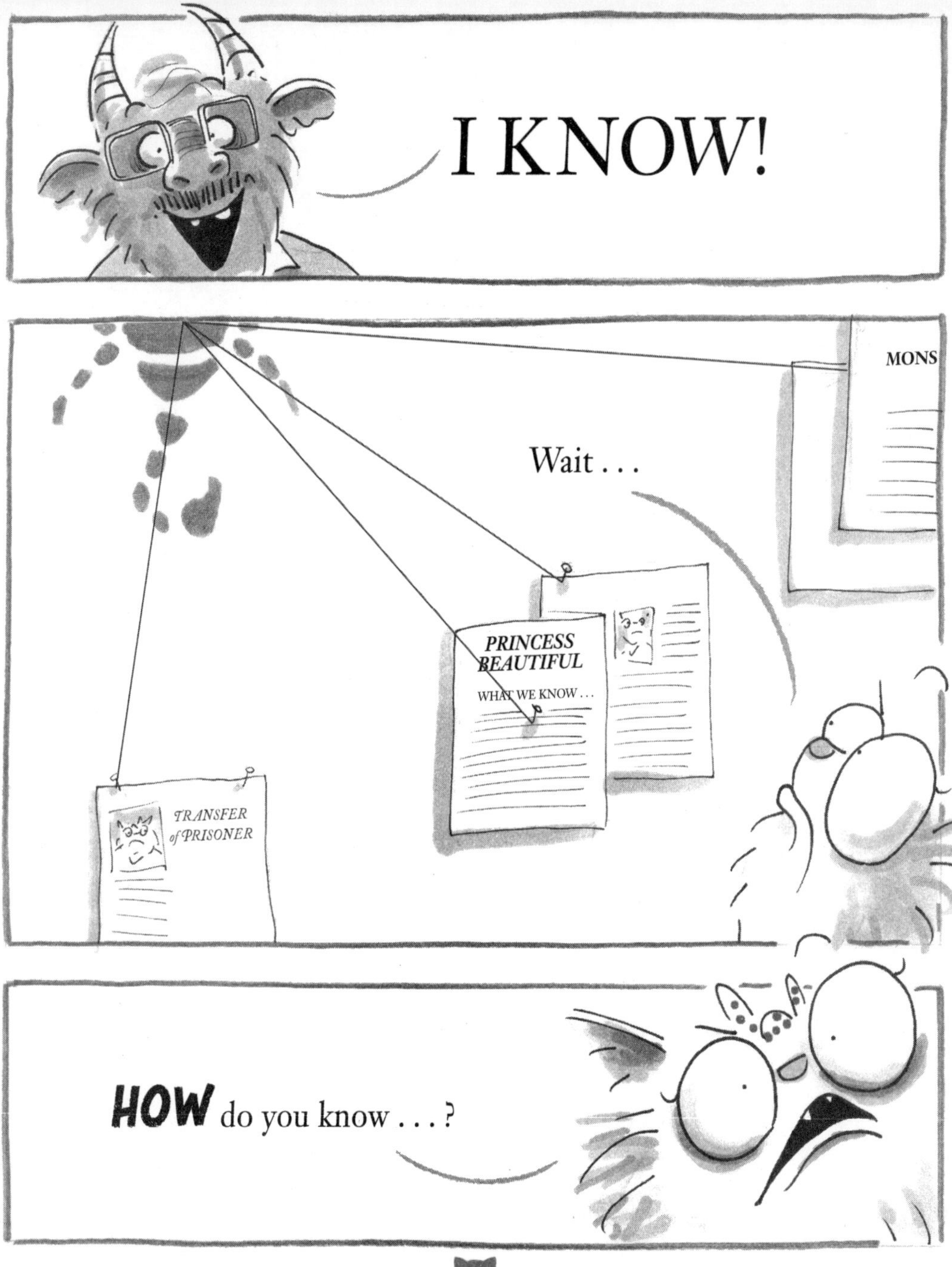
I KNOW!
MONS
Wait . . .
PRINCESS BEAUTIFUL
WHAT WE KNOW . . .
TRANSFER of PRISONER
HOW do you know . . . ?

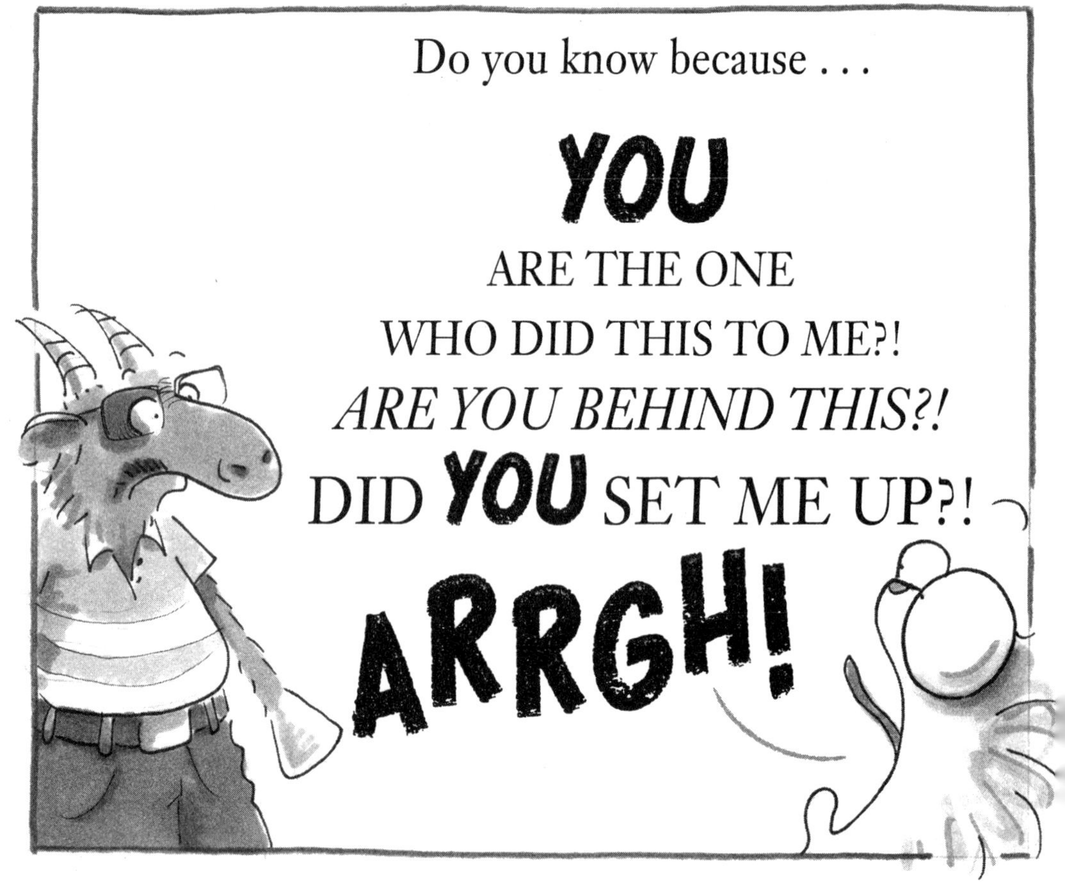
Do you know because . . .
YOU
ARE THE ONE
WHO DID THIS TO ME?!
ARE YOU BEHIND THIS?!
DID **YOU** SET *ME* UP?!
ARRGH!

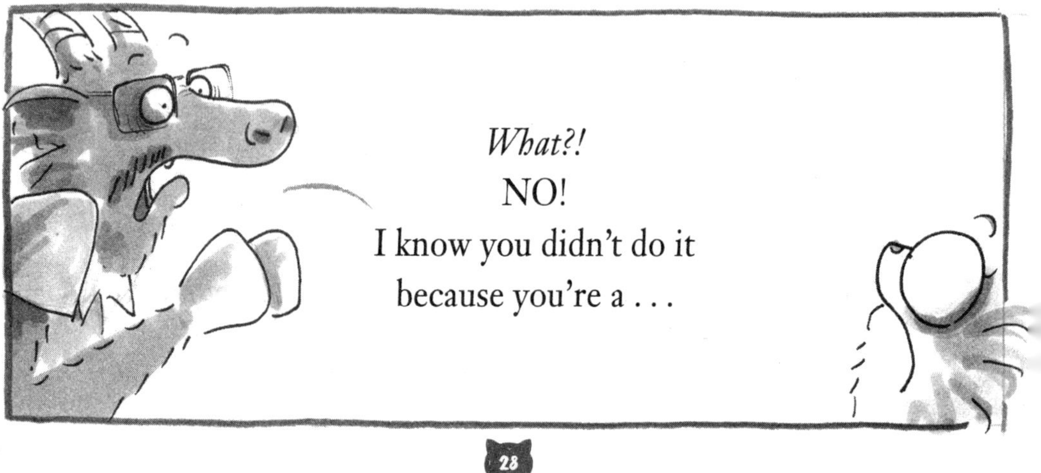
What?!
NO!
I know you didn't do it
because you're a . . .

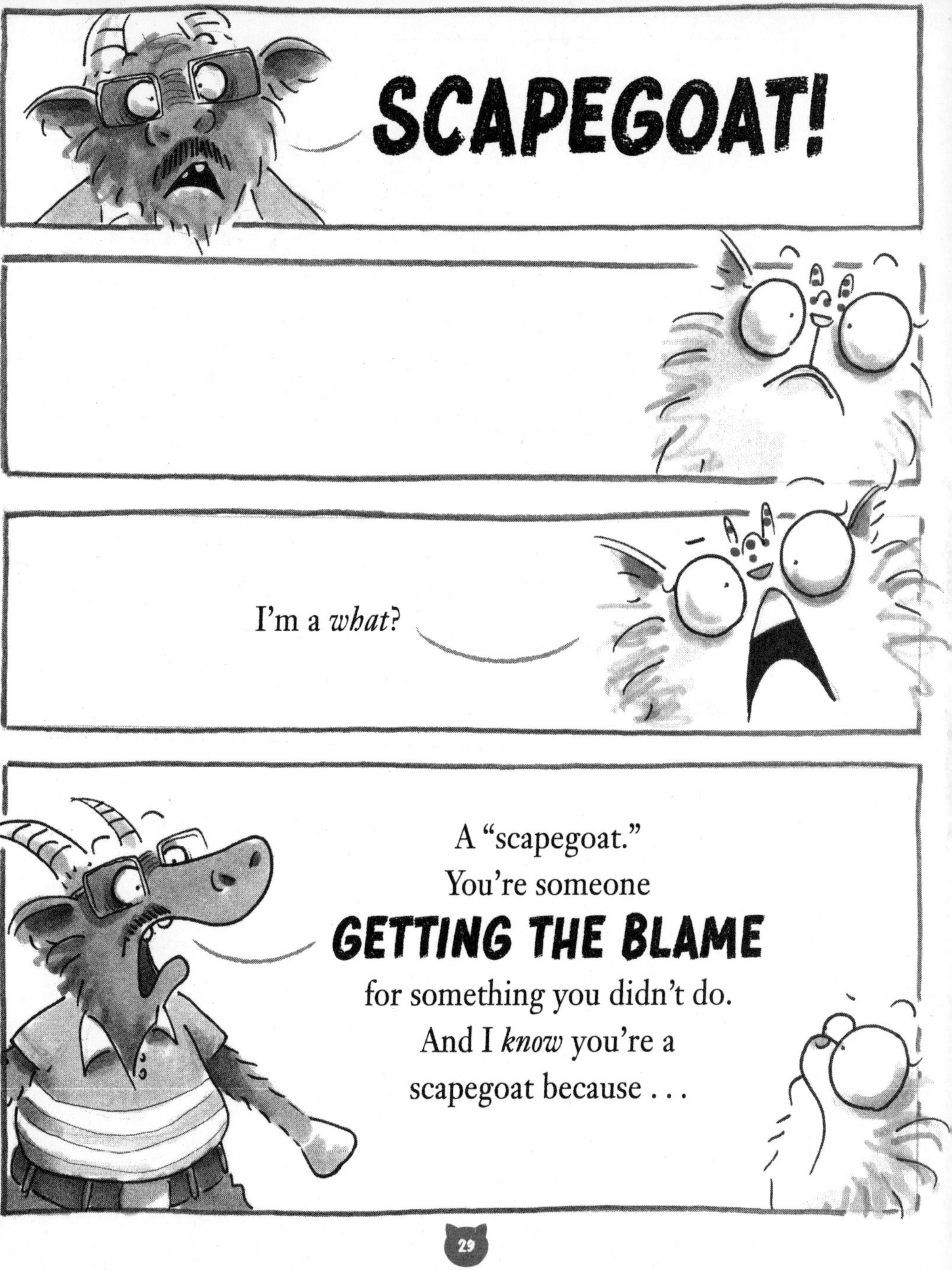
SCAPEGOAT!
I'm a *what*?
A "scapegoat."
You're someone
GETTING THE BLAME
for something you didn't do.
And I *know* you're a
scapegoat because . . .

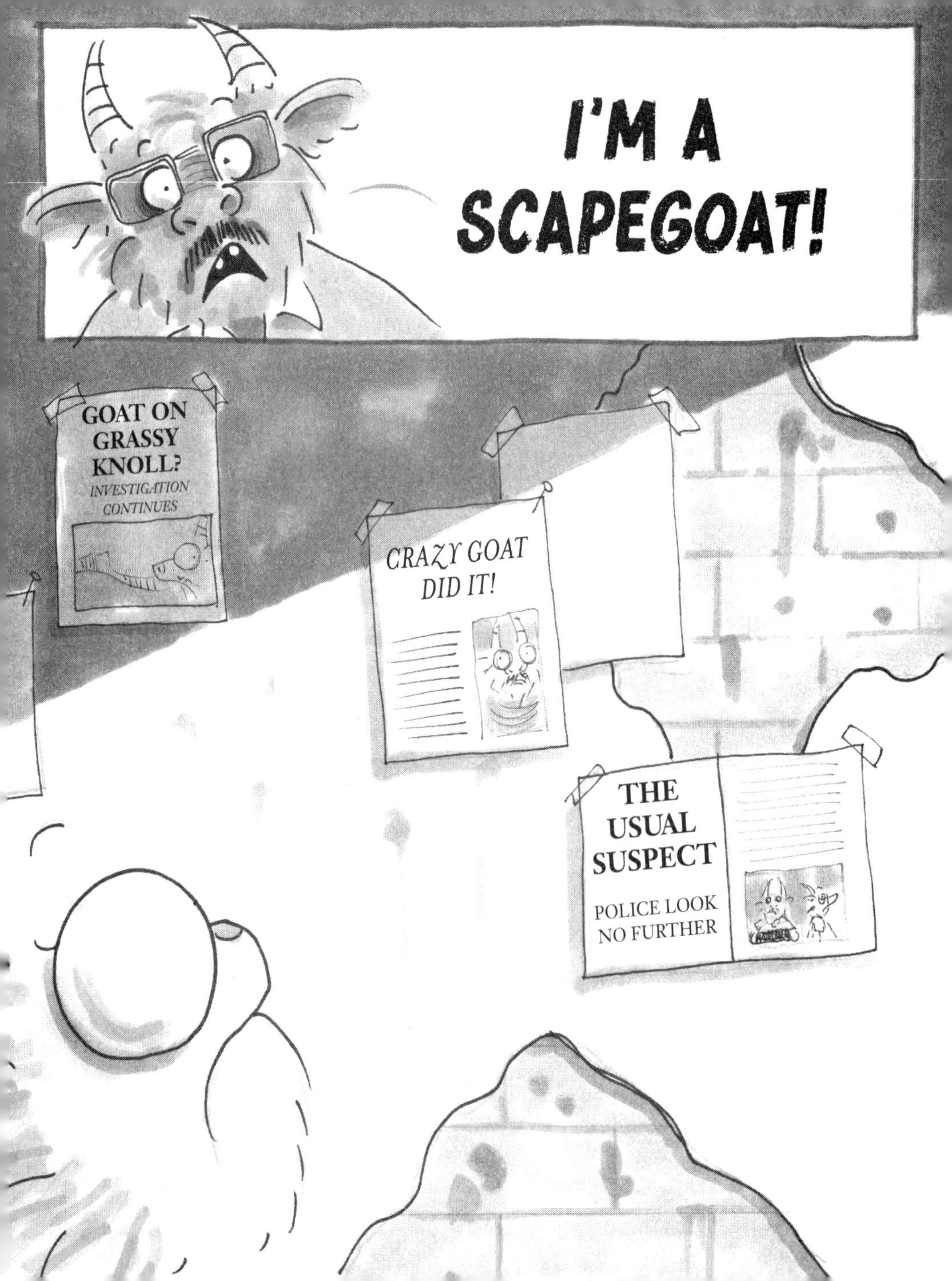

I'M A SCAPEGOAT!
GOAT ON GRASSY KNOLL?
INVESTIGATION CONTINUES
CRAZY GOAT DID IT!
THE USUAL SUSPECT
POLICE LOOK NO FURTHER

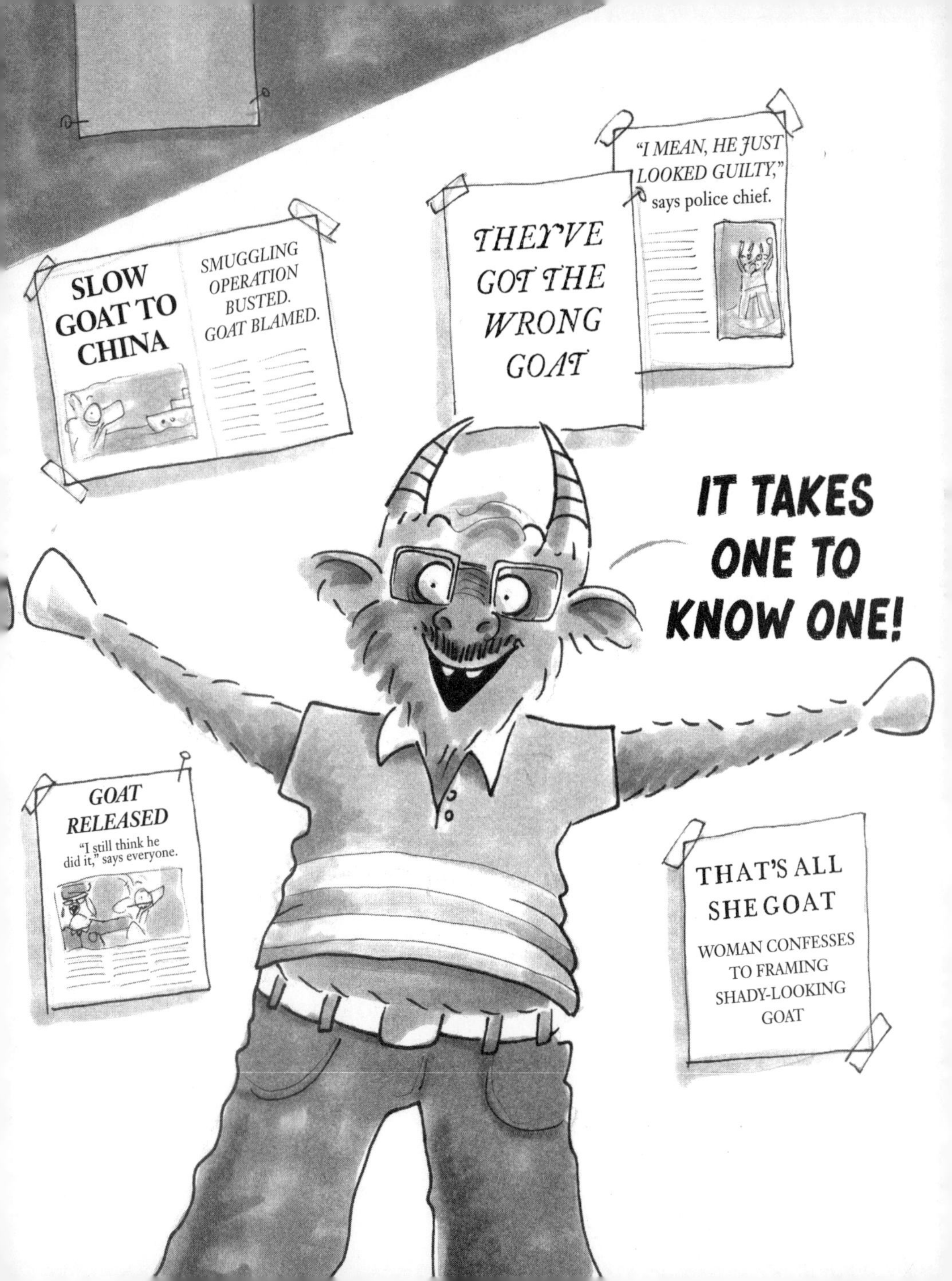
SLOW GOAT TO CHINA
SMUGGLING OPERATION BUSTED. GOAT BLAMED.
THEY'VE GOT THE WRONG GOAT
"I MEAN, HE JUST LOOKED GUILTY," says police chief.
IT TAKES ONE TO KNOW ONE!
GOAT RELEASED
"I still think he did it," says everyone.
THAT'S ALL SHE GOAT
WOMAN CONFESSES TO FRAMING SHADY-LOOKING GOAT

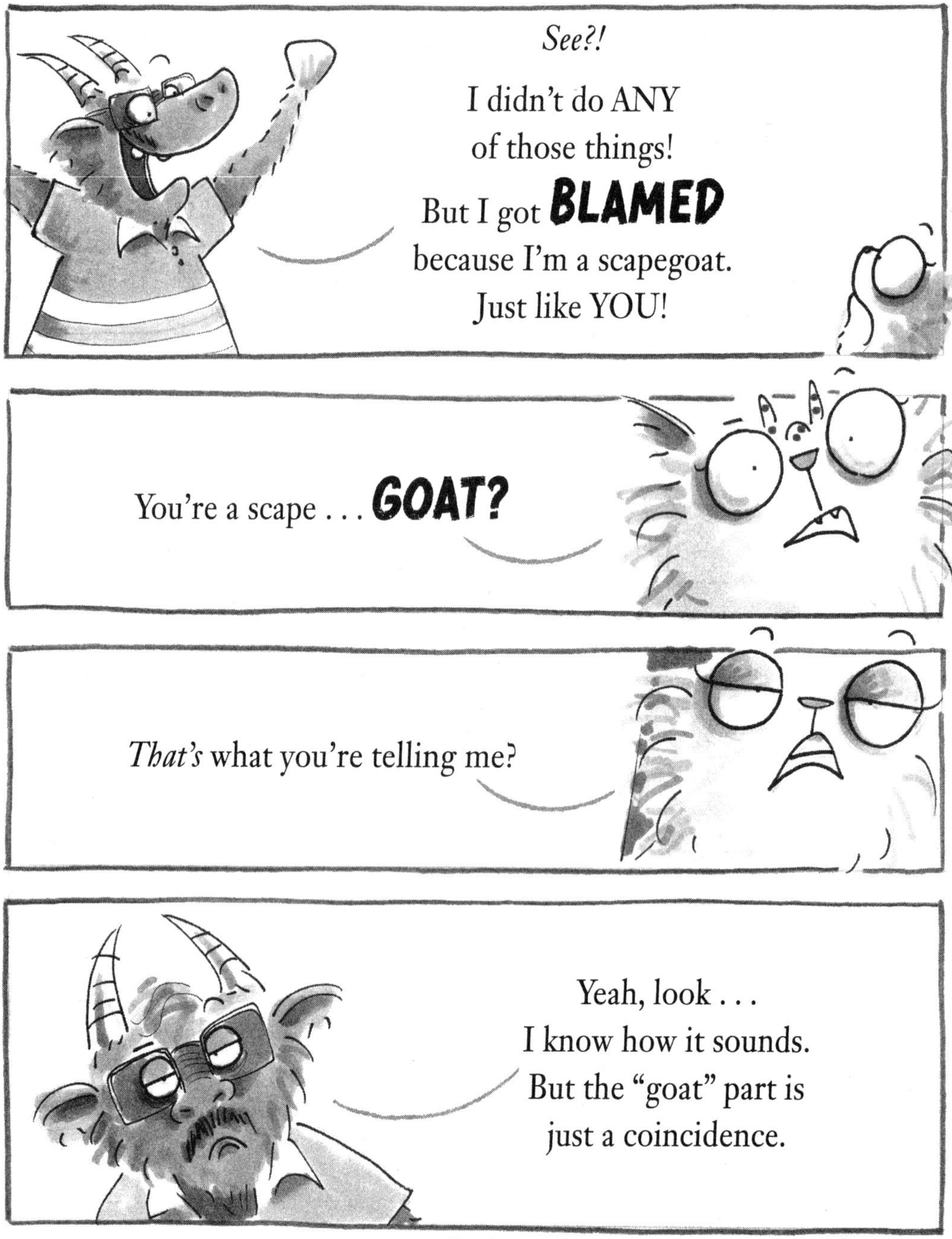
See?!
I didn't do ANY of those things! But I got **BLAMED** because I'm a scapegoat. Just like YOU!
You're a scape . . . **GOAT?**
That's what you're telling me?
Yeah, look . . . I know how it sounds. But the "goat" part is just a coincidence.

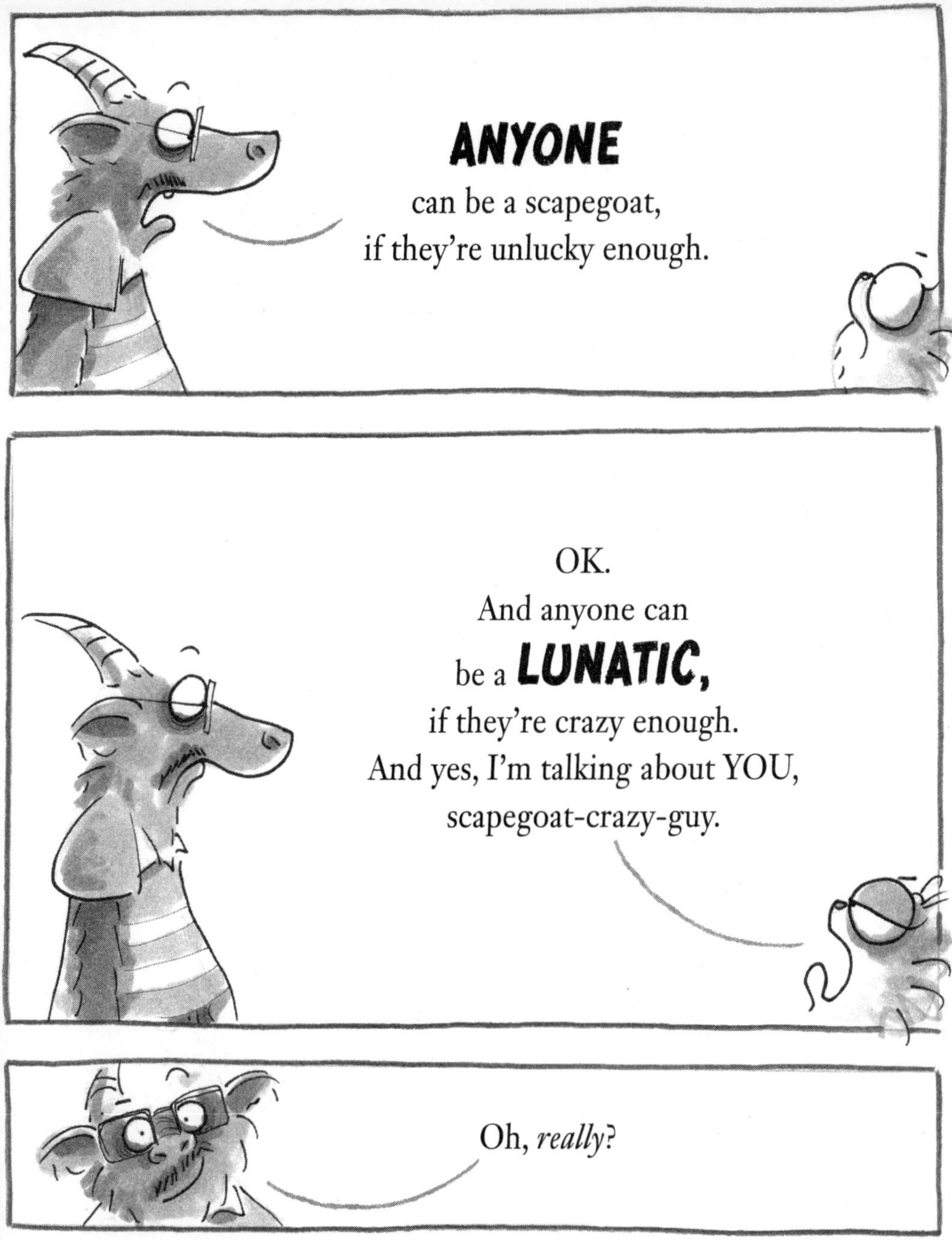
ANYONE
can be a scapegoat,
if they're unlucky enough.
OK.
And anyone can
be a LUNATIC,
if they're crazy enough.
And yes, I'm talking about YOU,
scapegoat-crazy-guy.
Oh, *really*?

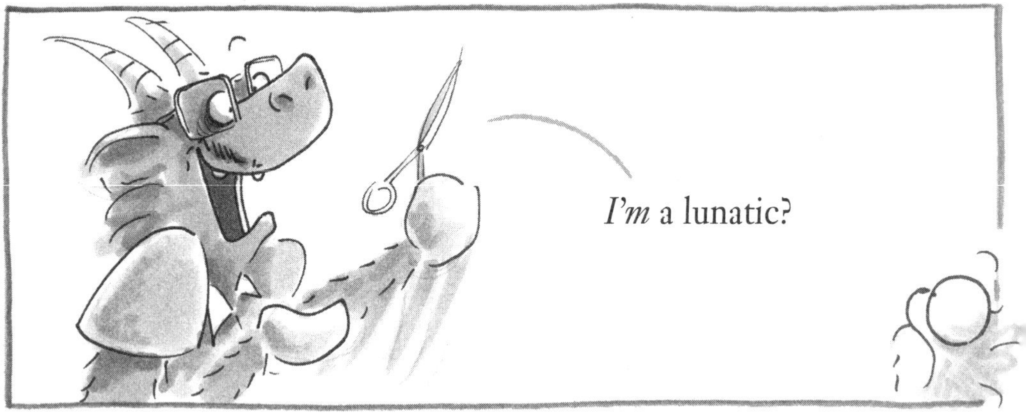
I'm a lunatic?

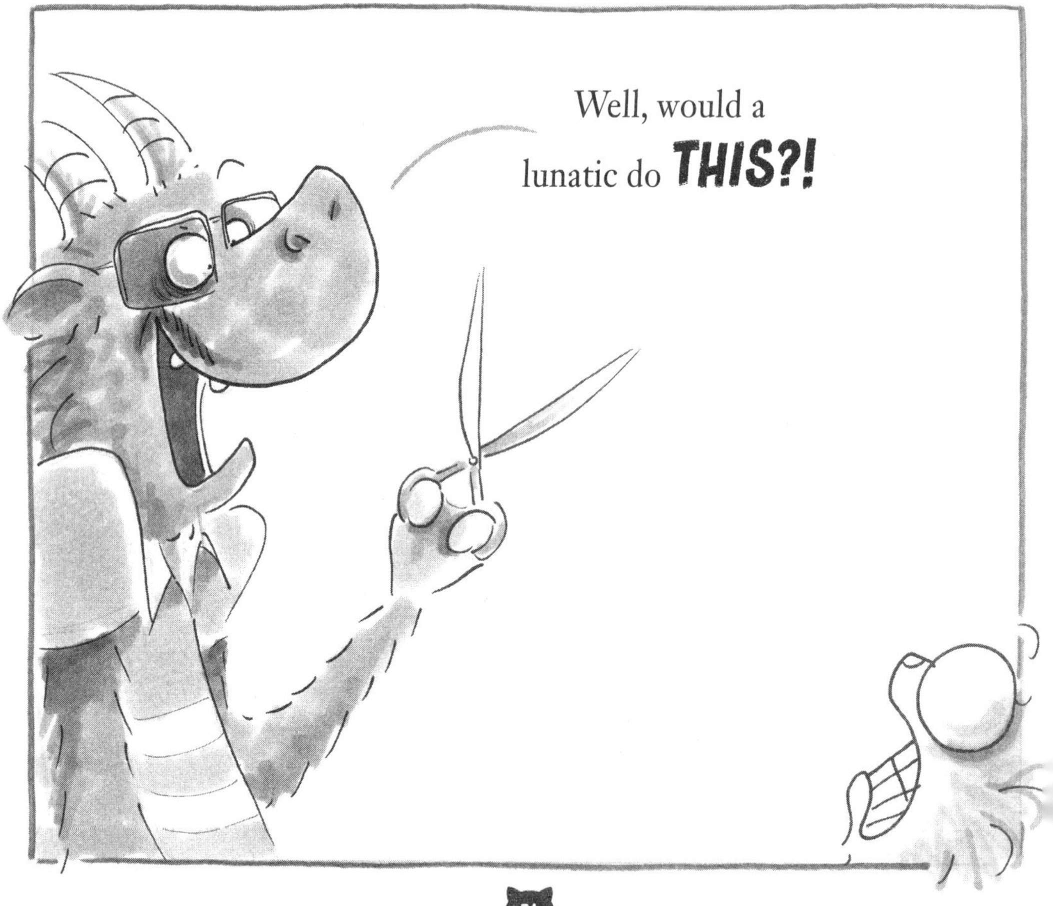
Well, would a lunatic do **THIS?!**

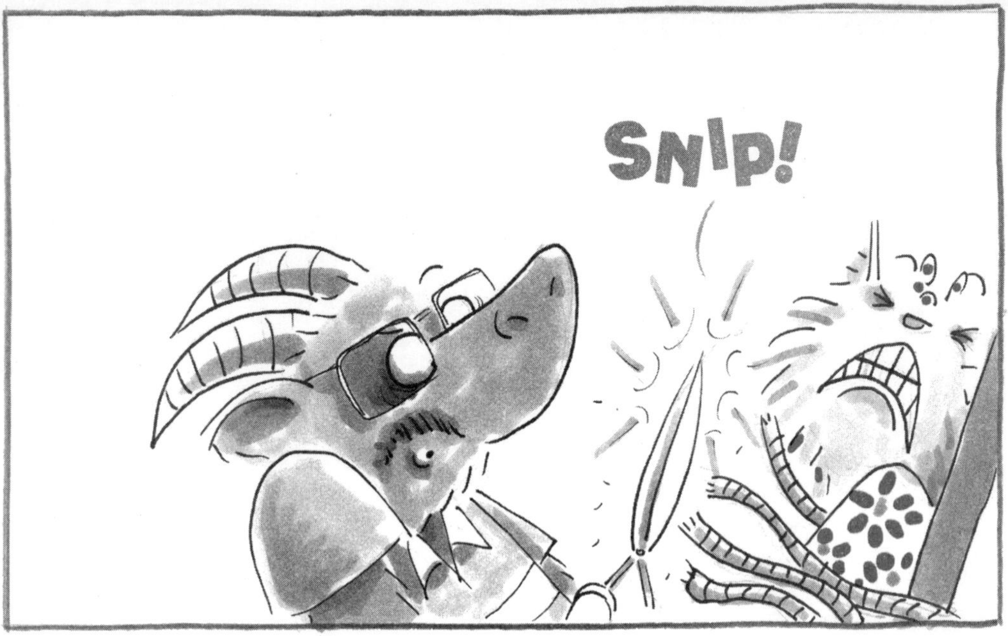
SNIP!

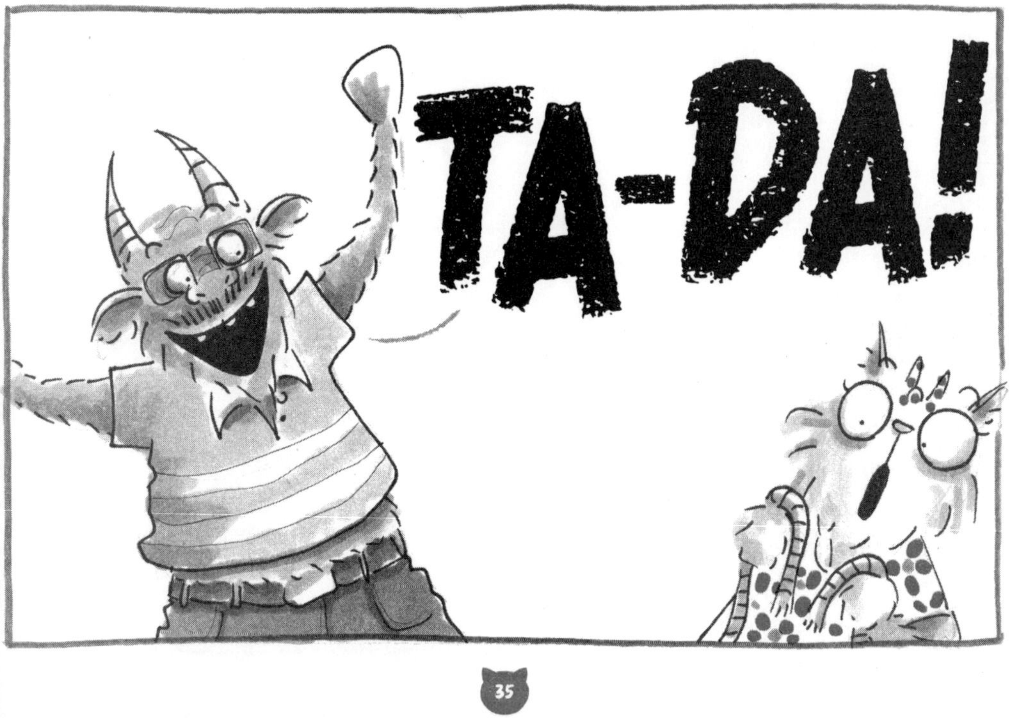
TA-DA!

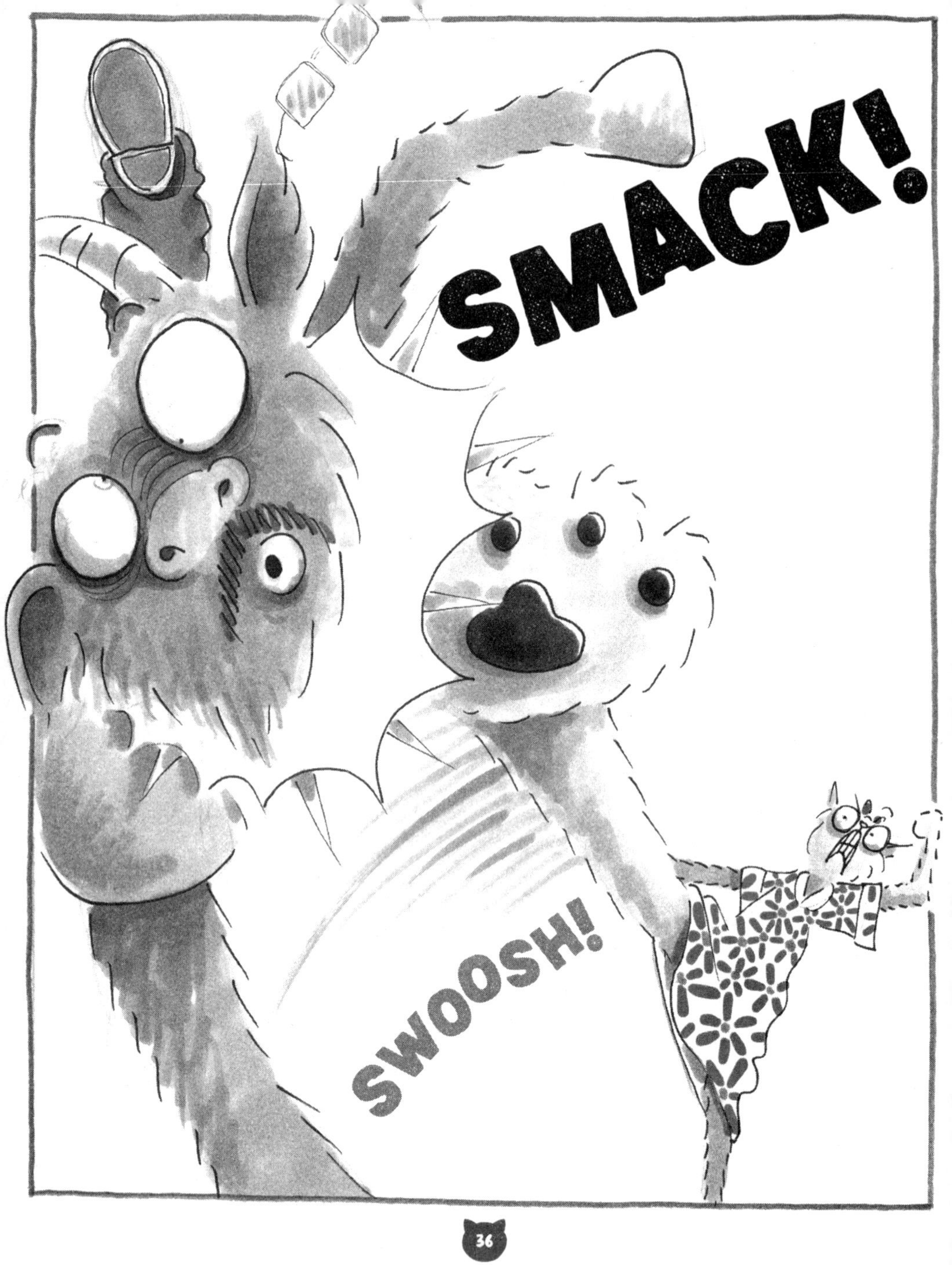
SMACK!
SWOOSH!

Two
BFFS

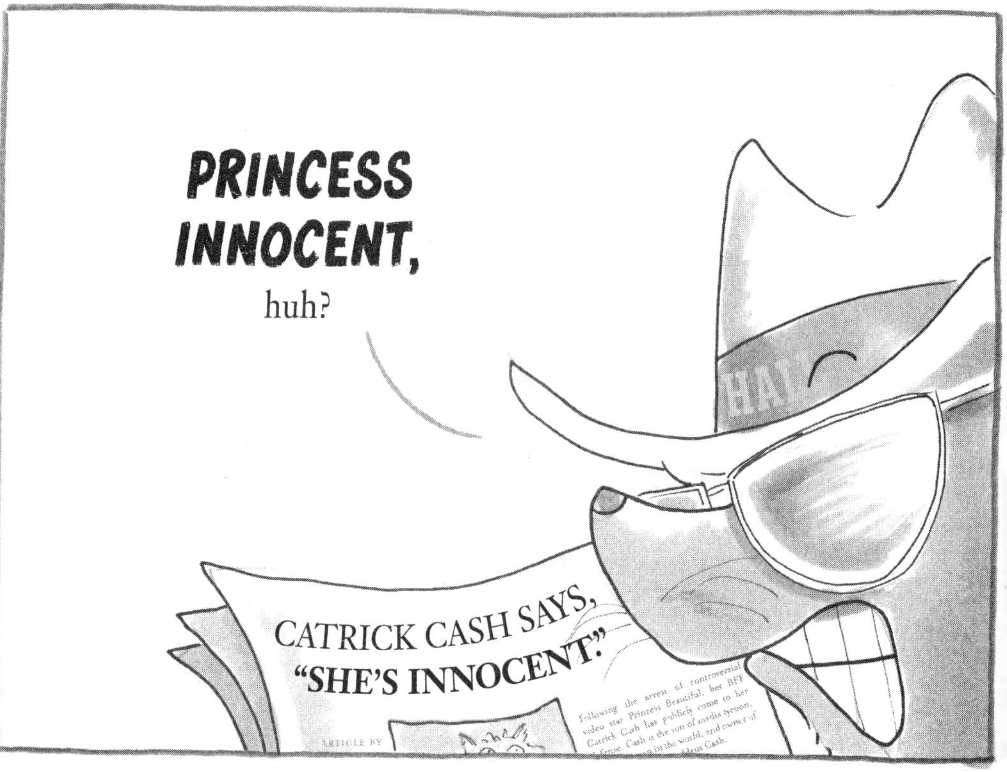
PRINCESS INNOCENT, huh?
CATRICK CASH SAYS, "SHE'S INNOCENT."
Following the arrest of controversial
video star Princess Beautiful, her BFF
Catrick Cash has publicly come to her
ARTICLE BY

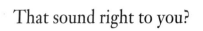
That sound right to you?

I . . . I'm sorry, what . . . ?

You heard me,
Beaver Boy.
Is she *"innocent"*?

Well, I don't know about
innocent . . .

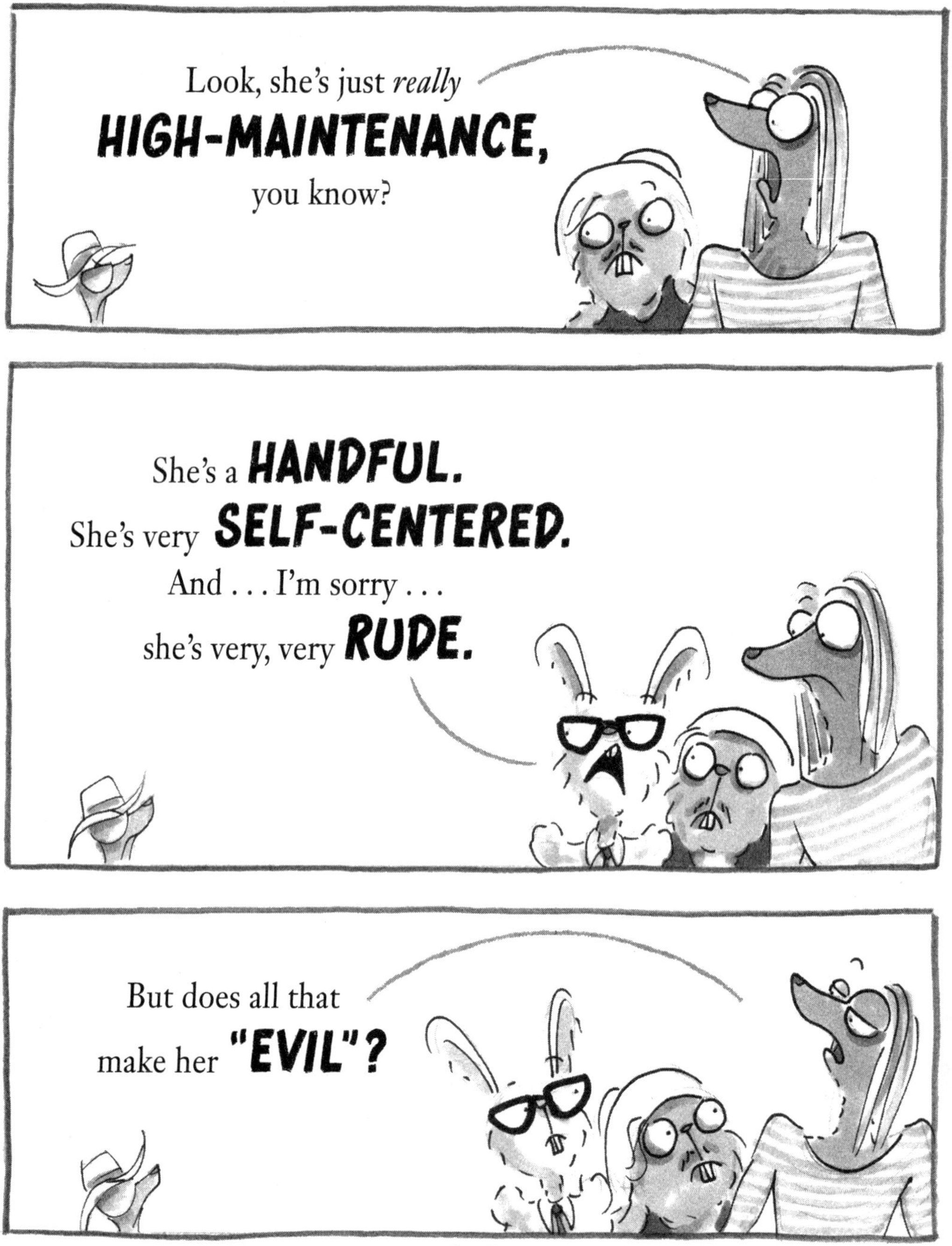

Look, she's just *really* HIGH-MAINTENANCE, you know?
She's a HANDFUL. She's very SELF-CENTERED. And . . . I'm sorry . . . she's very, very RUDE.
But does all that make her "EVIL"?

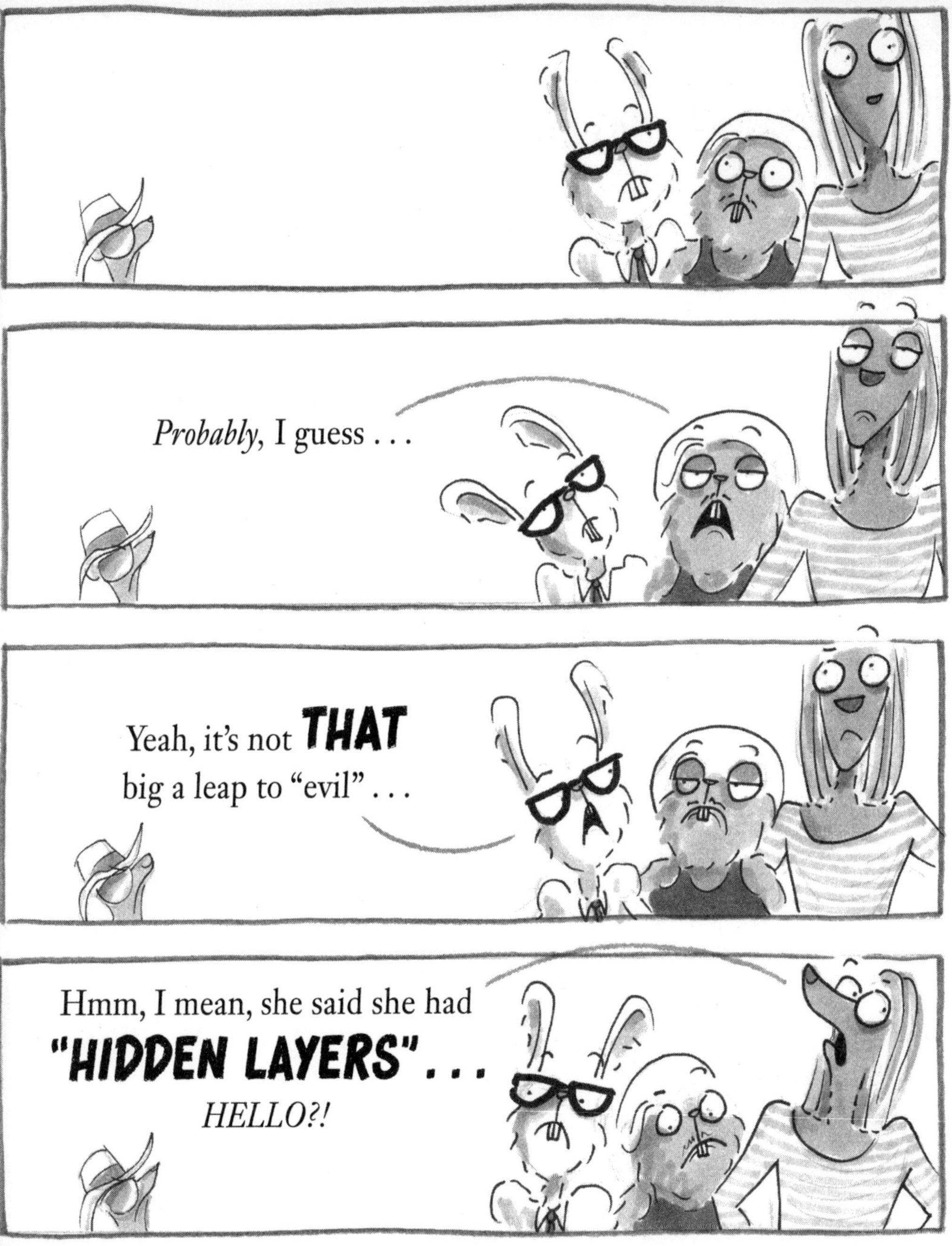
Probably, I guess . . .
Yeah, it's not **THAT** big a leap to "evil" . . .
Hmm, I mean, she said she had **"HIDDEN LAYERS" . . .** *HELLO?!*

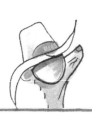

Deputy, it's not like we want to . . .

throw her under the bus . . .

Yeah, but . . . you know . . .

ALL ABOARD!

The bus is rollin', baby!

All the way to

GUILTY TOWN.

You know what I'm sayin'?

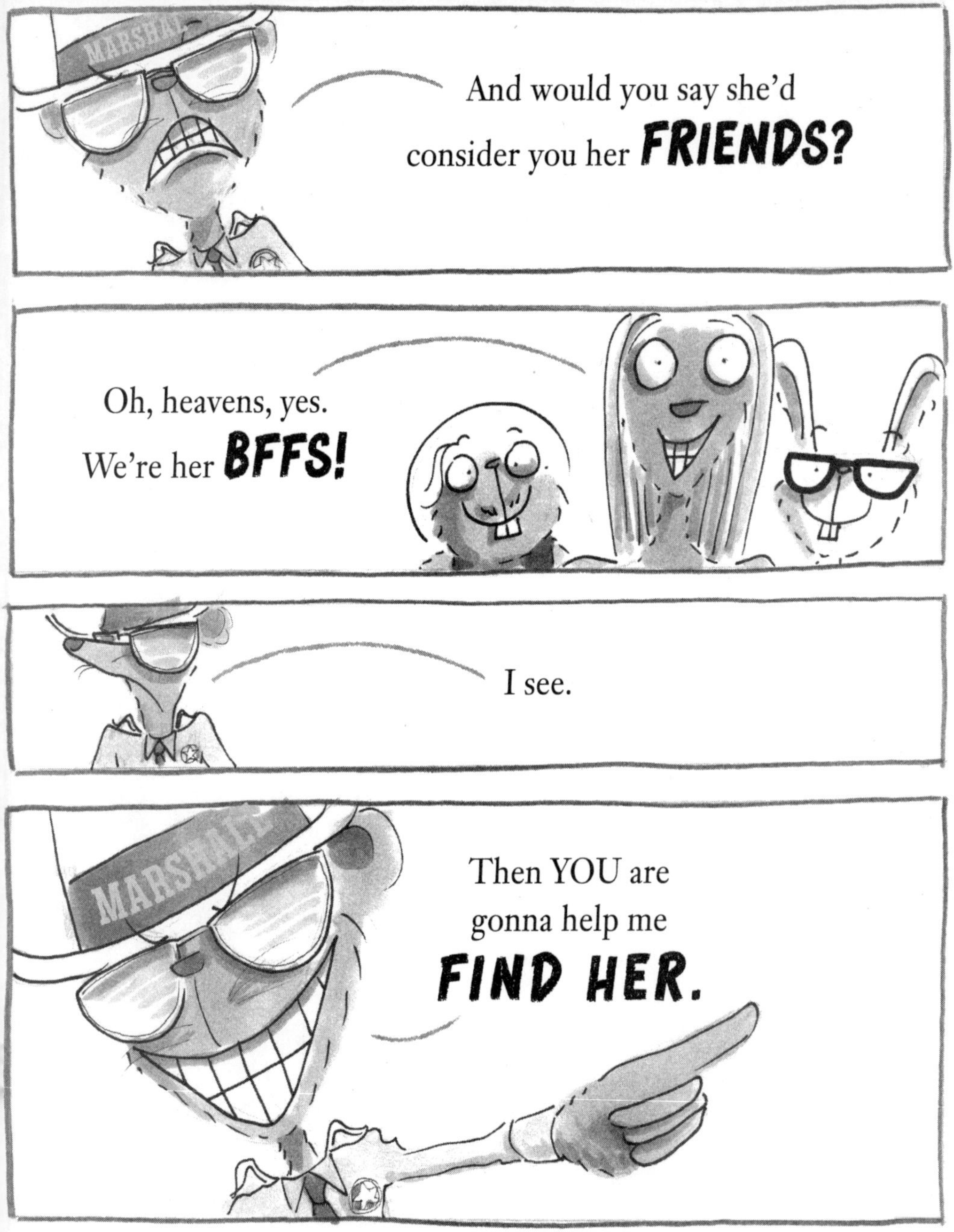
MARSHAL
And would you say she'd consider you her FRIENDS?
Oh, heavens, yes. We're her BFFS!
I see.
MARSHAL
Then YOU are gonna help me FIND HER.

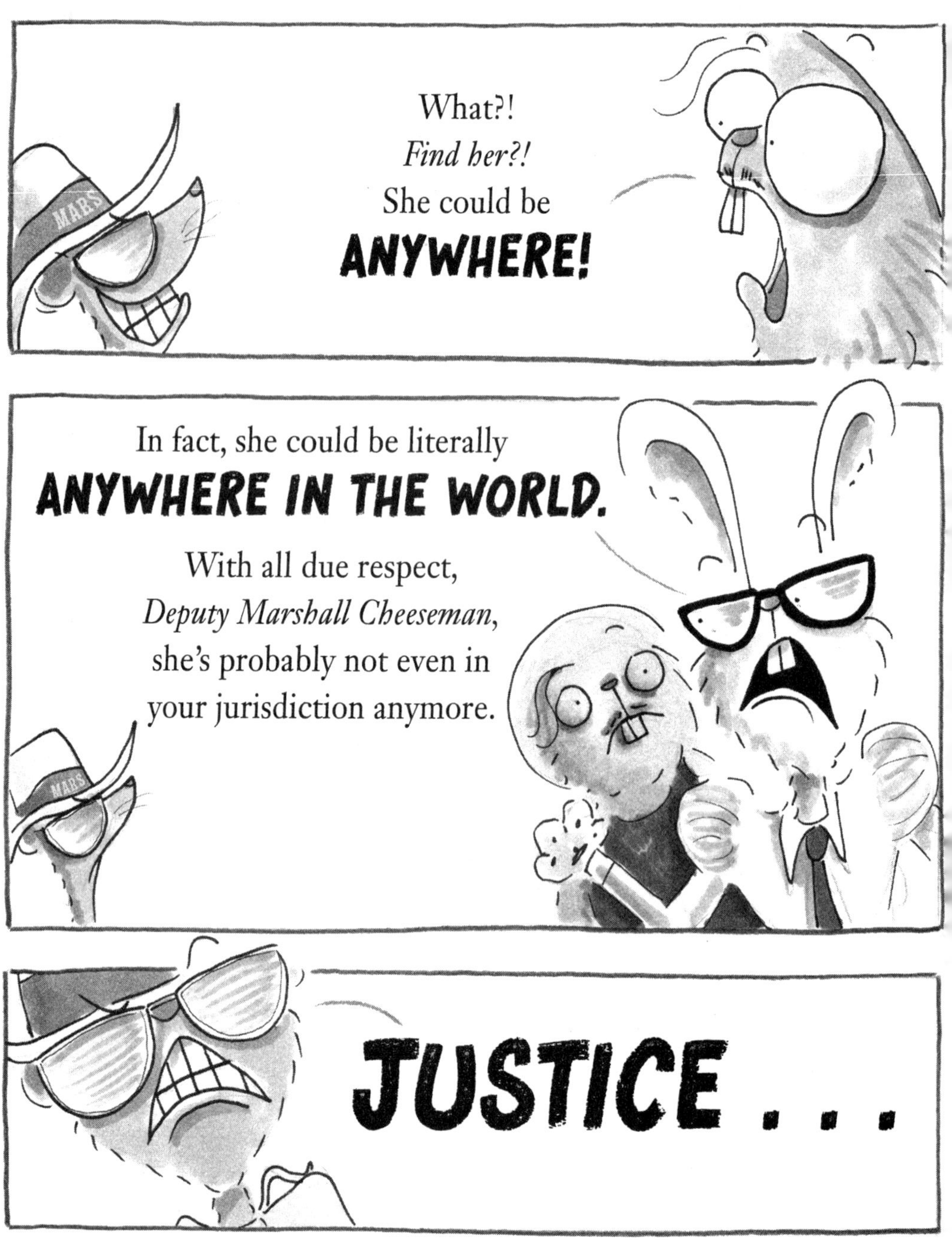
MARS
What?!
Find her?!
She could be
ANYWHERE!
In fact, she could be literally
ANYWHERE IN THE WORLD.
With all due respect,
Deputy Marshall Cheeseman,
she's probably not even in
your jurisdiction anymore.
MARS
JUSTICE . . .

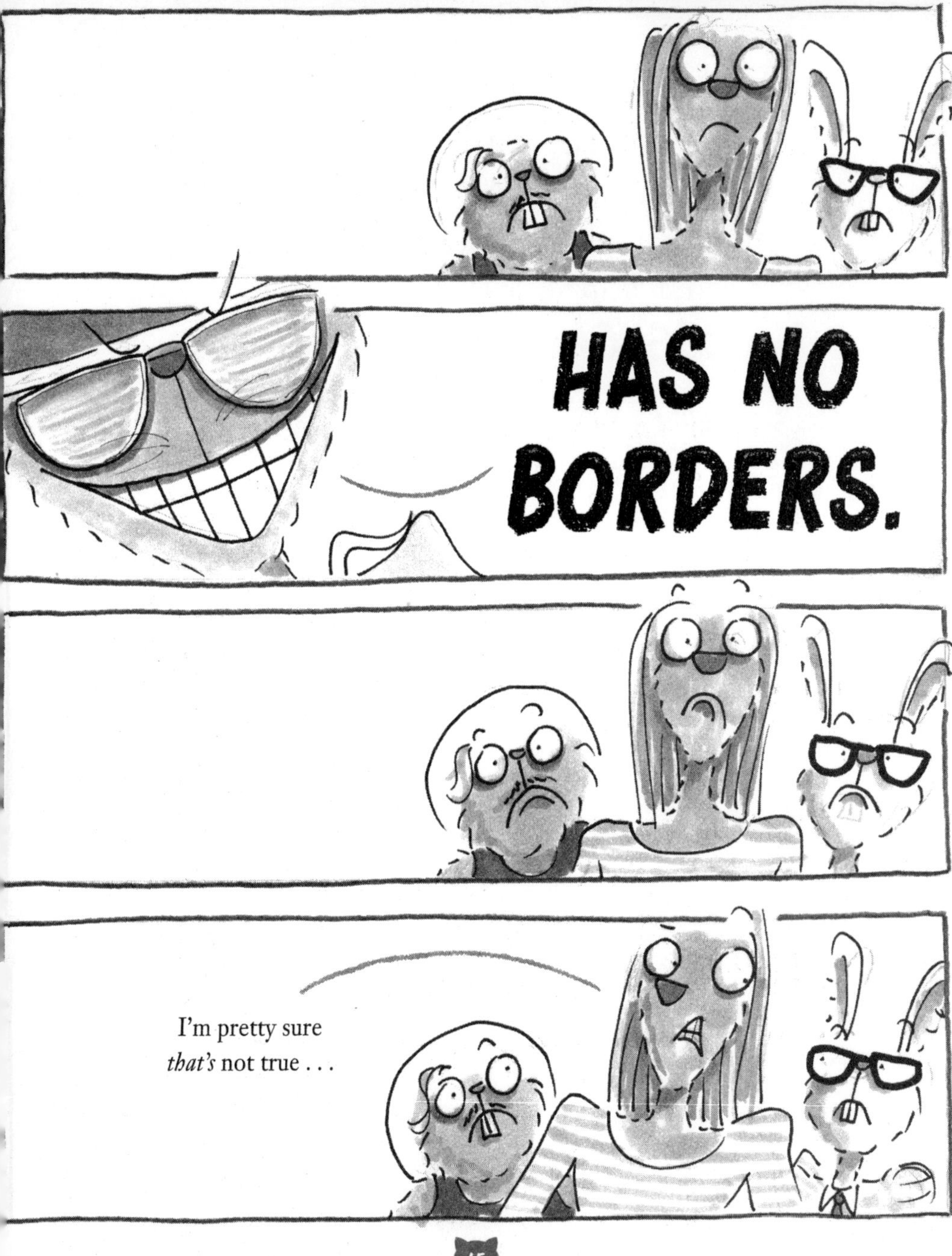
HAS NO BORDERS.
I'm pretty sure *that's* not true . . .

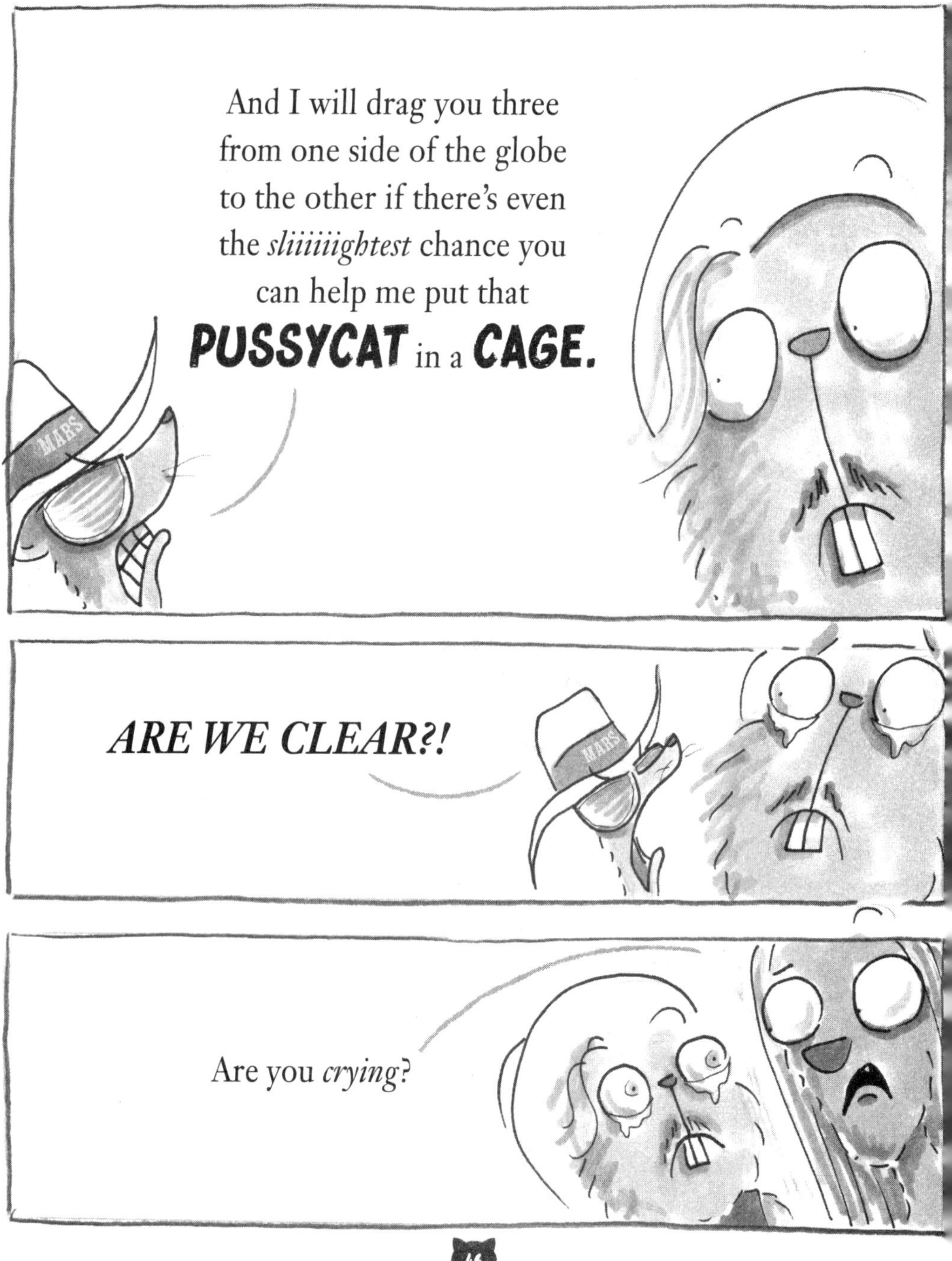
And I will drag you three from one side of the globe to the other if there's even the *sliiiiiightest* chance you can help me put that **PUSSYCAT** in a **CAGE.**
MARS
ARE WE CLEAR?!
MARS
Are you *crying*?

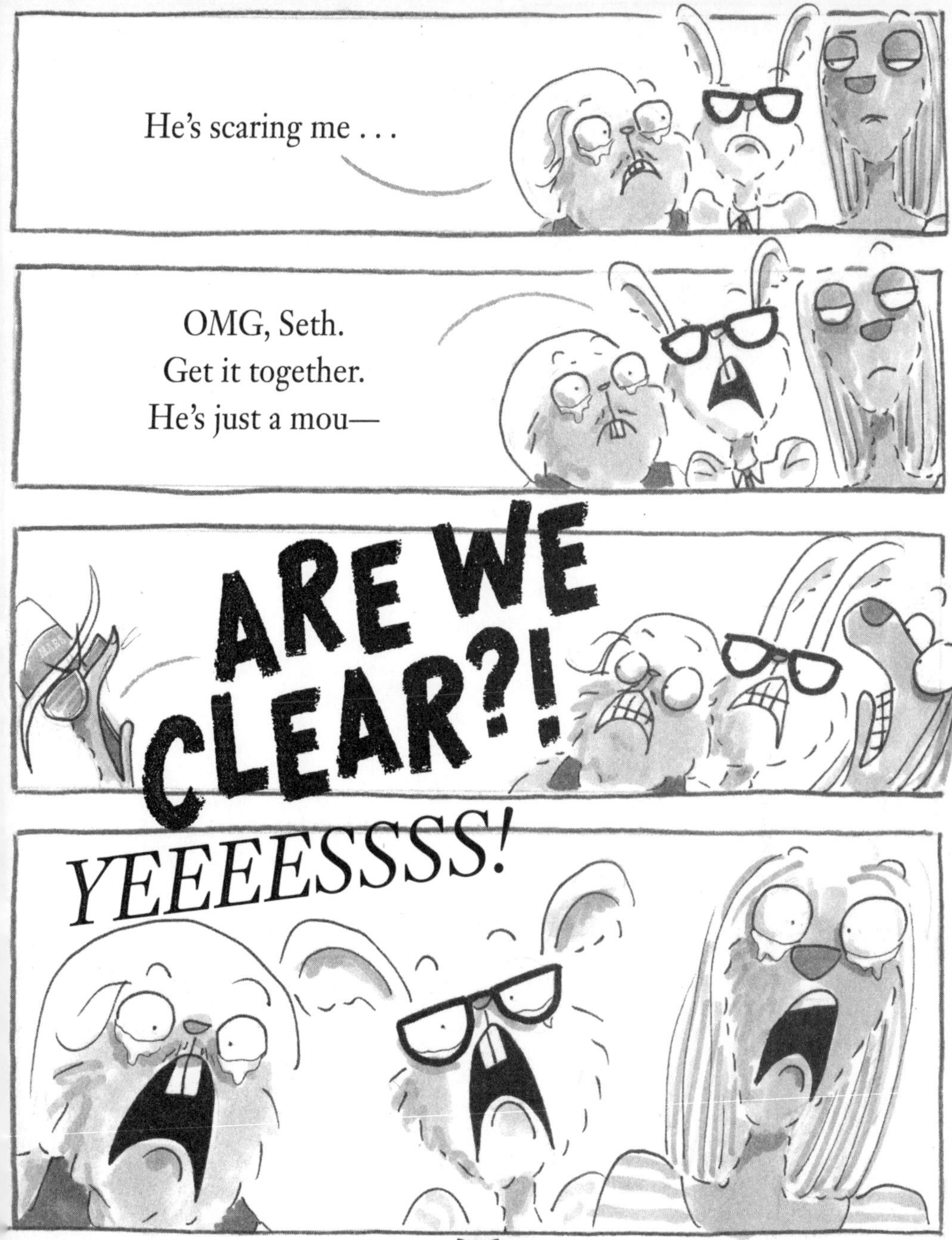
He's scaring me . . .
OMG, Seth.
Get it together.
He's just a mou—
ARE WE CLEAR?!
YEEEESSSS!

Three
PULL THAT STRING!

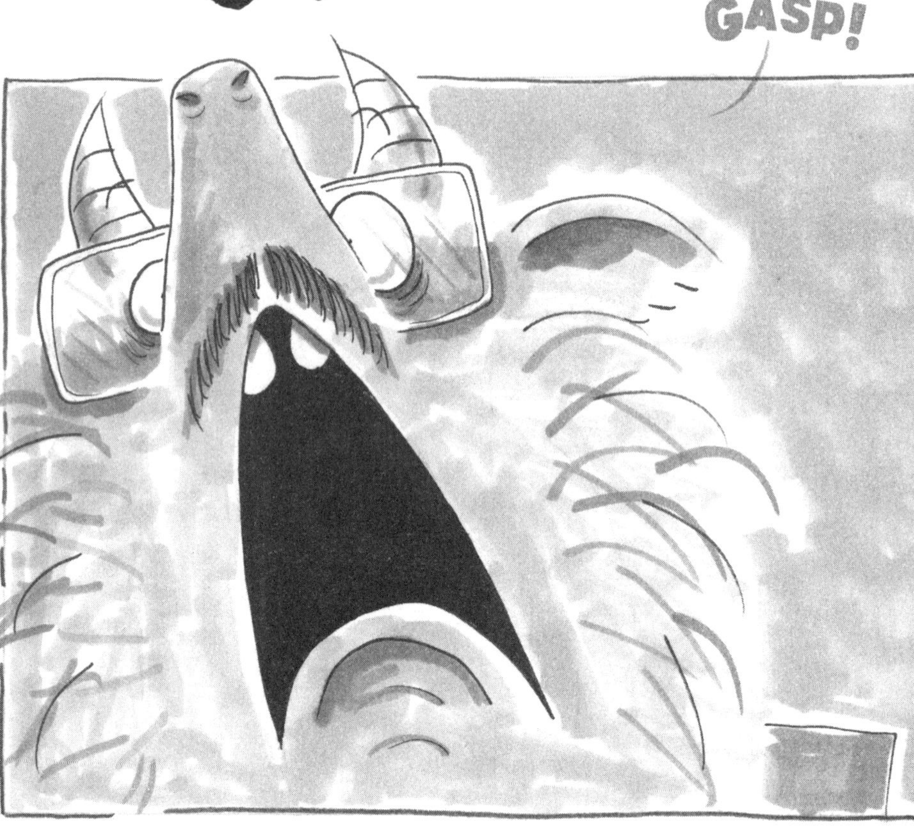
GASP!

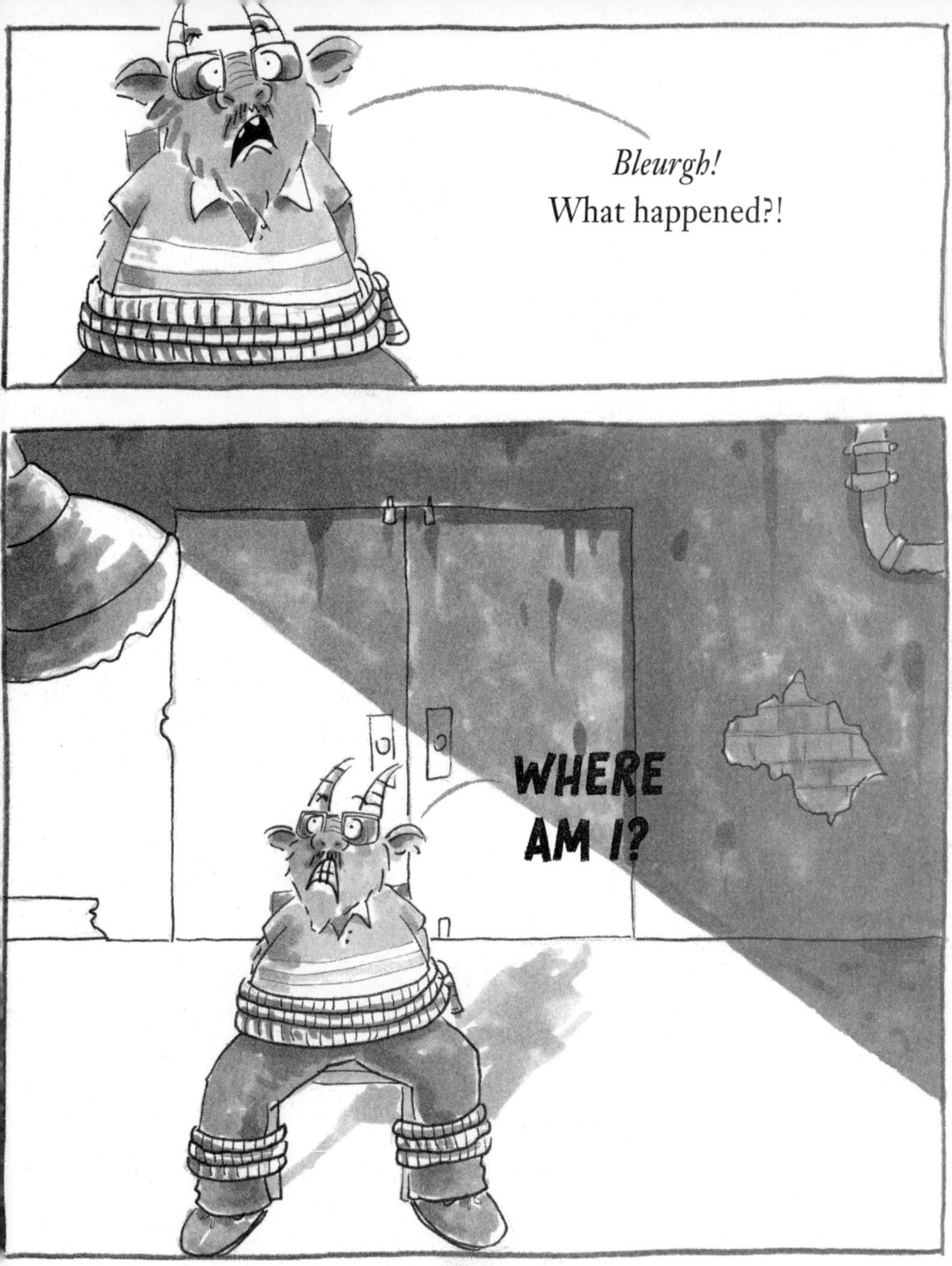
Bleurgh!
What happened?!
WHERE AM I?

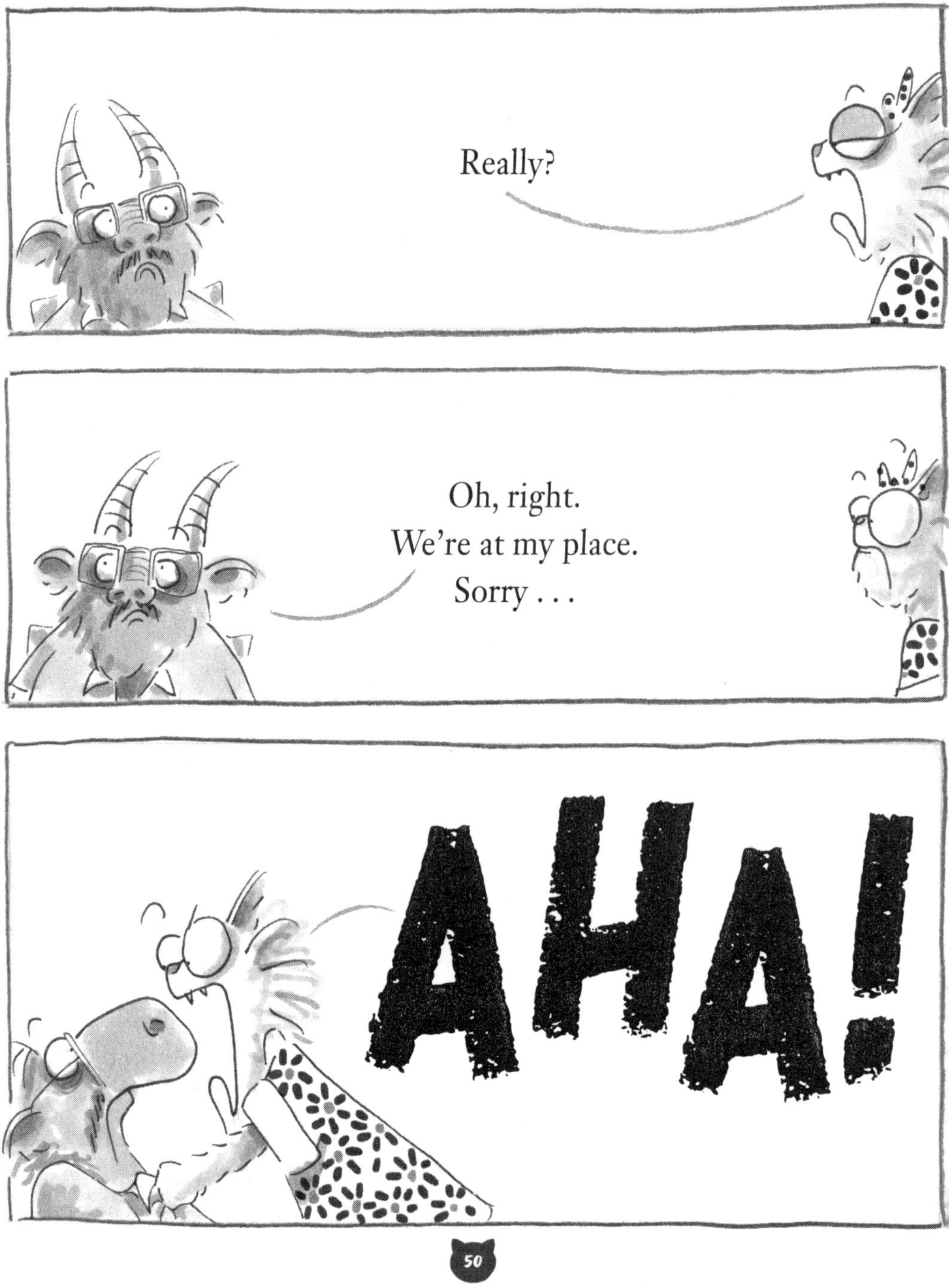
Really?
Oh, right.
We're at my place.
Sorry . . .
AHA!

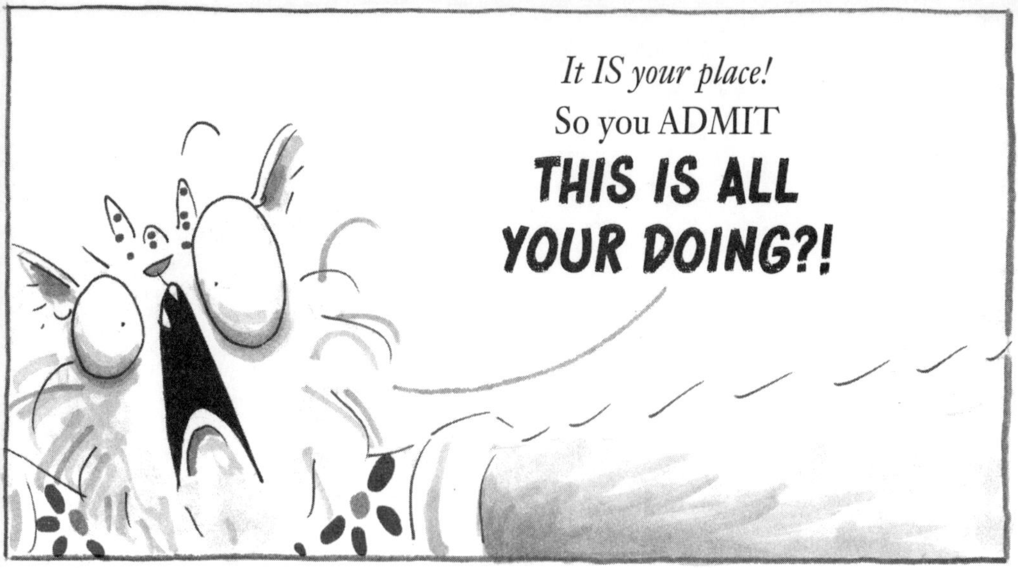
It IS your place!
So you ADMIT
THIS IS ALL YOUR DOING?!

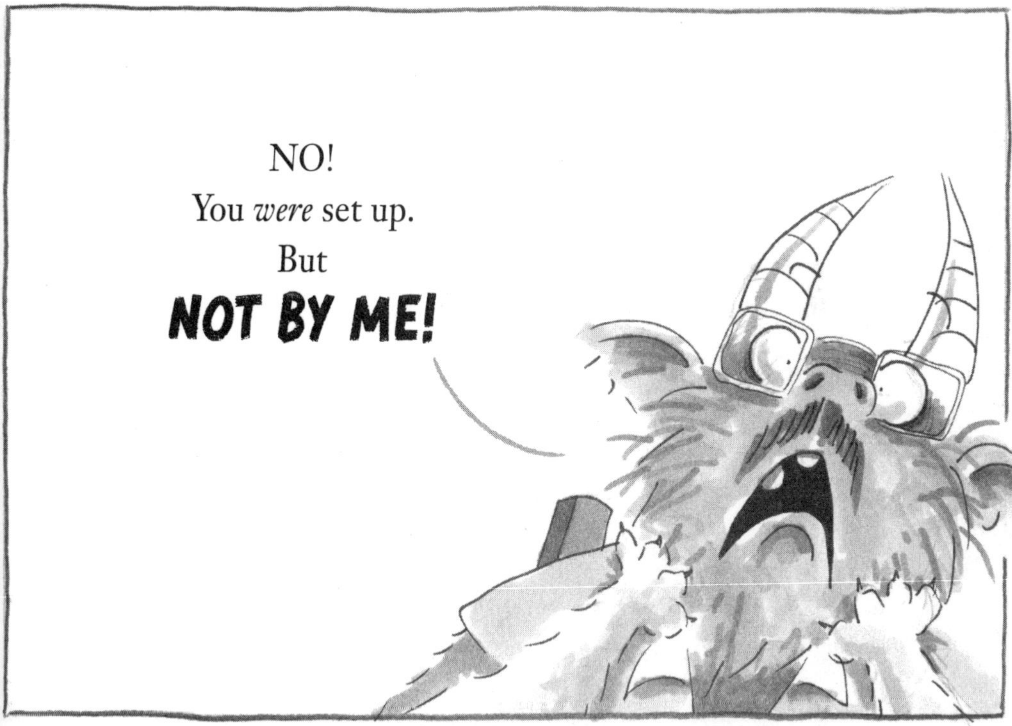
NO!
You *were* set up.
But
NOT BY ME!

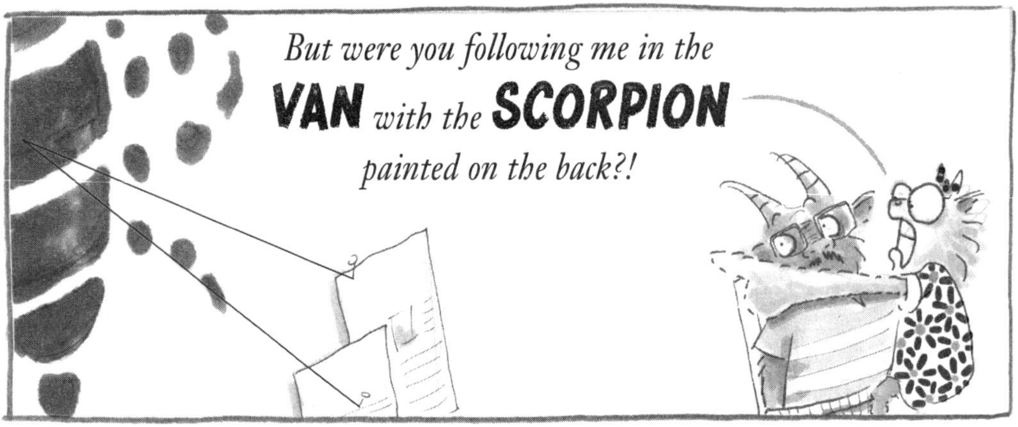
But were you following me in the
VAN with the SCORPION
painted on the back?!

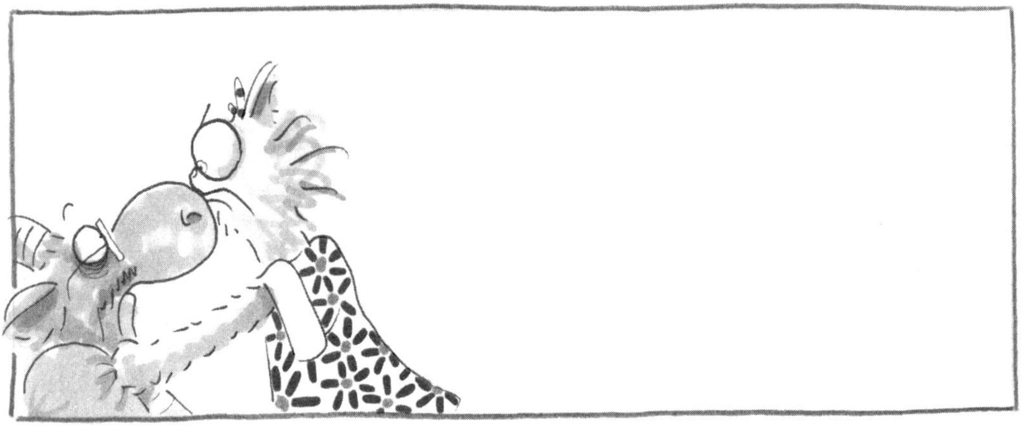

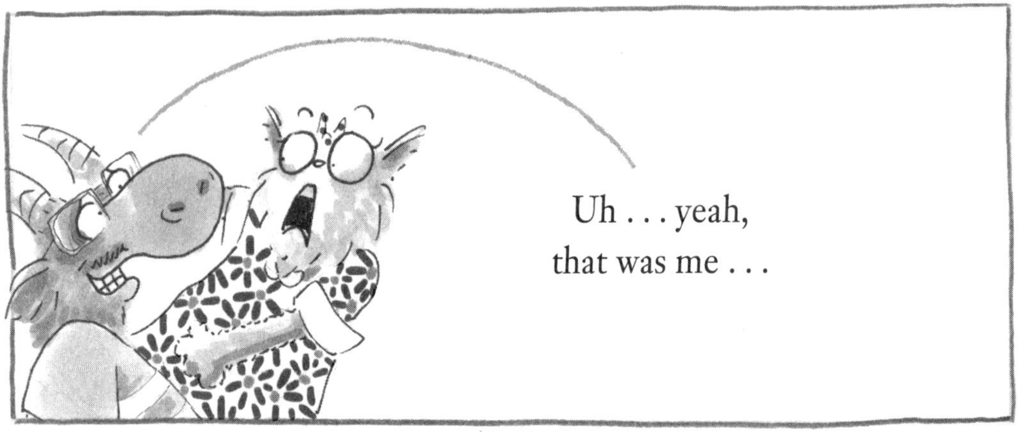
Uh . . . yeah,
that was me . . .

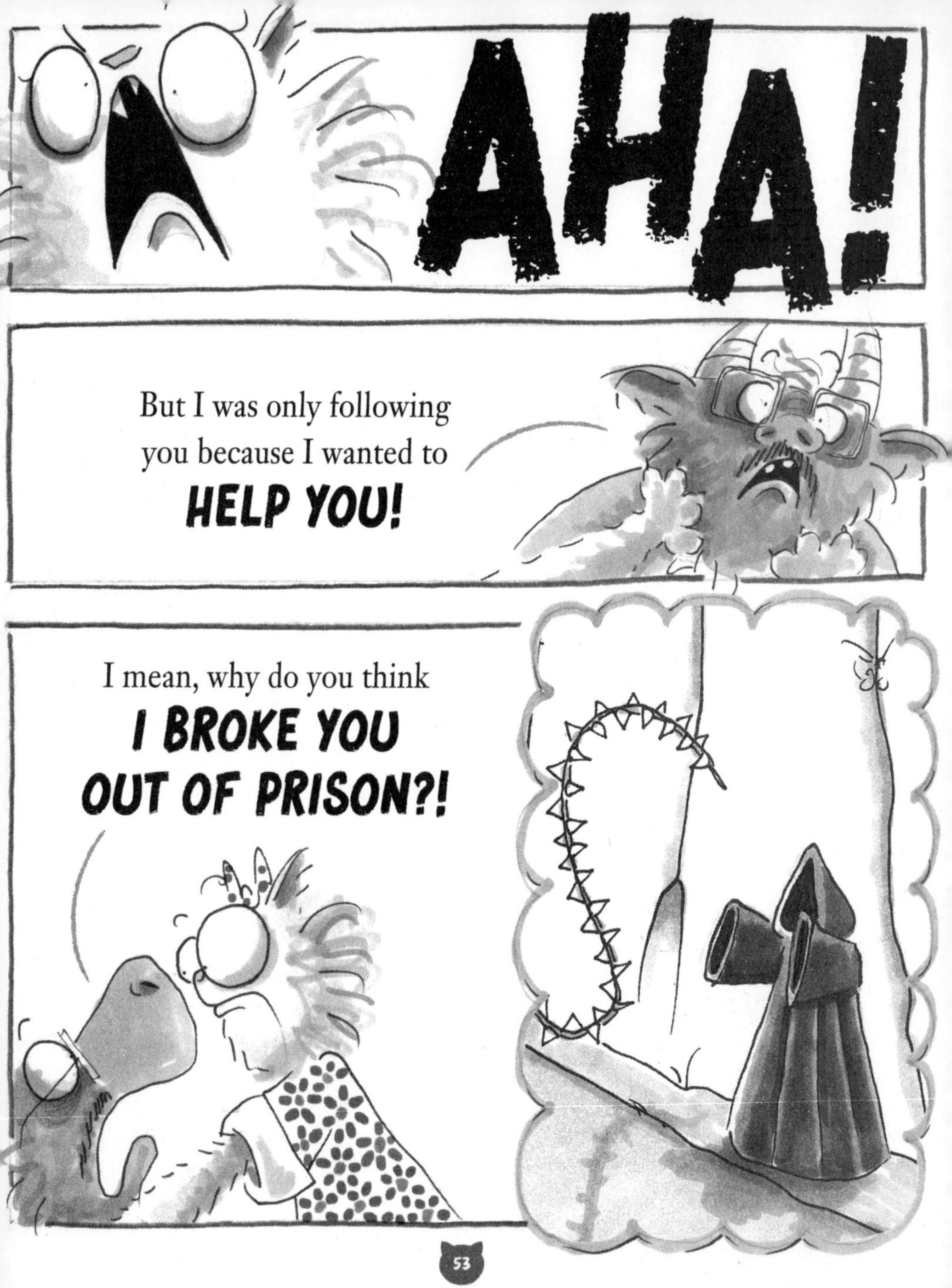
AHA!
But I was only following you because I wanted to HELP YOU!
I mean, why do you think I BROKE YOU OUT OF PRISON?!

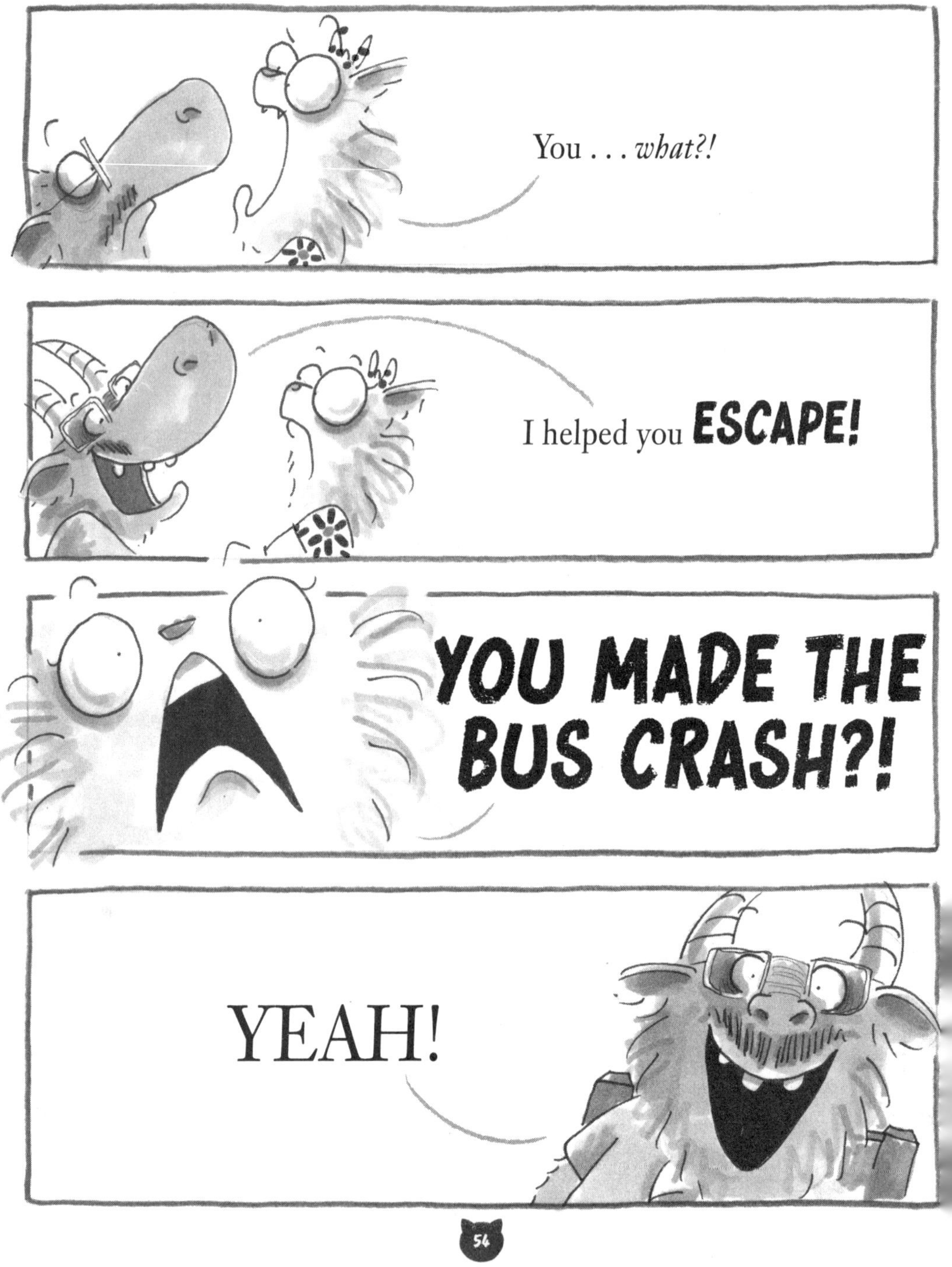
You . . . *what?!*
I helped you **ESCAPE!**
YOU MADE THE BUS CRASH?!
YEAH!

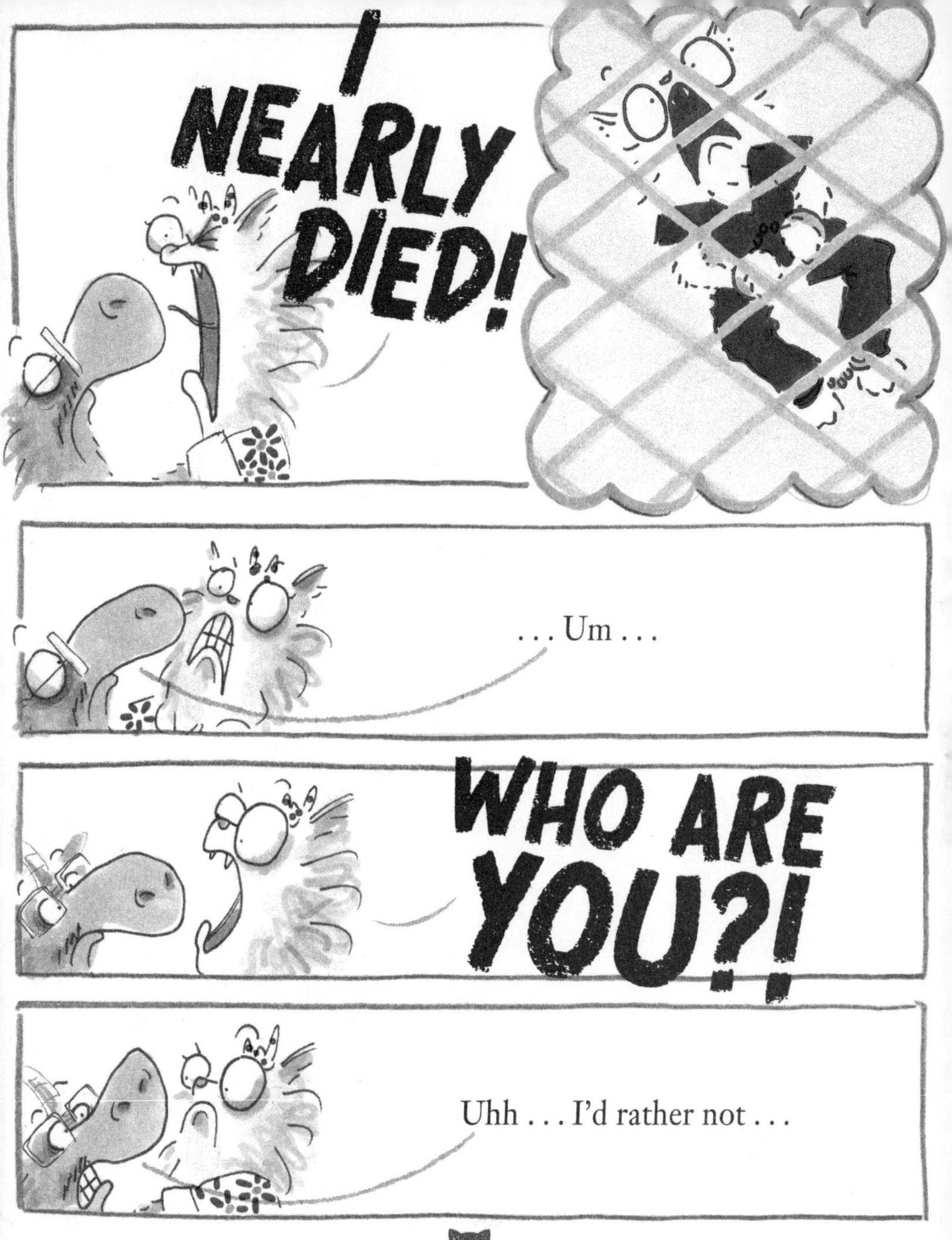
I NEARLY DIED!
. . . Um . . .
WHO ARE YOU?!
Uhh . . . I'd rather not . . .

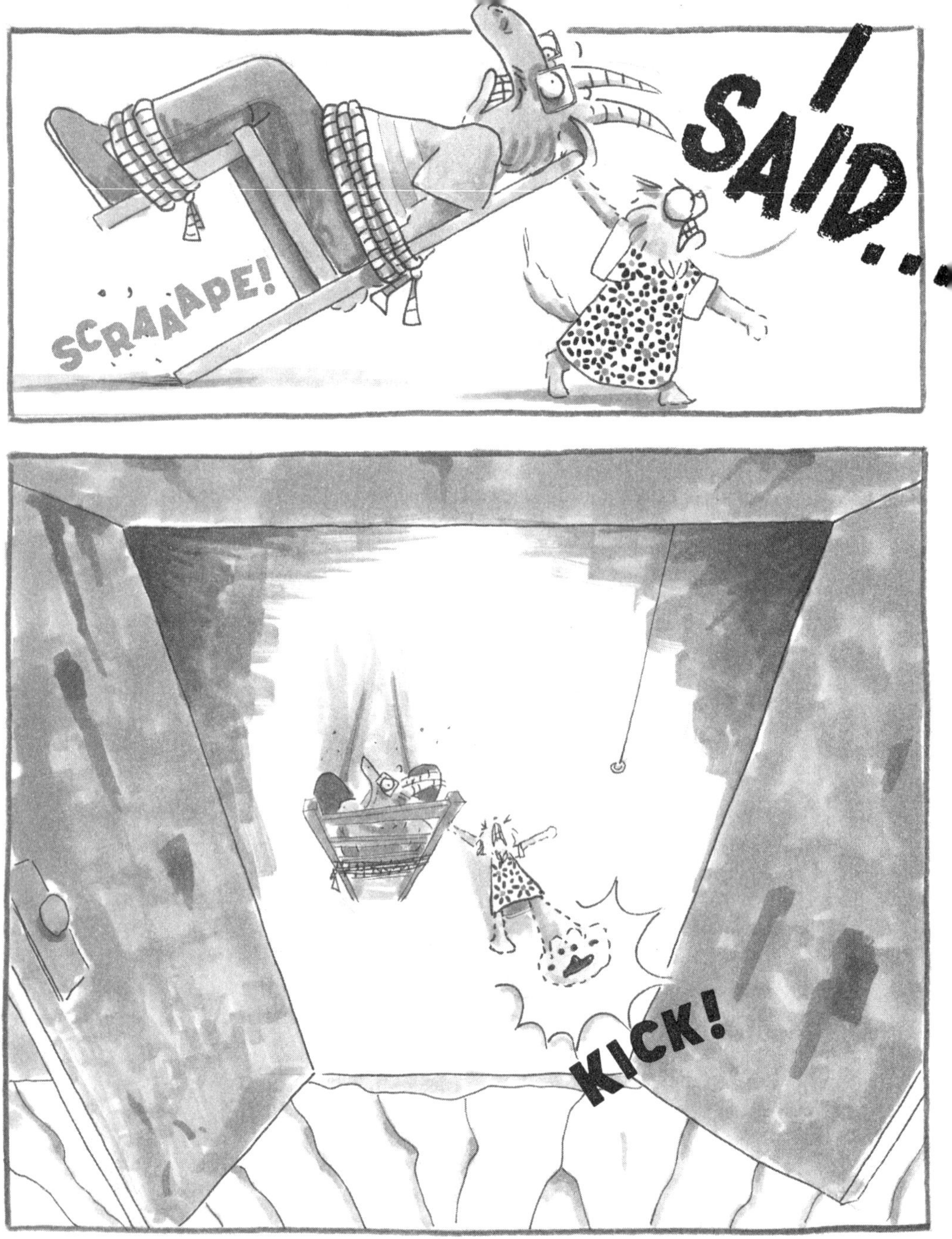
I SAID...
SCRAAAPE!
KICK!

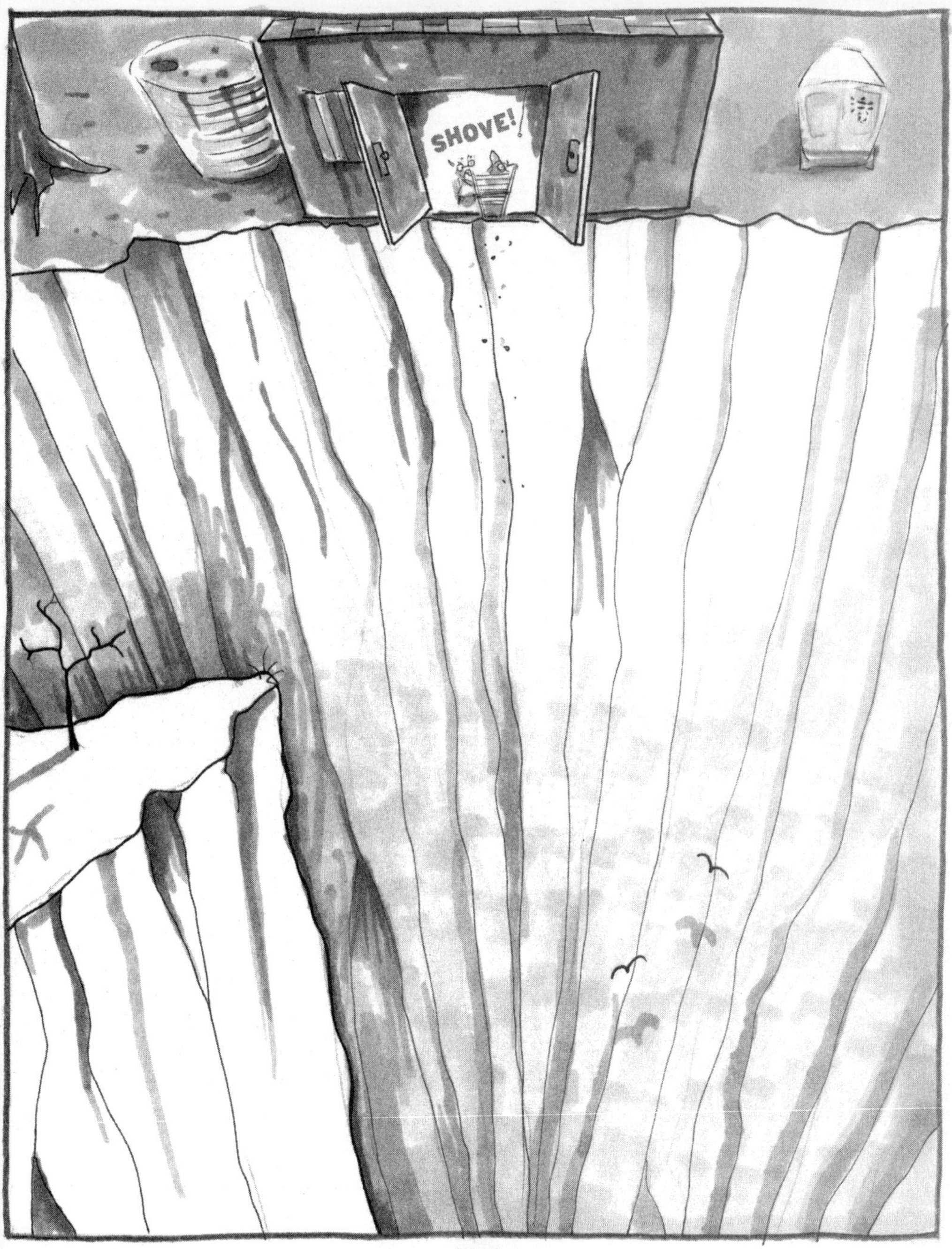
SHOVE!

WHO ARE YOU?!
MARV!
My name's *Marv*!
And why did you KIDNAP ME, Marv?
I told you!
I wanted to HELP YOU!

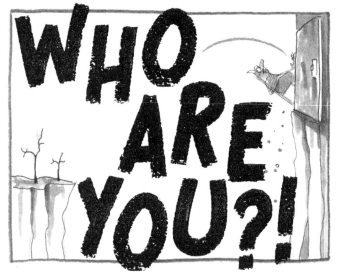

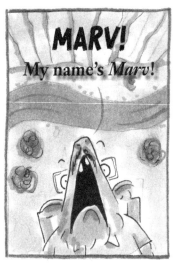

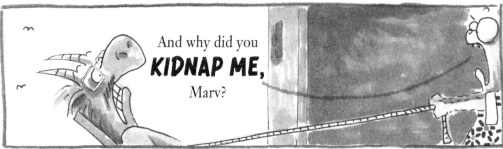

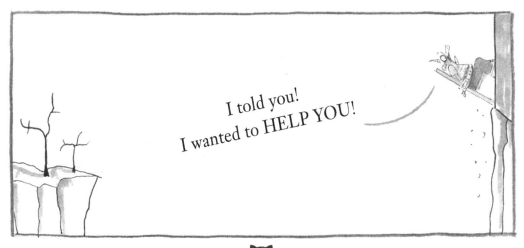

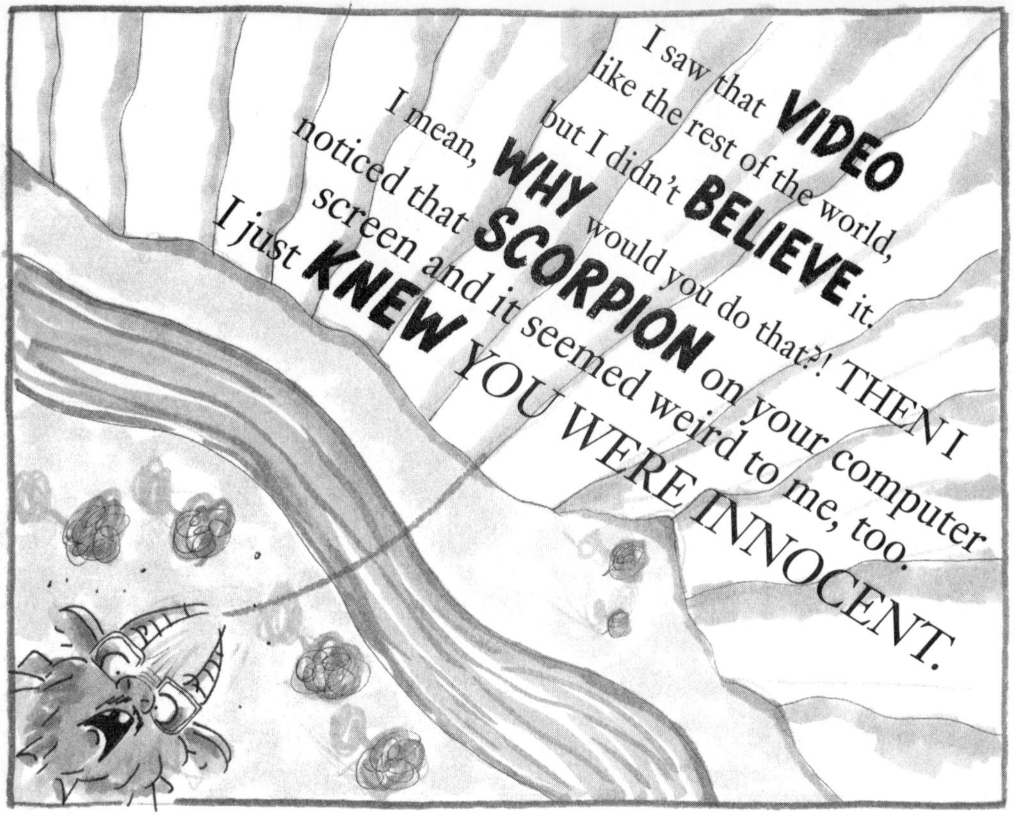
I saw that VIDEO
like the rest of the world,
but I didn't BELIEVE it.
I mean, WHY would you do that?! THEN I
noticed that SCORPION on your computer
screen and it seemed weird to me, too.
I just KNEW YOU WERE INNOCENT.

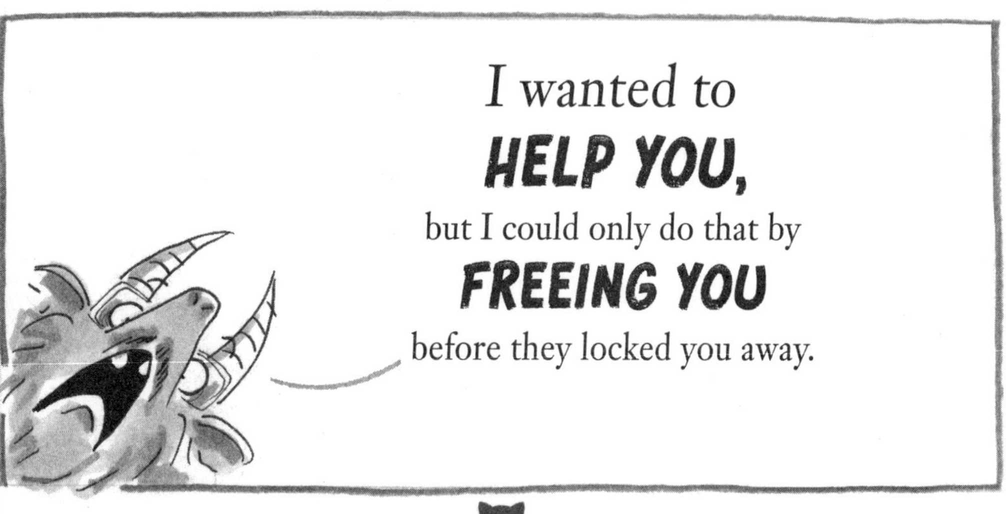
I wanted to
HELP YOU,
but I could only do that by
FREEING YOU
before they locked you away.

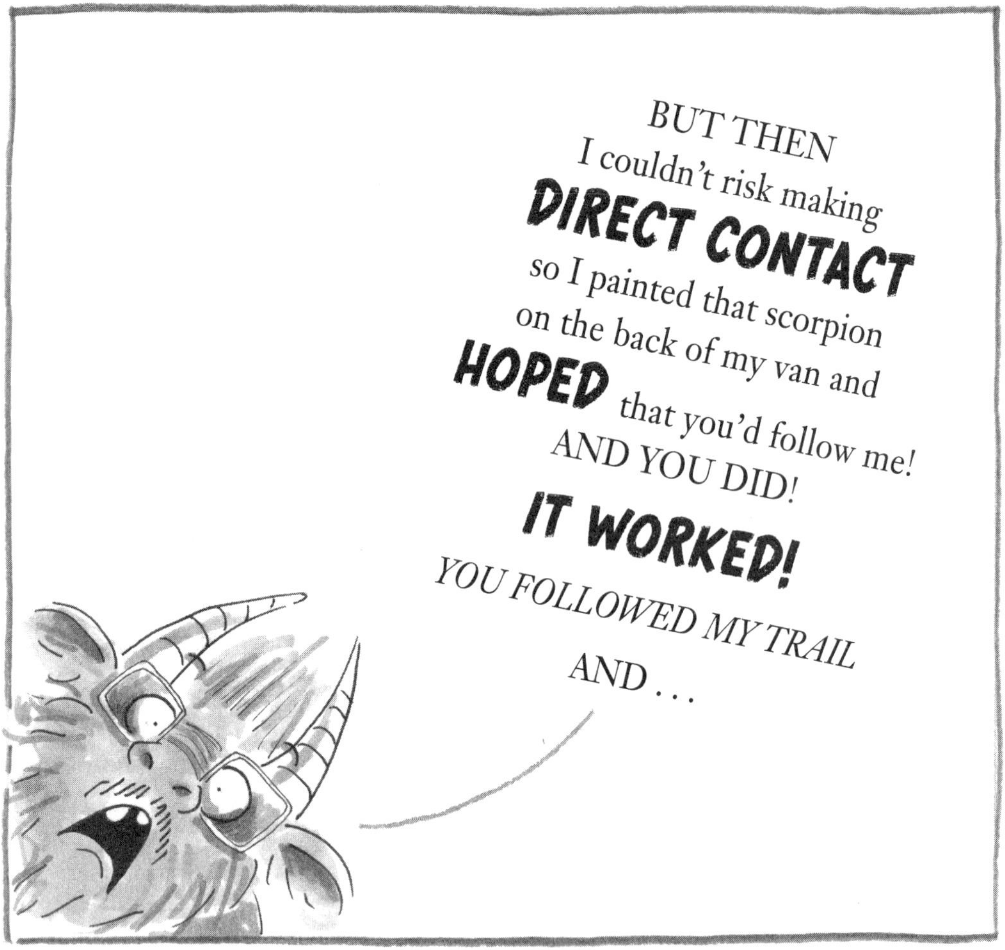
BUT THEN
I couldn't risk making
DIRECT CONTACT
so I painted that scorpion
on the back of my van and
HOPED that you'd follow me!
AND YOU DID!
IT WORKED!
YOU FOLLOWED MY TRAIL
AND . . .

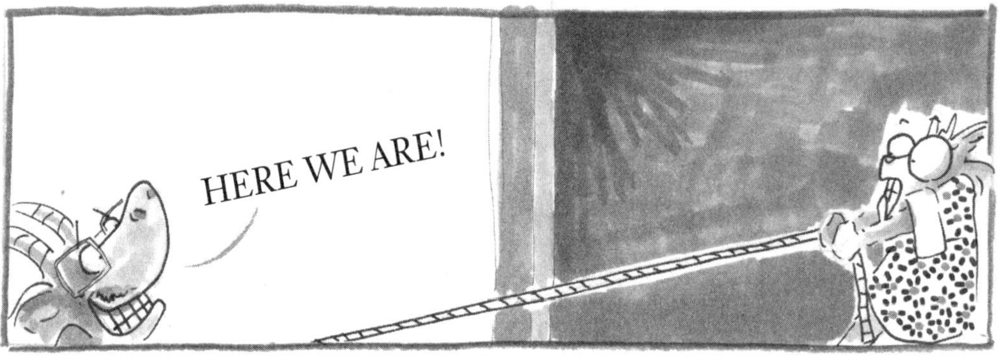
HERE WE ARE!

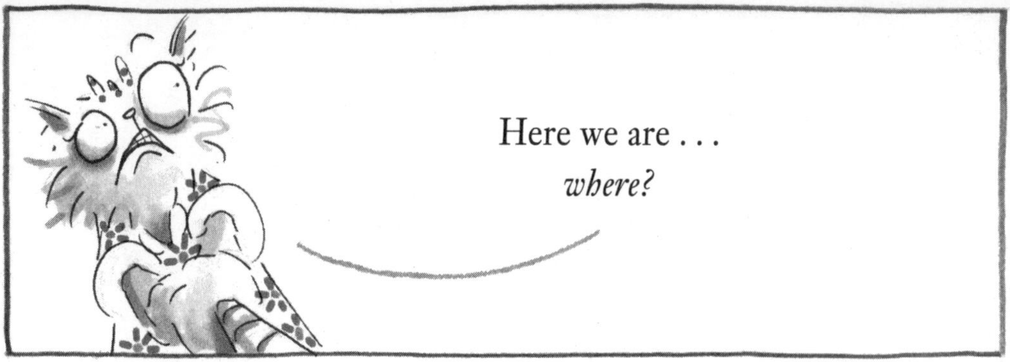
Here we are . . .
where?

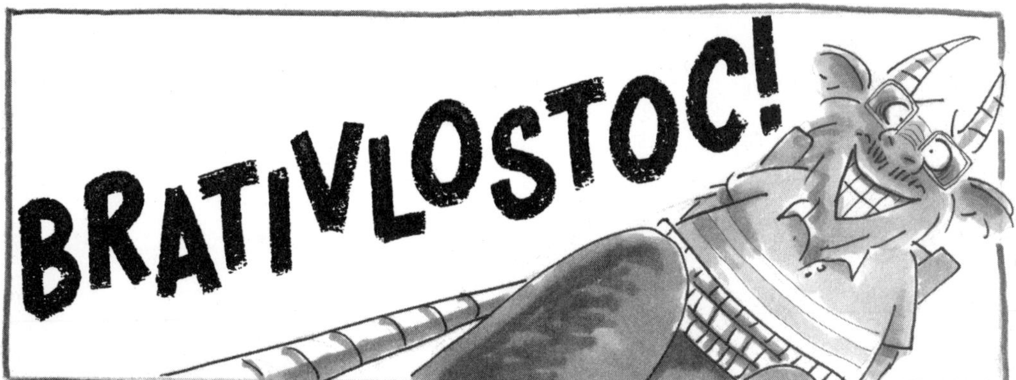
BRATIVLOSTOC!

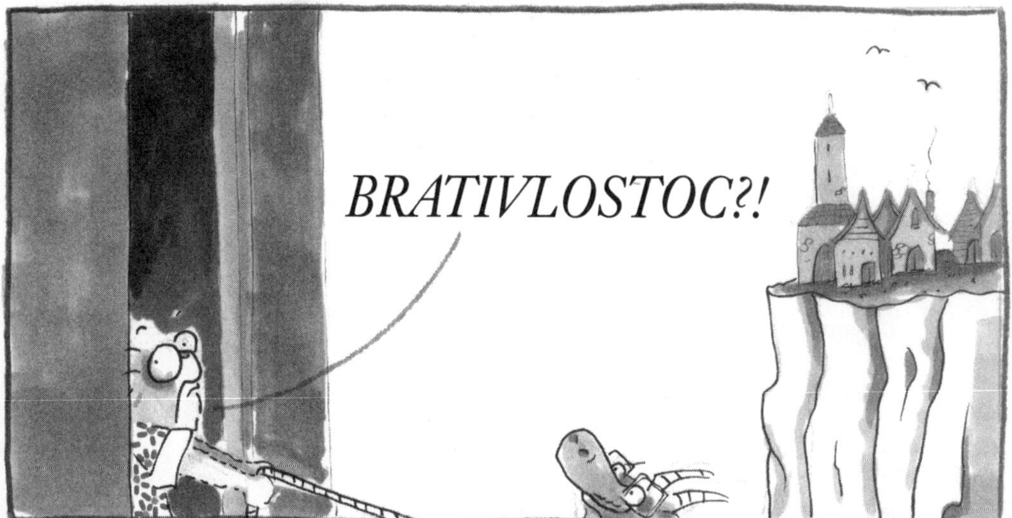
BRATIVLOSTOC?!

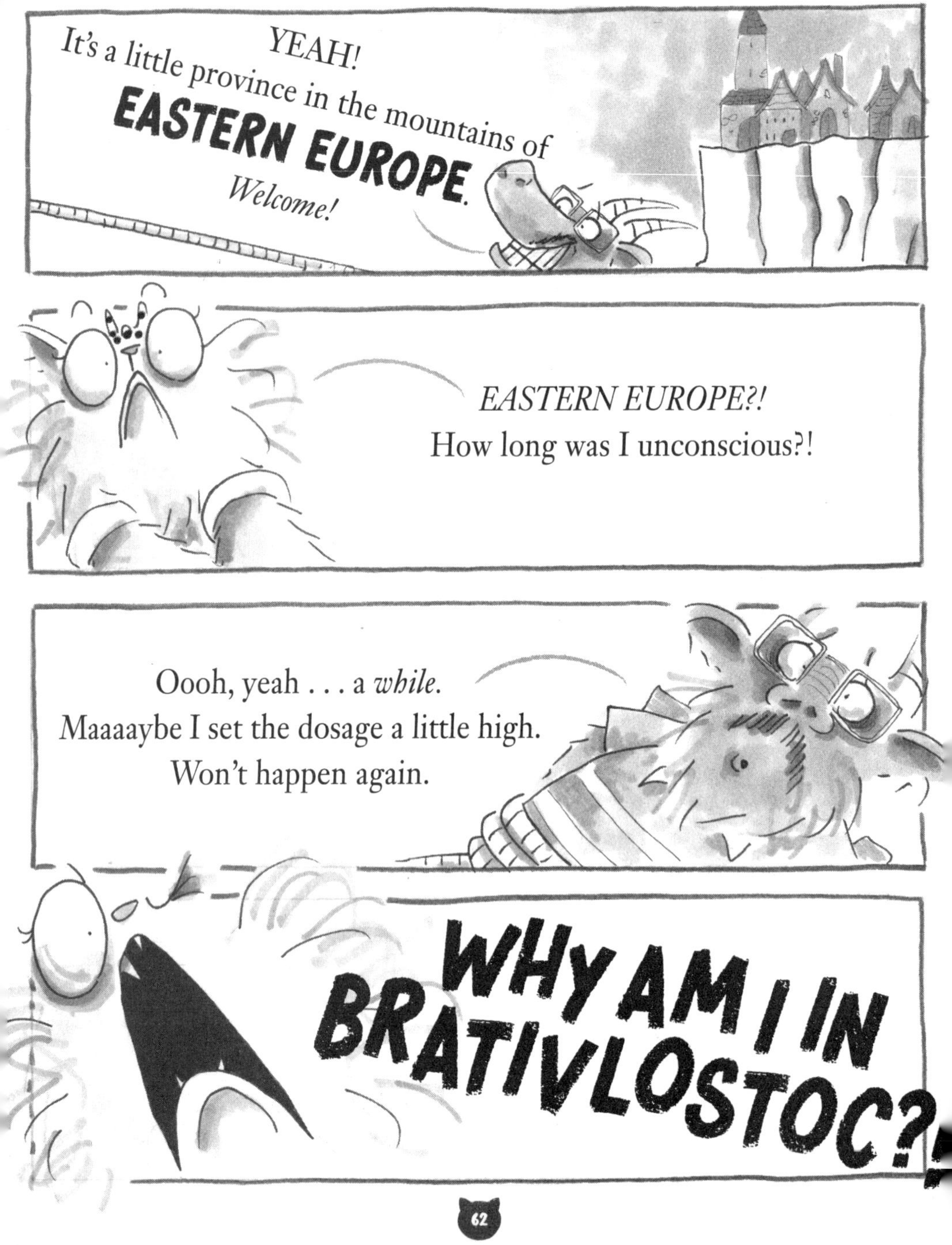
YEAH!
It's a little province in the mountains of EASTERN EUROPE.
Welcome!
EASTERN EUROPE?!
How long was I unconscious?!
Oooh, yeah . . . a while.
Maaaaybe I set the dosage a little high.
Won't happen again.
WHY AM I IN BRATIVLOSTOC?!

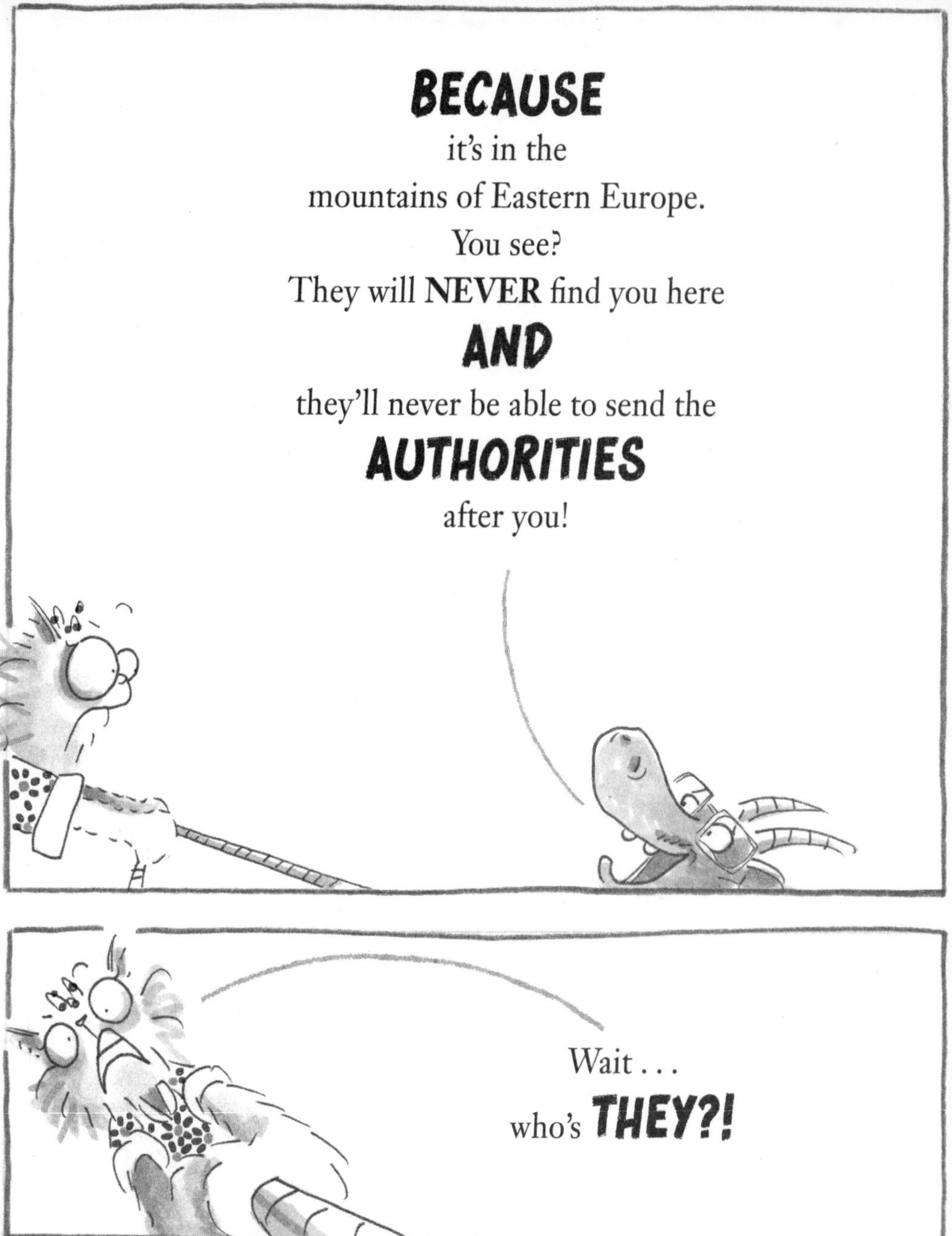
BECAUSE
it's in the
mountains of Eastern Europe.
You see?
They will NEVER find you here
AND
they'll never be able to send the
AUTHORITIES
after you!
Wait . . .
who's THEY?!

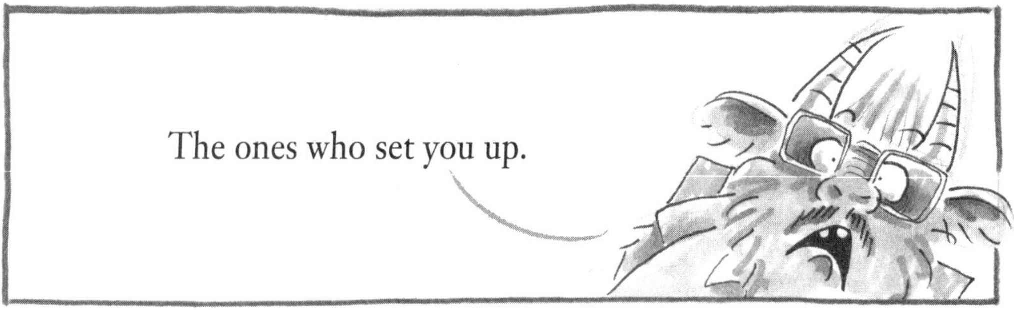
The ones who set you up.

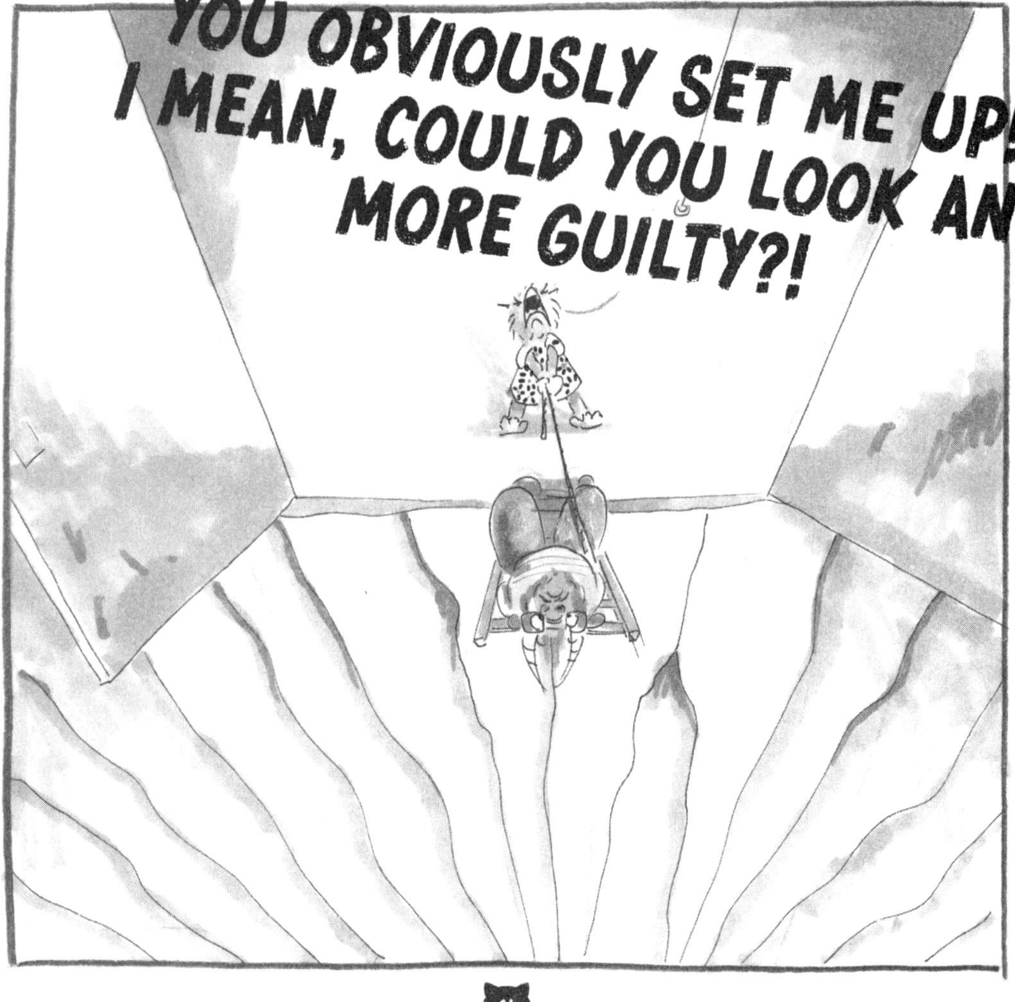
YOU OBVIOUSLY SET ME UP! I MEAN, COULD YOU LOOK ANY MORE GUILTY?!

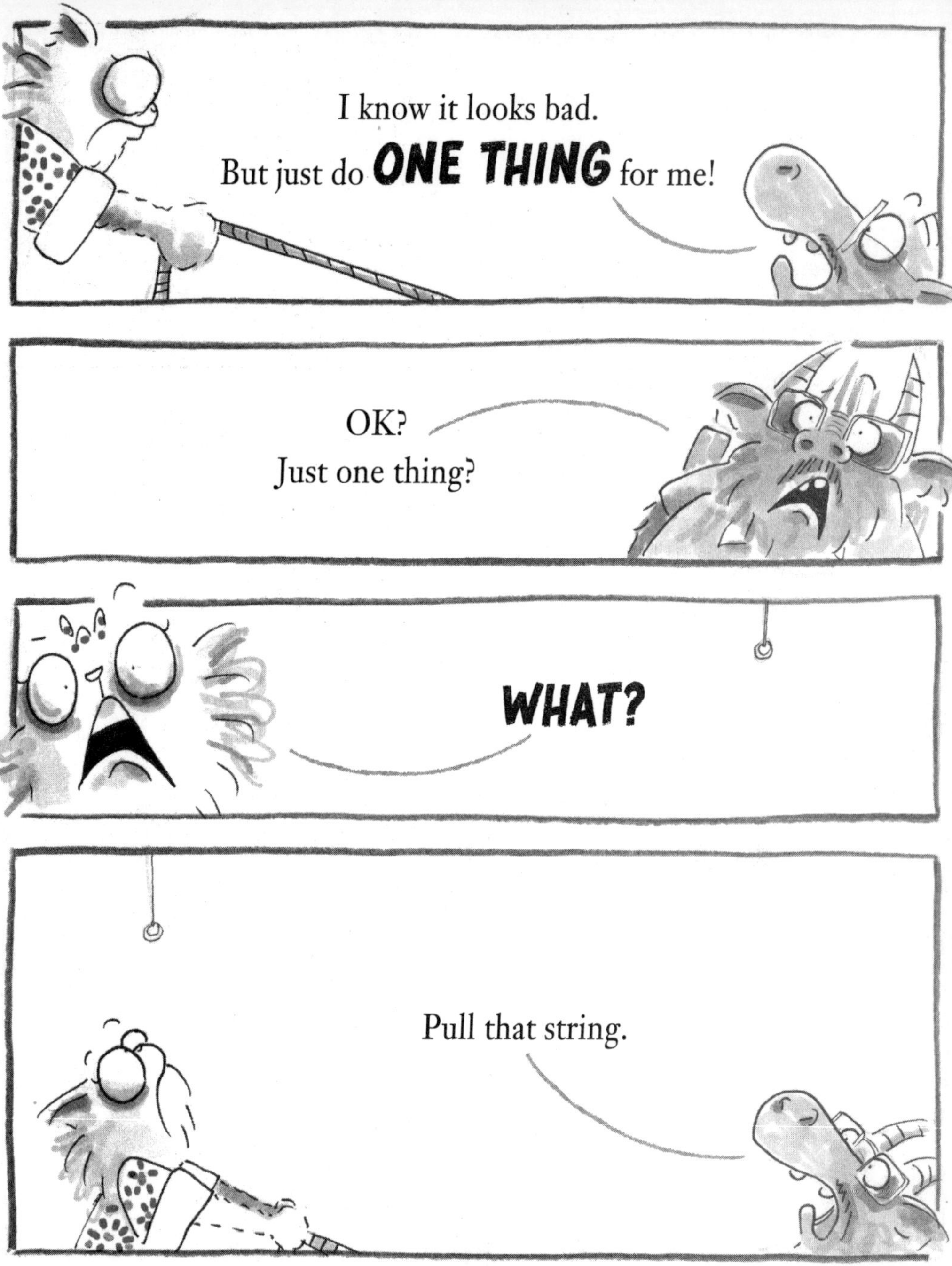
I know it looks bad.
But just do ONE THING for me!
OK?
Just one thing?
WHAT?
Pull that string.

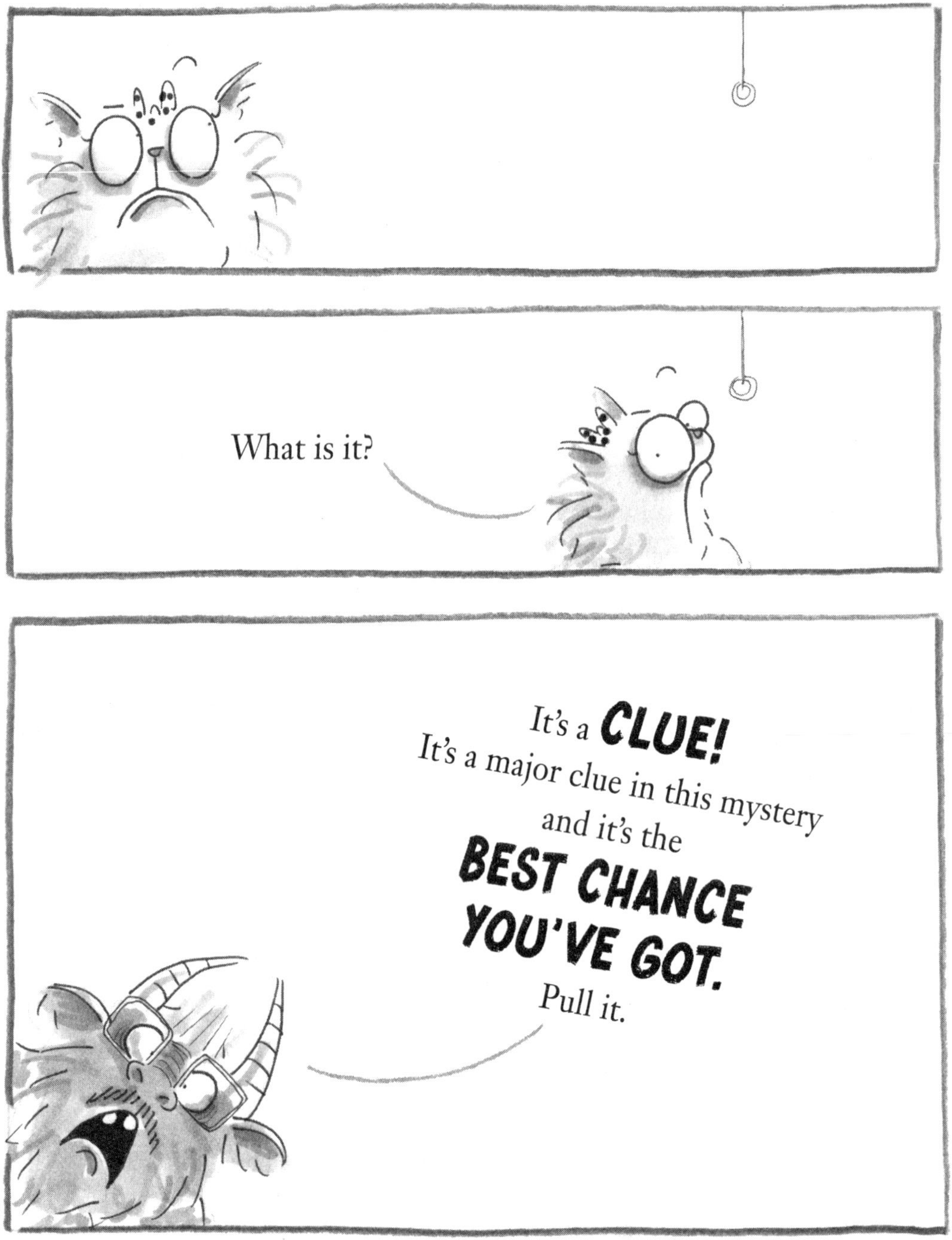

What is it?
It's a CLUE!
It's a major clue in this mystery
and it's the
BEST CHANCE
YOU'VE GOT.
Pull it.

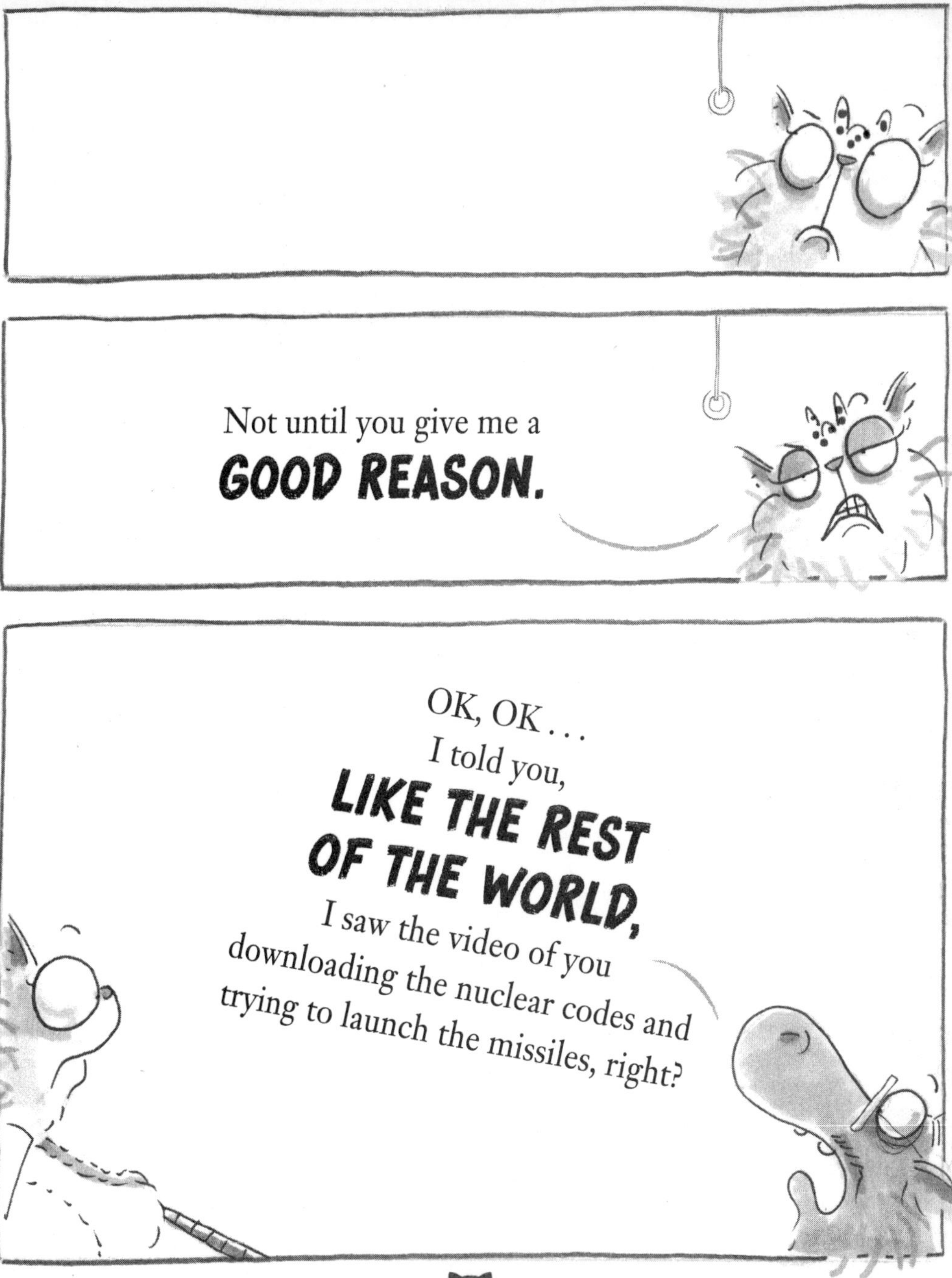
Not until you give me a
GOOD REASON.
OK, OK . . .
I told you,
LIKE THE REST OF THE WORLD,
I saw the video of you downloading the nuclear codes and trying to launch the missiles, right?

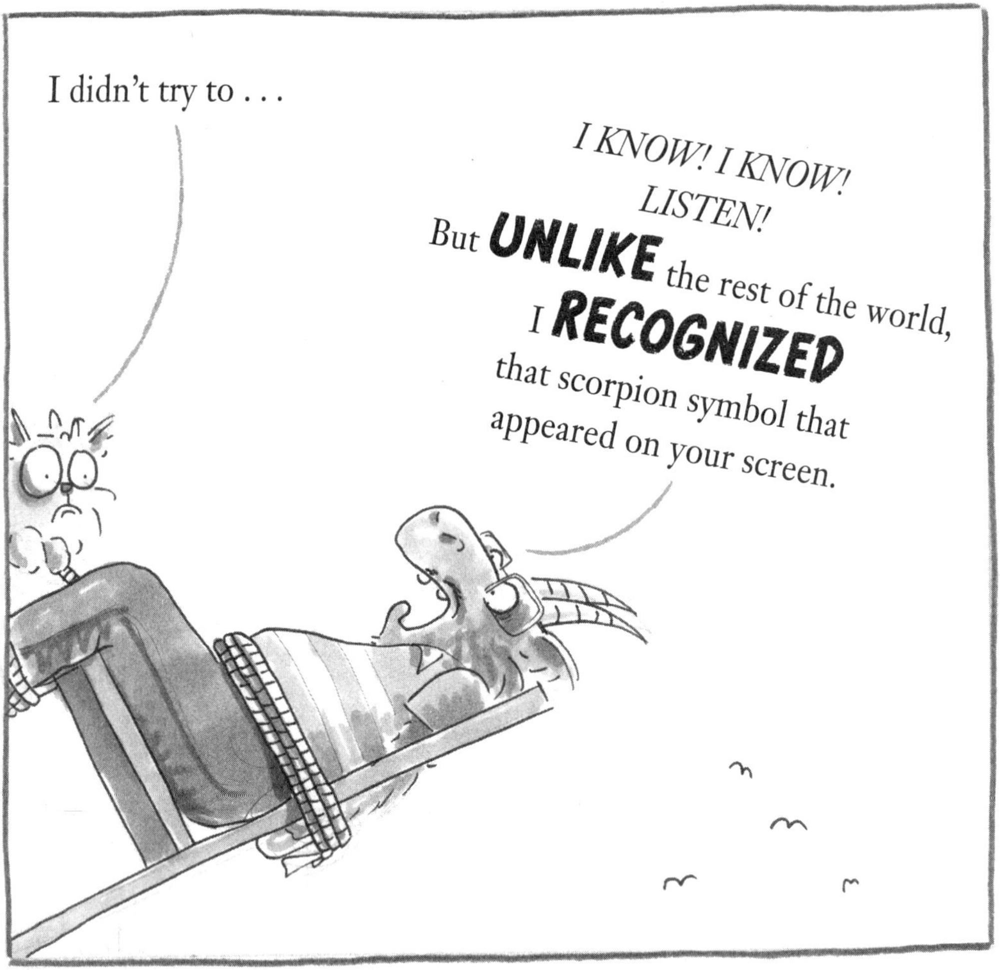
I didn't try to . . .
I KNOW! I KNOW! LISTEN!
But UNLIKE the rest of the world, I RECOGNIZED that scorpion symbol that appeared on your screen.

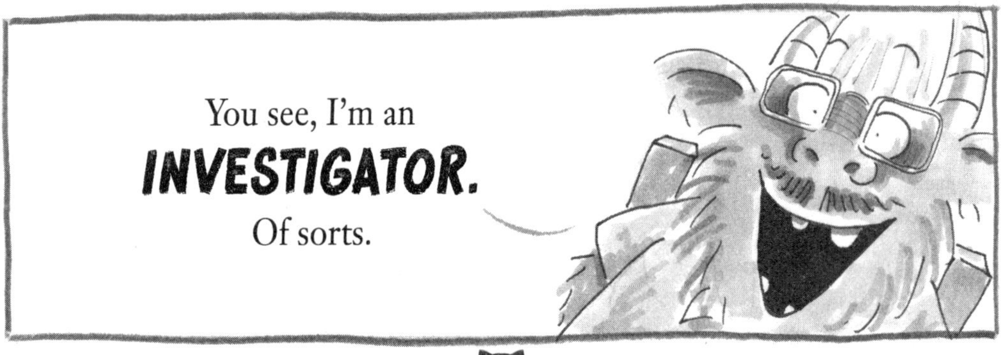
You see, I'm an INVESTIGATOR. Of sorts.

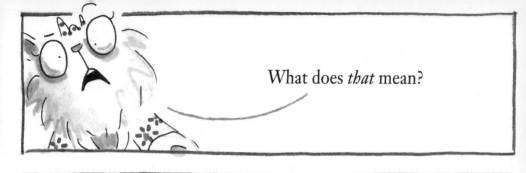

What does *that* mean?

Well, the world is a **DARK** and **MYSTERIOUS** place. I develop **THEORIES** to try to get to the bottom of those mysteries.

Oh, I see. You're a **NUT.**

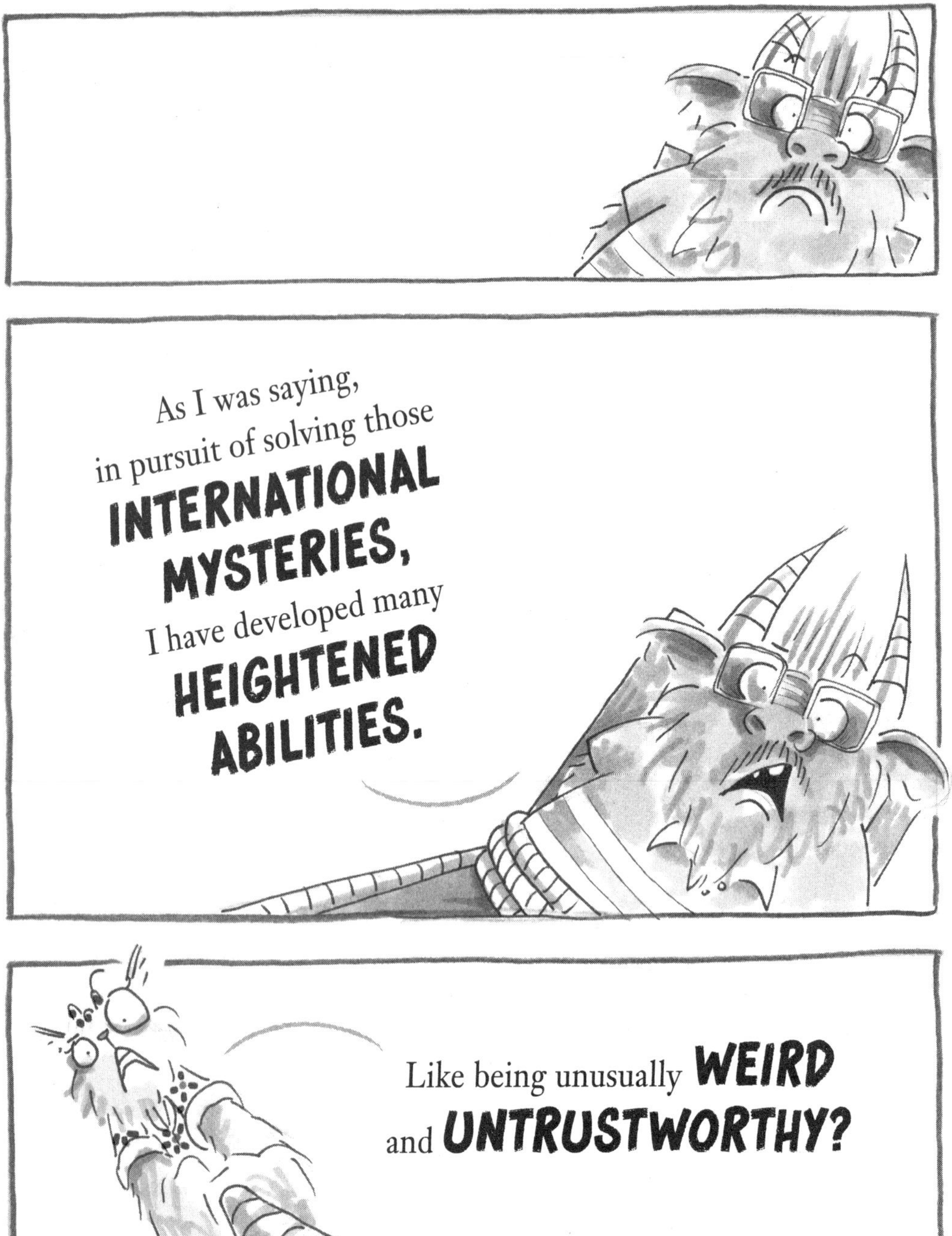

As I was saying, in pursuit of solving those INTERNATIONAL MYSTERIES, I have developed many HEIGHTENED ABILITIES.
Like being unusually WEIRD and UNTRUSTWORTHY?

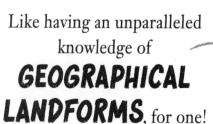

Like having an unparalleled knowledge of **GEOGRAPHICAL LANDFORMS**, for one!

Oh, that must come in handy.

SERIOUSLY, WHY WOULD ANYONE EVER NEED THAT? LIKE, EVER?!

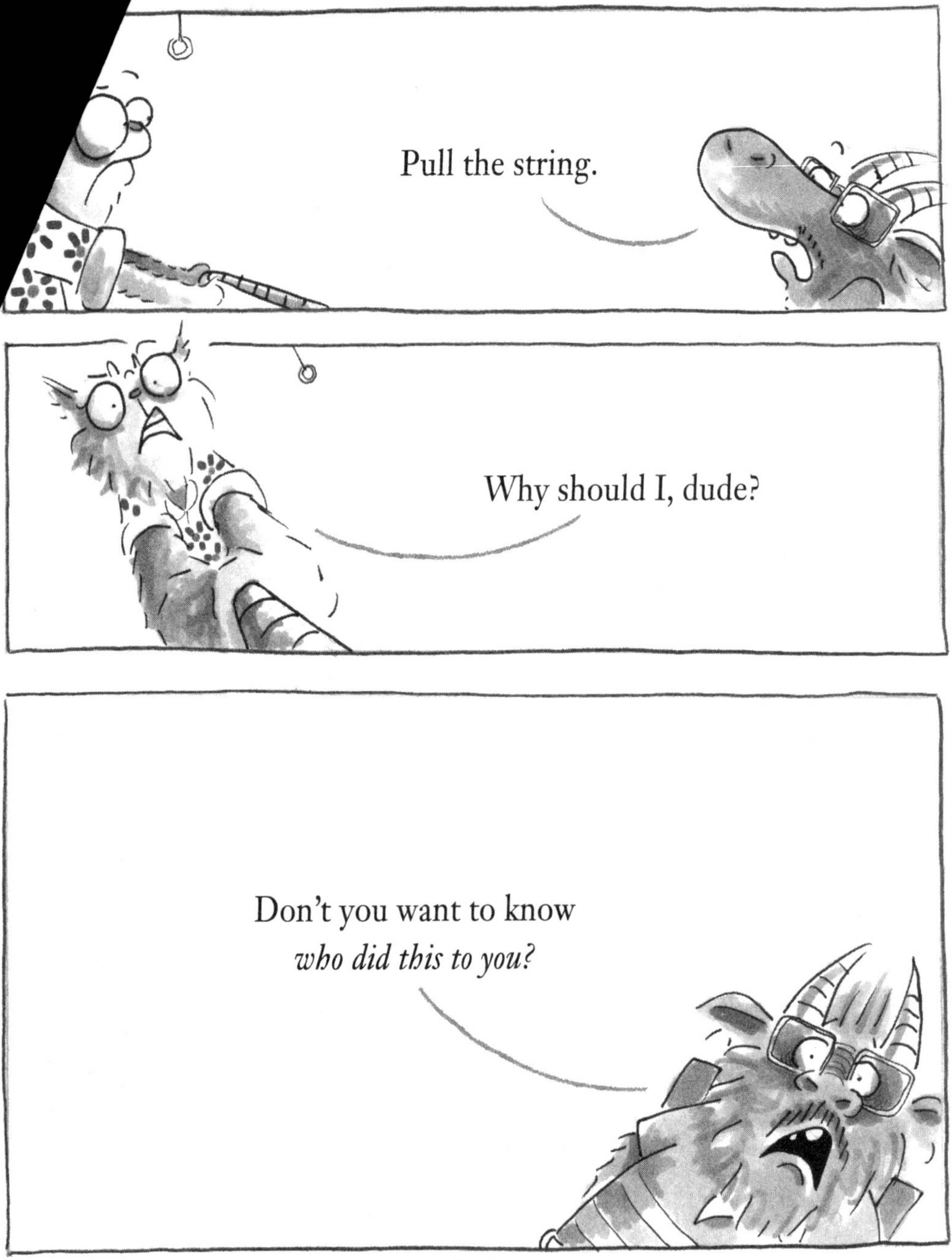
Pull the string.
Why should I, dude?
Don't you want to know *who did this to you?*

ZOOOT!

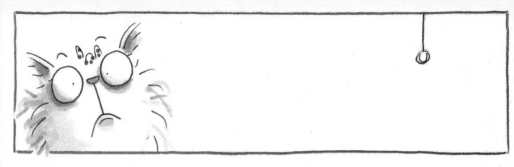

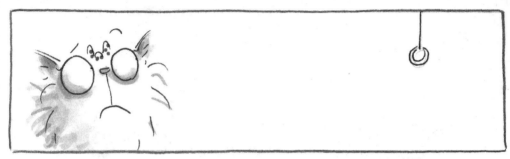

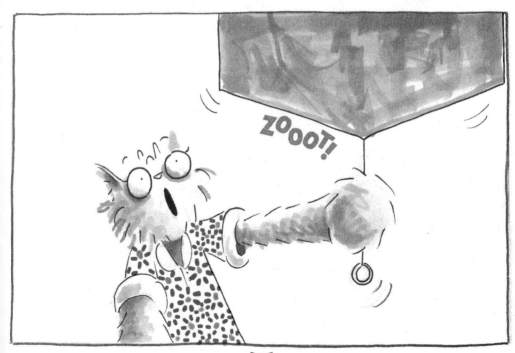

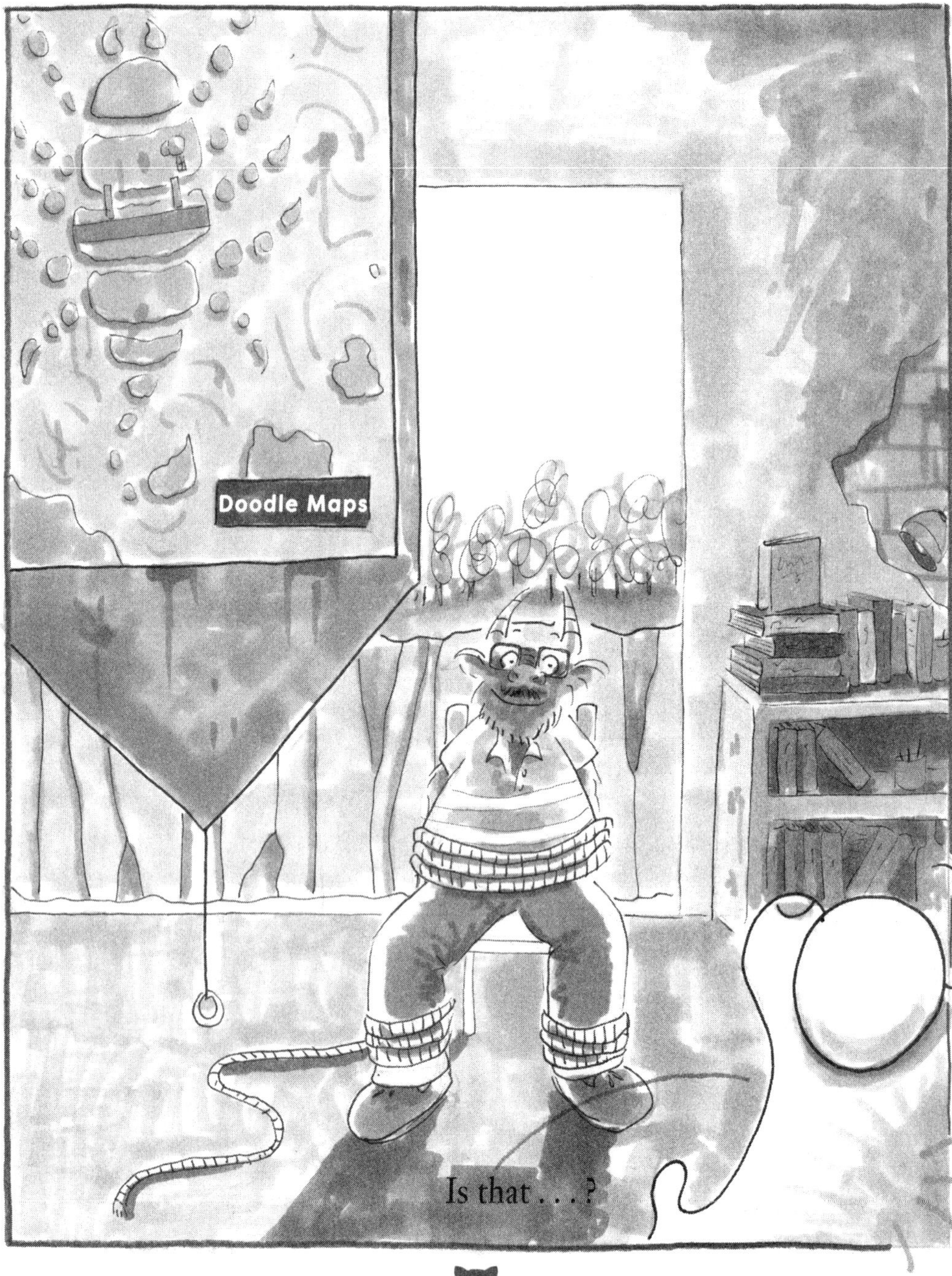
Doodle Maps
Is that . . . ?

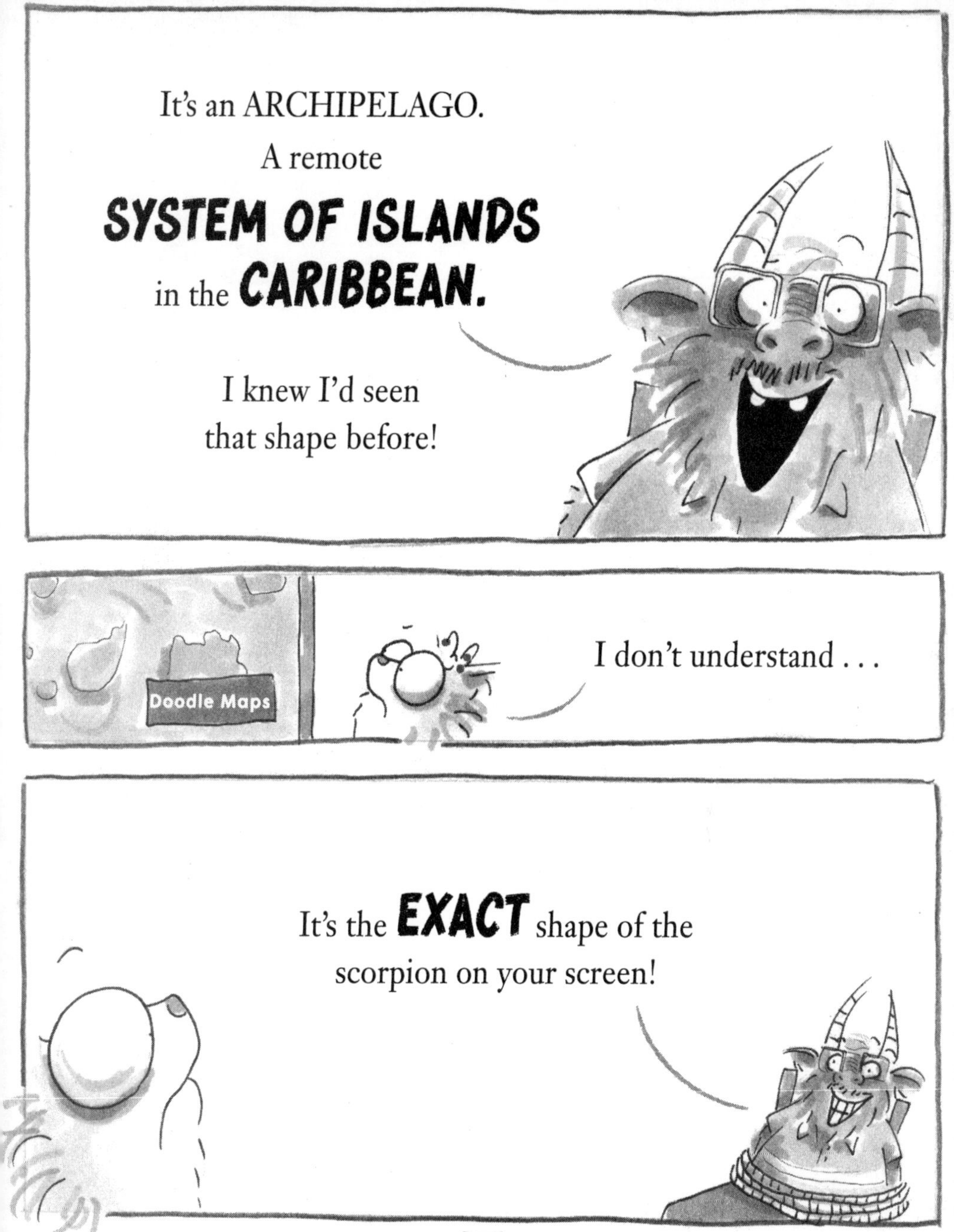
It's an ARCHIPELAGO.
A remote
SYSTEM OF ISLANDS
in the CARIBBEAN.
I knew I'd seen
that shape before!
Doodle Maps
I don't understand . . .
It's the EXACT shape of the
scorpion on your screen!

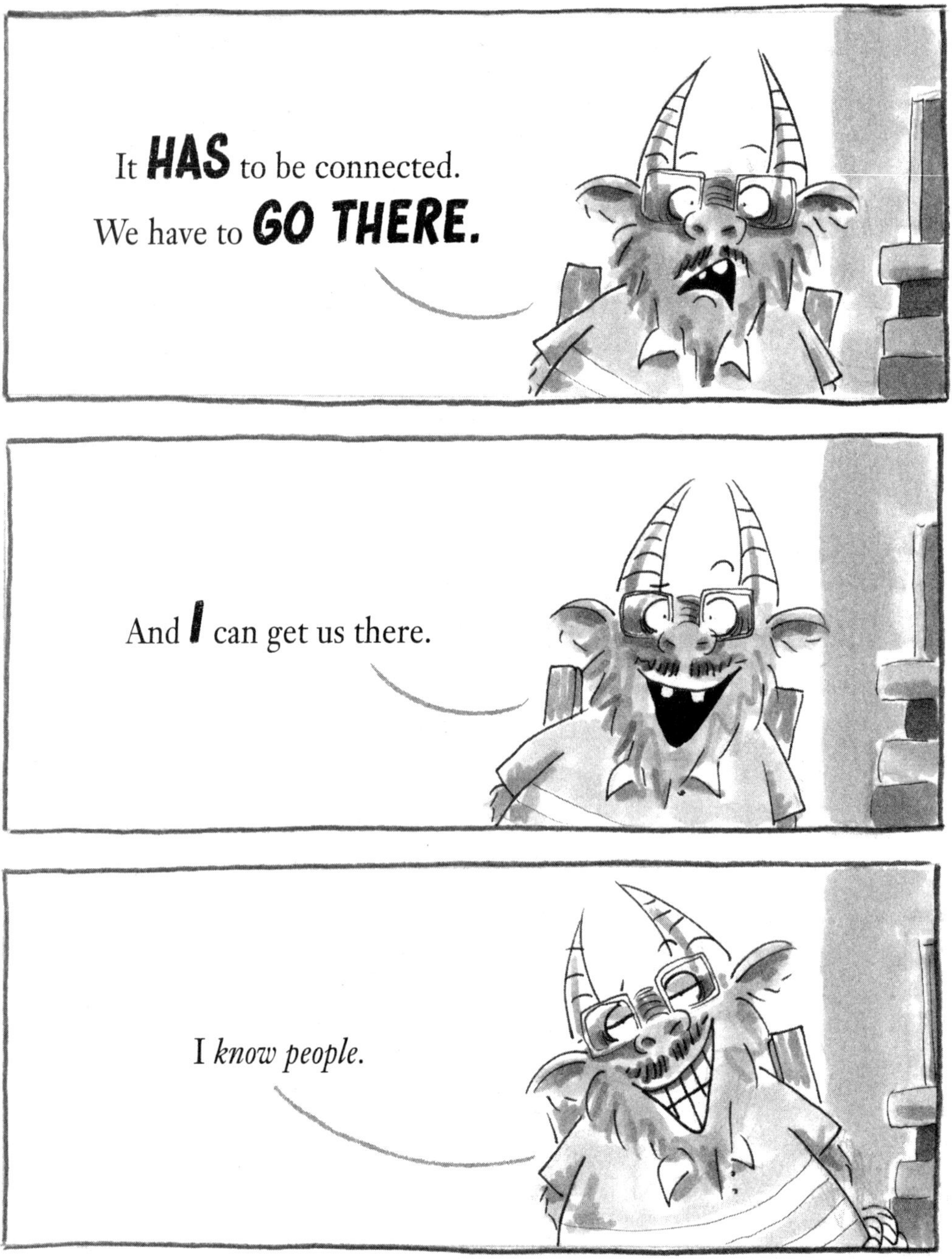
It HAS to be connected. We have to GO THERE.
And I can get us there.
I *know people.*

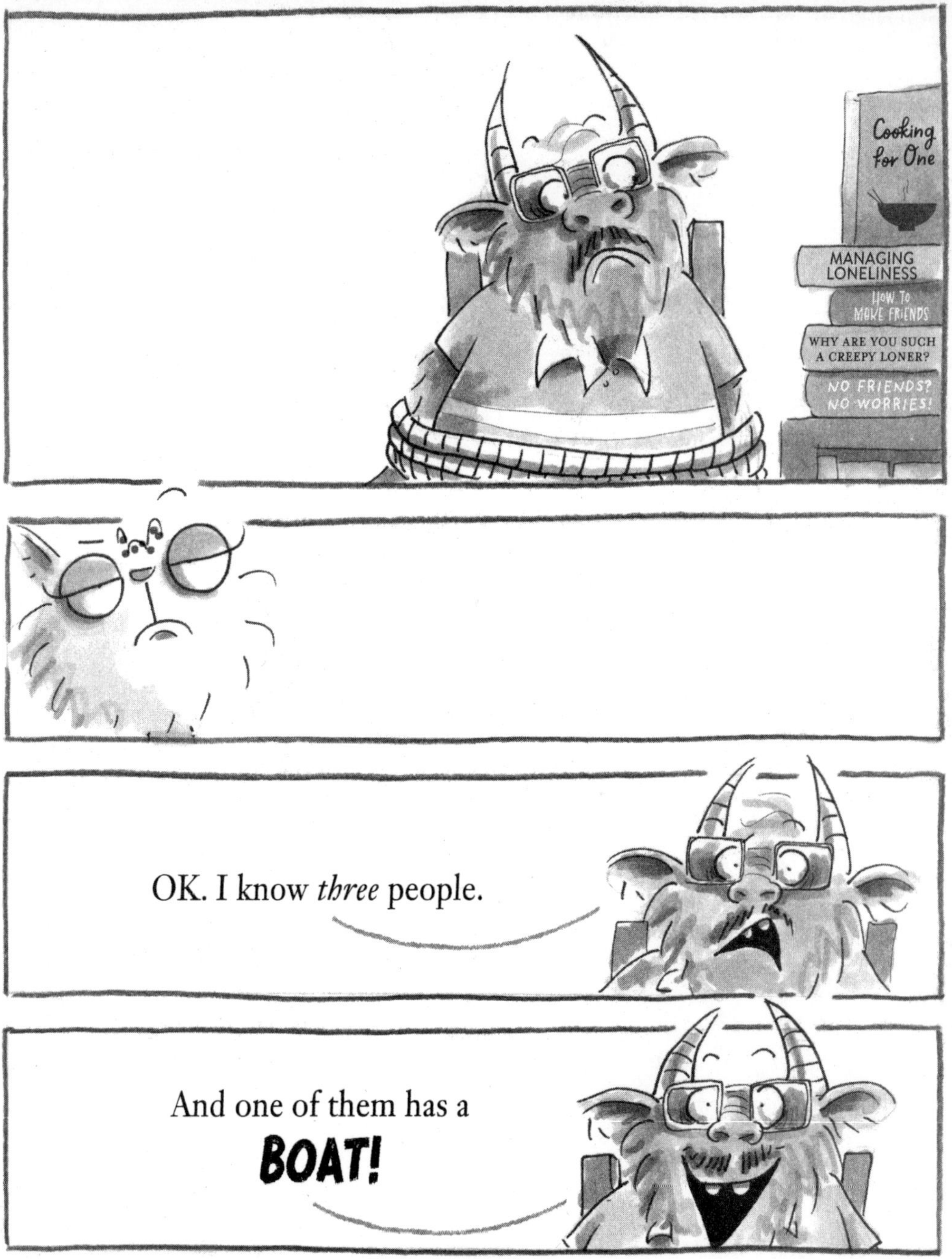

Cooking for One
MANAGING LONELINESS
HOW TO MAKE FRIENDS
WHY ARE YOU SUCH A CREEPY LONER?
NO FRIENDS? NO WORRIES!
OK. I know *three* people.
And one of them has a **BOAT!**

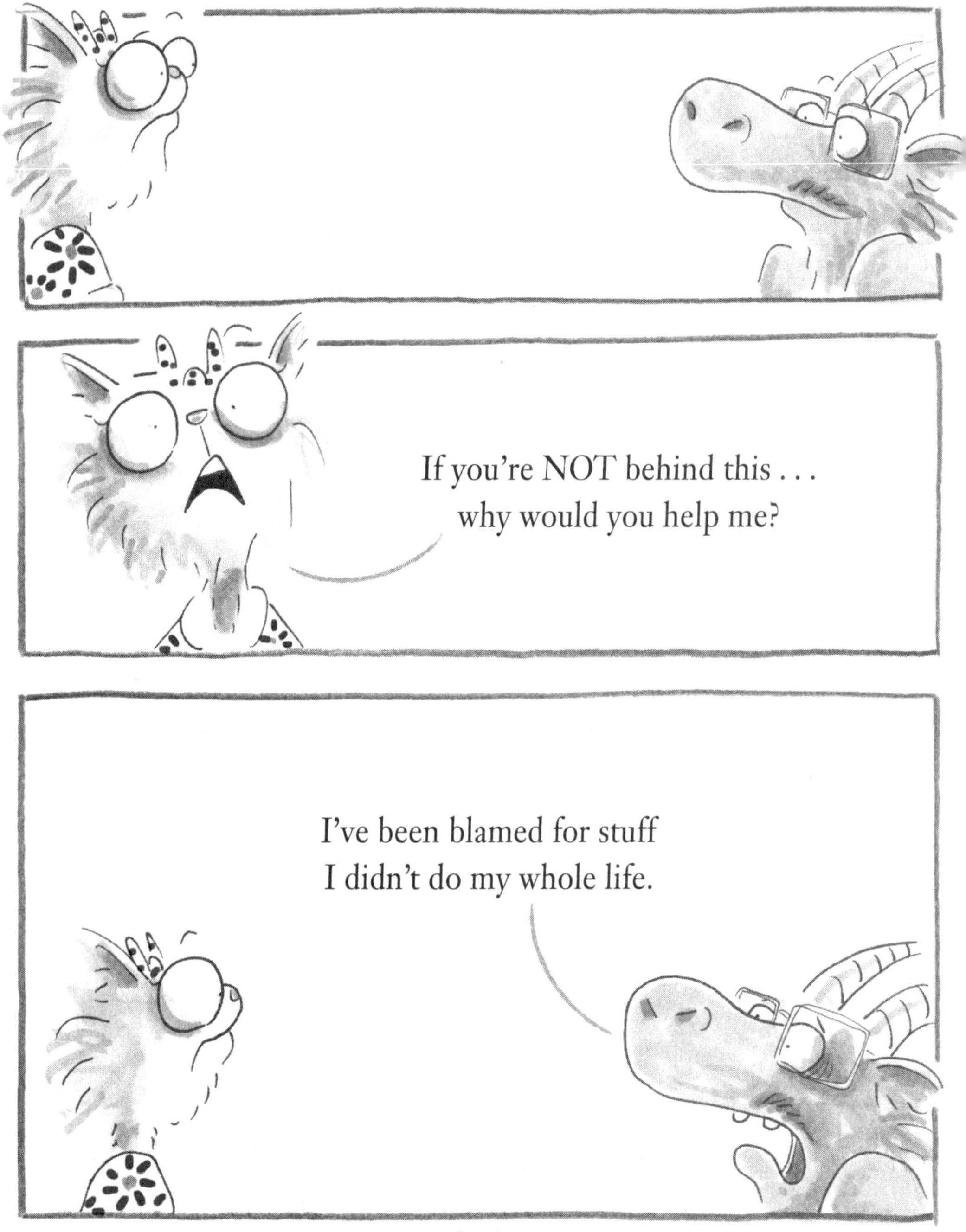
If you're NOT behind this . . .
why would you help me?
I've been blamed for stuff
I didn't do my whole life.

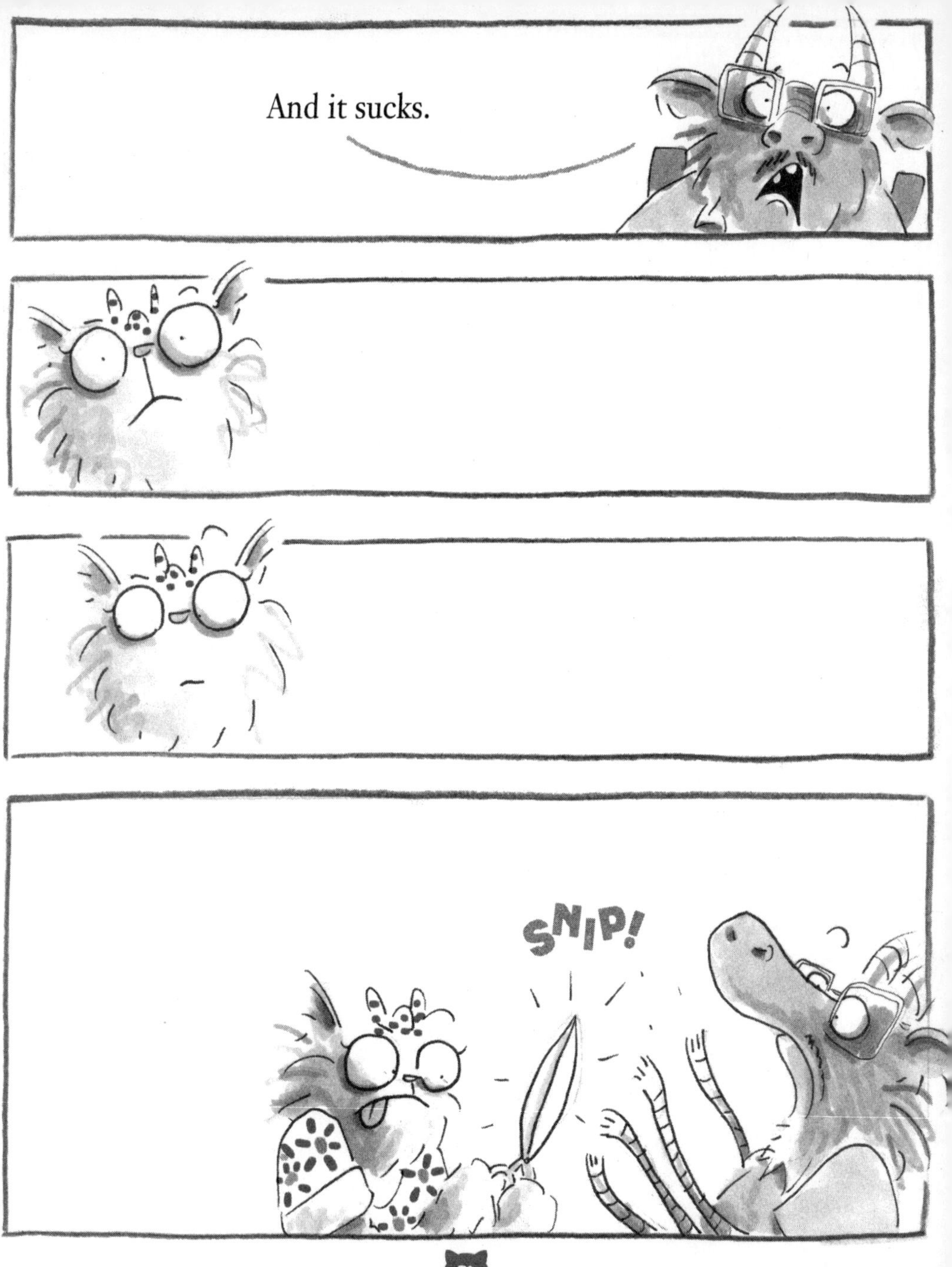
And it sucks.
SNIP!

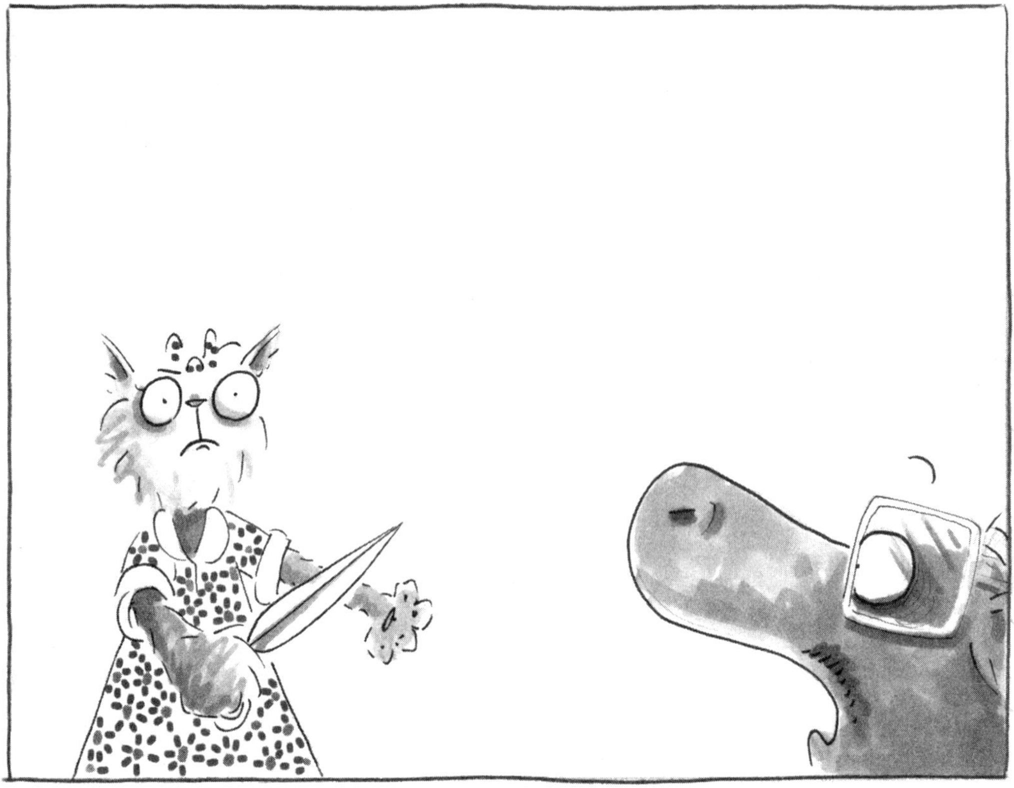

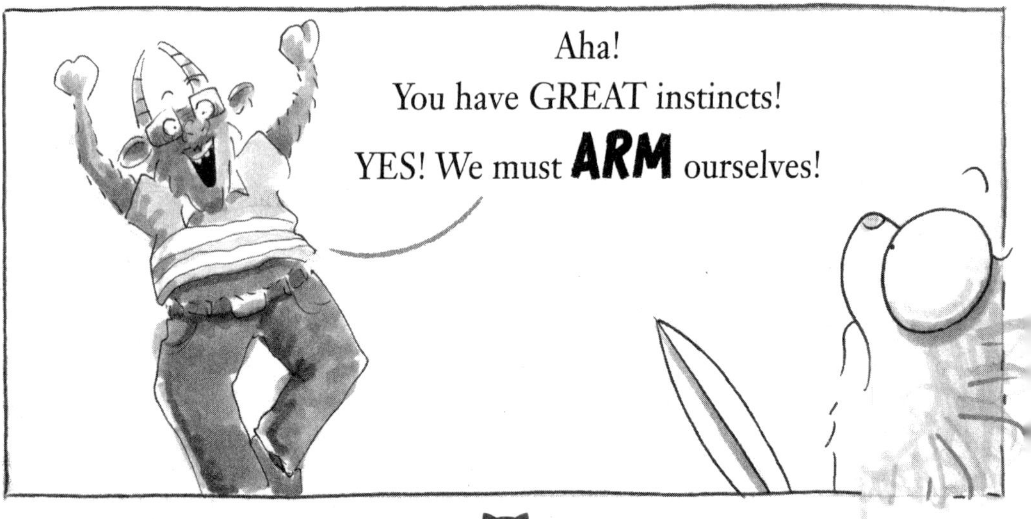
Aha!
You have GREAT instincts!
YES! We must ARM ourselves!

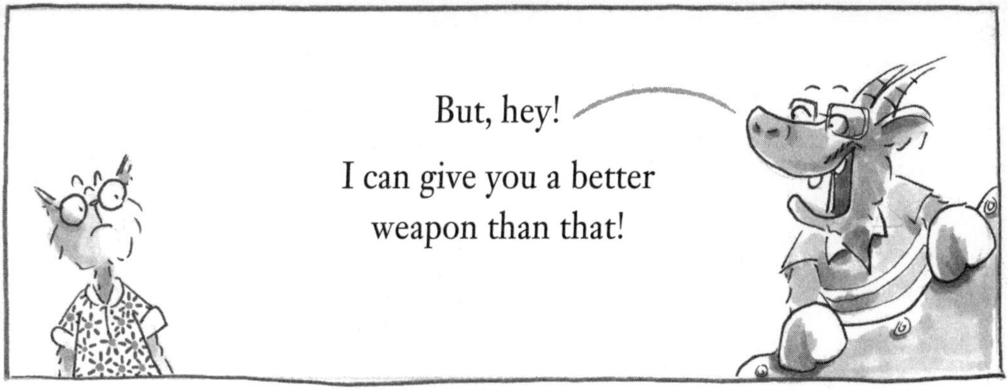
But, hey!
I can give you a better weapon than that!

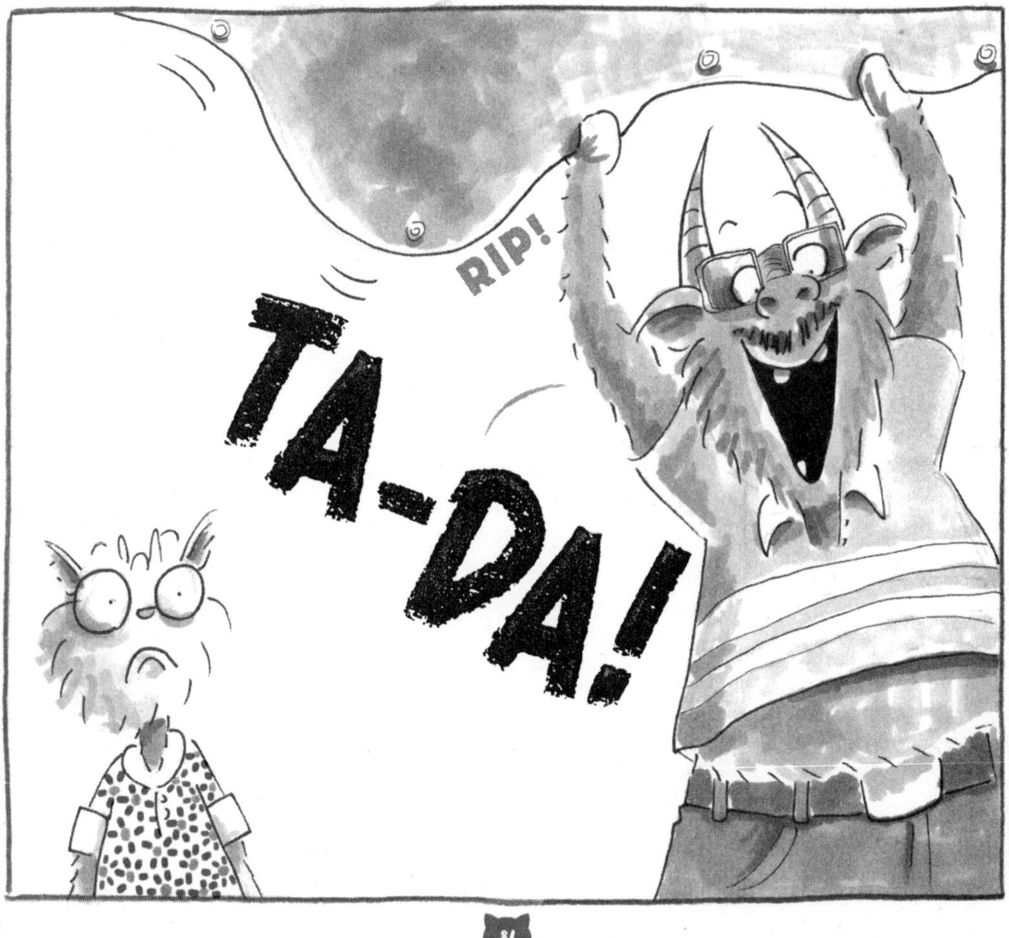
RIP!
TA-DA!

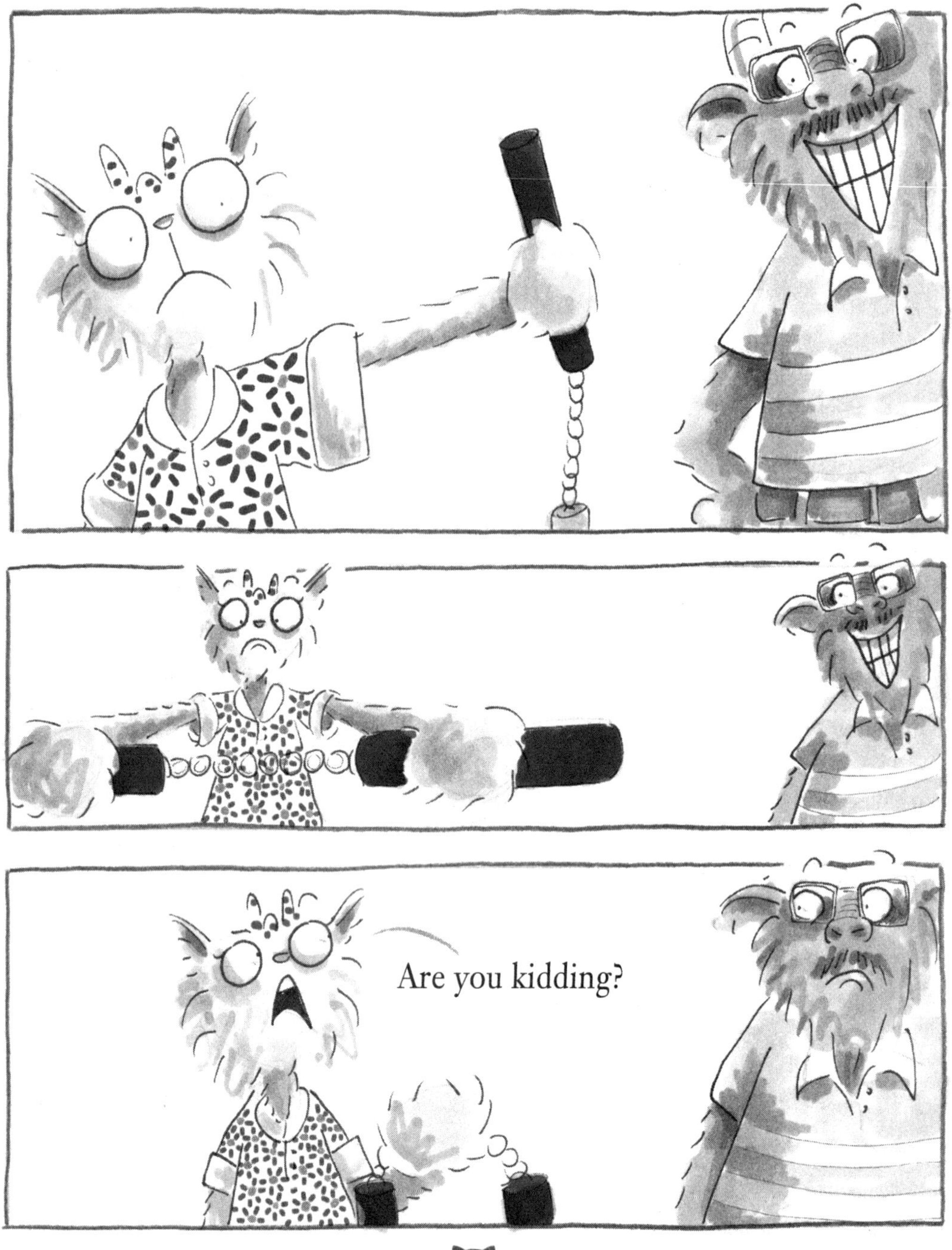
Are you kidding?

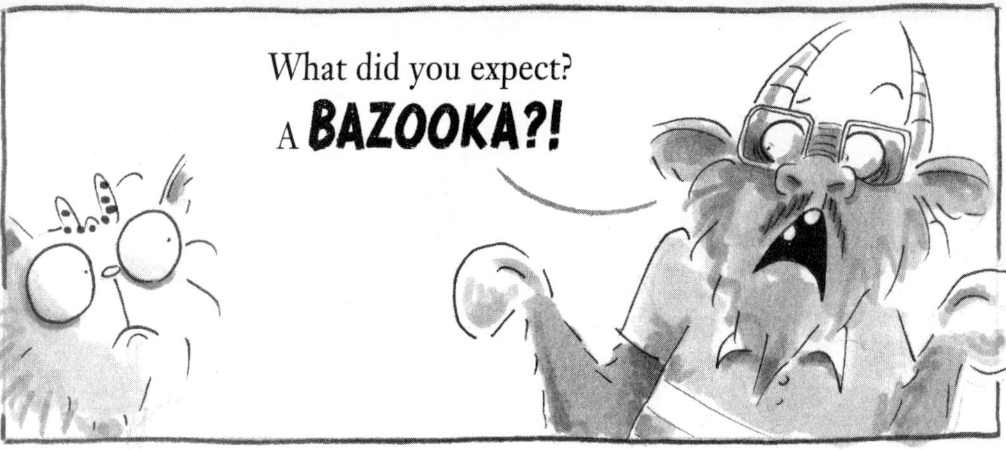
What did you expect? A BAZOOKA?!

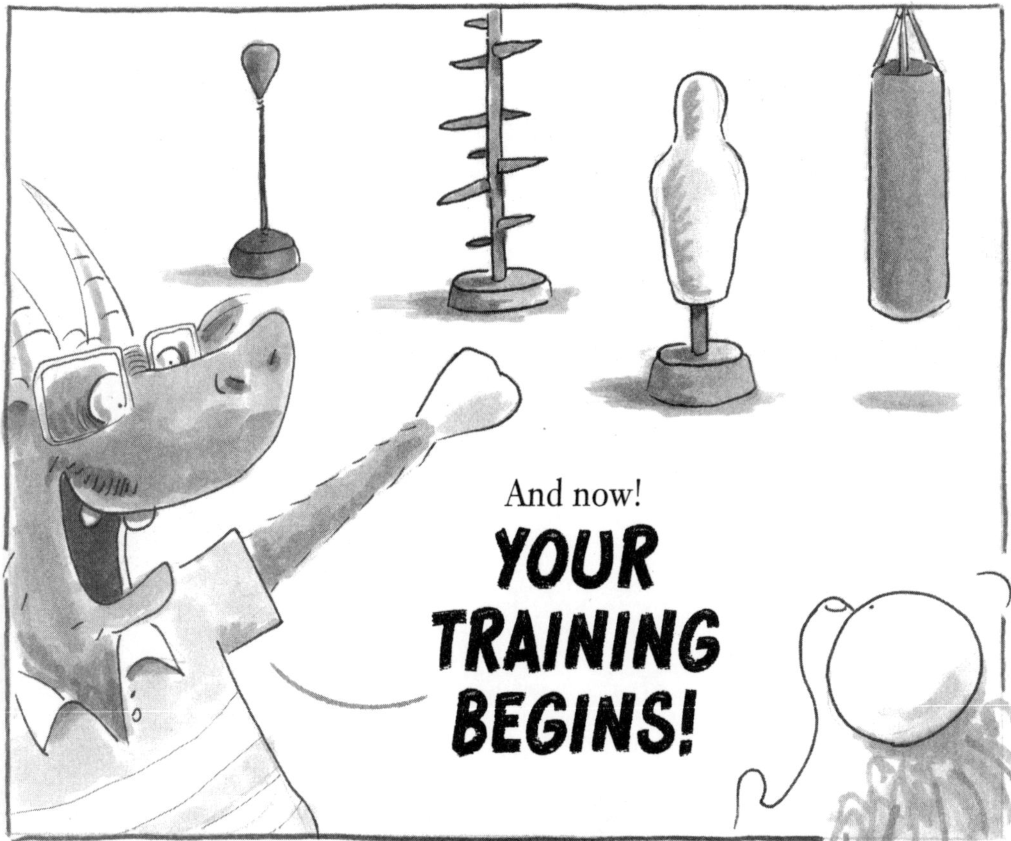
And now! YOUR TRAINING BEGINS!

Four
HOT SPOT

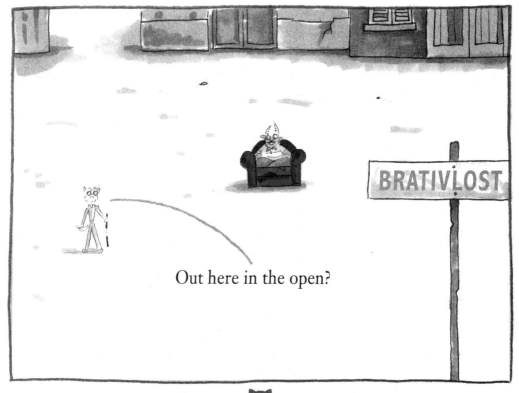

Out here in the open?

BRATIVLOST

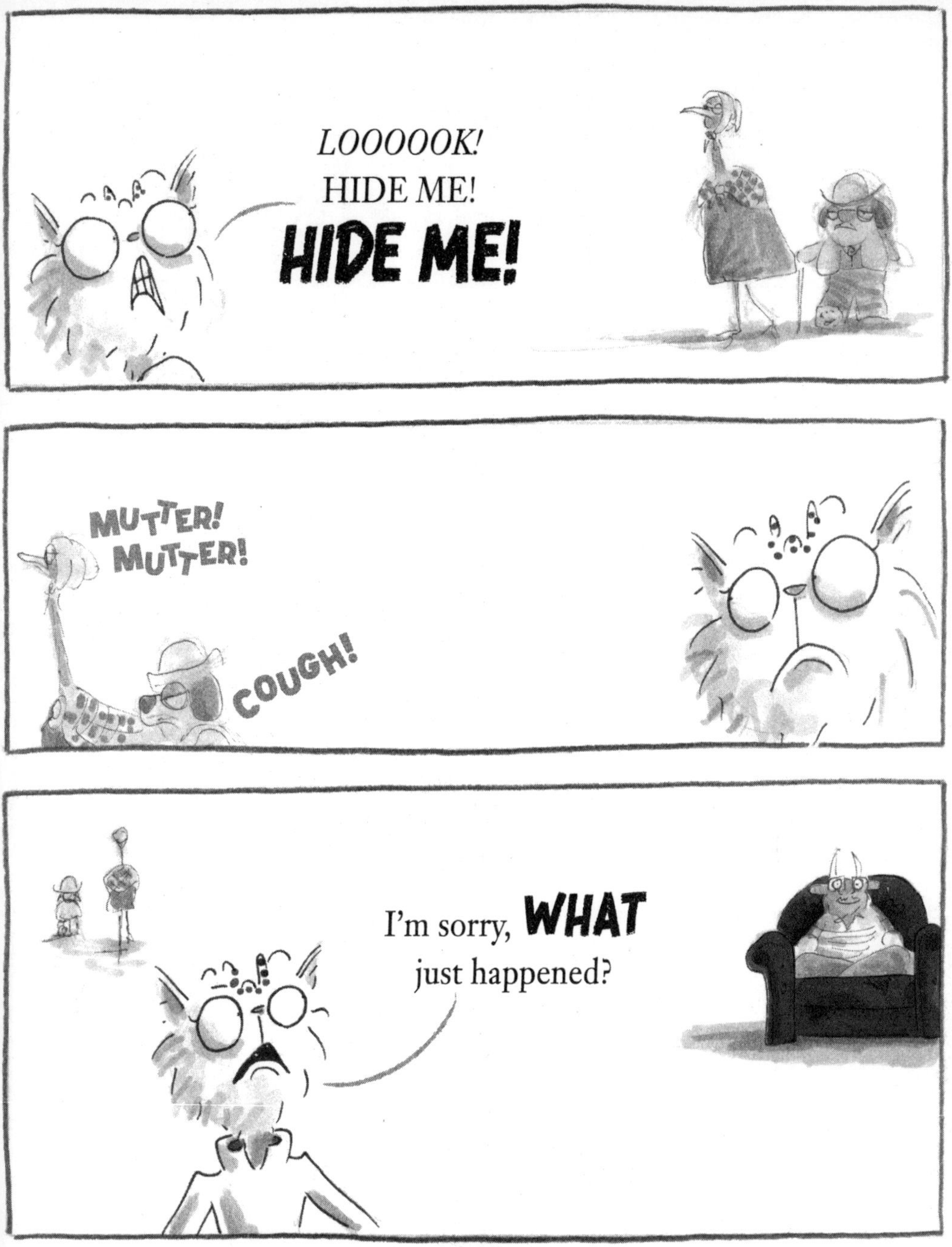
LOOOOOK!
HIDE ME!
HIDE ME!
MUTTER! MUTTER!
COUGH!
I'm sorry, WHAT just happened?

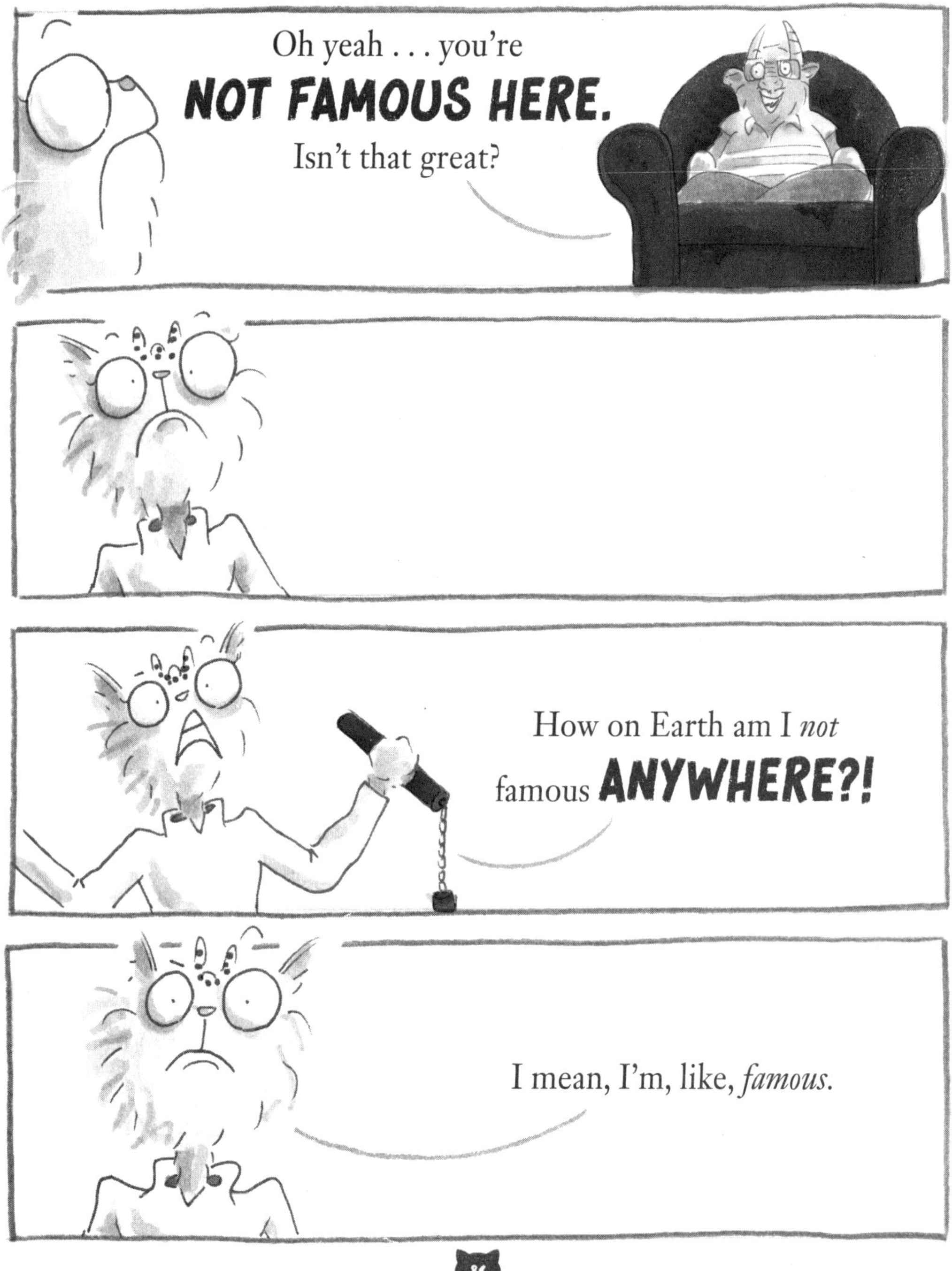
Oh yeah . . . you're
NOT FAMOUS HERE.
Isn't that great?
How on Earth am I *not* famous ANYWHERE?!
I mean, I'm, like, *famous*.

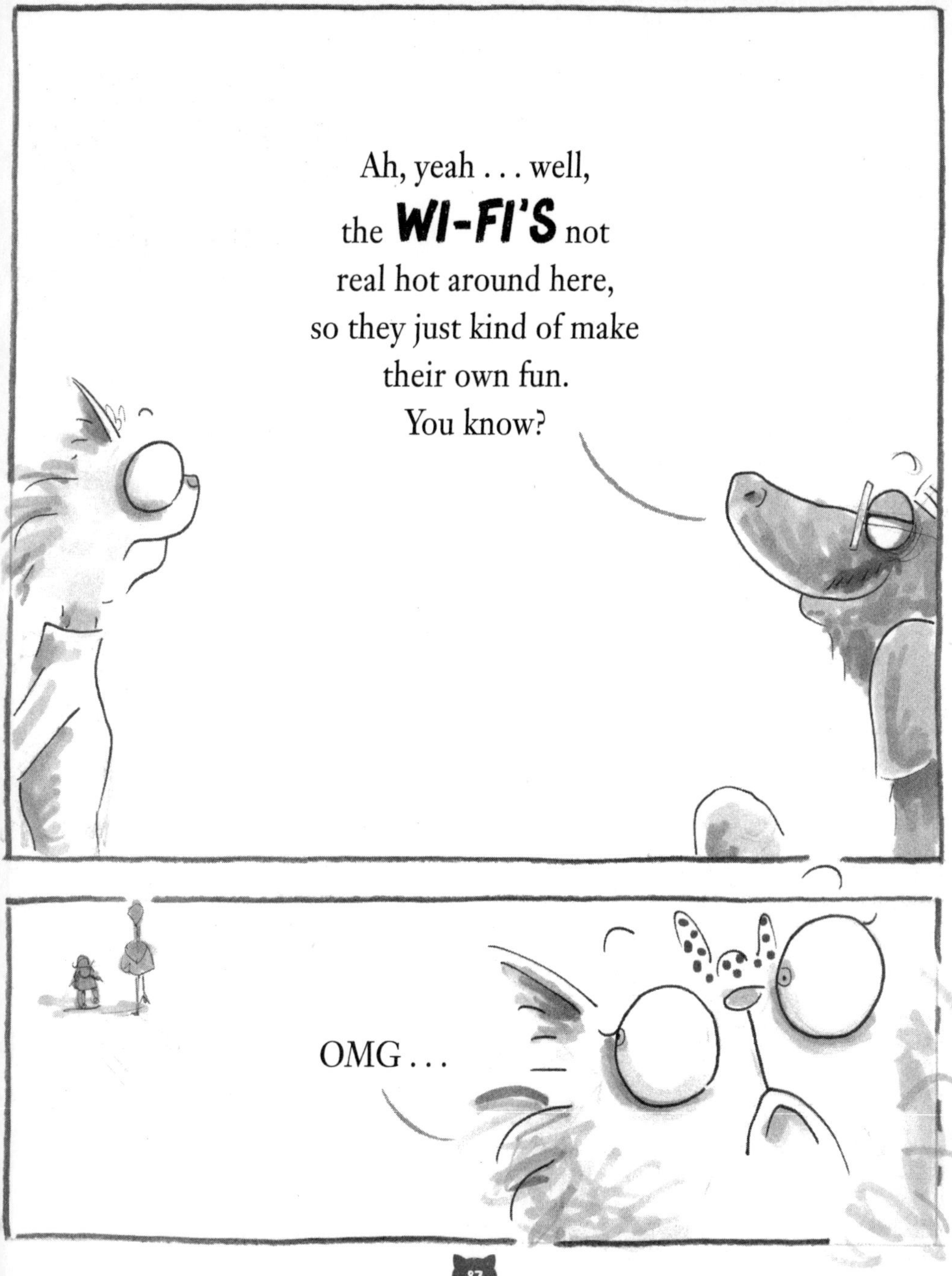
Ah, yeah . . . well,
the **WI-FI'S** not
real hot around here,
so they just kind of make
their own fun.
You know?
OMG . . .

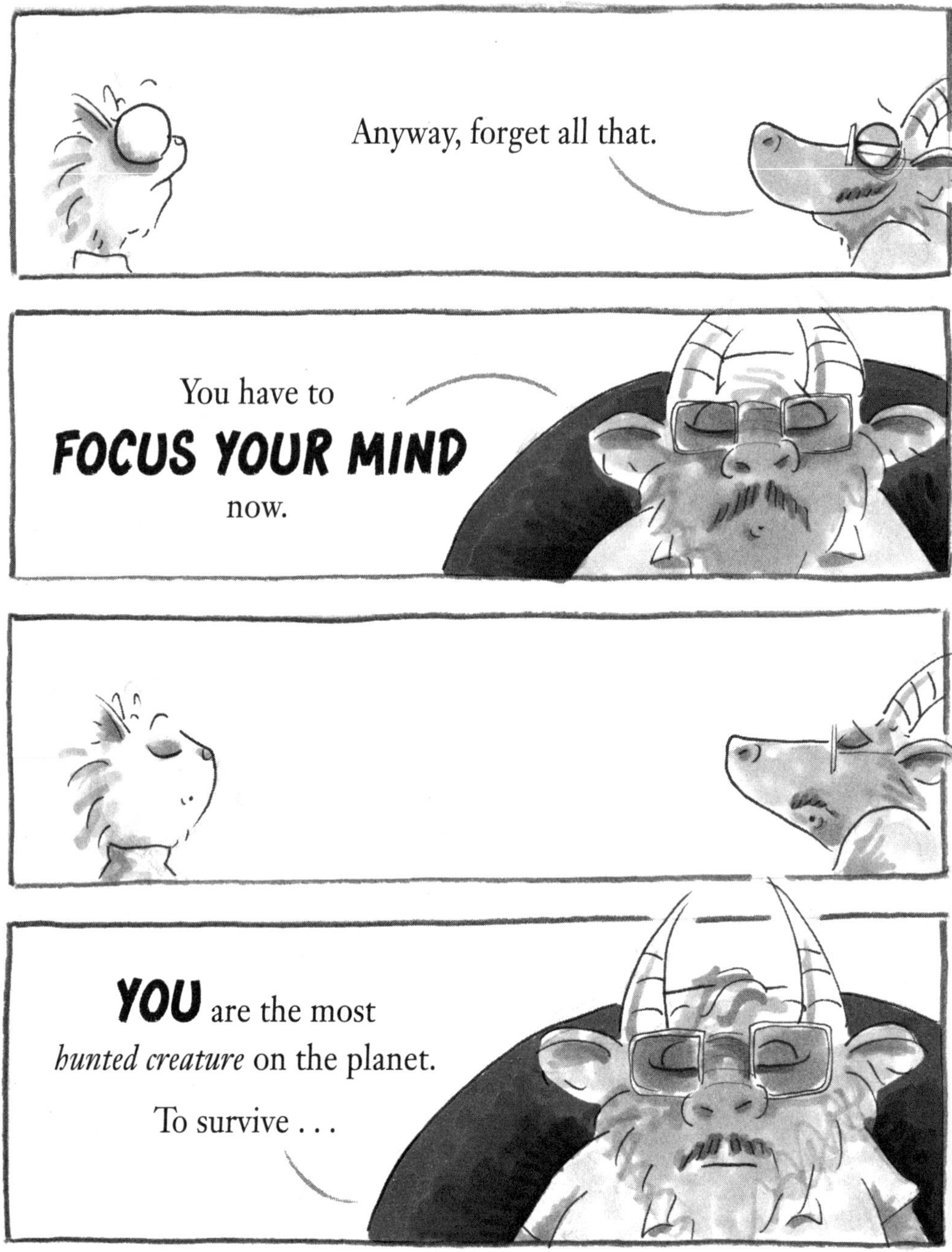

Anyway, forget all that.
You have to FOCUS YOUR MIND now.
YOU are the most *hunted creature* on the planet.
To survive . . .

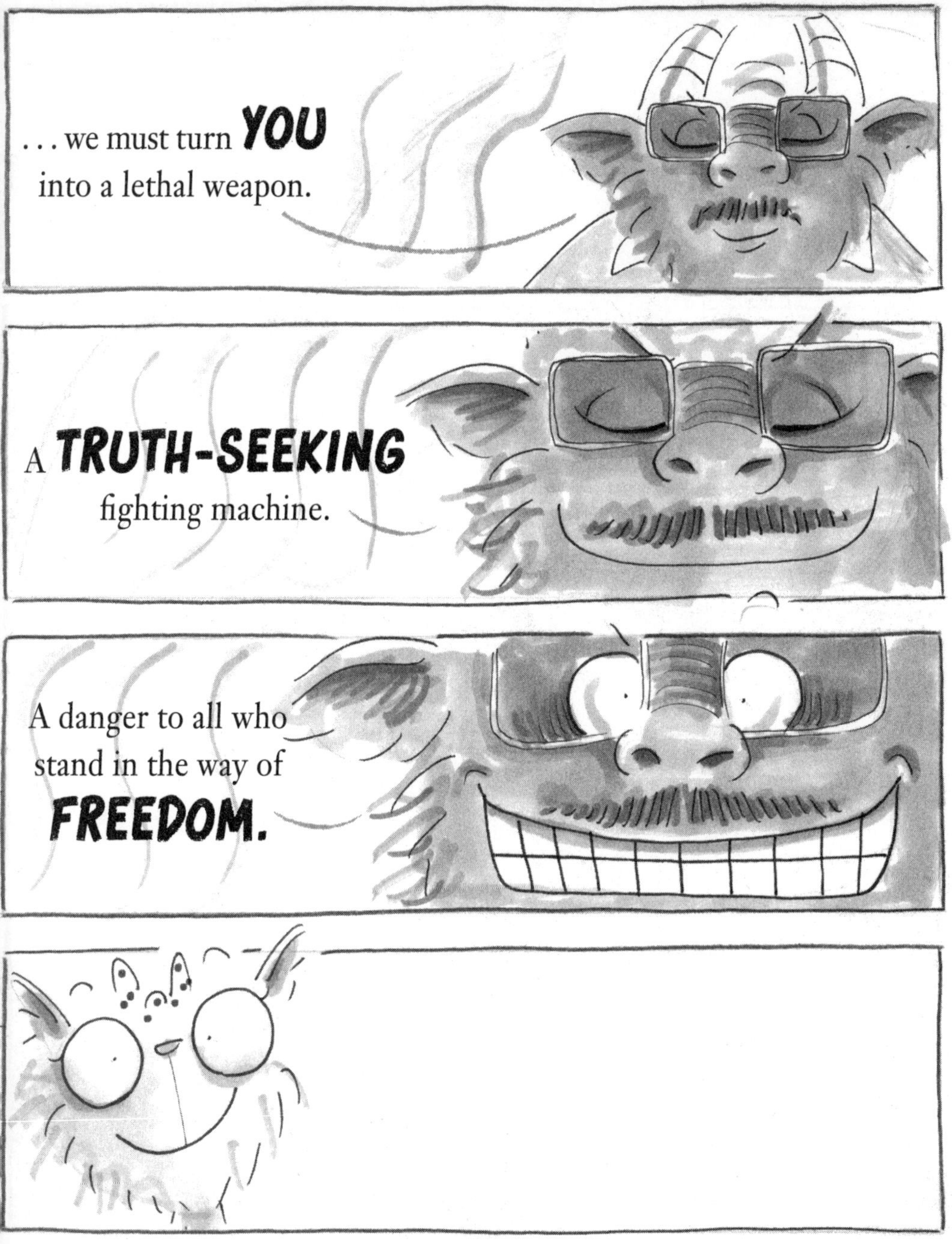
. . . we must turn YOU into a lethal weapon.
A TRUTH-SEEKING fighting machine.
A danger to all who stand in the way of FREEDOM.

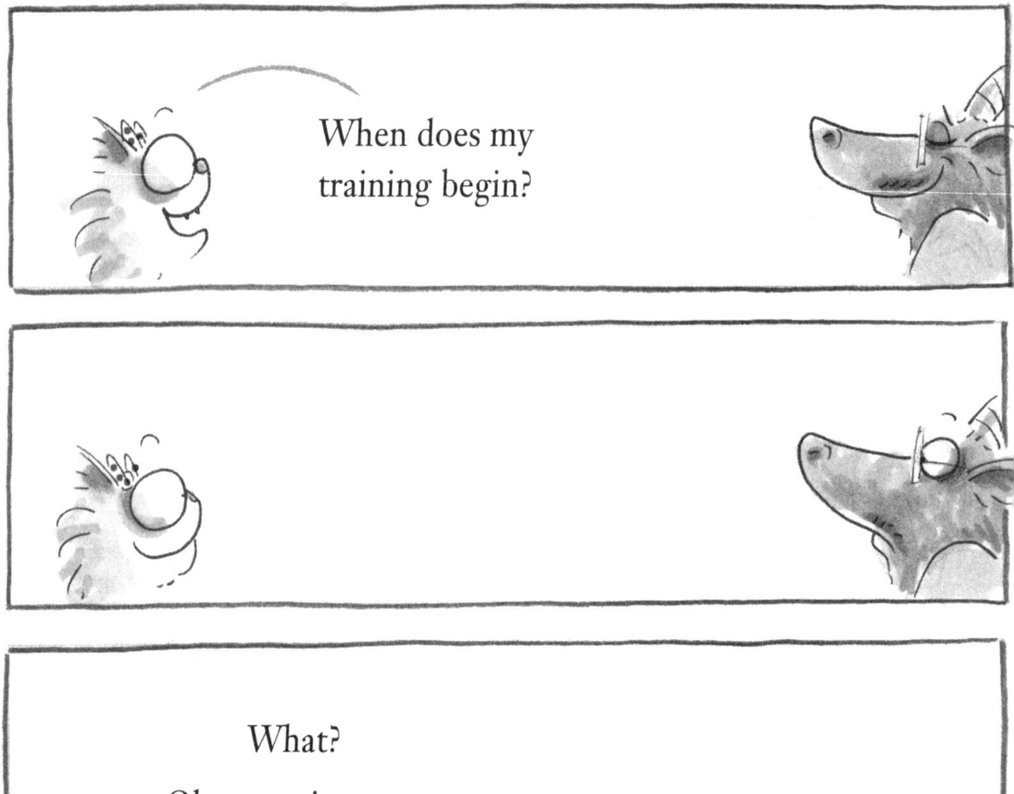
When does my training begin?
What?
Oh no, wait up . . . that's all I've got.
Just the little speech.
After that, you're on your own.

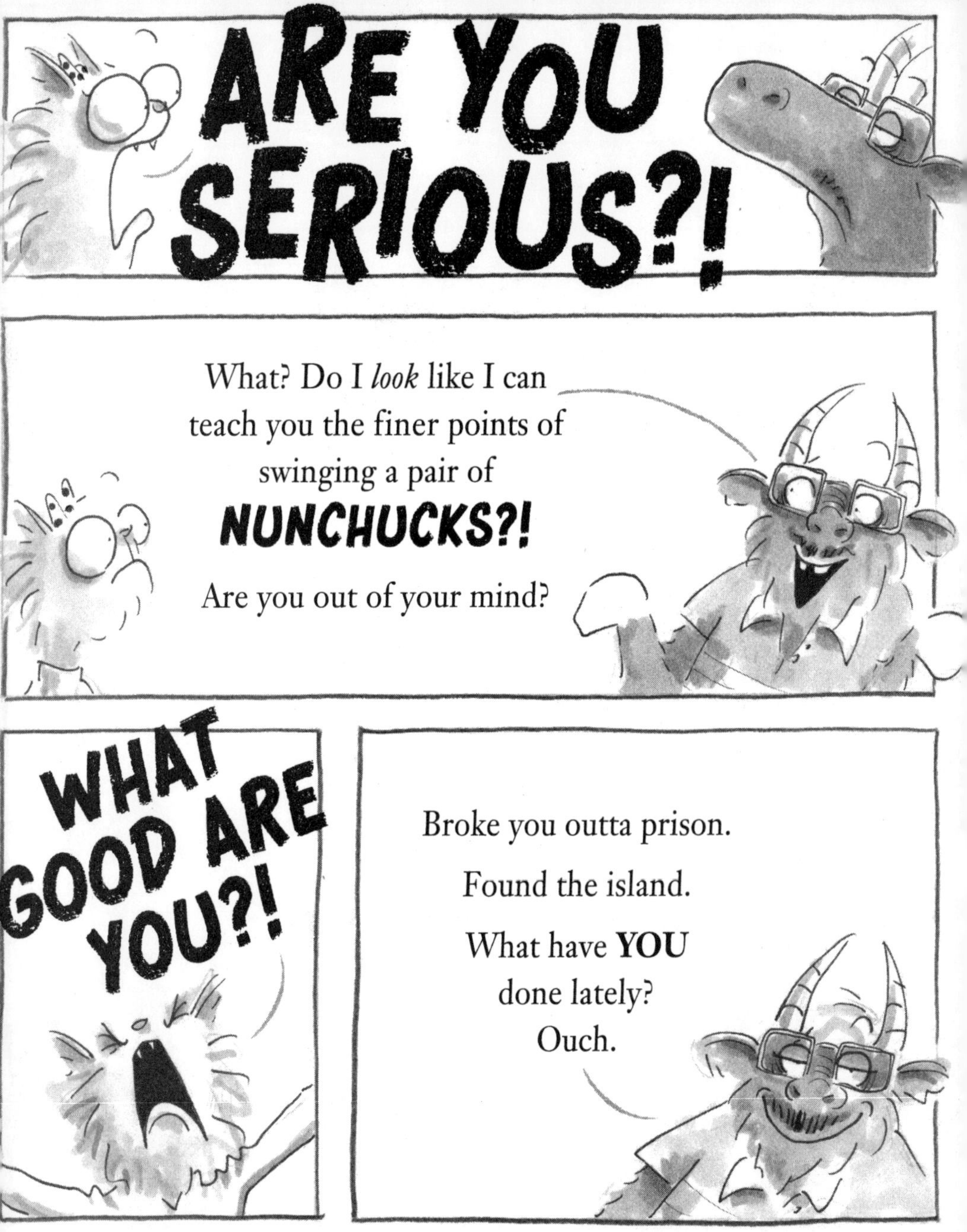
ARE YOU SERIOUS?!
What? Do I *look* like I can teach you the finer points of swinging a pair of
NUNCHUCKS?!
Are you out of your mind?
WHAT GOOD ARE YOU?!
Broke you outta prison.
Found the island.
What have **YOU** done lately?
Ouch.

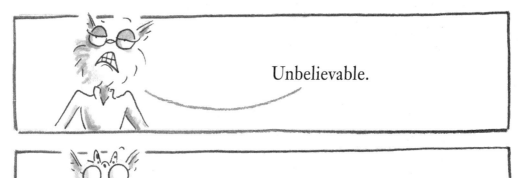

Unbelievable.

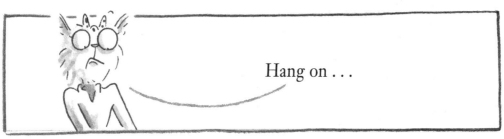

Hang on . . .

HA! I forgot! I've still got that pizza guy's **PHONE!**

Oh, that won't help. No Wi-Fi, remember?

Well, there will be when I switch on his . . .

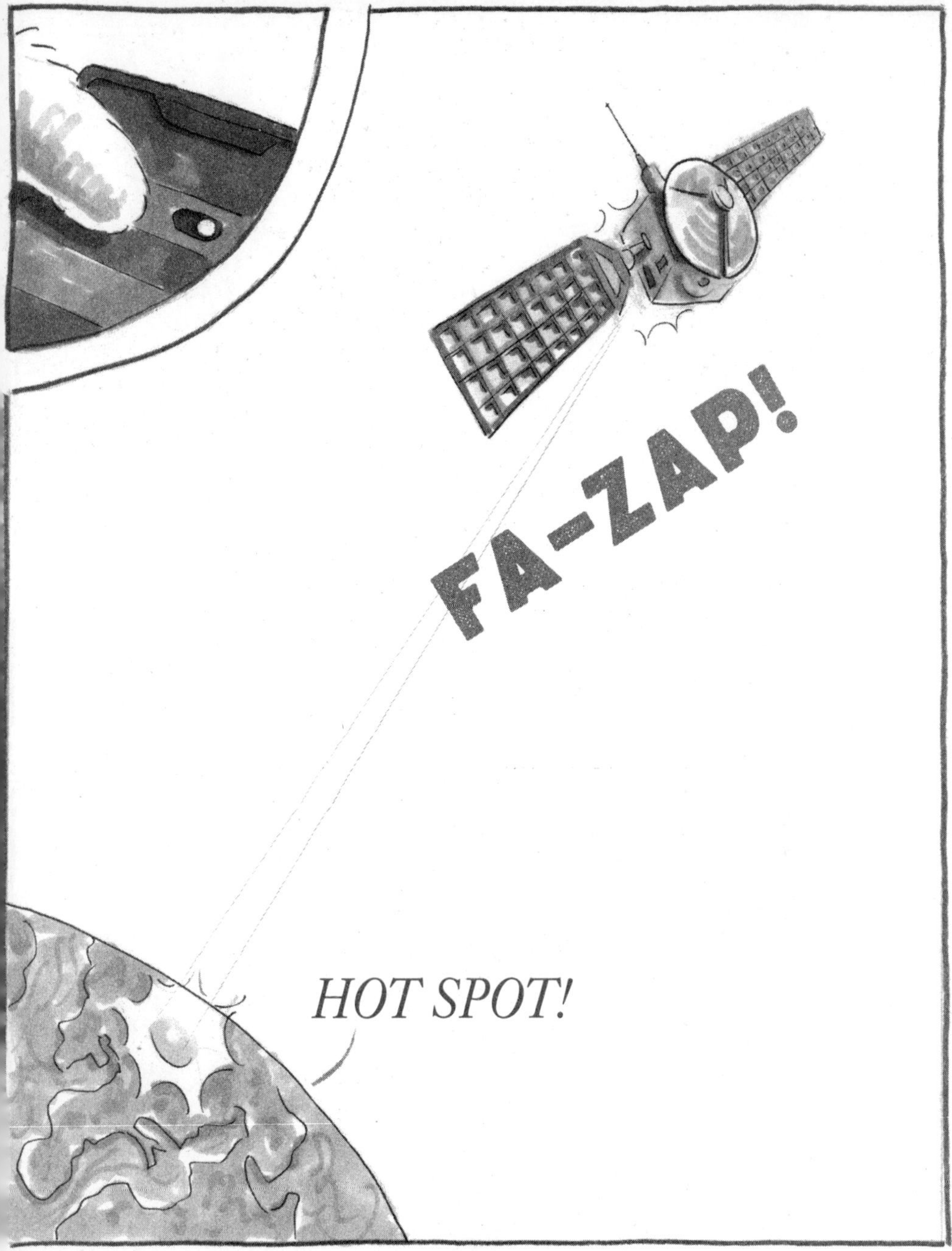
FA-ZAP!
HOT SPOT!

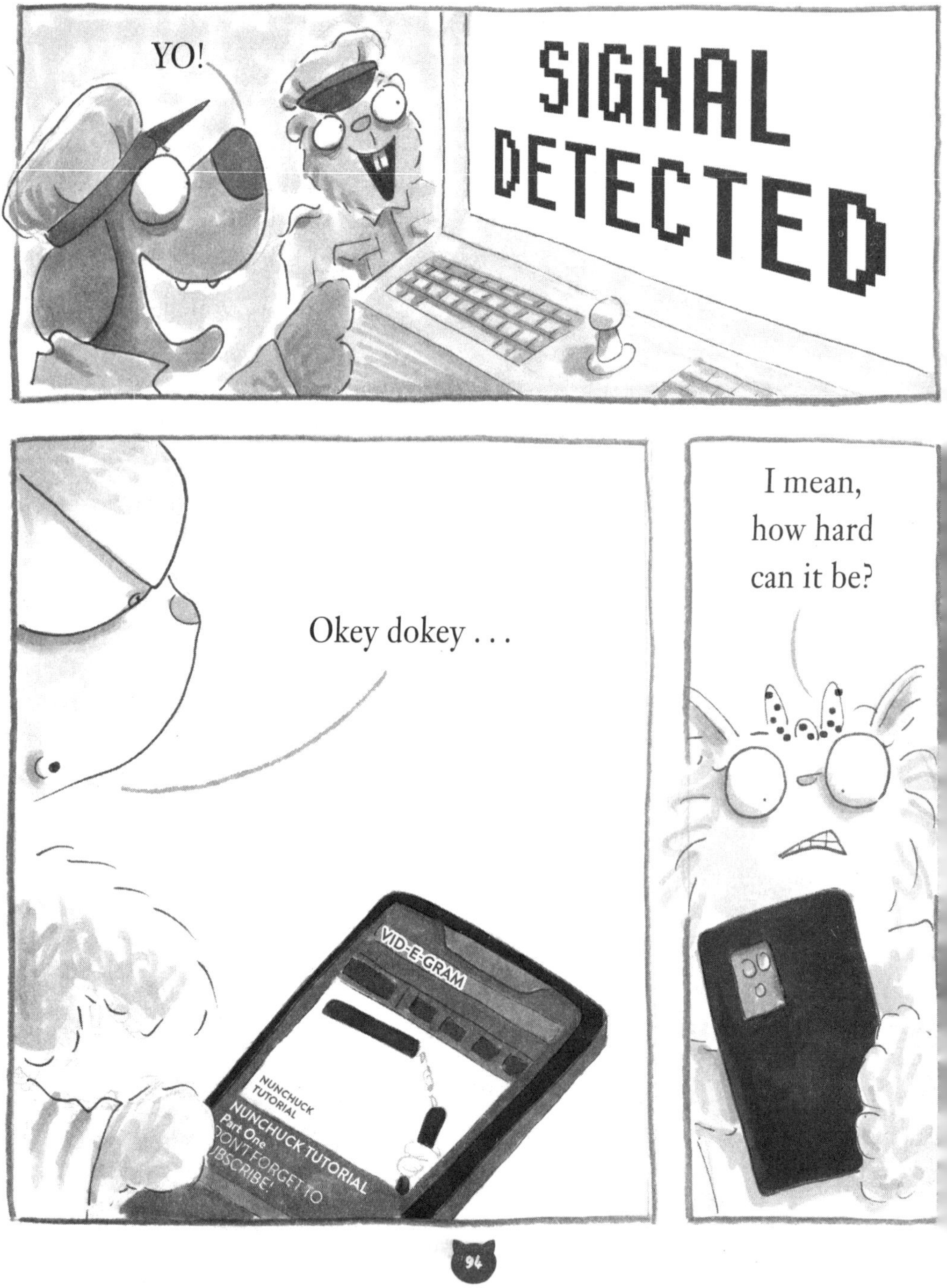
YO!
SIGNAL DETECTED
Okey dokey . . .
VID-E-GRAM
NUNCHUCK TUTORIAL
NUNCHUCK TUTORIAL
Part One
DONT FORGET TO
UBSCRIBE!
I mean, how hard can it be?

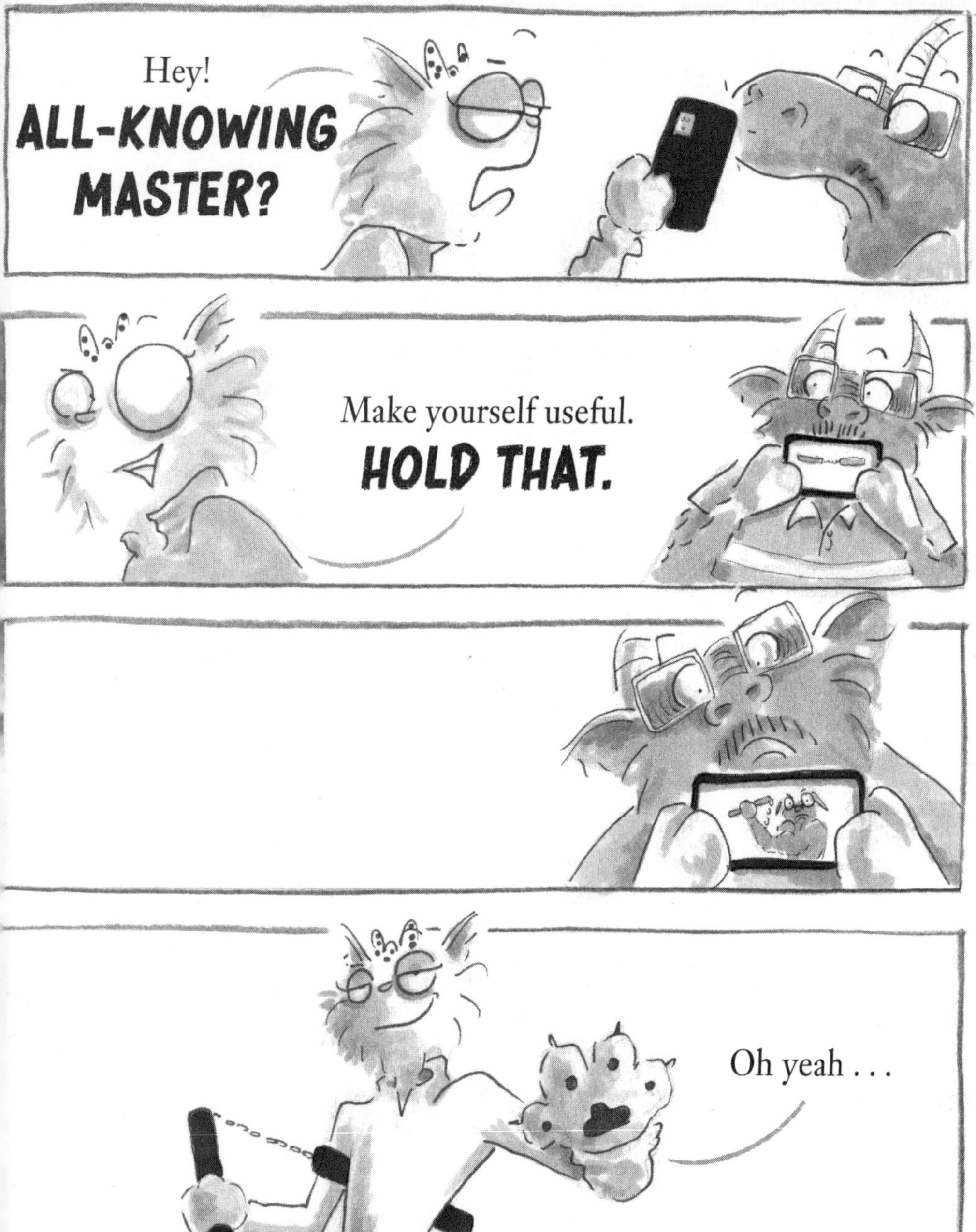
Hey!
ALL-KNOWING MASTER?
Make yourself useful.
HOLD THAT.
Oh yeah . . .

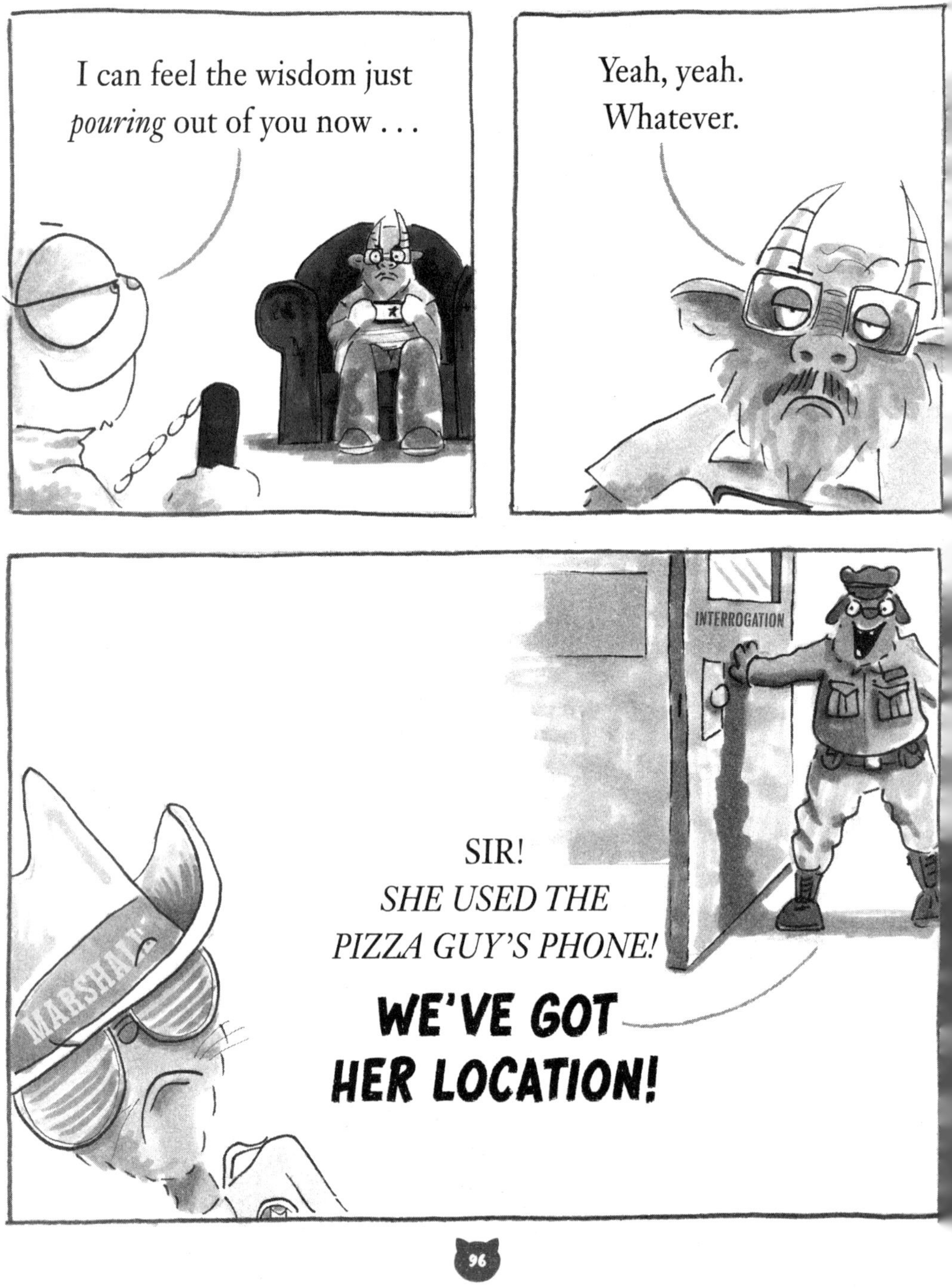
I can feel the wisdom just *pouring* out of you now . . .
Yeah, yeah. Whatever.
INTERROGATION
MARSHALL
SIR! *SHE USED THE PIZZA GUY'S PHONE!*
WE'VE GOT HER LOCATION!

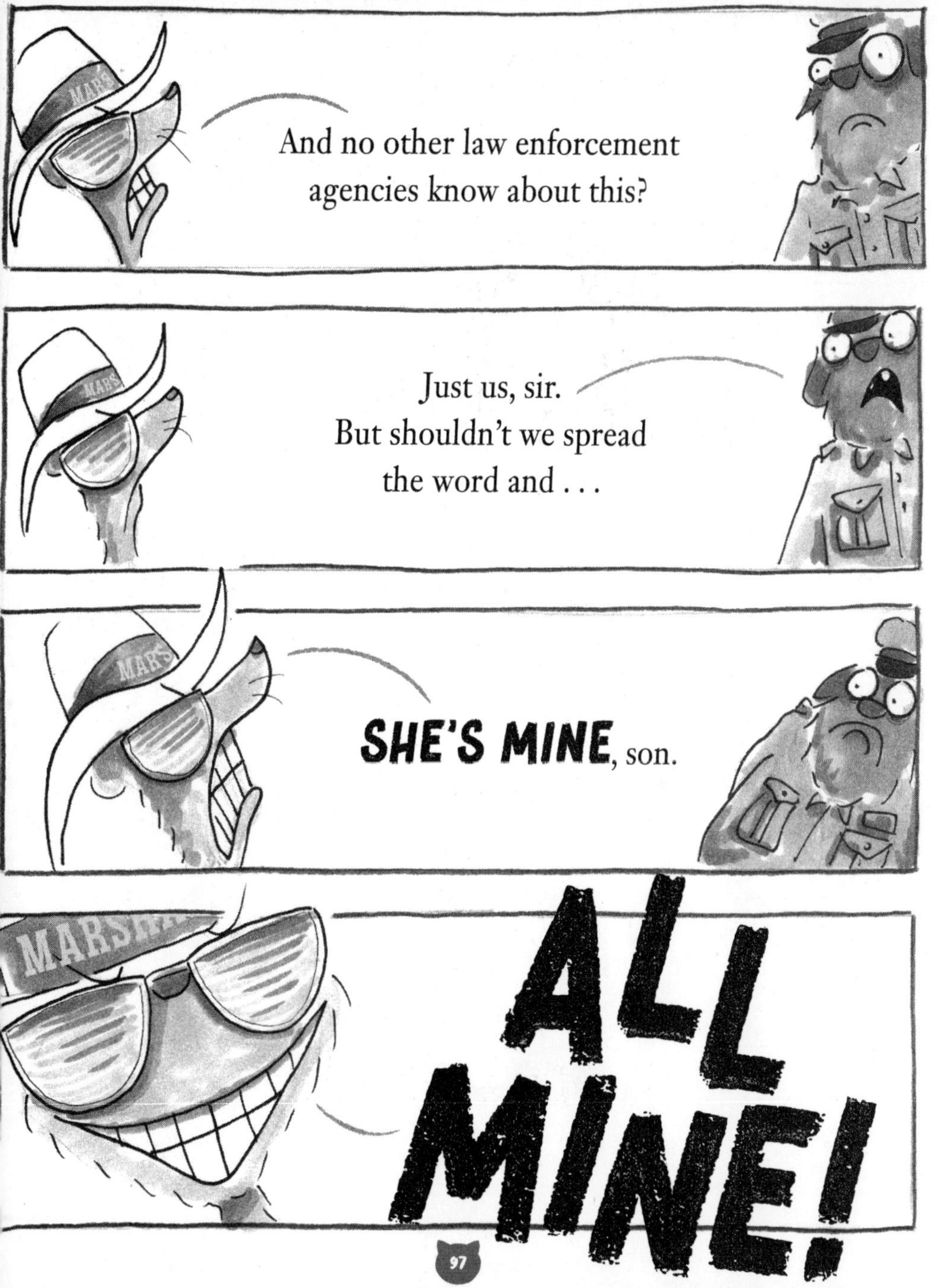
MARS
And no other law enforcement agencies know about this?
MARS
Just us, sir.
But shouldn't we spread the word and . . .
MARS
SHE'S MINE, son.
MARSHA
ALL MINE!

Five
LEMONADE

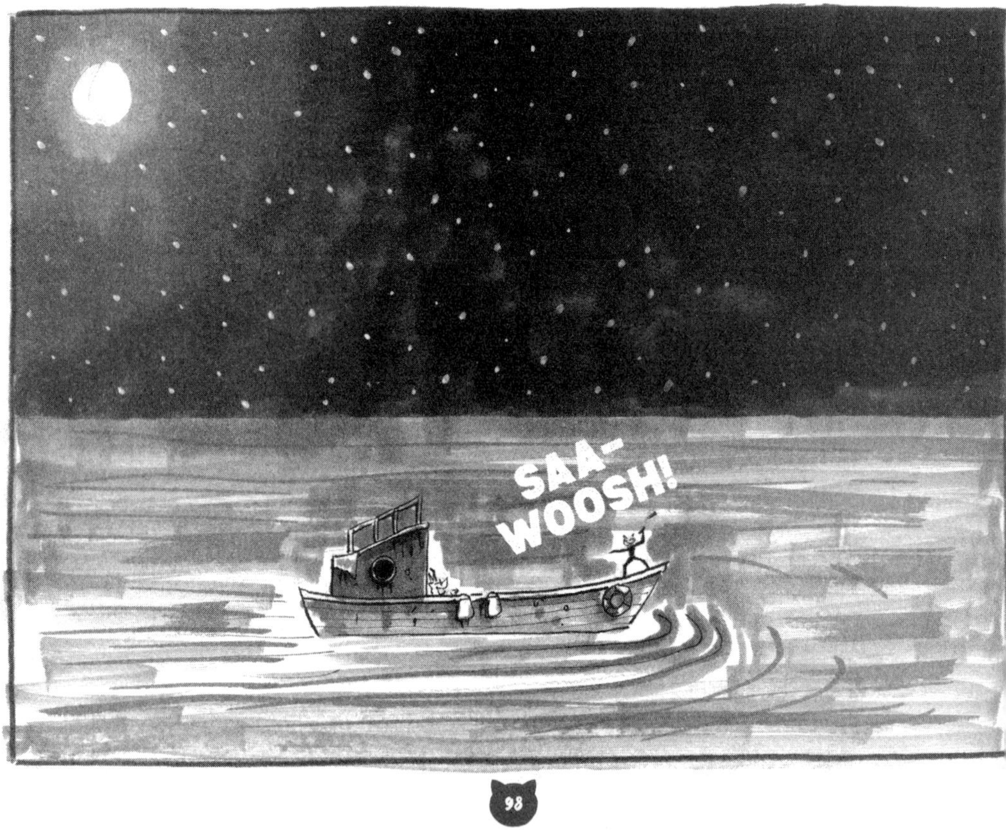
SAA-
WOOSH!

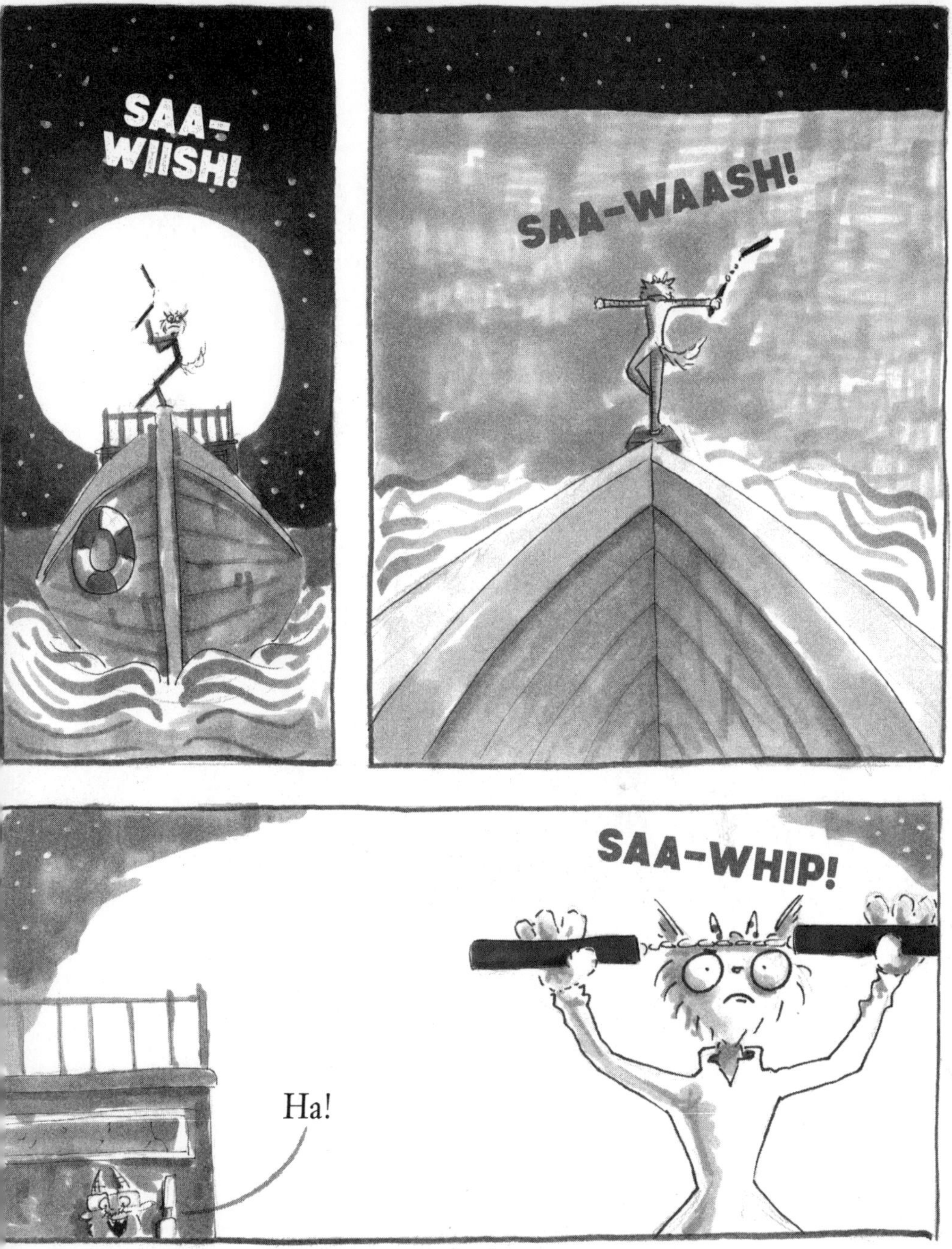
SAA-
WIISH!
SAA-WAASH!
SAA-WHIP!
Ha!

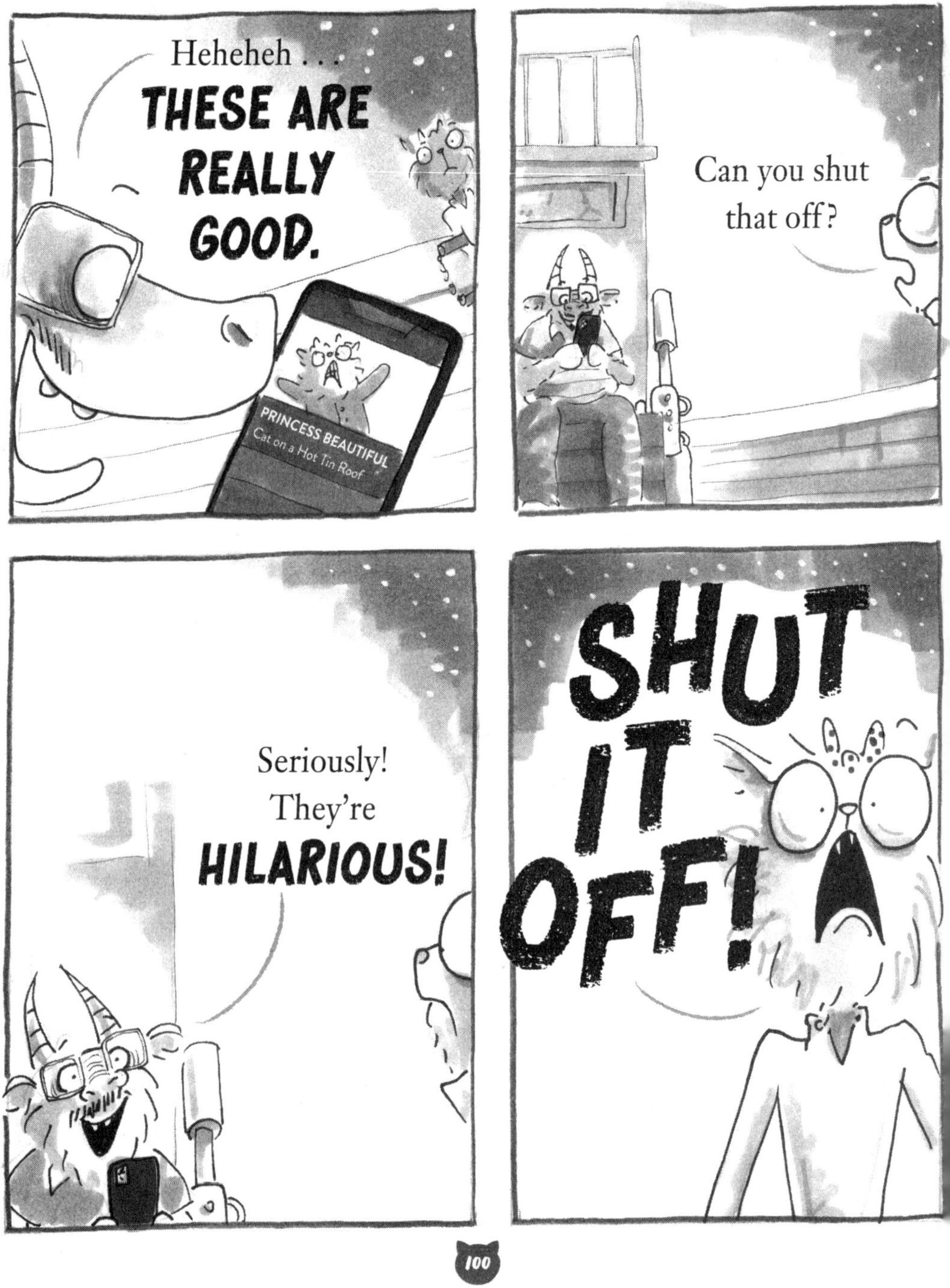

Heheheh . . .
THESE ARE REALLY GOOD.
PRINCESS BEAUTIFUL
Cat on a Hot Tin Roof
Can you shut that off?
Seriously! They're HILARIOUS!
SHUT IT OFF!

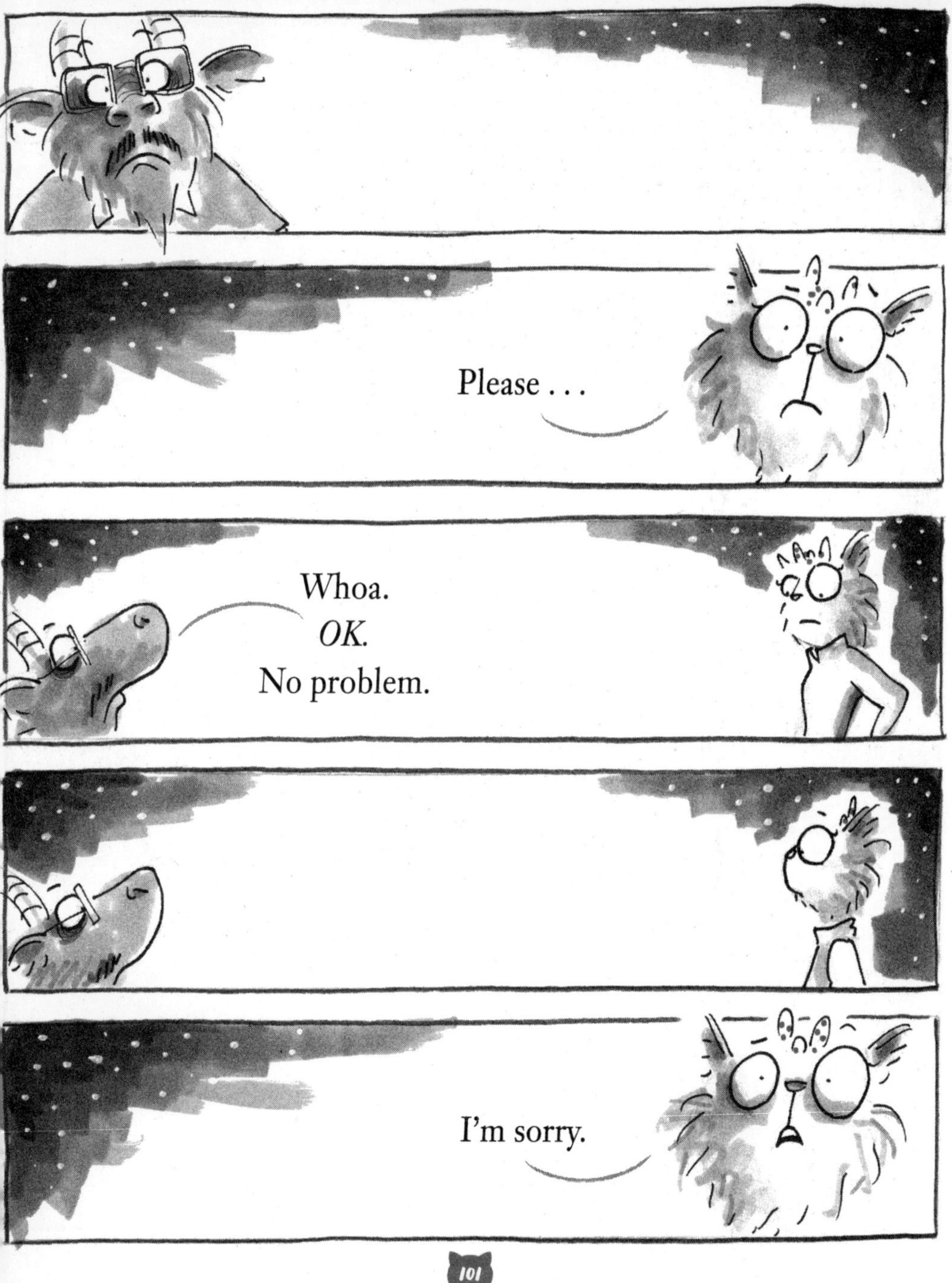
Please . . .
Whoa.
OK.
No problem.
I'm sorry.

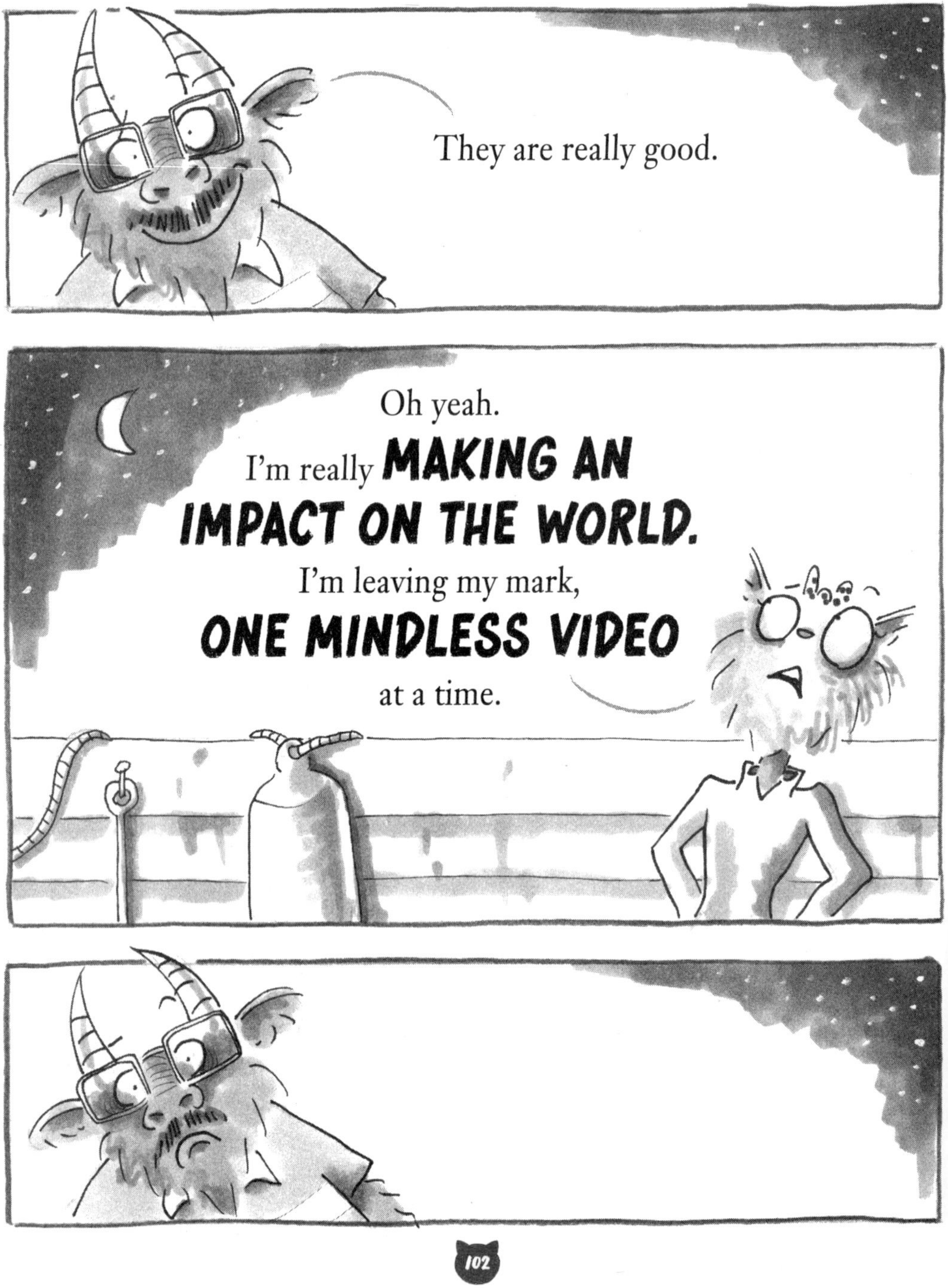
They are really good.
Oh yeah.
I'm really MAKING AN IMPACT ON THE WORLD.
I'm leaving my mark, ONE MINDLESS VIDEO at a time.

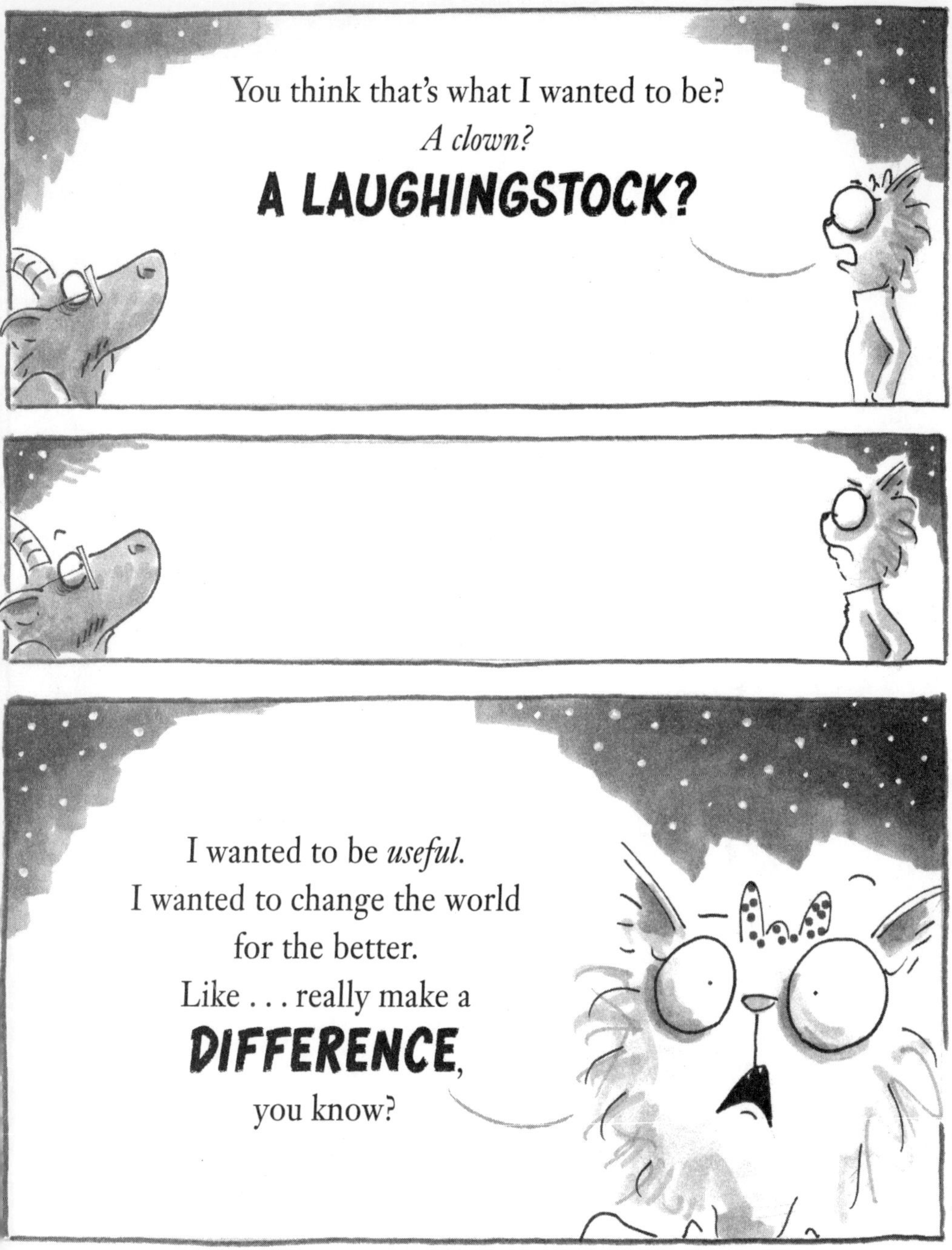
You think that's what I wanted to be?
A clown?
A LAUGHINGSTOCK?
I wanted to be *useful.*
I wanted to change the world
for the better.
Like . . . really make a
DIFFERENCE,
you know?

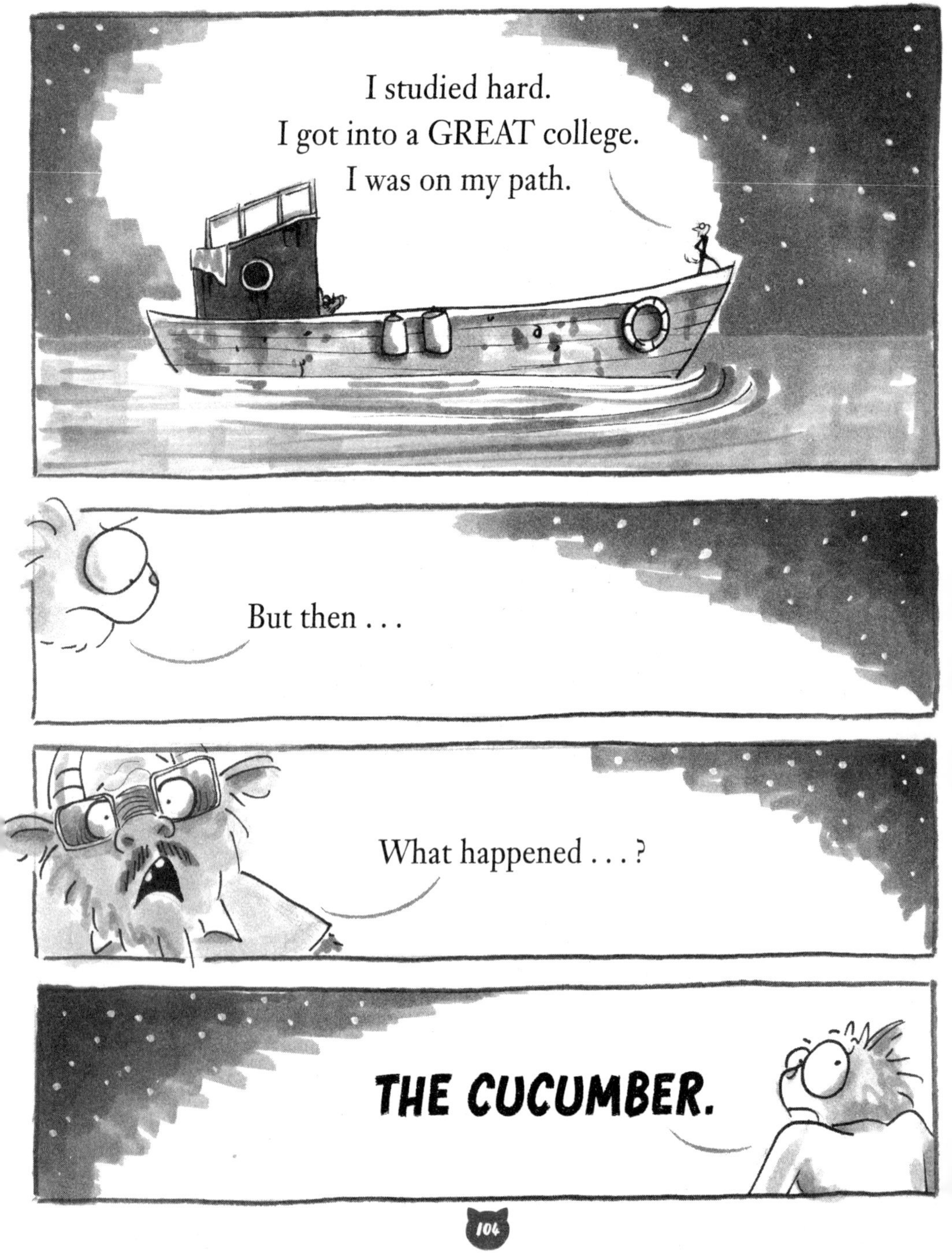
I studied hard.
I got into a GREAT college.
I was on my path.
But then . . .
What happened . . . ?
THE CUCUMBER.

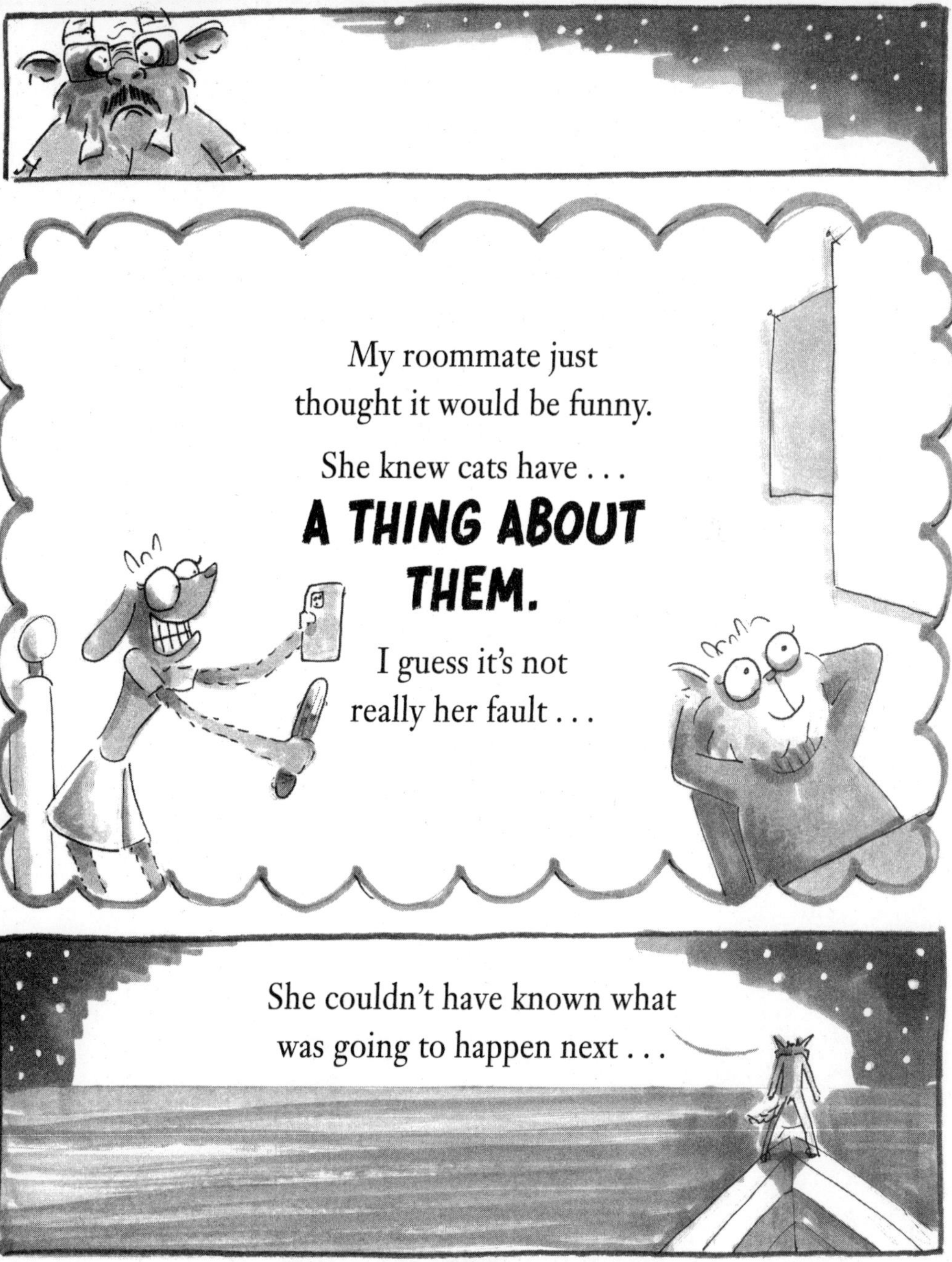
My roommate just thought it would be funny.
She knew cats have . . .
A THING ABOUT THEM.
I guess it's not really her fault . . .
She couldn't have known what was going to happen next . . .

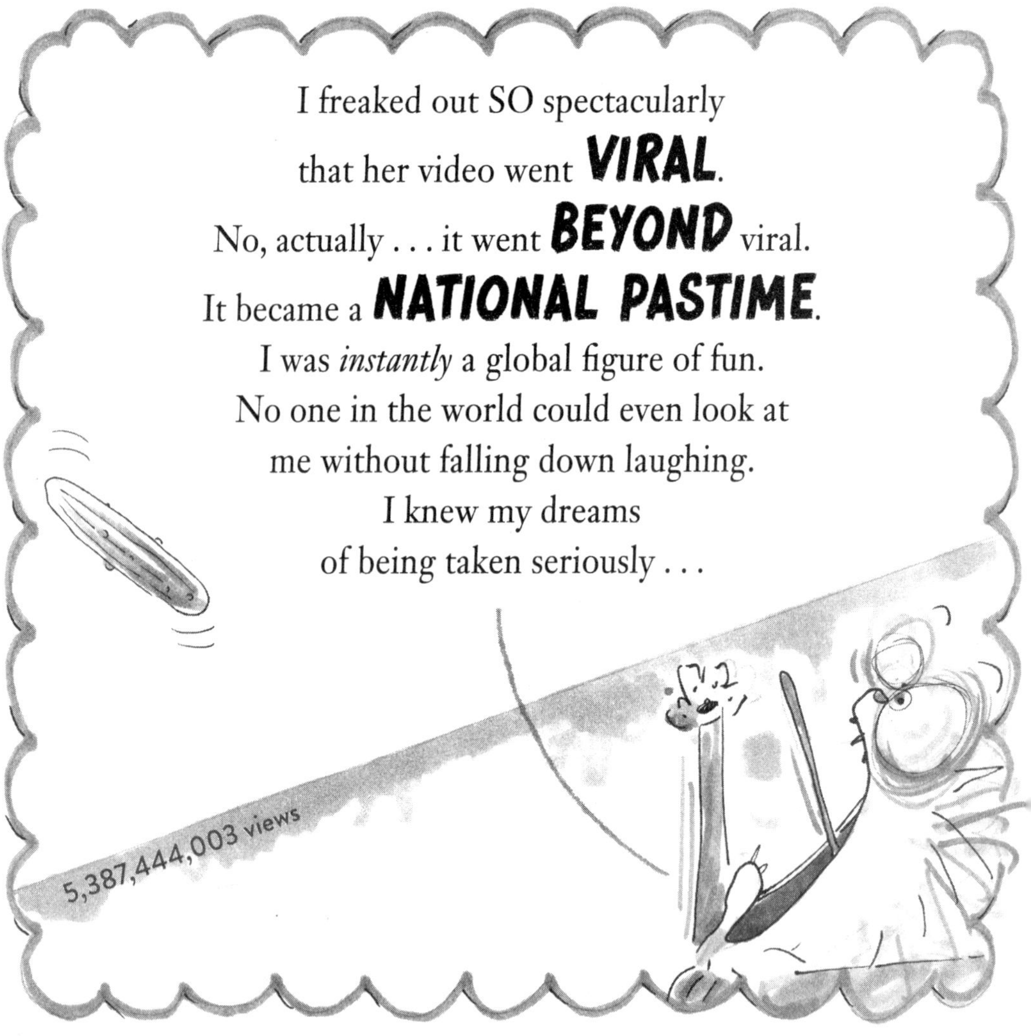
I freaked out SO spectacularly
that her video went **VIRAL**.
No, actually . . . it went **BEYOND** viral.
It became a **NATIONAL PASTIME**.
I was *instantly* a global figure of fun.
No one in the world could even look at
me without falling down laughing.
I knew my dreams
of being taken seriously . . .
5,387,444,003 views

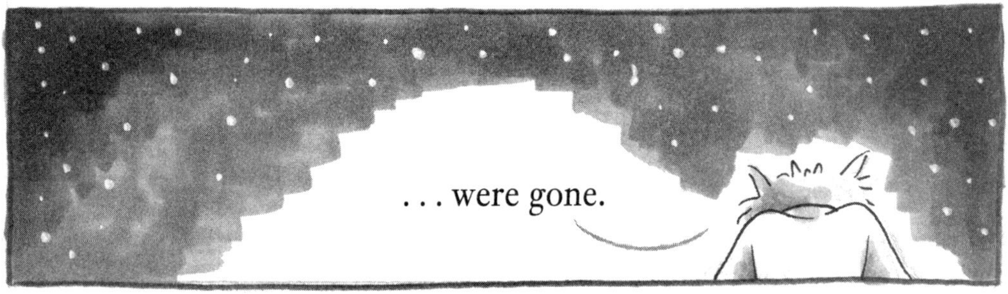
. . . were gone.

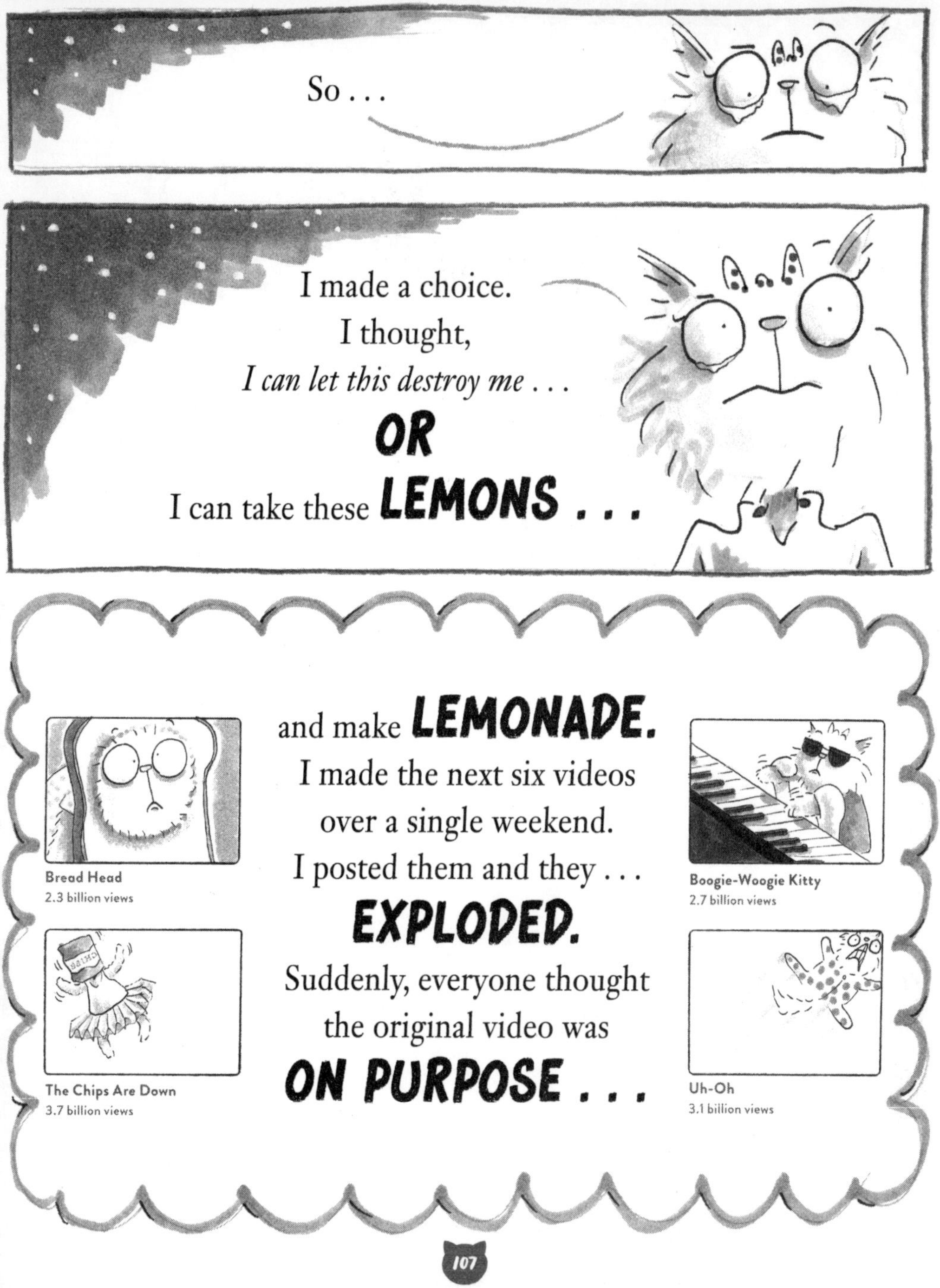
So . . .
I made a choice.
I thought,
I can let this destroy me . . .
OR
I can take these **LEMONS . . .**
and make **LEMONADE.**
I made the next six videos
over a single weekend.
I posted them and they . . .
EXPLODED.
Suddenly, everyone thought
the original video was
ON PURPOSE . . .
Bread Head
2.3 billion views
The Chips Are Down
3.7 billion views
Boogie-Woogie Kitty
2.7 billion views
Uh-Oh
3.1 billion views

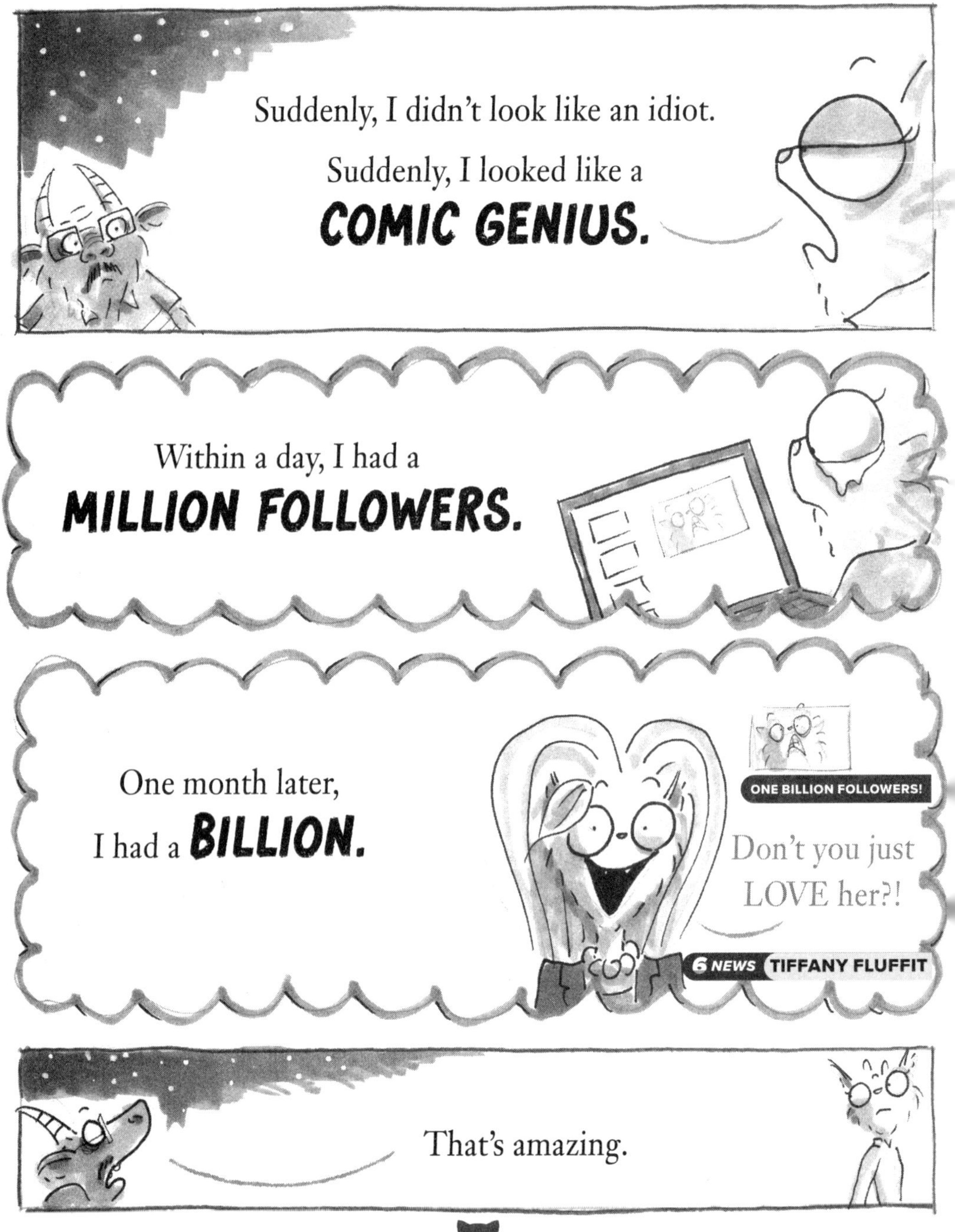
Suddenly, I didn't look like an idiot.
Suddenly, I looked like a
COMIC GENIUS.
Within a day, I had a
MILLION FOLLOWERS.
One month later,
I had a BILLION.
ONE BILLION FOLLOWERS!
Don't you just
LOVE her?!
6 NEWS TIFFANY FLUFFIT
That's amazing.

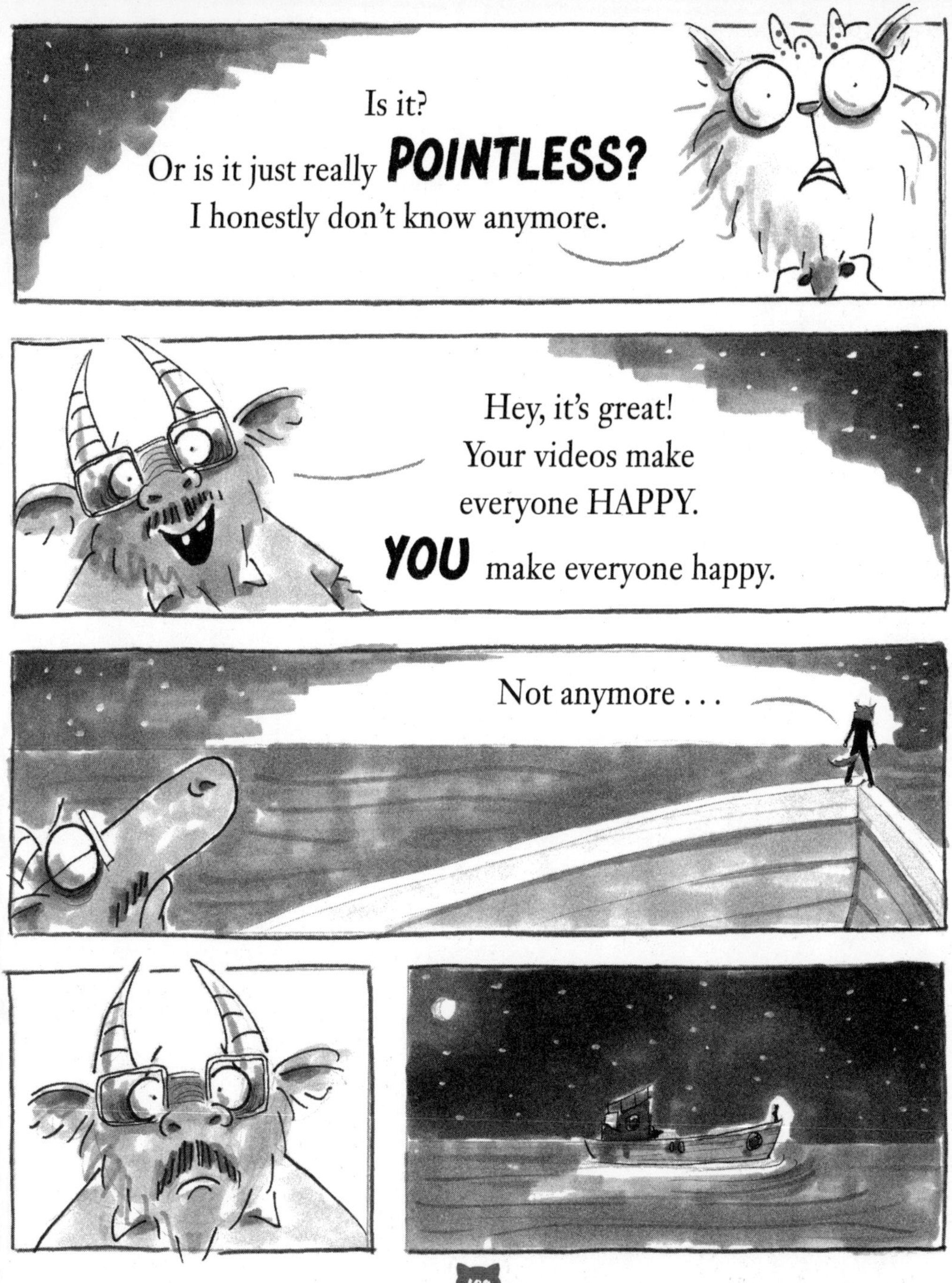
Is it?
Or is it just really POINTLESS?
I honestly don't know anymore.
Hey, it's great!
Your videos make
everyone HAPPY.
YOU make everyone happy.
Not anymore . . .

Six
SCORPION ISLAND

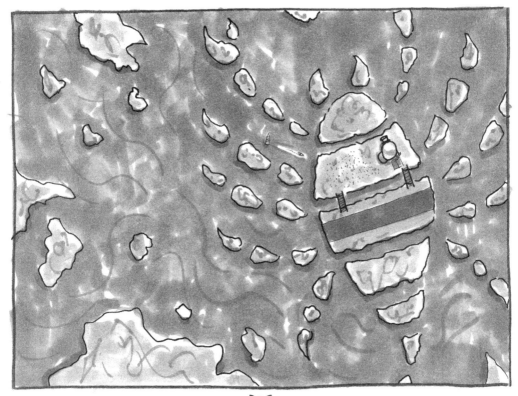

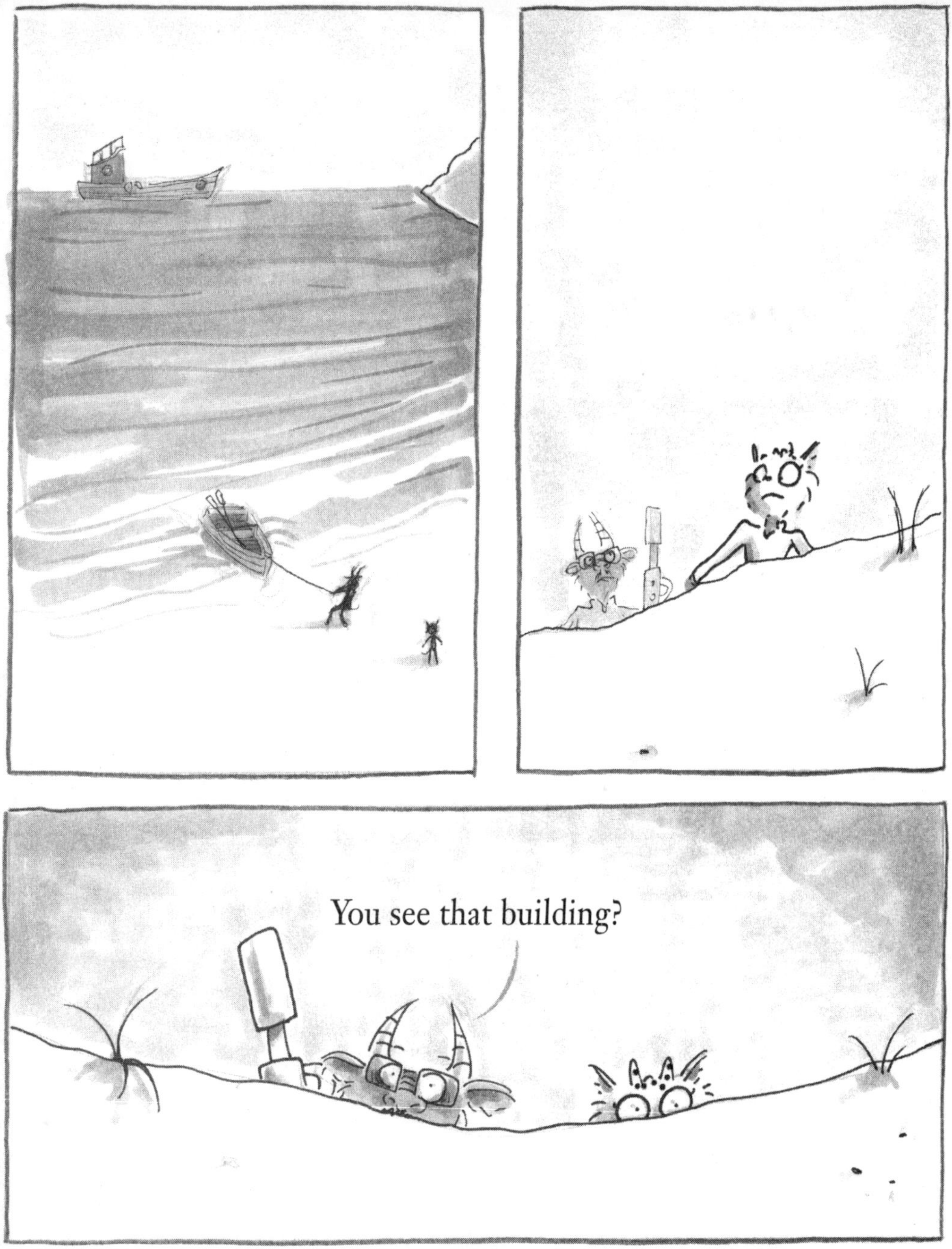
You see that building?

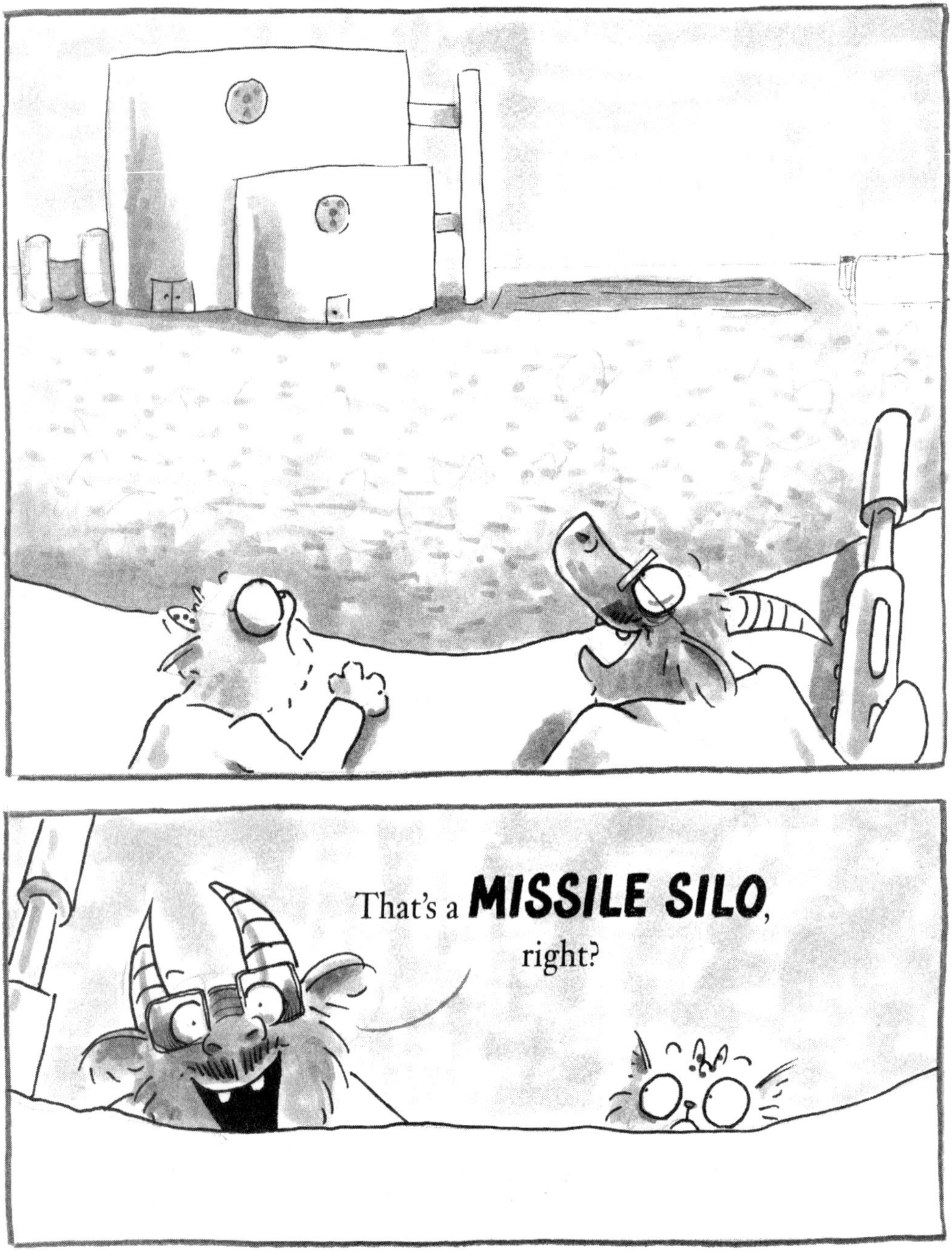
That's a MISSILE SILO, right?

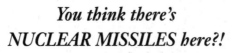

You think there's
NUCLEAR MISSILES here?!
This is CRAZY!
I'm not qualified to deal with THIS!

I MAKE STUPID VIDEOS!

WHAT DOES *ANY OF THIS*
HAVE TO DO WITH ME?!

WHY ARE
WE HERE?!

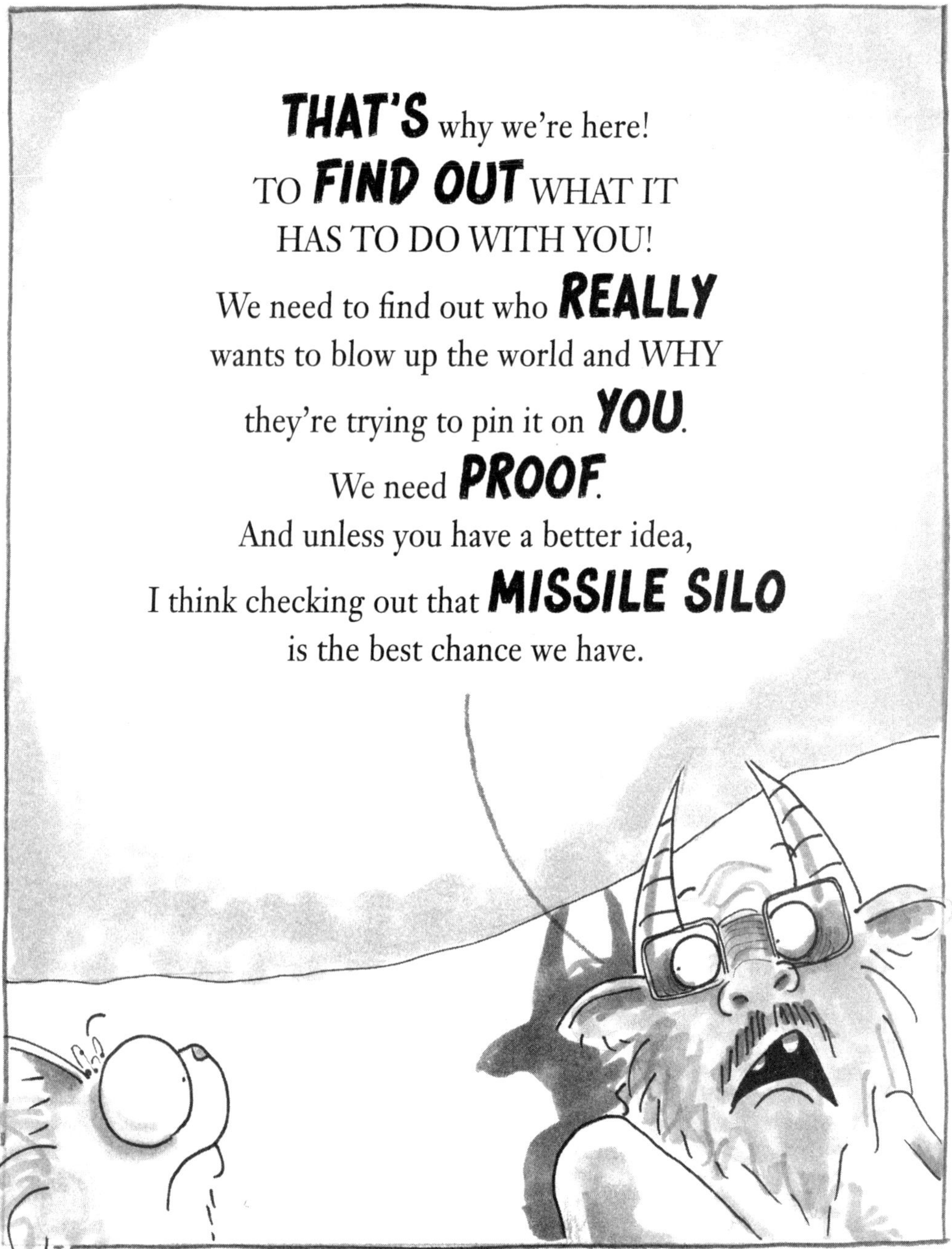
THAT'S why we're here!
TO FIND OUT WHAT IT
HAS TO DO WITH YOU!
We need to find out who REALLY
wants to blow up the world and WHY
they're trying to pin it on YOU.
We need PROOF.
And unless you have a better idea,
I think checking out that MISSILE SILO
is the best chance we have.

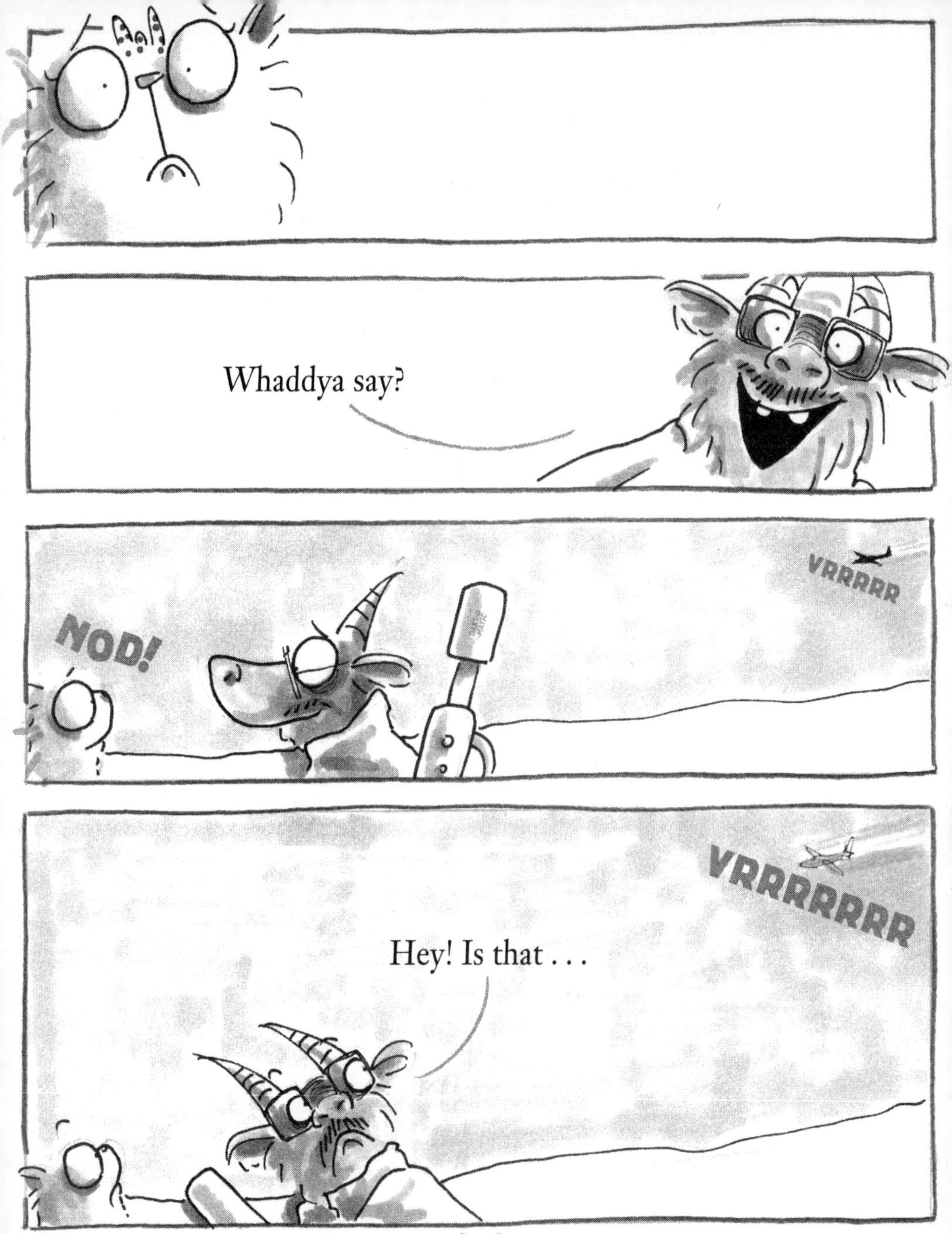
Whaddya say?
NOD!
VRRRRR
VRRRRRRRR
Hey! Is that . . .

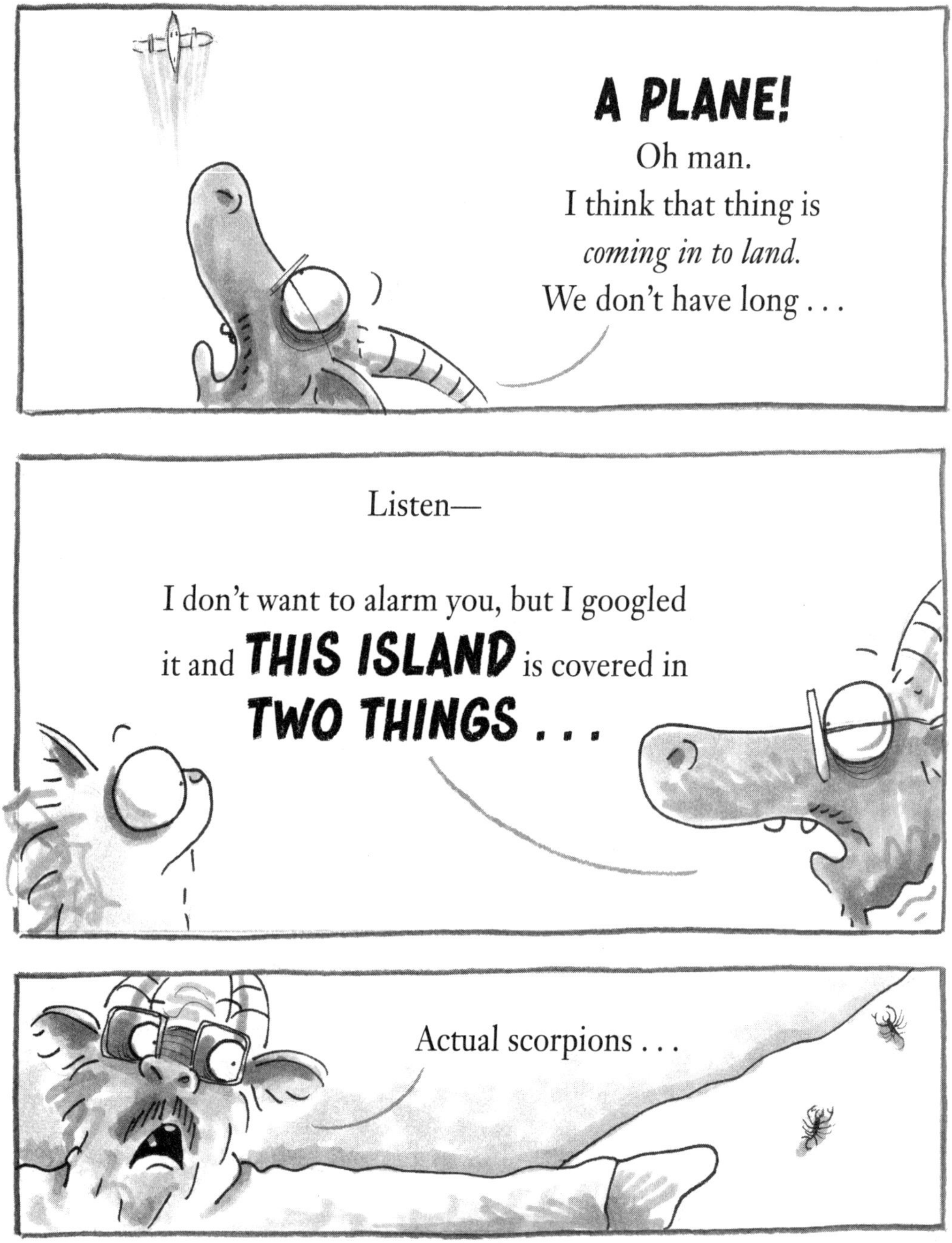
A PLANE!
Oh man.
I think that thing is
coming in to land.
We don't have long . . .
Listen—
I don't want to alarm you, but I googled it and THIS ISLAND is covered in TWO THINGS . . .
Actual scorpions . . .

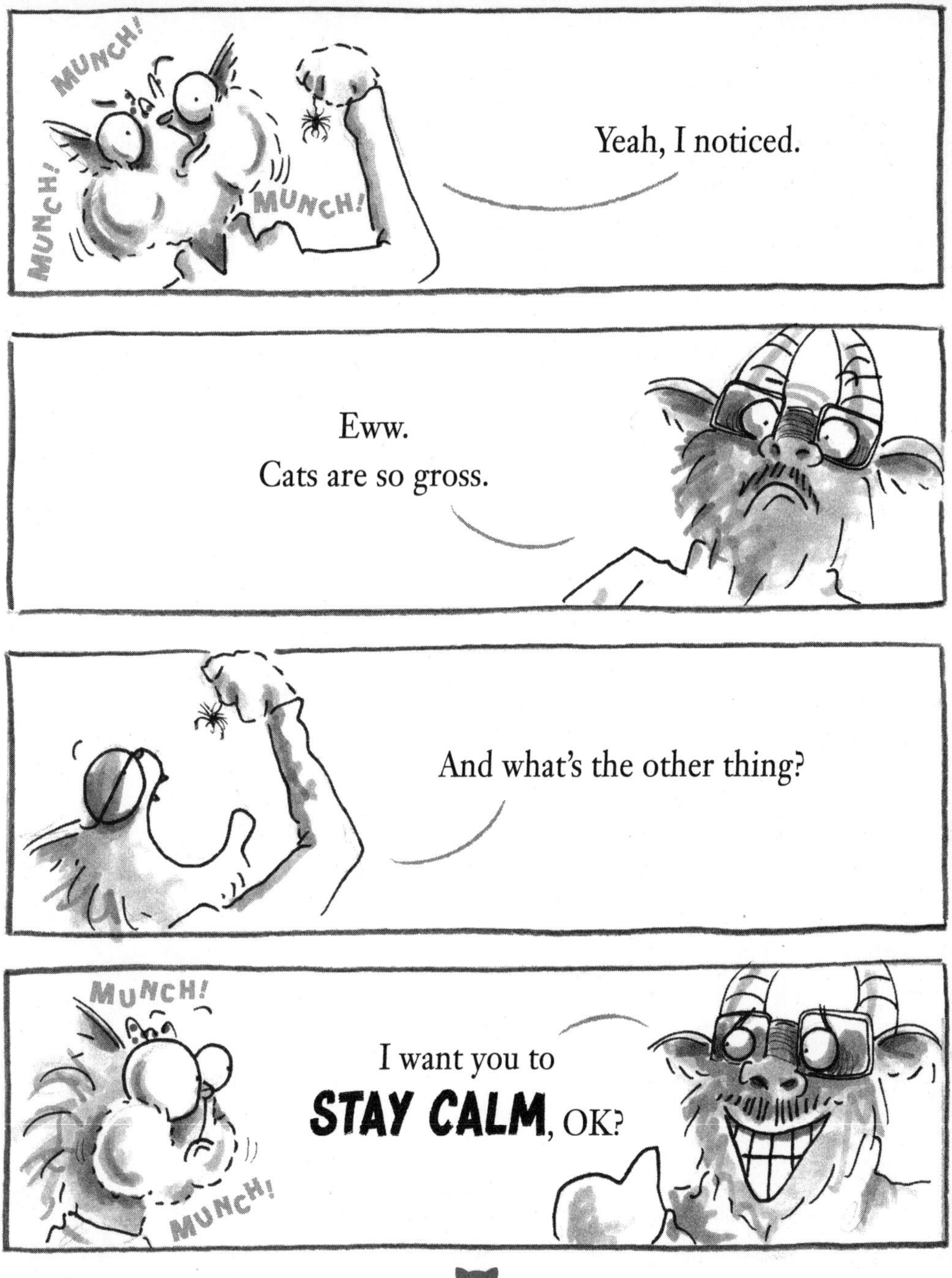
MUNCH!
MUNCH!
MUNCH!
Yeah, I noticed.
Eww.
Cats are so gross.
And what's the other thing?
MUNCH!
I want you to STAY CALM, OK?
MUNCH!

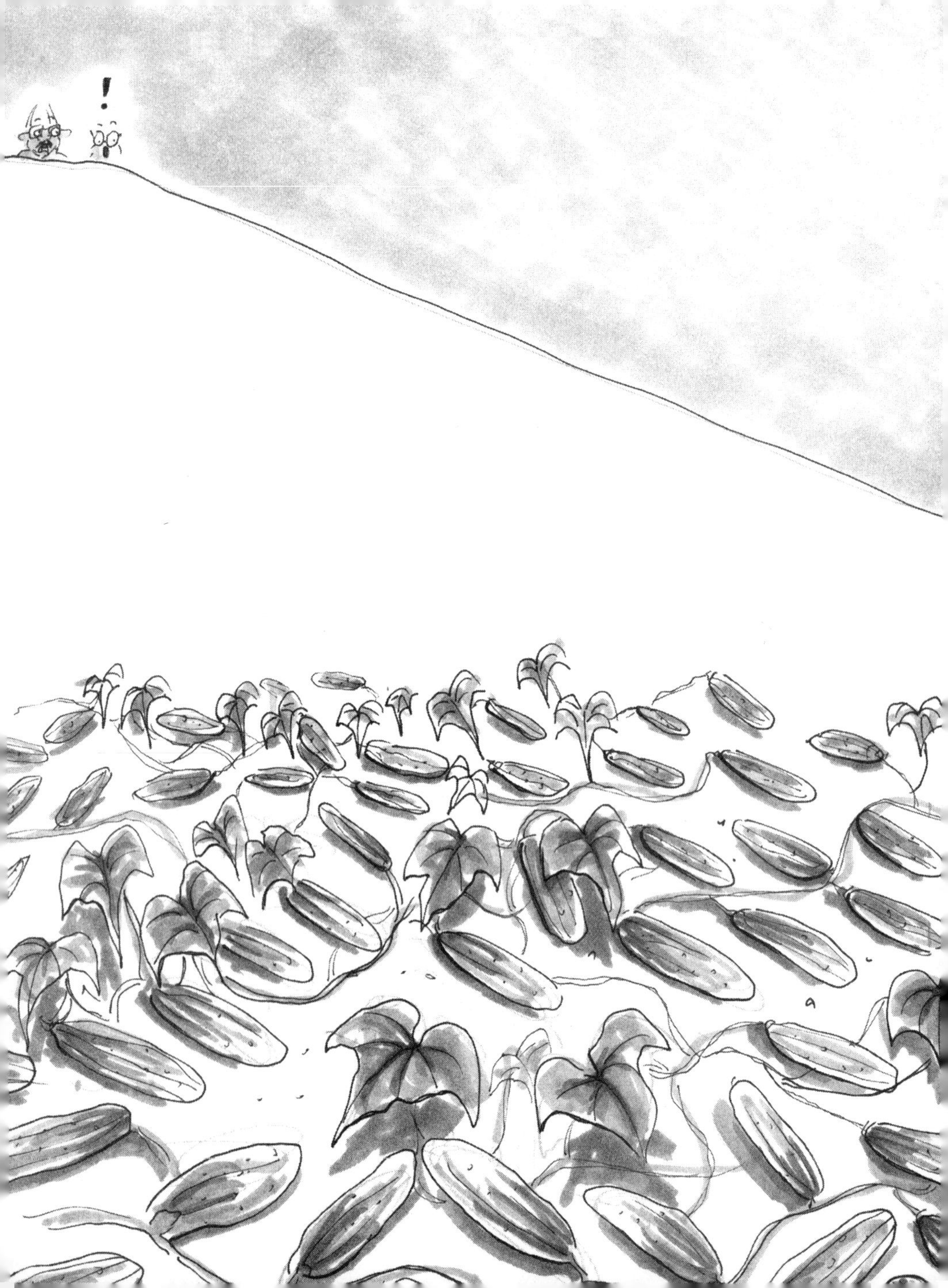
!

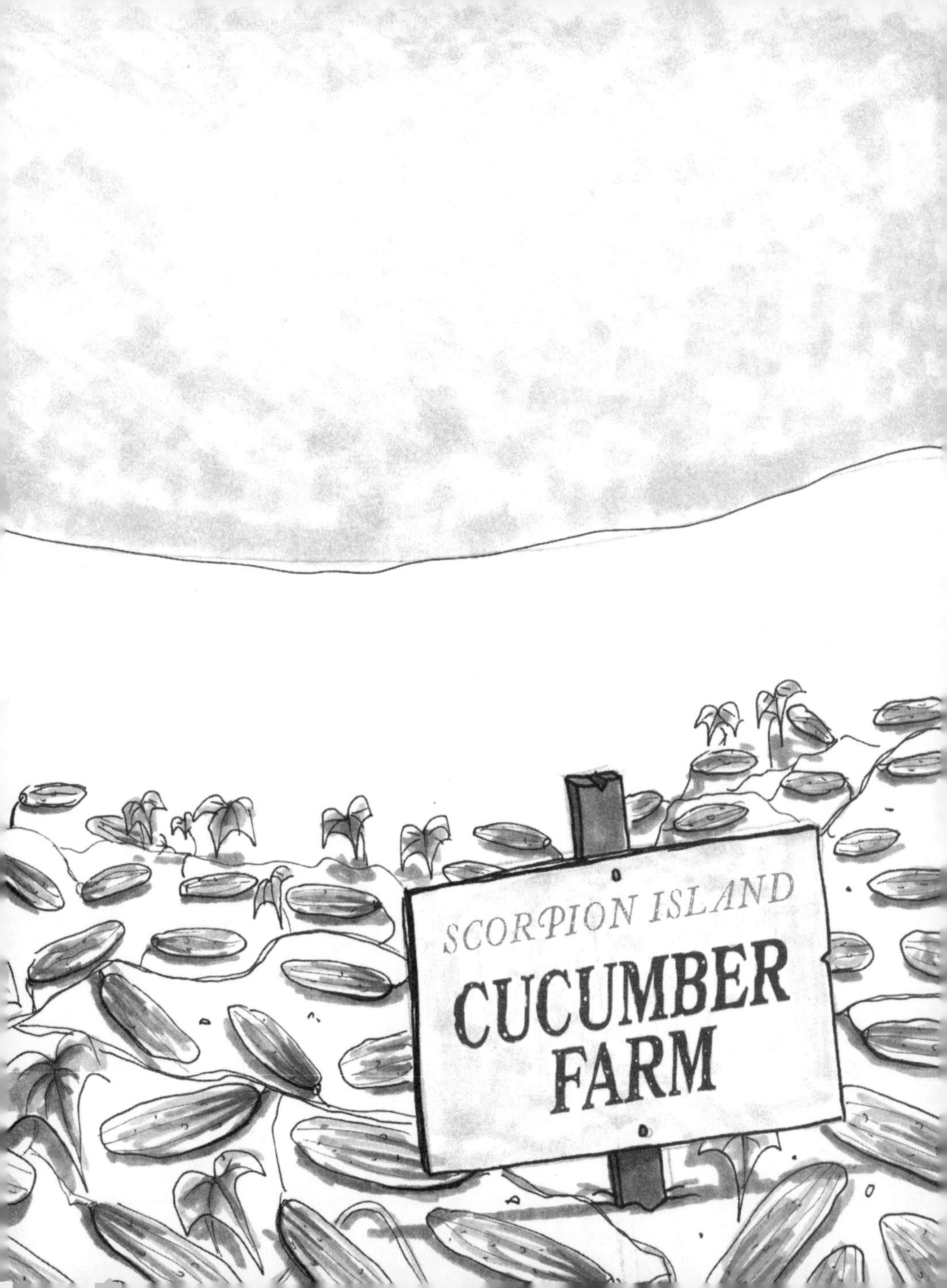
SCORPION ISLAND
CUCUMBER FARM

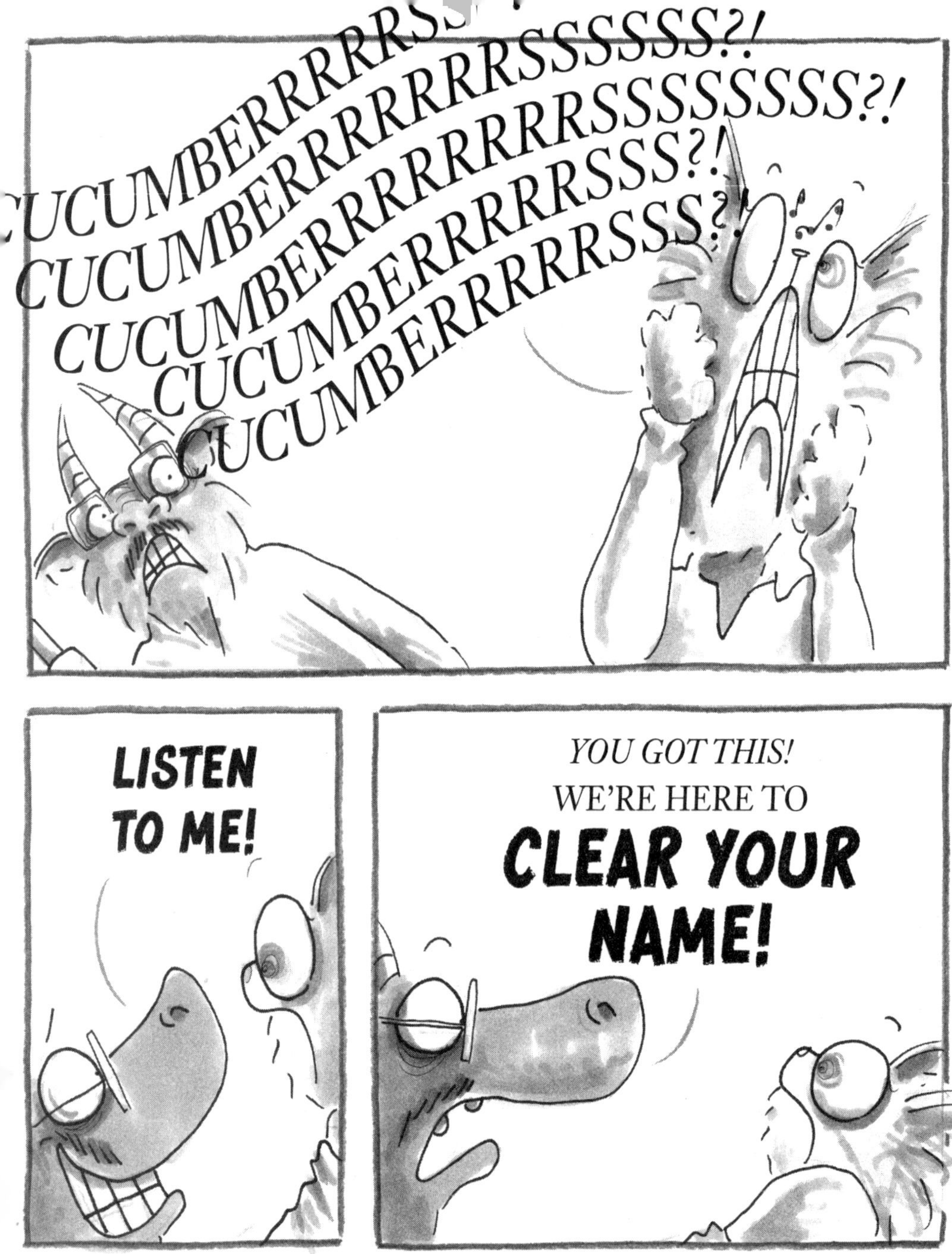
CUCUMBERRRRRRSS
CUCUMBERRRRRRRRRSSSSSS?!
CUCUMBERRRRRRRRRRSSSSSSSSSS?!
CUCUMBERRRRRRRRSSS?!
CUCUMBERRRRRRRSSS?!
CUCUMBERRRRRRSSS?!
LISTEN TO ME!
YOU GOT THIS!
WE'RE HERE TO
CLEAR YOUR NAME!

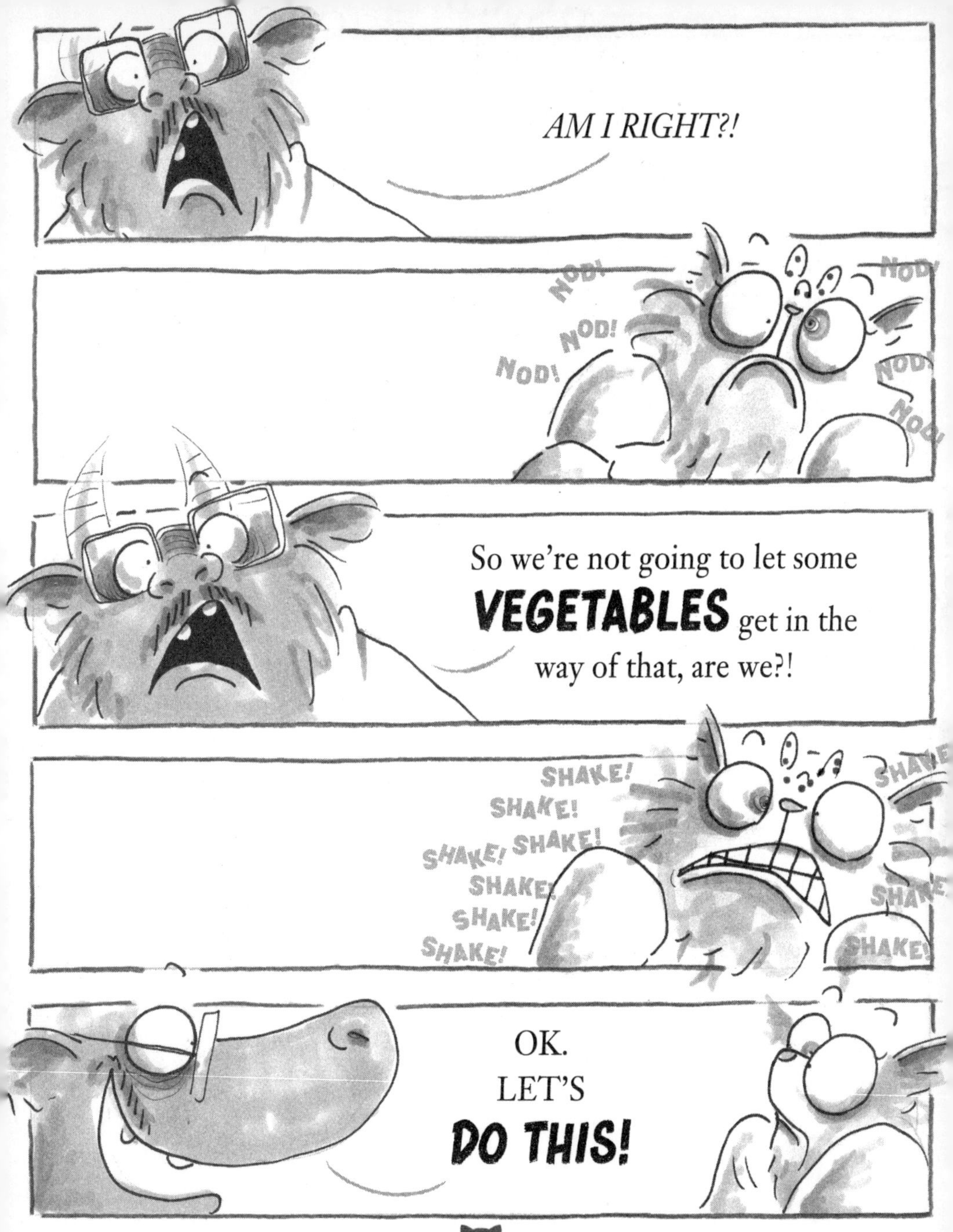

AM I RIGHT?!
NOD! NOD! NOD! NOD! NOD!
So we're not going to let some VEGETABLES get in the way of that, are we?!
SHAKE! SHAKE! SHAKE! SHAKE! SHAKE! SHAKE! SHAKE! SHAKE!
OK. LET'S DO THIS!

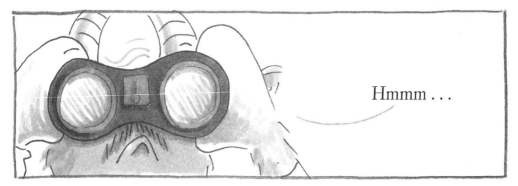

Hmmm . . .

This is *definitely* the place.

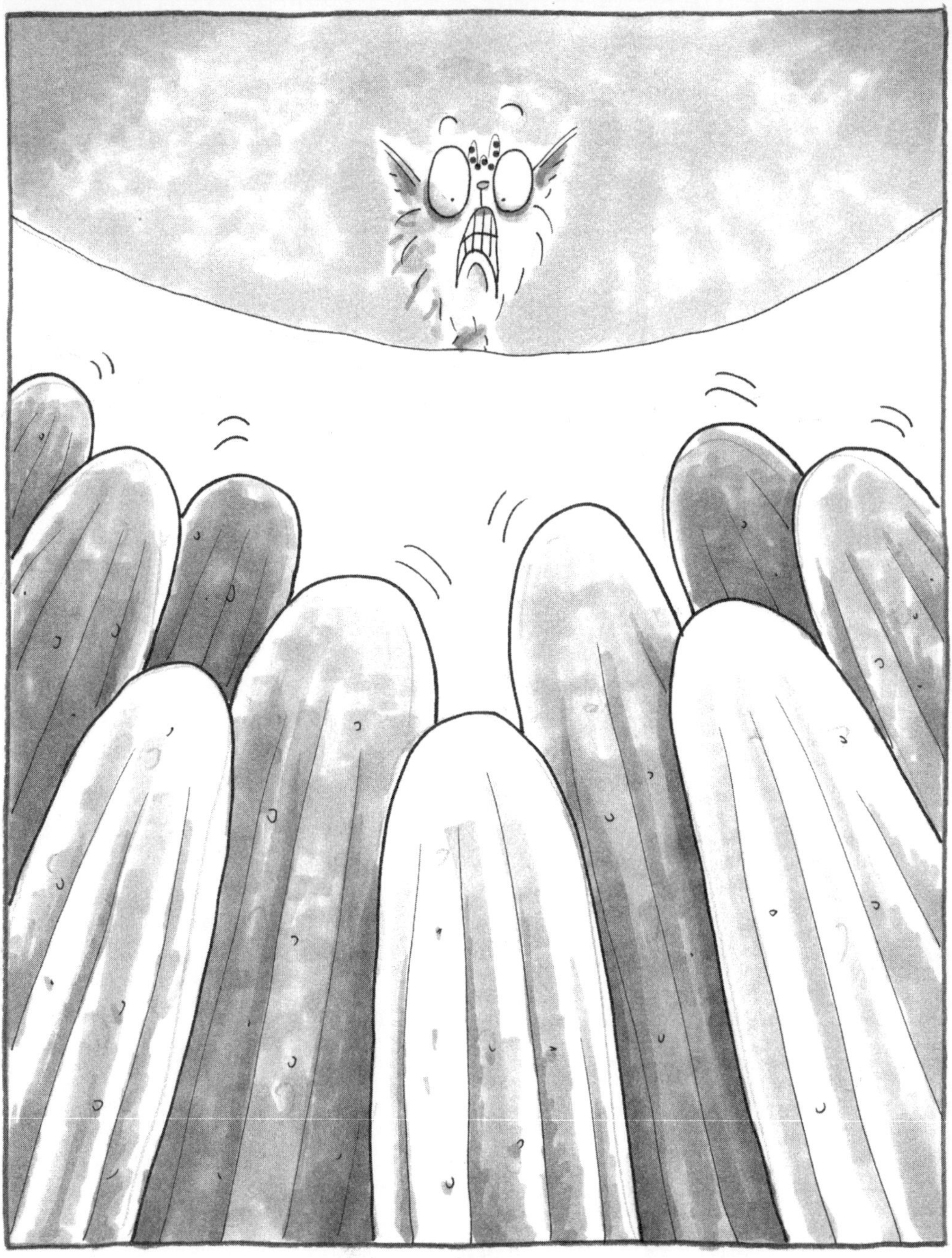

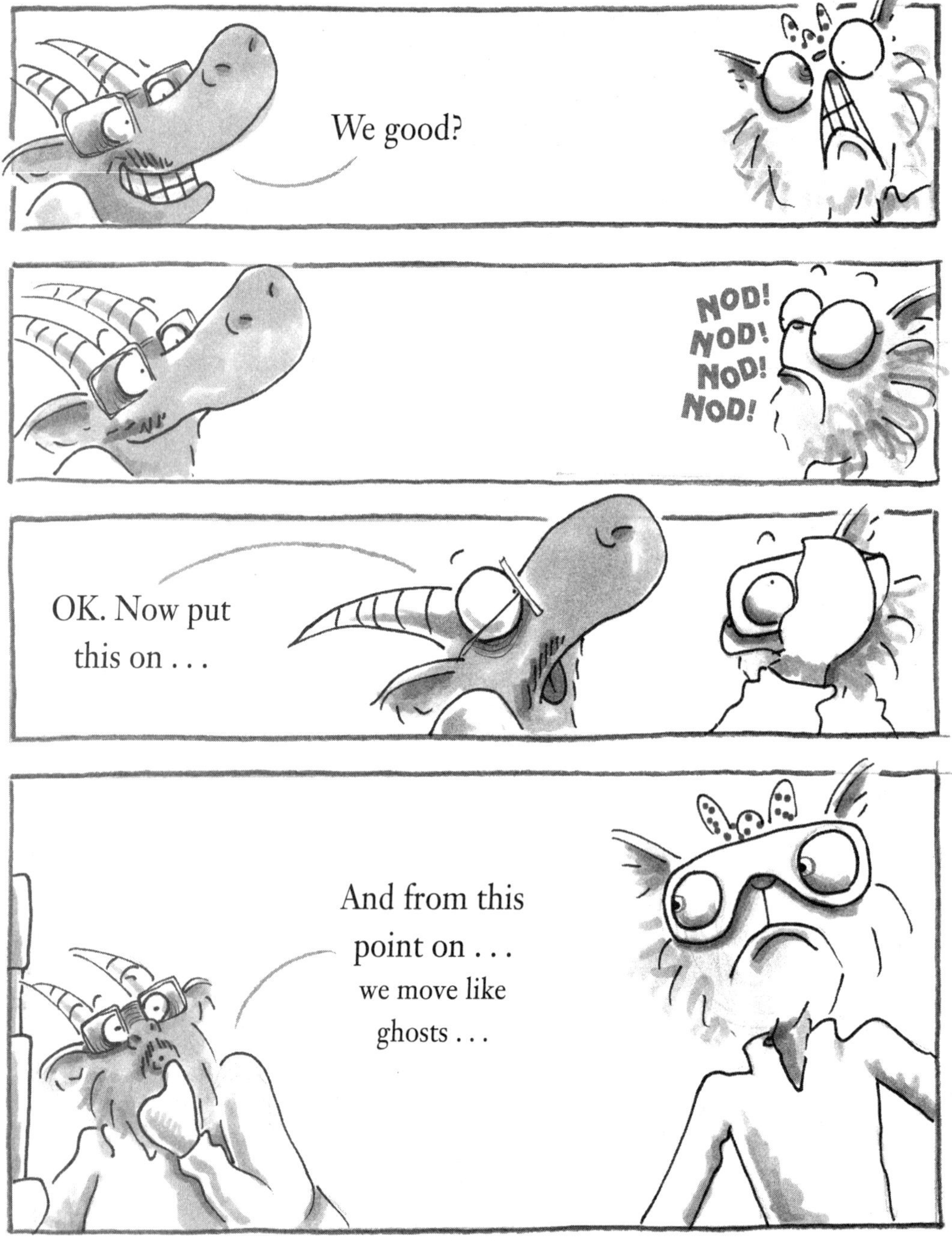

We good?
NOD!
NOD!
NOD!
NOD!
OK. Now put this on . . .
And from this point on . . .
we move like ghosts . . .

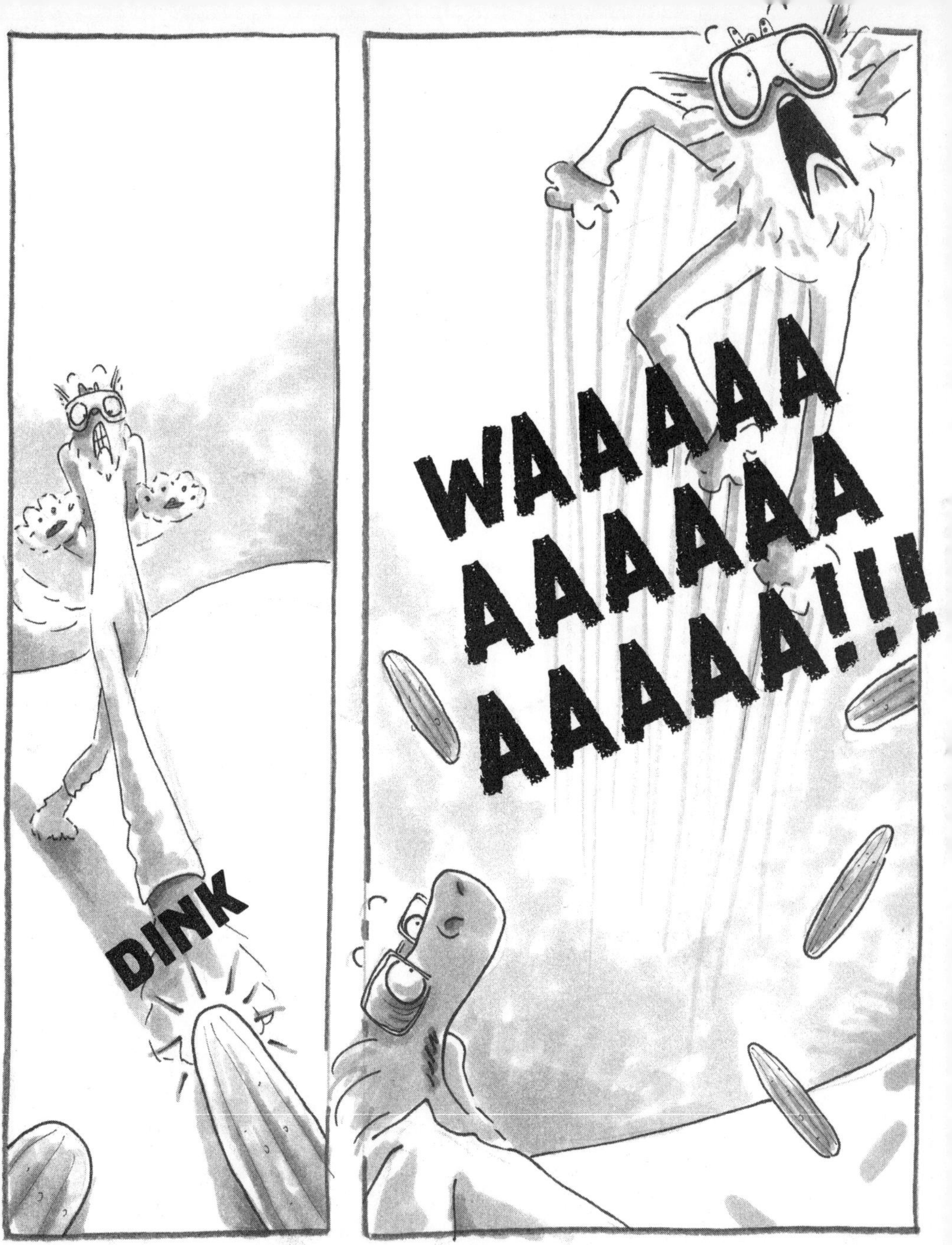
DINK
WAAAAAAAAAAAAAAAAAAAAAAA!!!

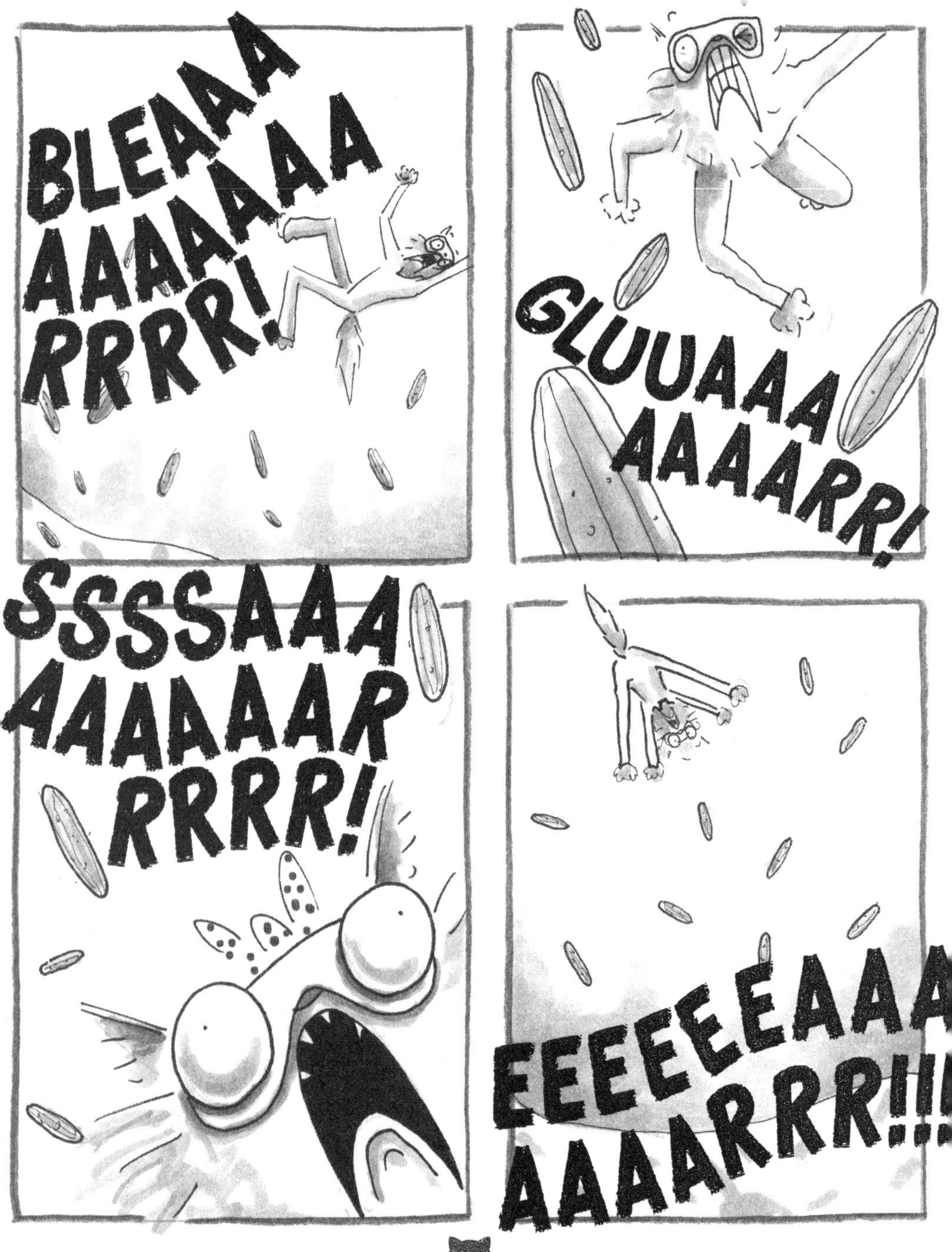
BLEAAAAAAAAAAAAAARRRRR!
GLUUAAAAAAAARR!
SSSSAAAAAAAAAARRRRR!
EEEEEEAAAAAAARRRR!!!

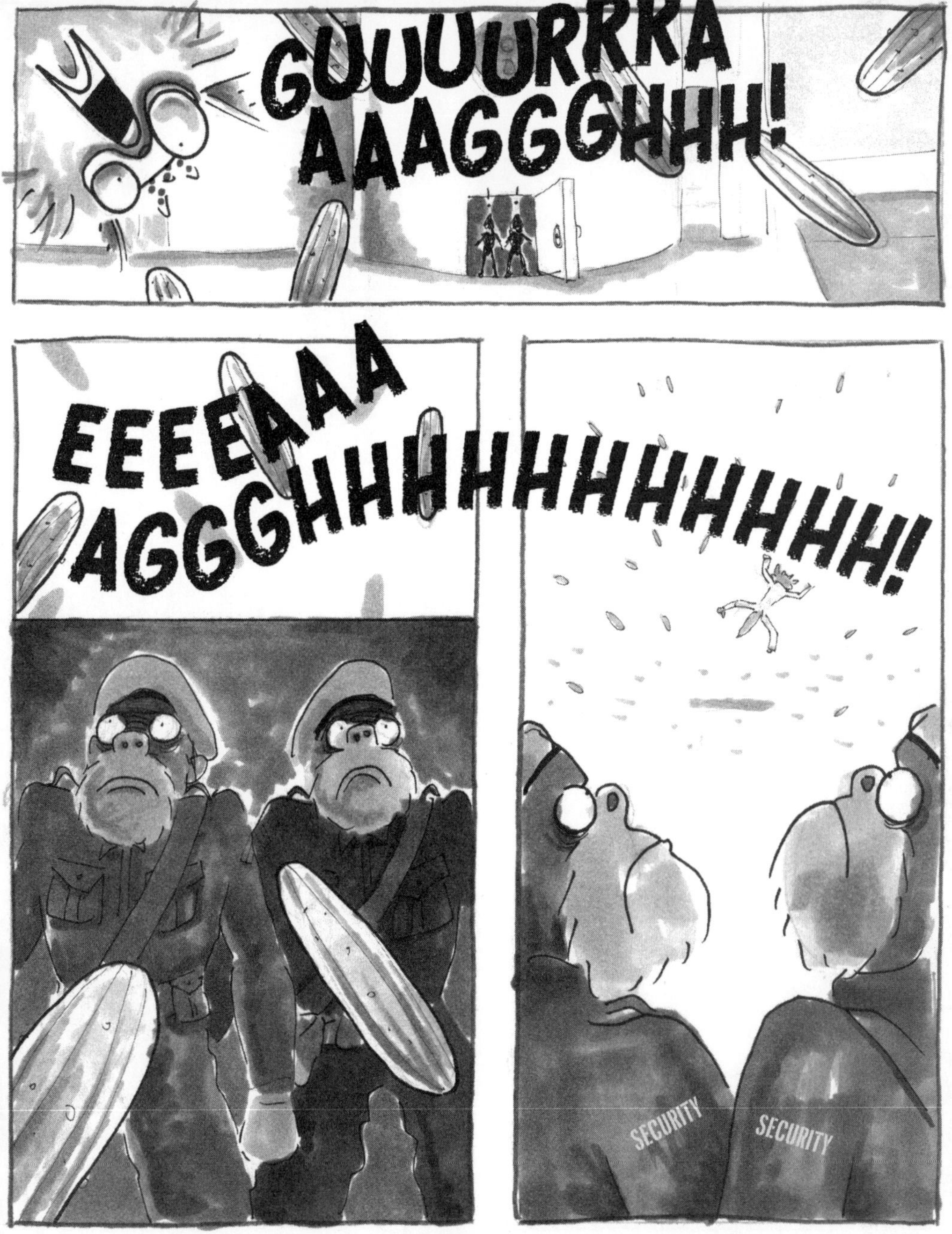
GUUUURRRA AAAGGGHHH!
EEEEAAA AGGGHHHHHHHHHHHH!
SECURITY
SECURITY

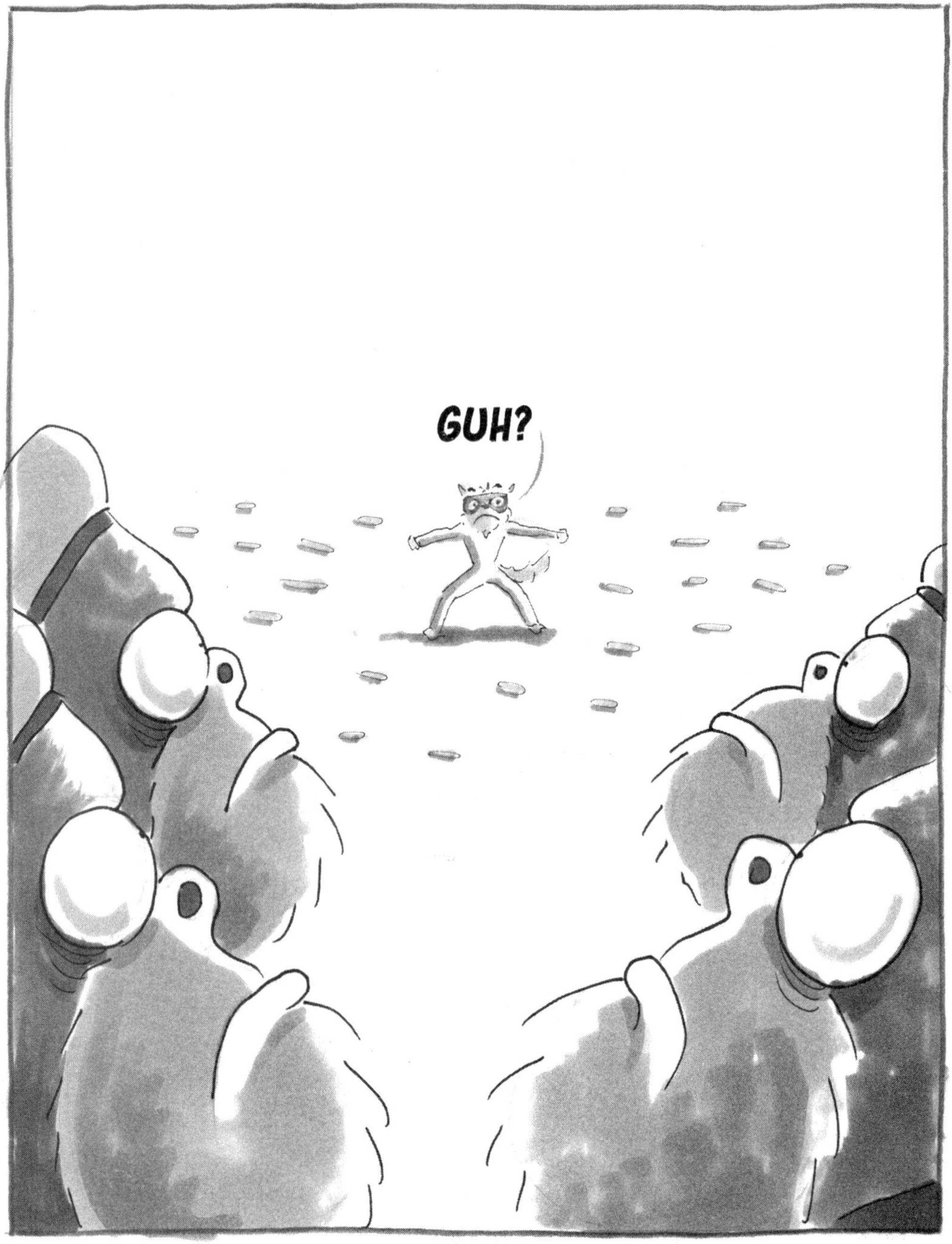
GUH?

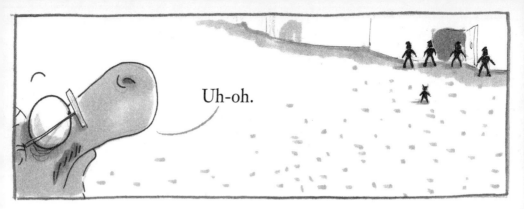

Uh-oh.

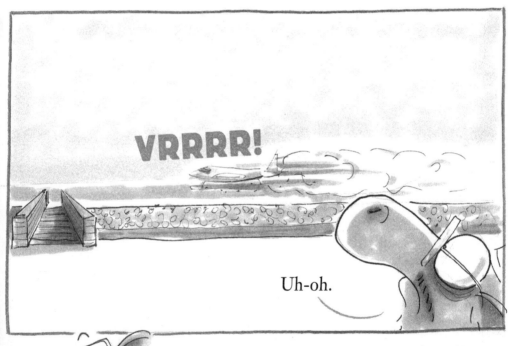

VRRRR!

Uh-oh.

Uh-oh.

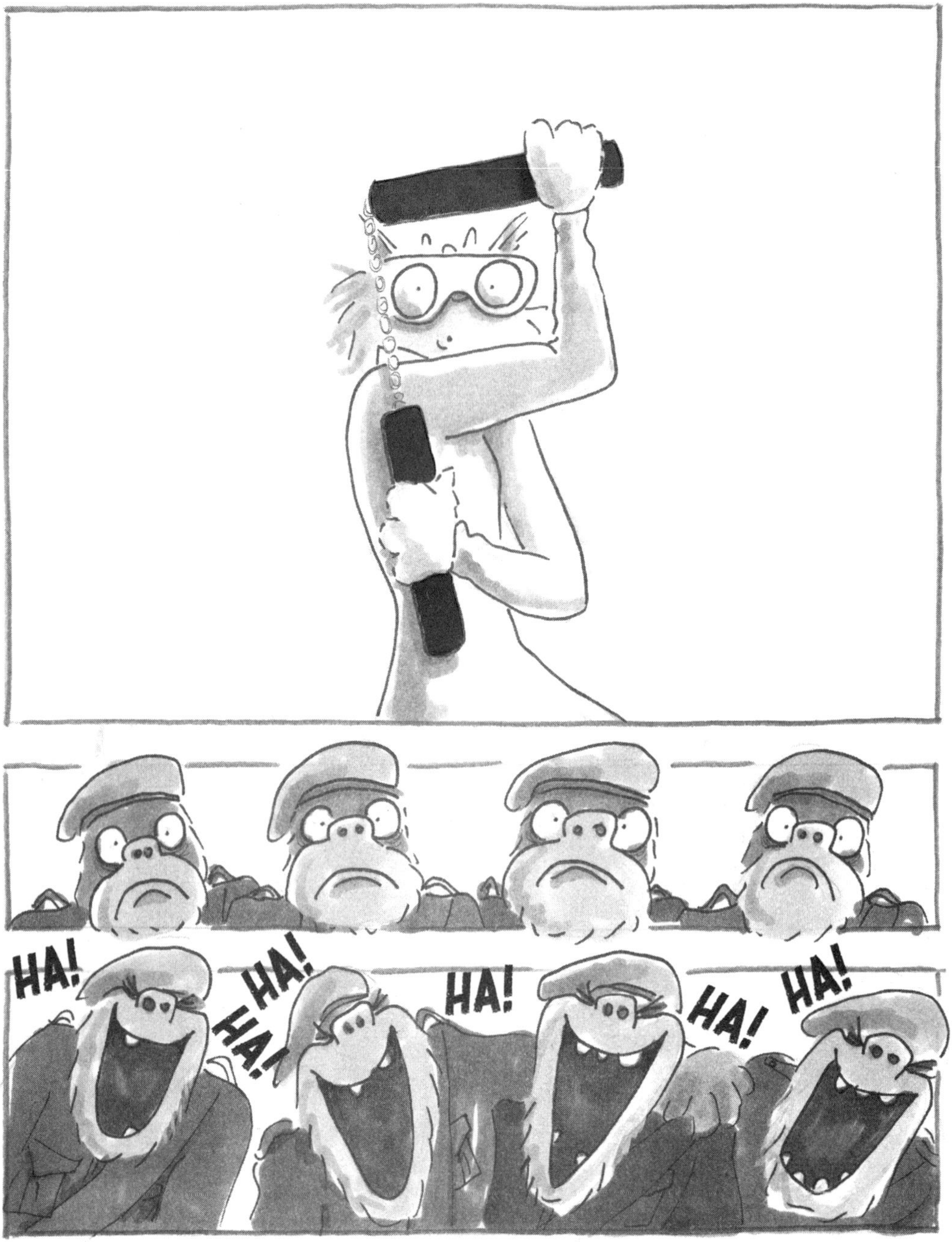
HA!
HA!
HA!
HA!
HA!
HA!

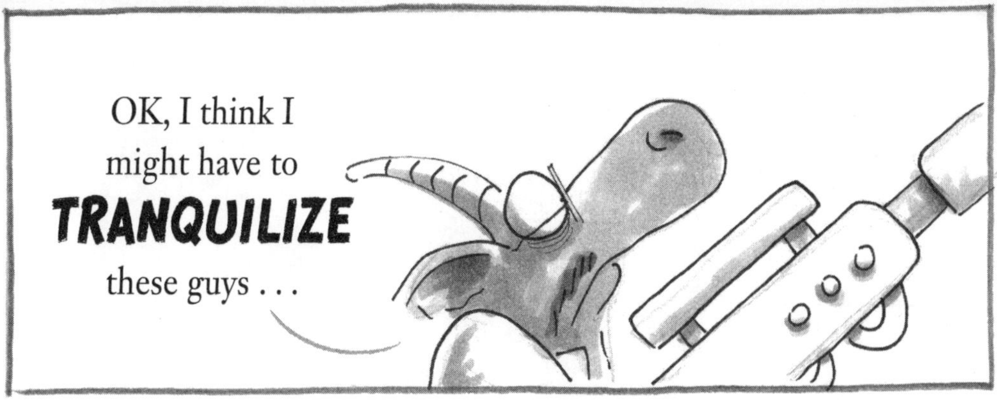
OK, I think I might have to **TRANQUILIZE** these guys . . .

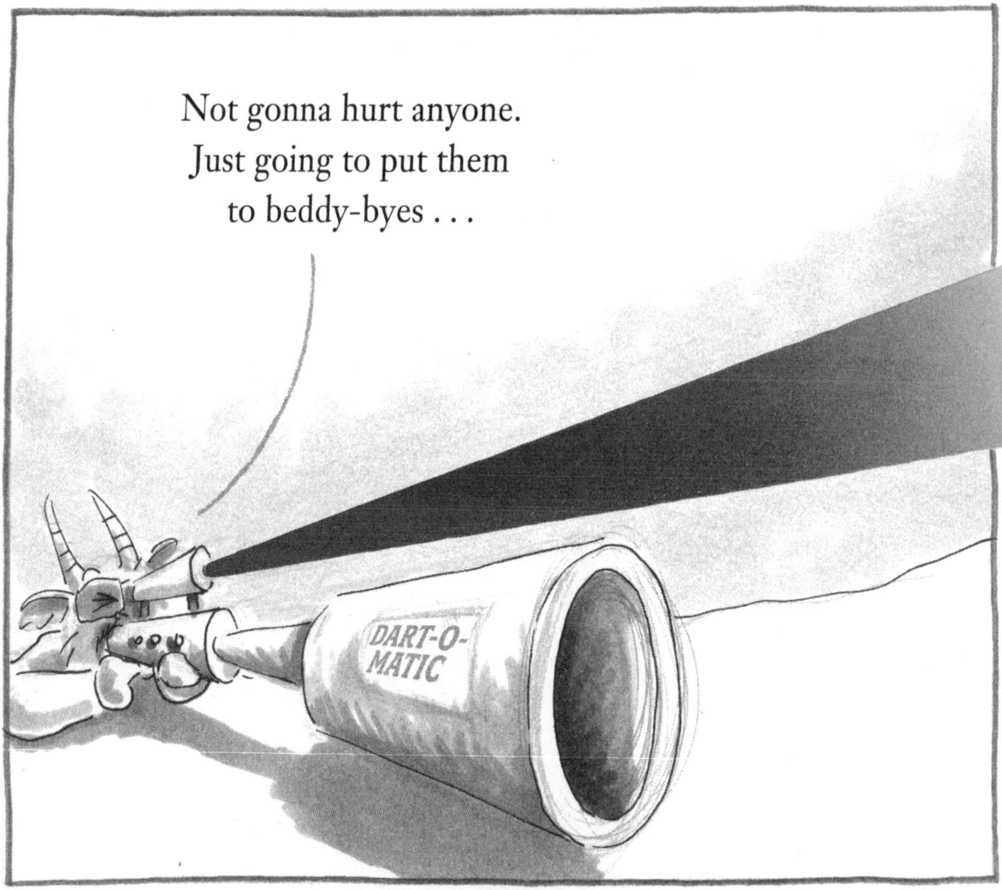
Not gonna hurt anyone. Just going to put them to beddy-byes . . .
DART-O-MATIC

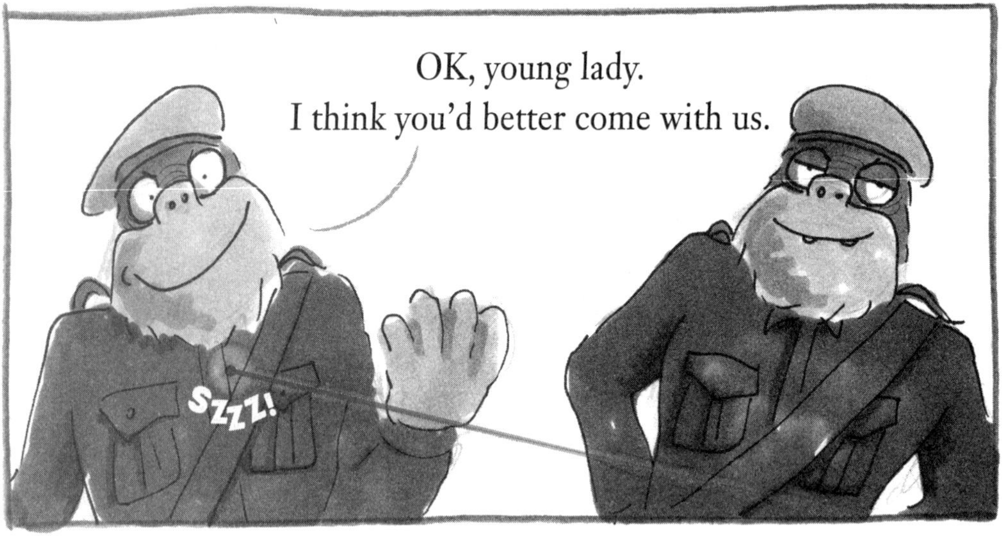
OK, young lady.
I think you'd better come with us.
SZZZ!

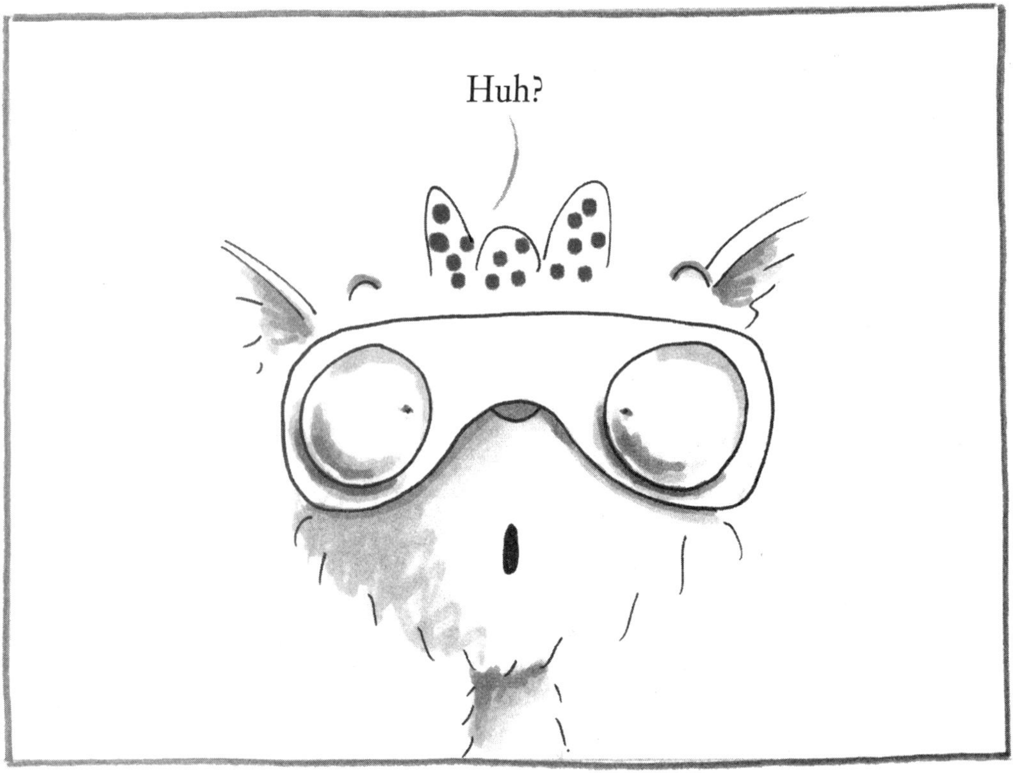
Huh?

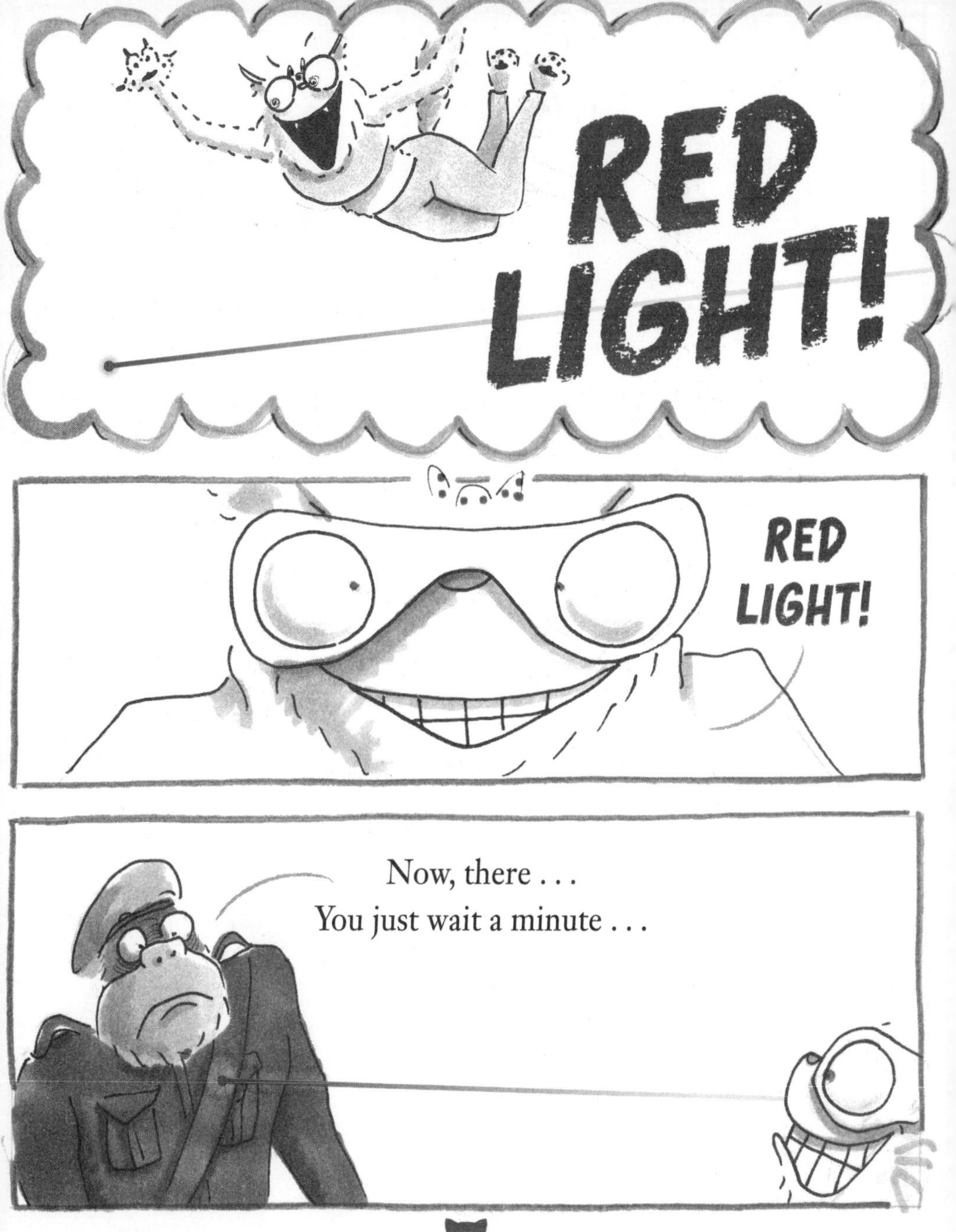
RED LIGHT!
RED LIGHT!
Now, there . . .
You just wait a minute . . .

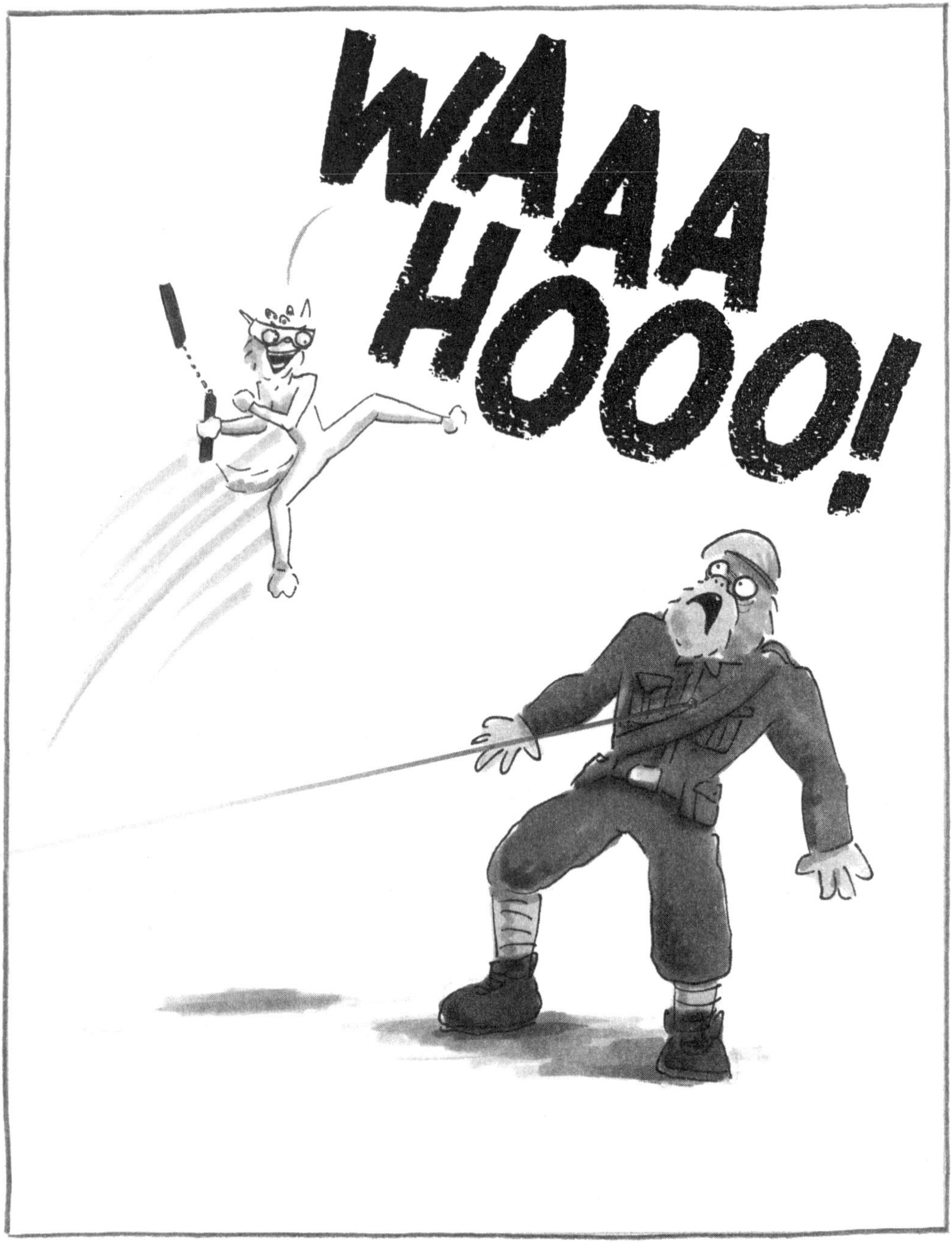
WAAA
HOOO!

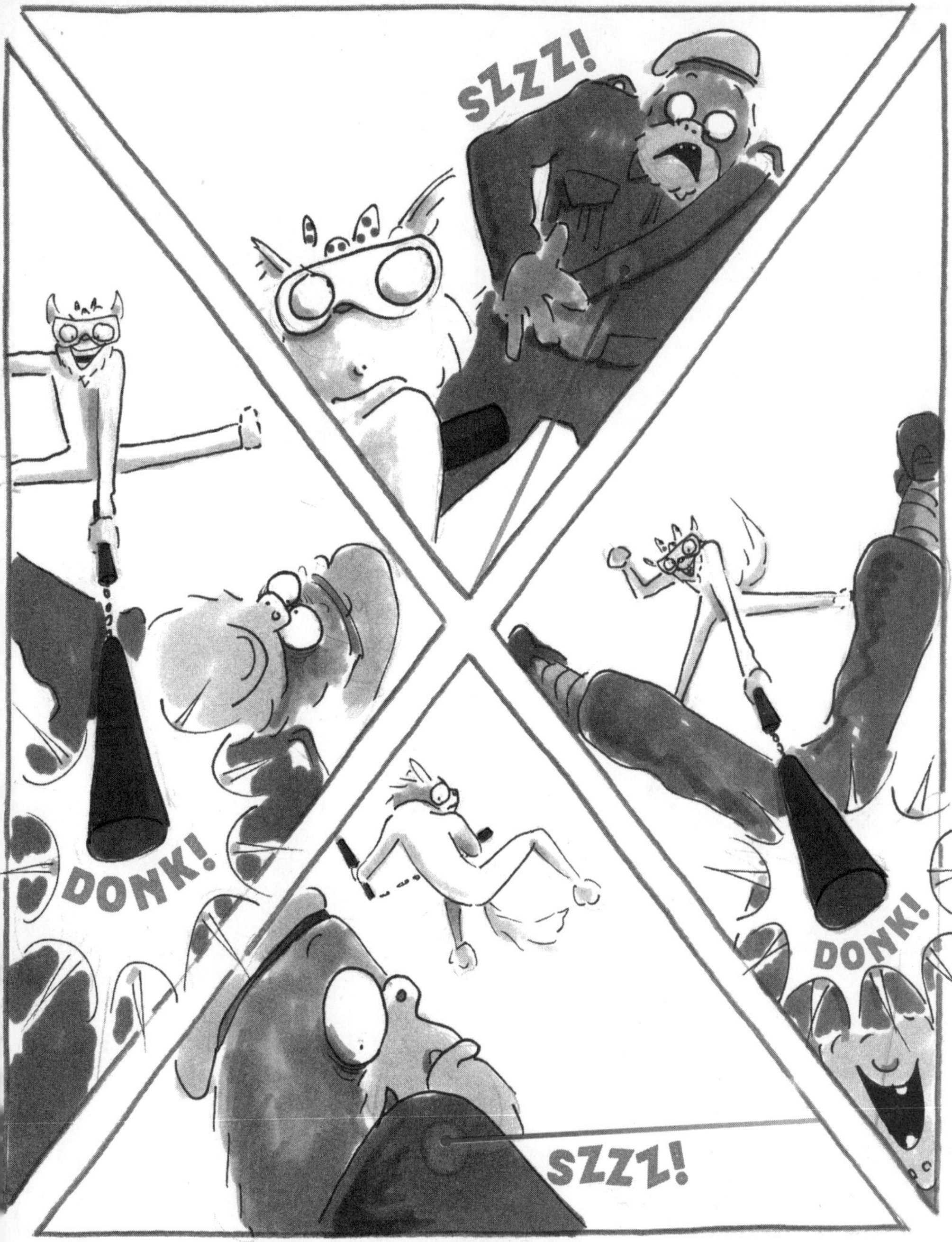
SZZZ!
DONK!
DONK!
SZZZ!

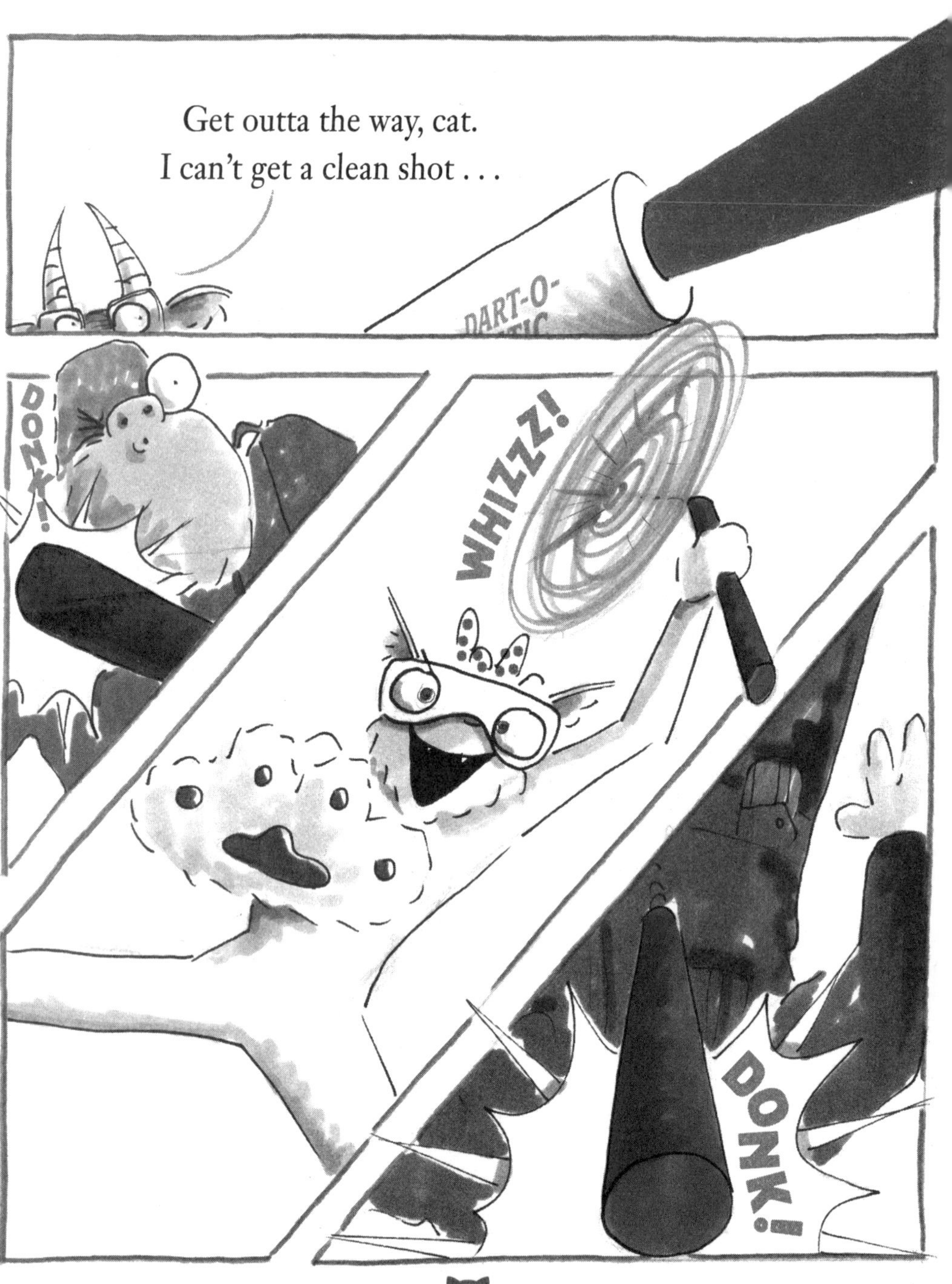
Get outta the way, cat.
I can't get a clean shot . . .
DART-O-
DONK!
WHIZZZ!
DONK!

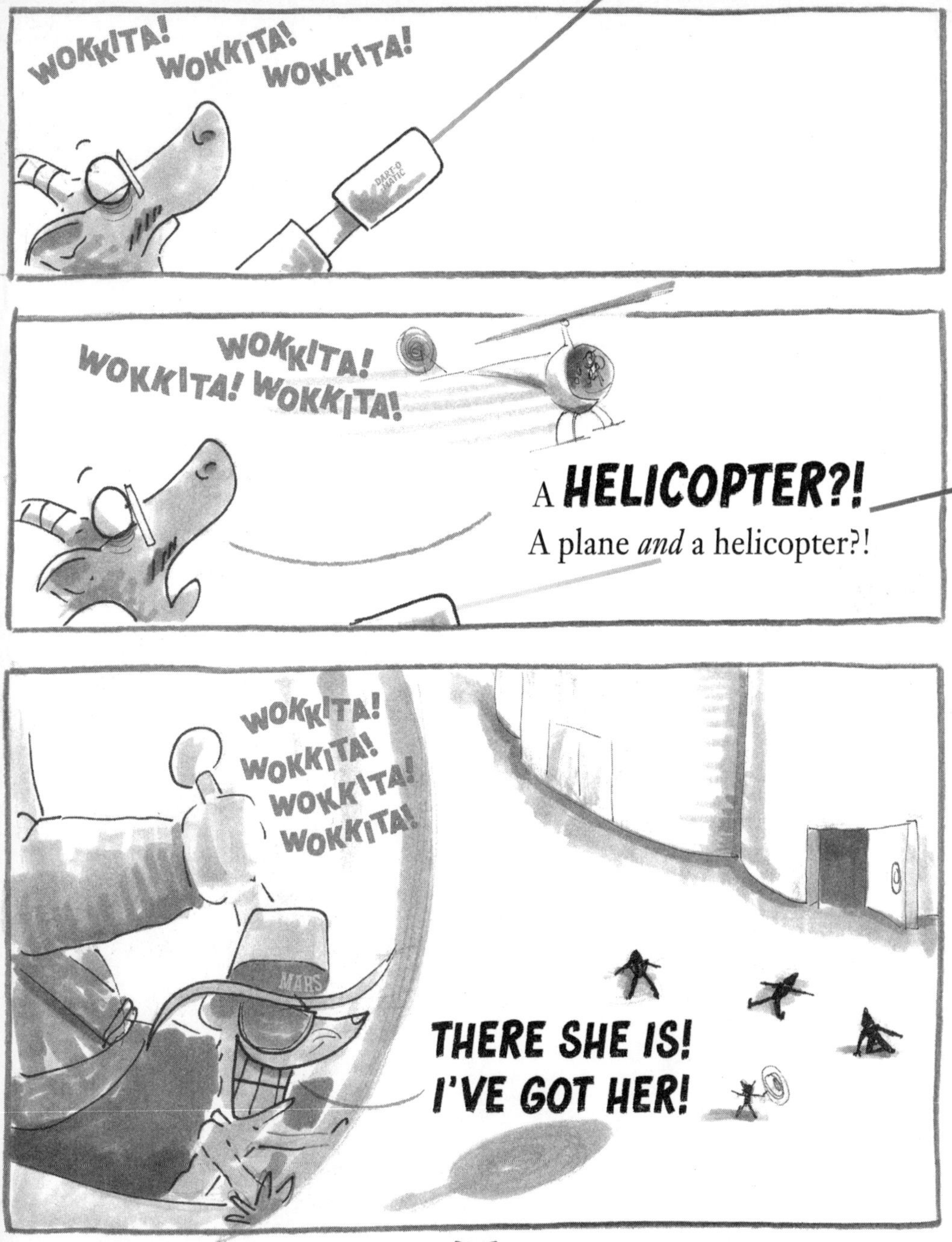
WOKKITA! WOKKITA! WOKKITA!
DART-O MATIC
WOKKITA! WOKKITA! WOKKITA!
A HELICOPTER?!
A plane *and* a helicopter?!
WOKKITA! WOKKITA! WOKKITA! WOKKITA!
MARS
THERE SHE IS! I'VE GOT HER!

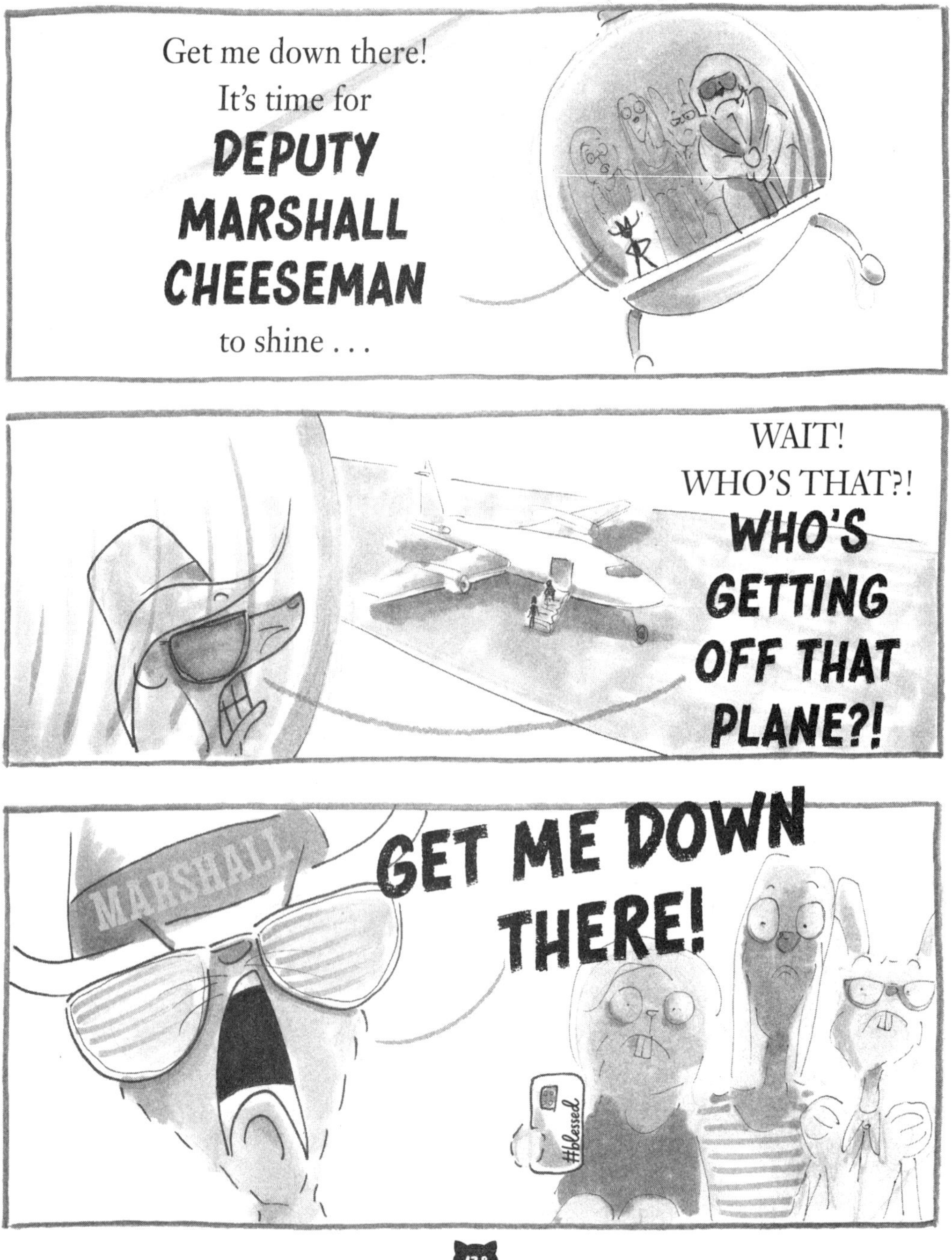

Get me down there!
It's time for
DEPUTY MARSHALL CHEESEMAN
to shine . . .
WAIT!
WHO'S THAT?!
WHO'S GETTING OFF THAT PLANE?!
MARSHALL
GET ME DOWN THERE!
#blessed

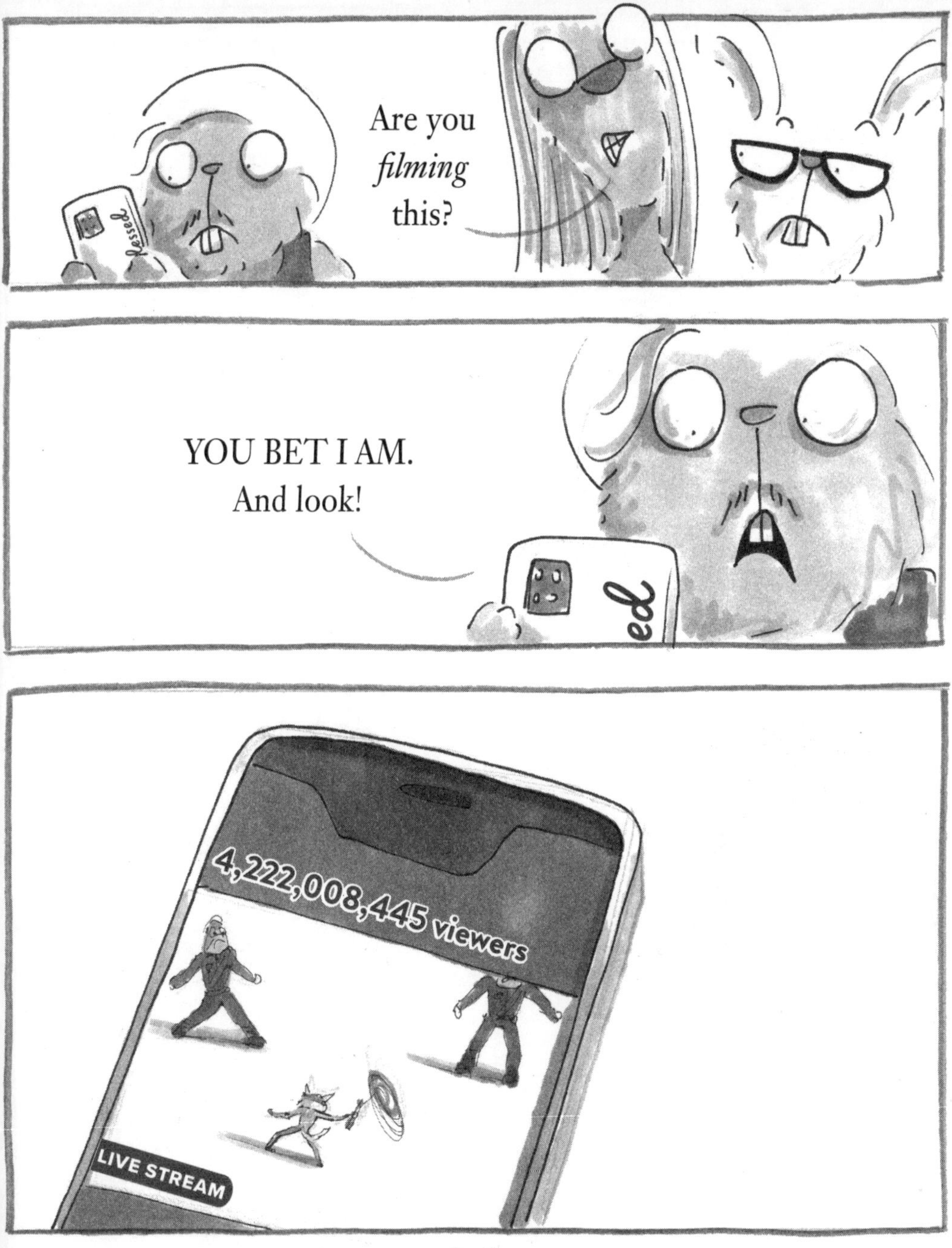
Are you *filming* this?
YOU BET I AM.
And look!
4,222,008,445 viewers
LIVE STREAM

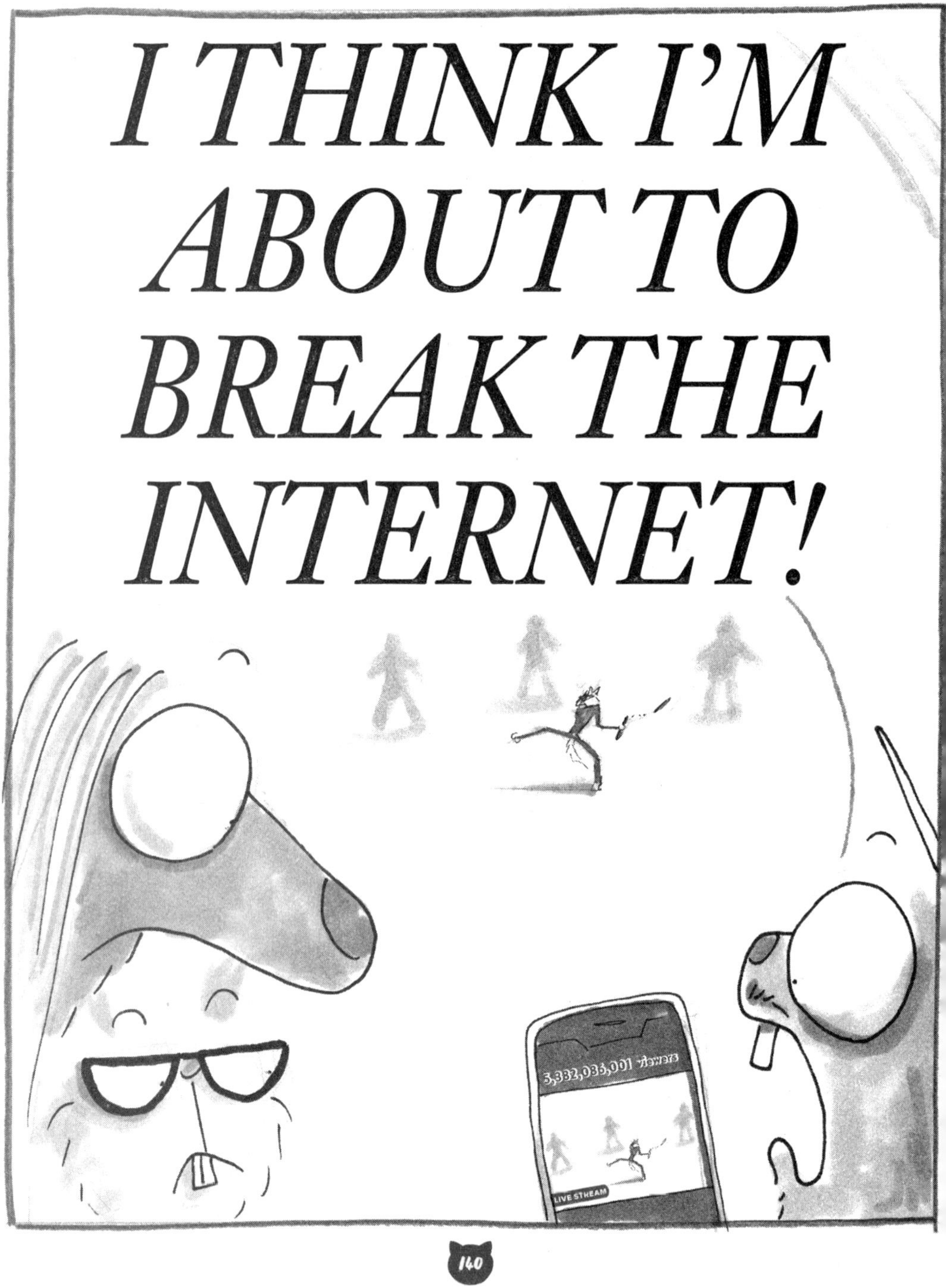
I THINK I'M ABOUT TO BREAK THE INTERNET!
5,382,086,001 viewers
LIVE STREAM

Seven

FOLLOW THE SCORPION

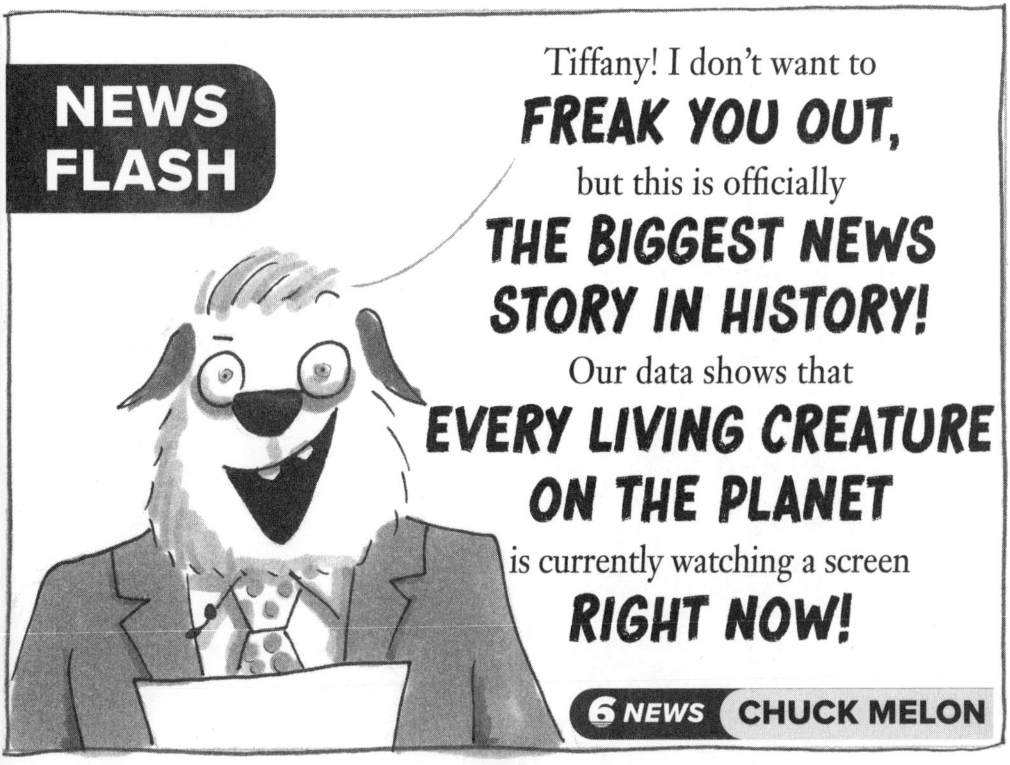
NEWS FLASH
Tiffany! I don't want to FREAK YOU OUT, but this is officially THE BIGGEST NEWS STORY IN HISTORY! Our data shows that EVERY LIVING CREATURE ON THE PLANET is currently watching a screen RIGHT NOW!
6 NEWS CHUCK MELON

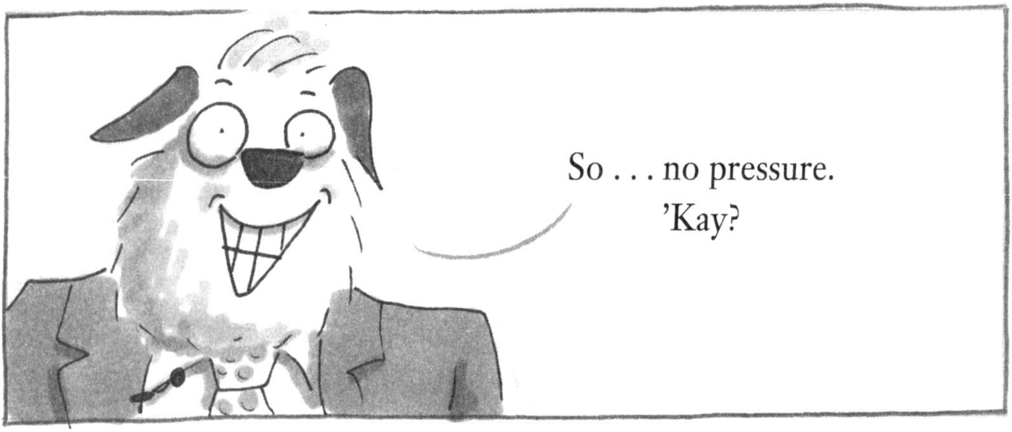
So . . . no pressure.
'Kay?

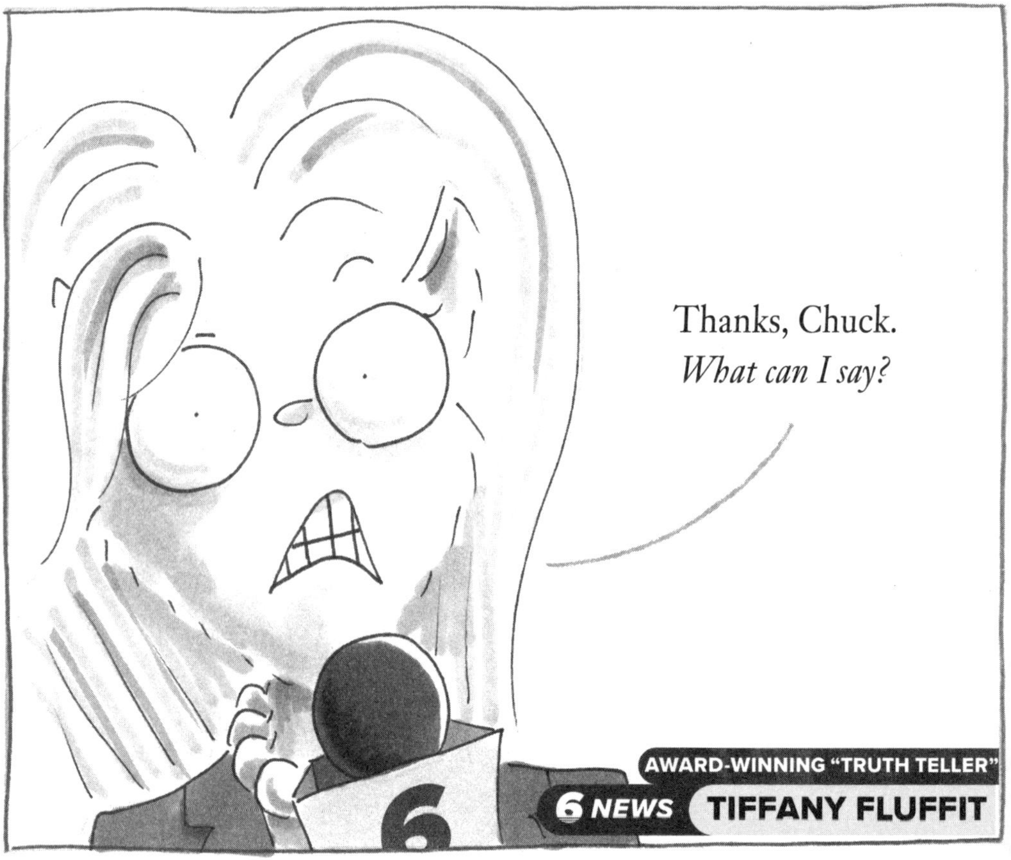
Thanks, Chuck.
What can I say?
AWARD-WINNING "TRUTH TELLER"
6 NEWS
TIFFANY FLUFFIT
6

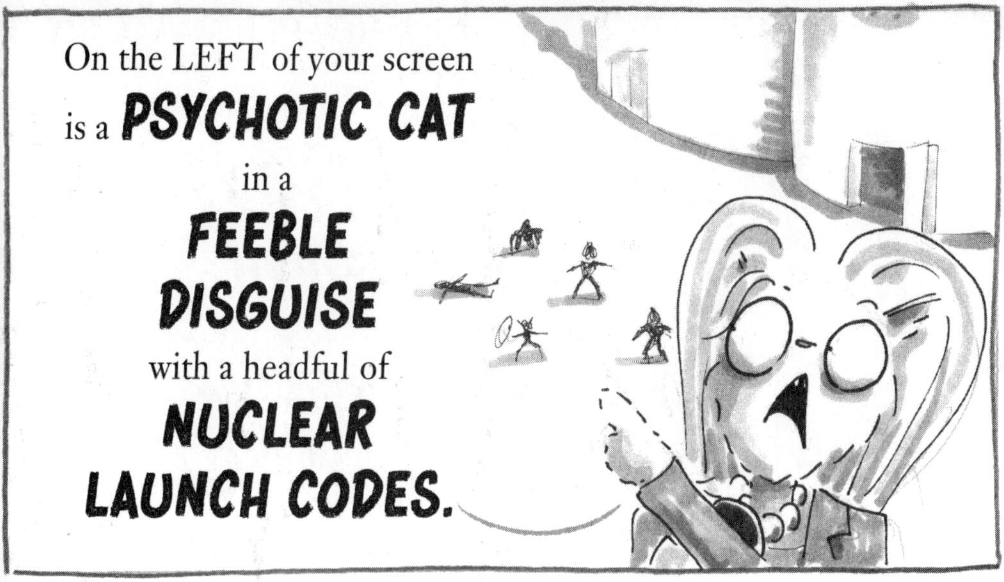
On the LEFT of your screen
is a PSYCHOTIC CAT
in a
FEEBLE
DISGUISE
with a headful of
NUCLEAR
LAUNCH CODES.

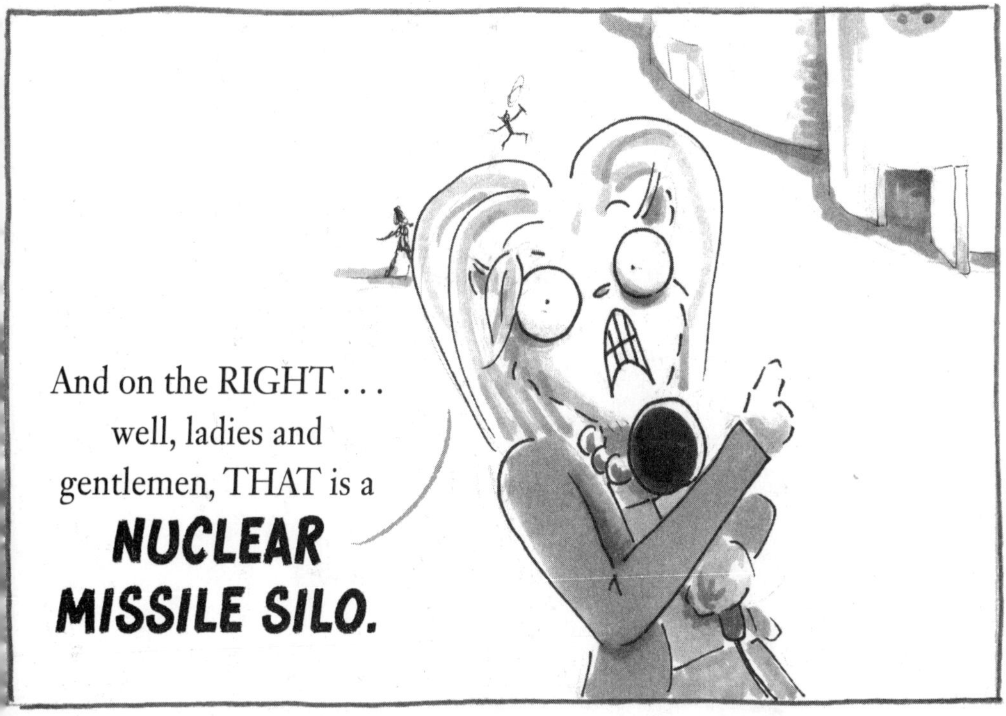
And on the RIGHT . . .
well, ladies and
gentlemen, THAT is a
NUCLEAR
MISSILE SILO.

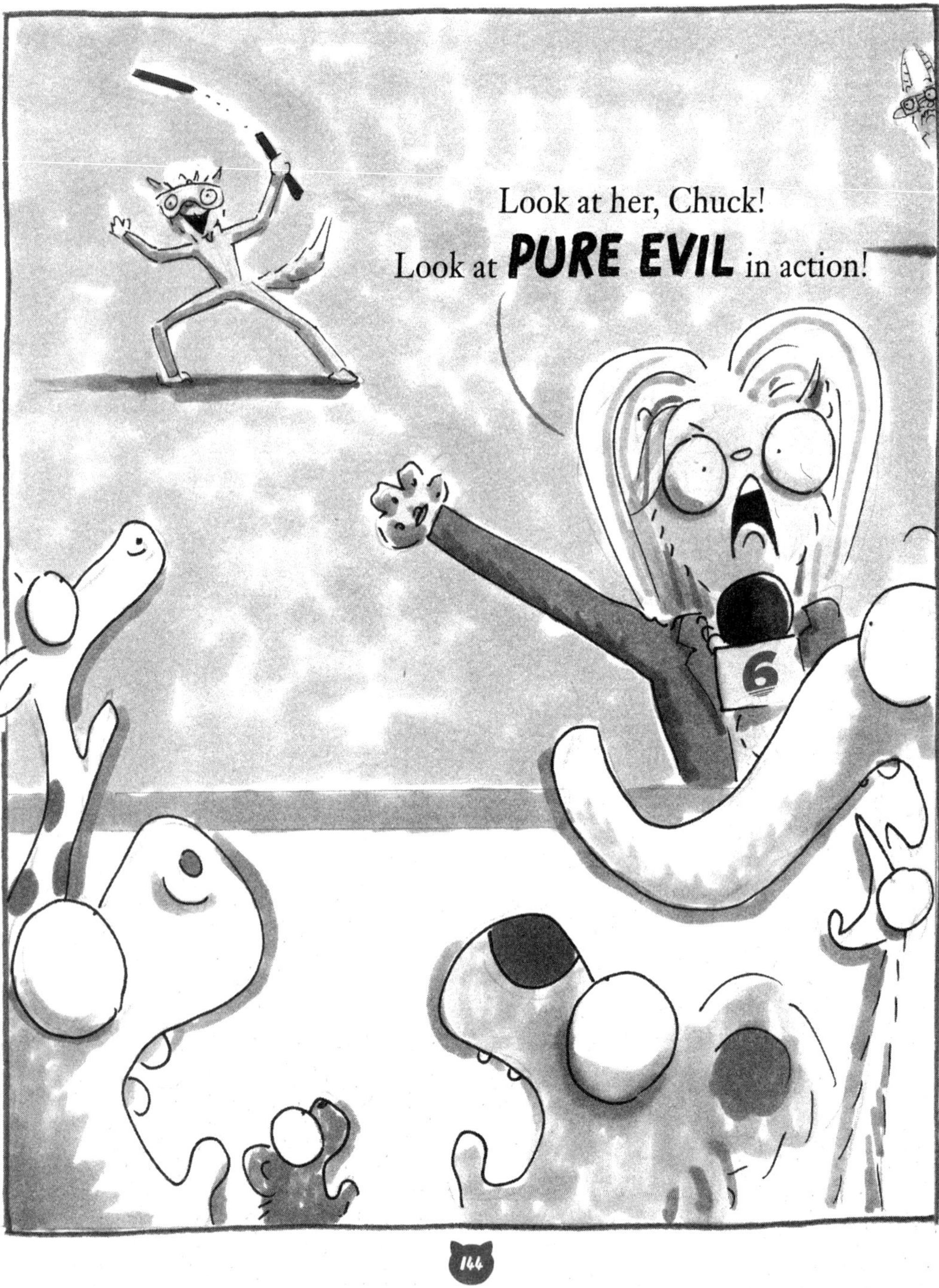
Look at her, Chuck!
Look at **PURE EVIL** in action!
6

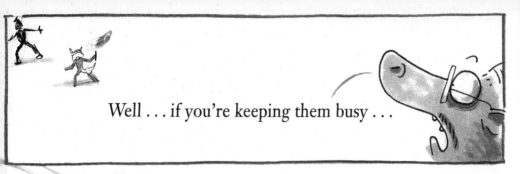

Well . . . if you're keeping them busy . . .

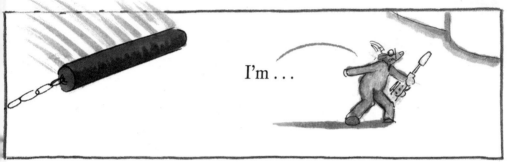

I'm . . .

going in . . .

DONK!

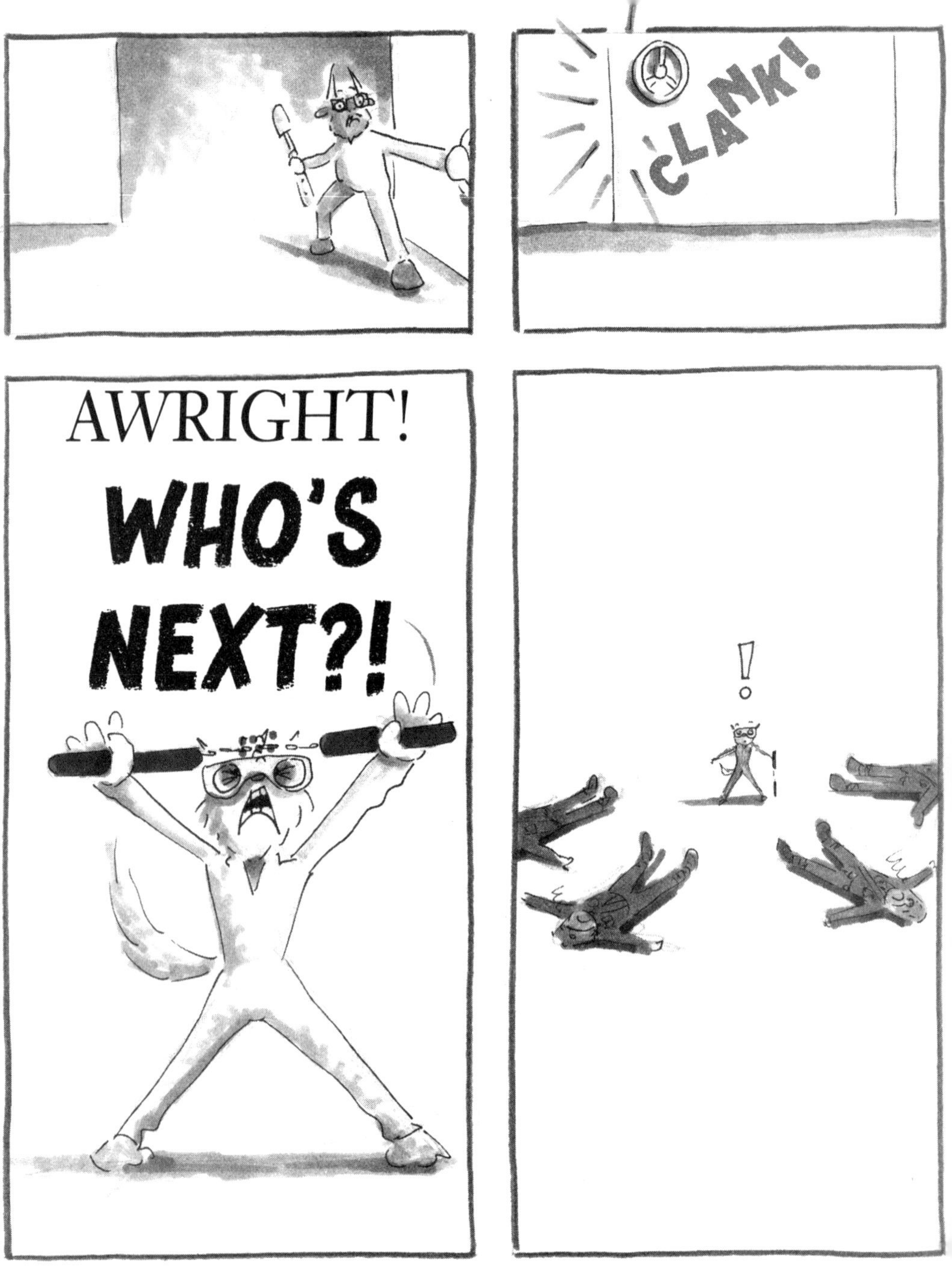
CLANK!
AWRIGHT!
WHO'S
NEXT?!
!

Princess?

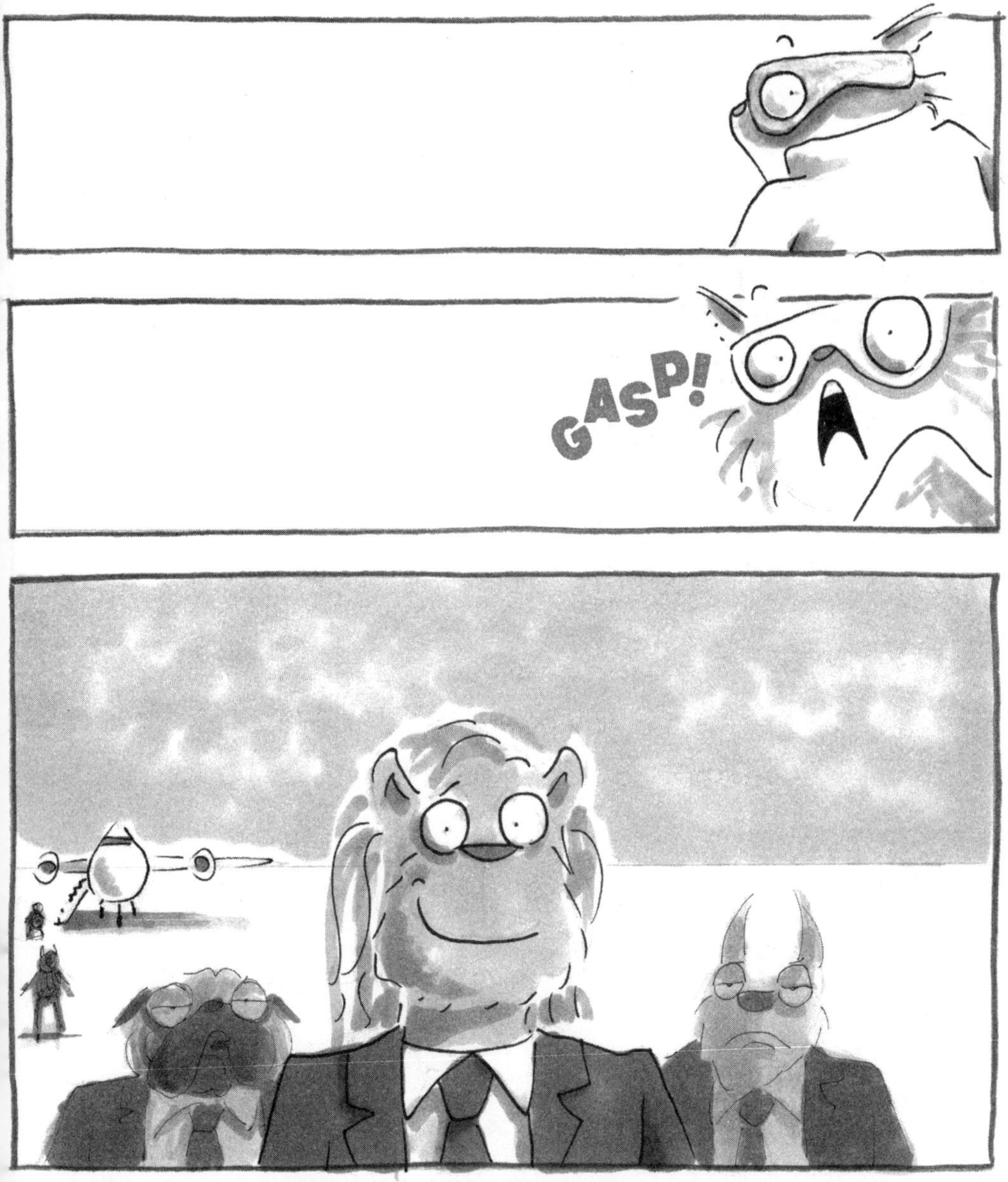
GASP!

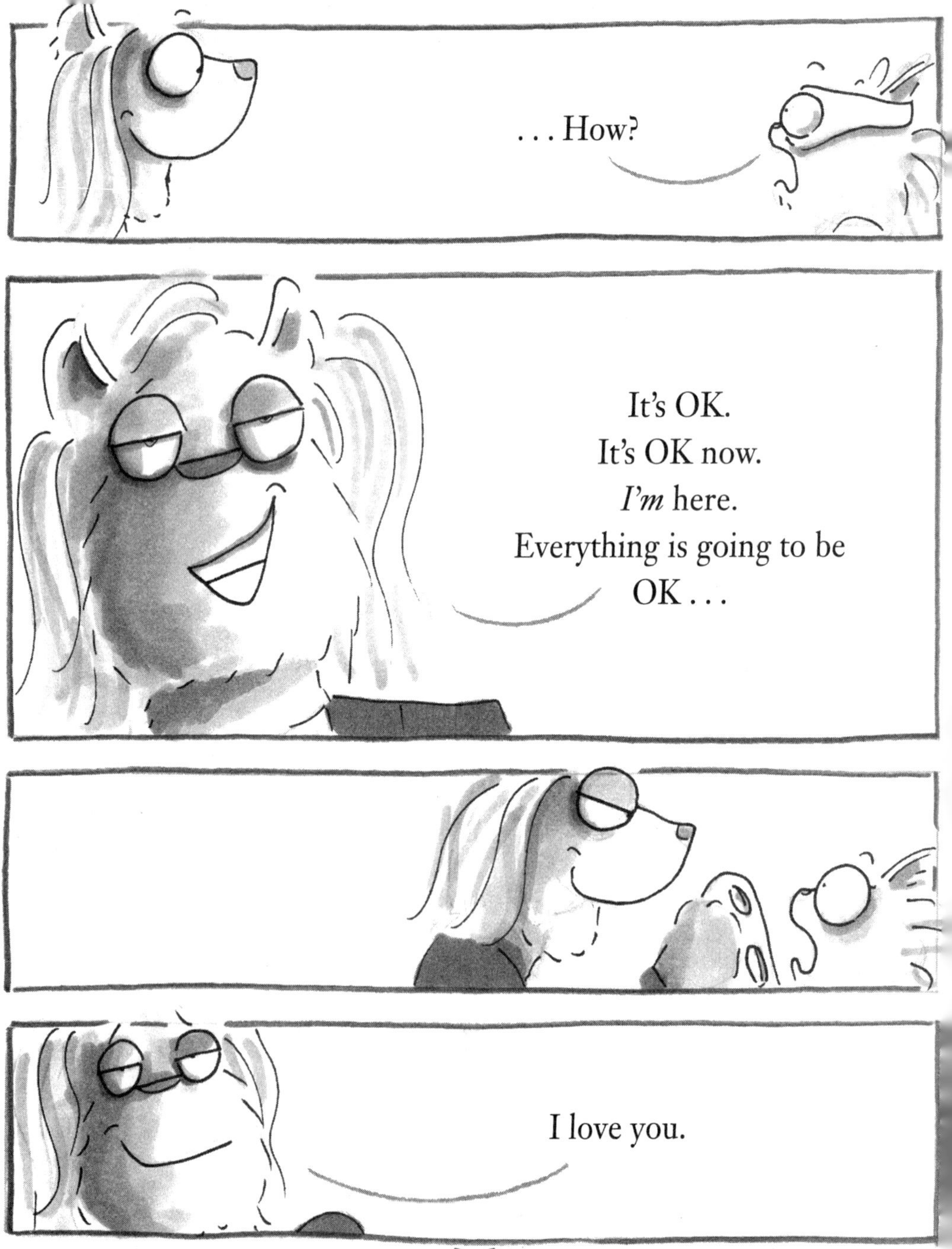

. . . How?
It's OK.
It's OK now.
I'm here.
Everything is going to be OK . . .
I love you.

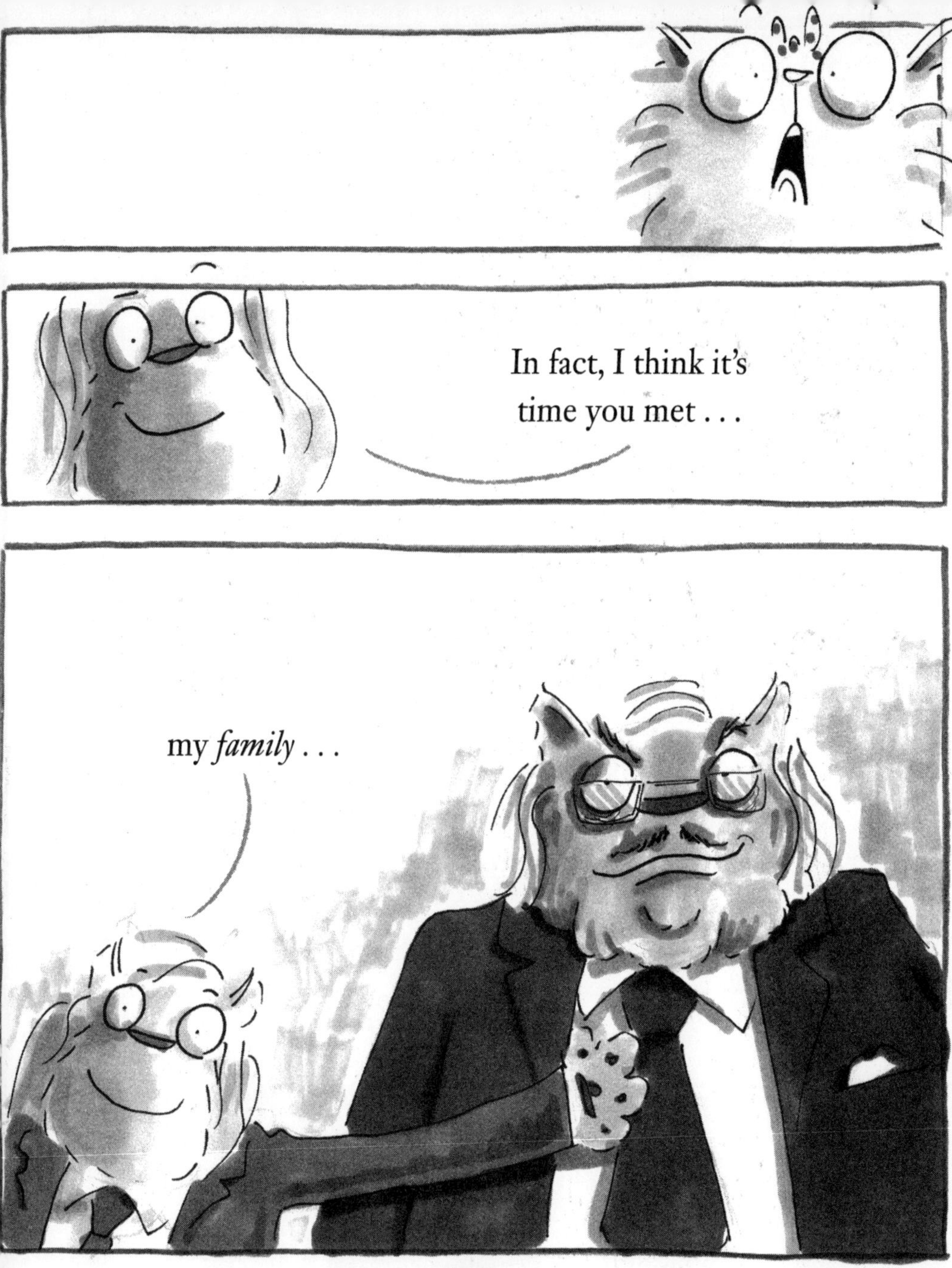
In fact, I think it's time you met . . .
my *family* . . .

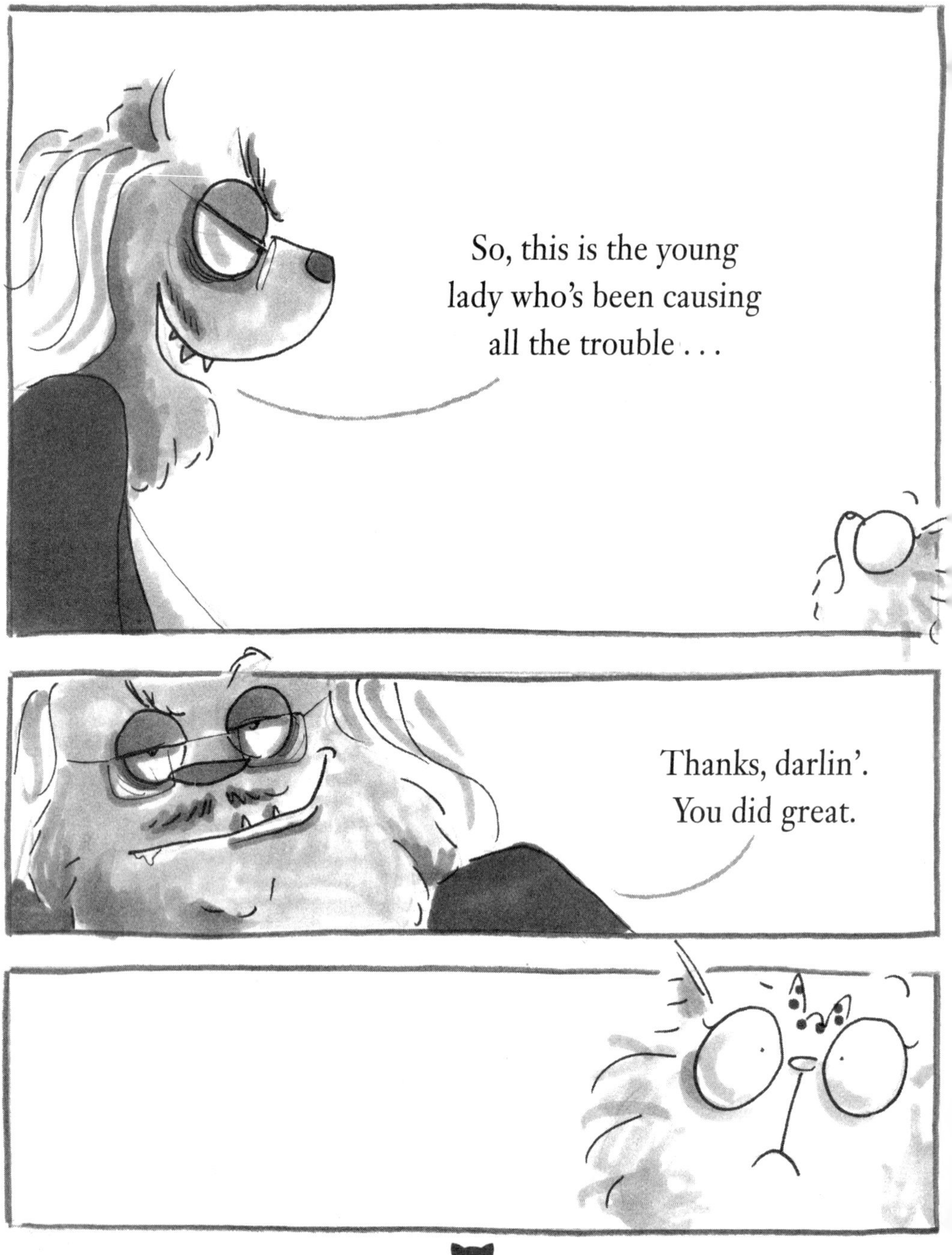

So, this is the young lady who's been causing all the trouble . . .
Thanks, darlin'. You did great.

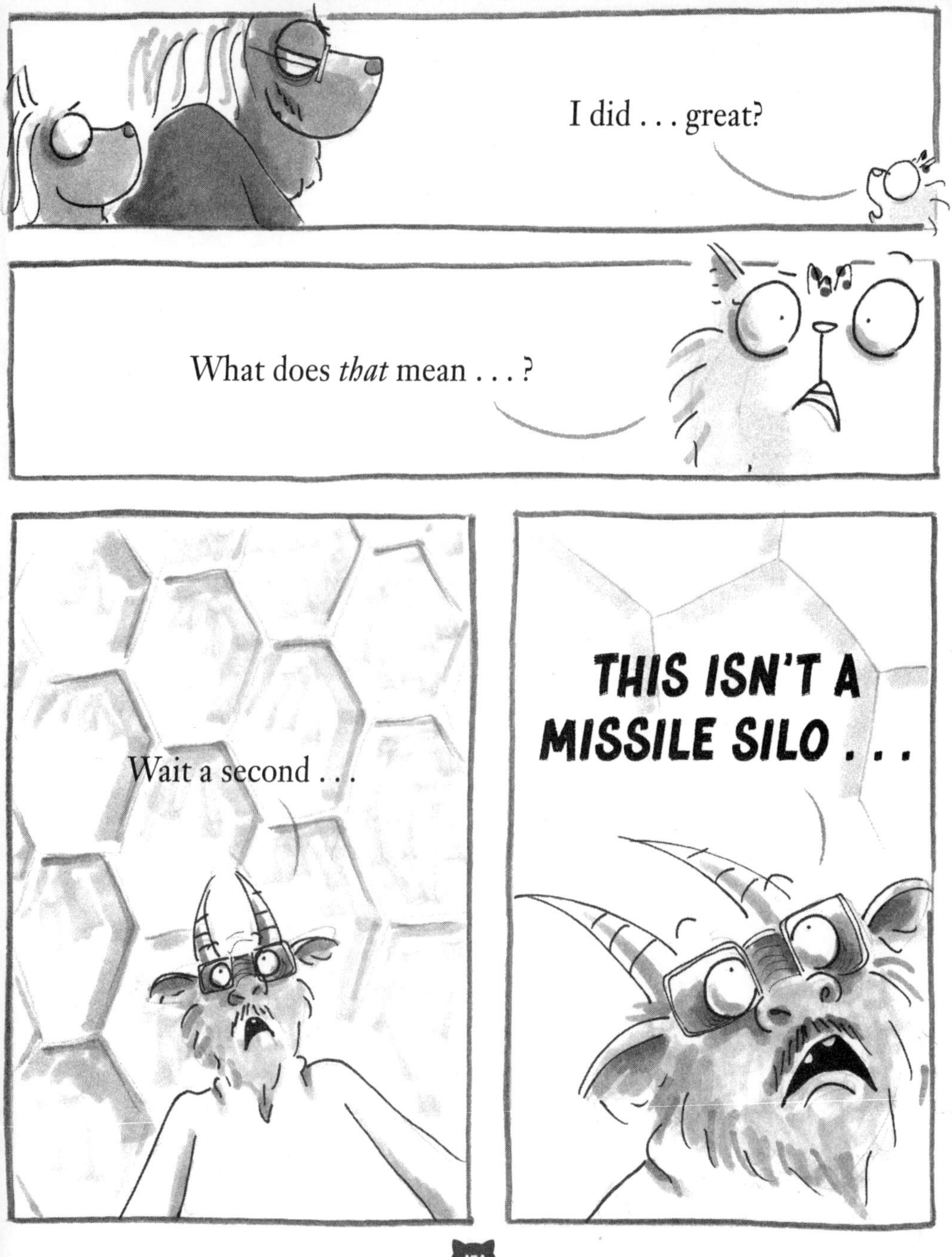
I did . . . great?
What does *that* mean . . . ?
Wait a second . . .
THIS ISN'T A MISSILE SILO . . .

Eight

THE WHOLE WORLD WATCHES

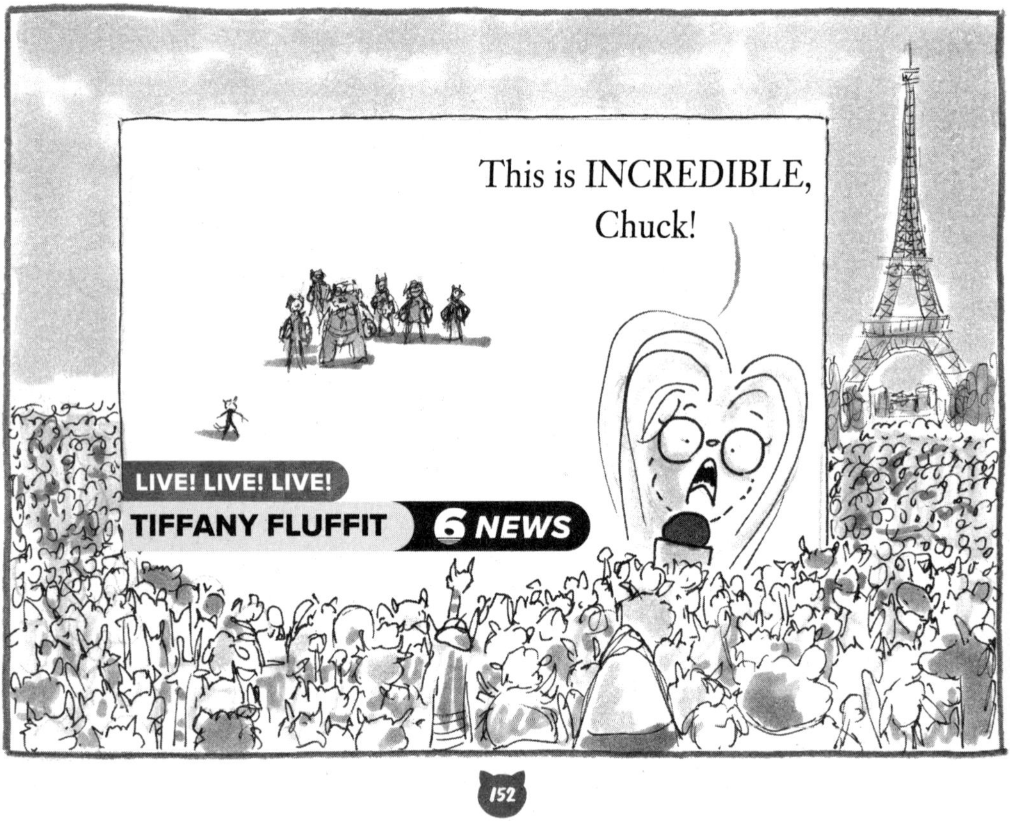
This is INCREDIBLE, Chuck!
LIVE! LIVE! LIVE!
TIFFANY FLUFFIT
6 NEWS

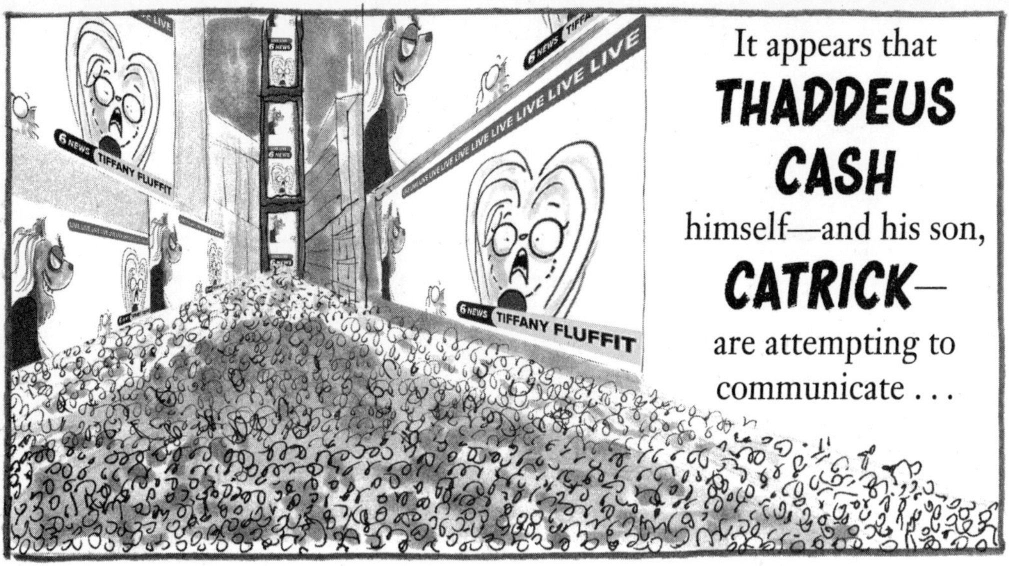
6 NEWS
TIFFANY FLUFFIT
LIVE LIVE LIVE LIVE LIVE LIVE
6 NEWS
TIFFANY FLUFFIT
It appears that
THADDEUS CASH
himself—and his son,
CATRICK—
are attempting to
communicate . . .

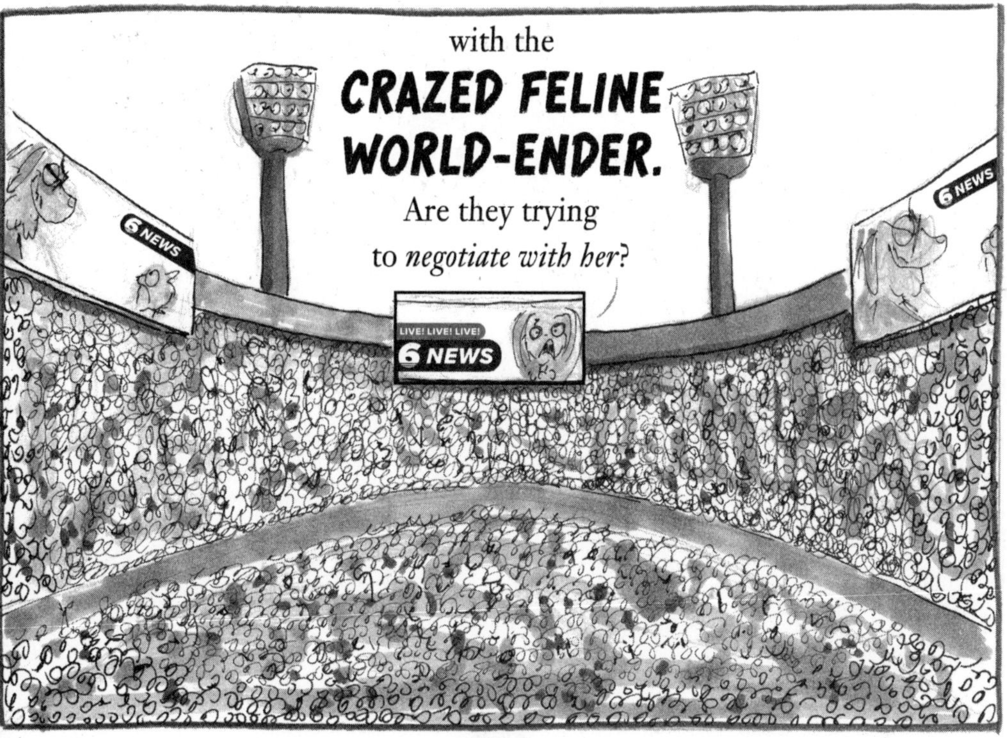
with the
CRAZED FELINE WORLD-ENDER.
Are they trying
to *negotiate with her*?
6 NEWS
LIVE! LIVE! LIVE!
6 NEWS
6 NEWS

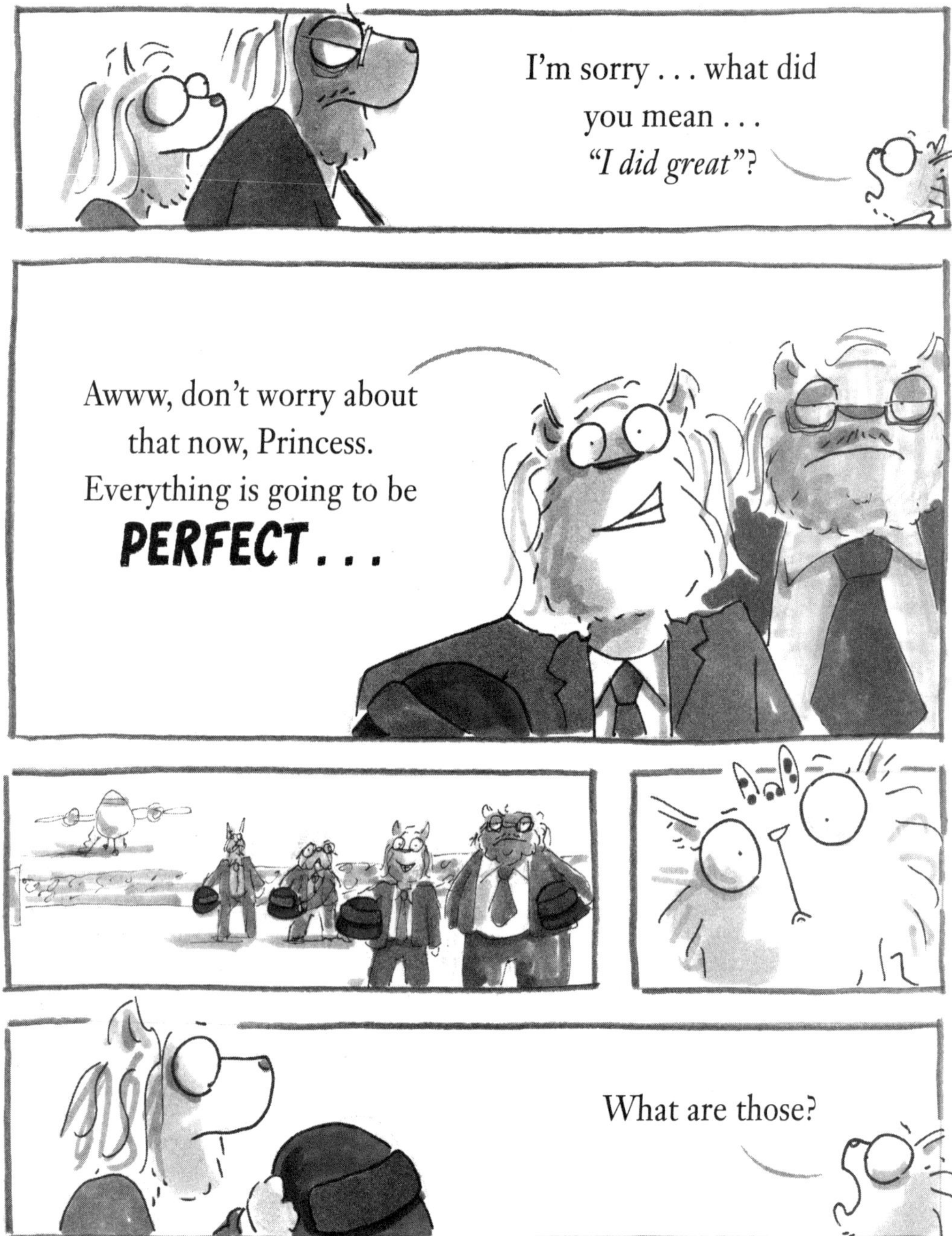
I'm sorry . . . what did you mean . . . *"I did great"*?
Awww, don't worry about that now, Princess. Everything is going to be **PERFECT . . .**
What are those?

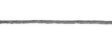

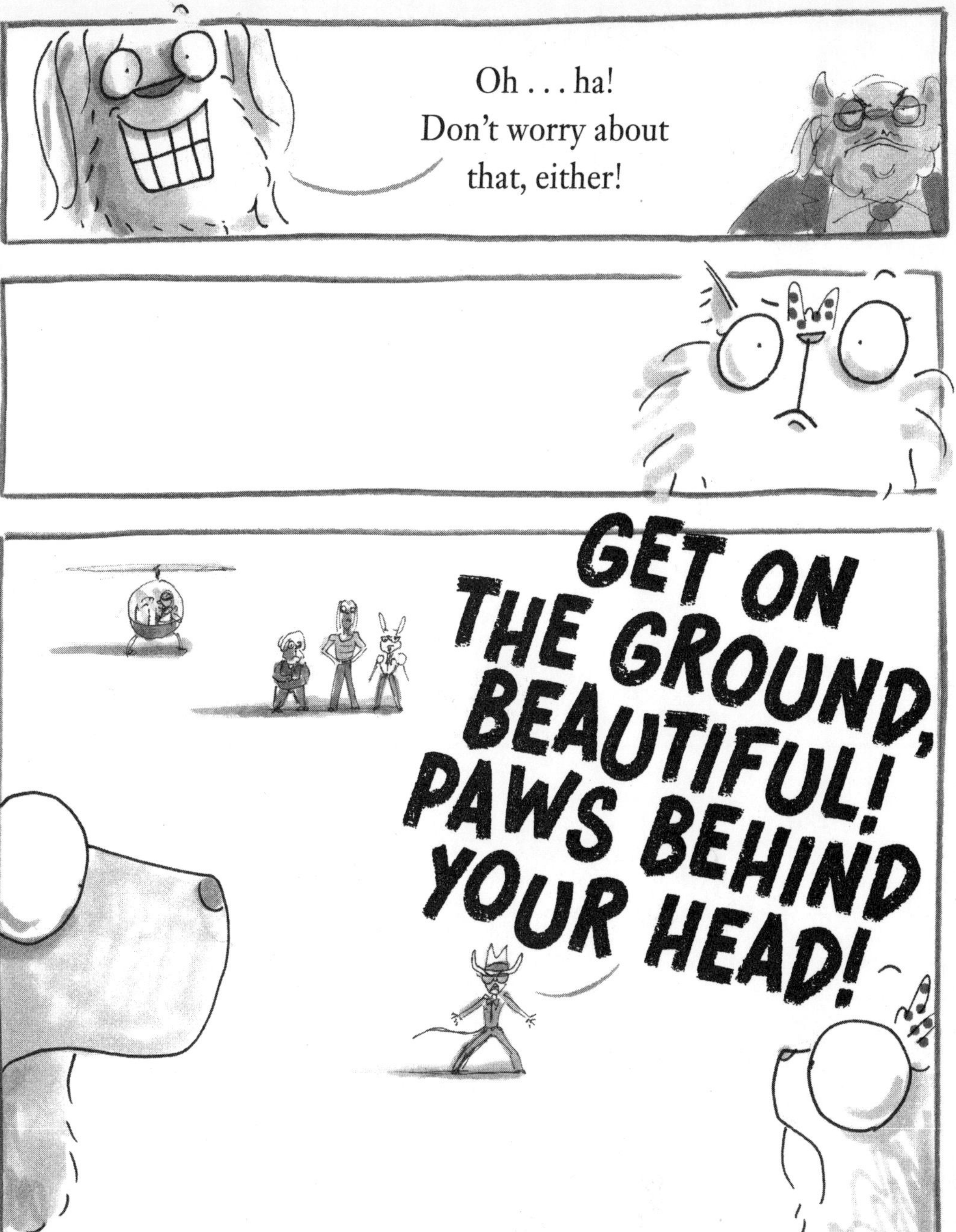
Oh . . . ha!
Don't worry about
that, either!
GET ON THE GROUND, BEAUTIFUL! PAWS BEHIND YOUR HEAD!

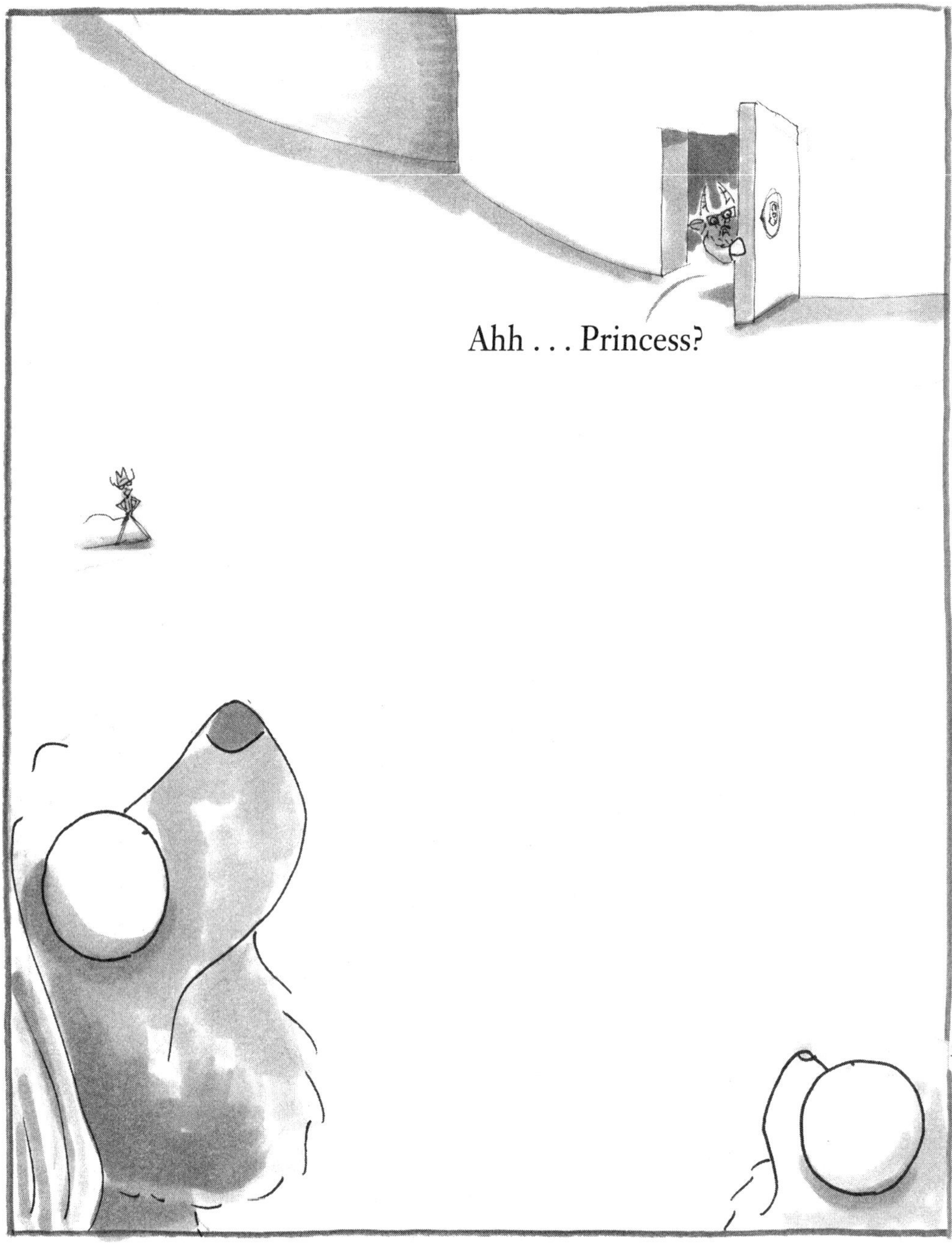
Ahh . . . Princess?

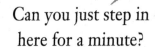

Can you just step in here for a minute?

Don't even **THINK** about it, pussycat.

Princess . . .

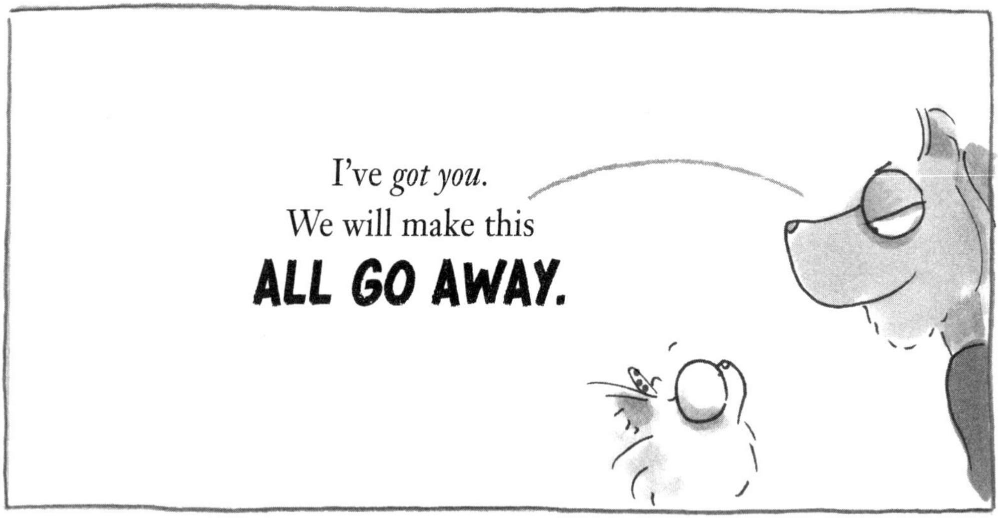
I've *got you.*
We will make this
ALL GO AWAY.

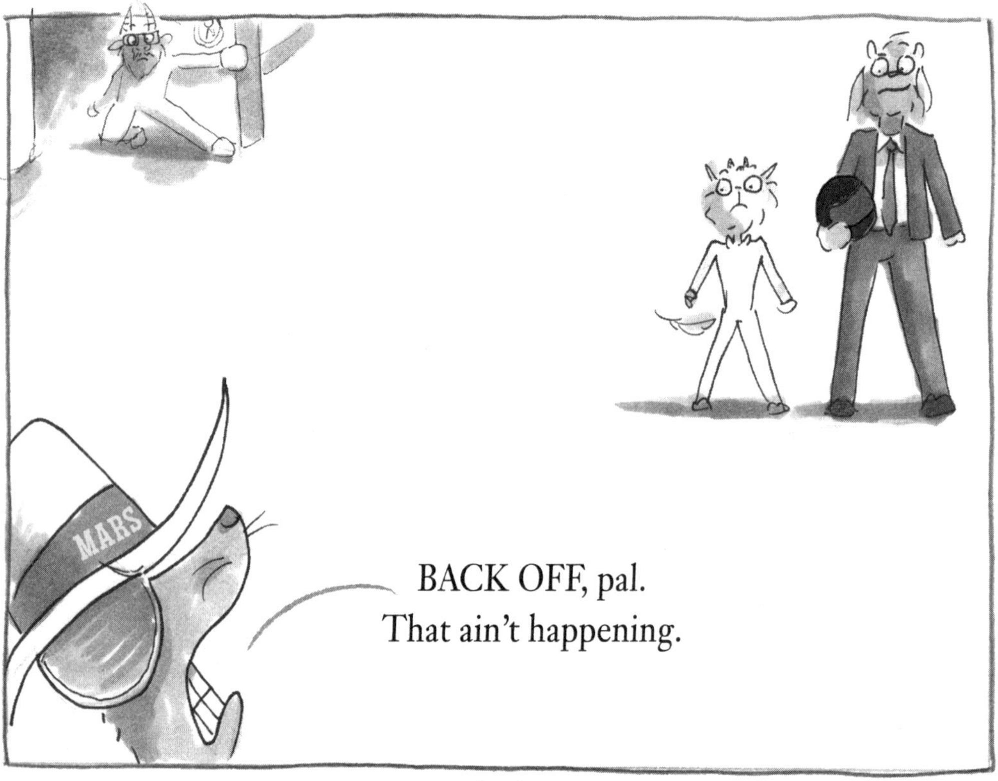
MARS
BACK OFF, pal.
That ain't happening.

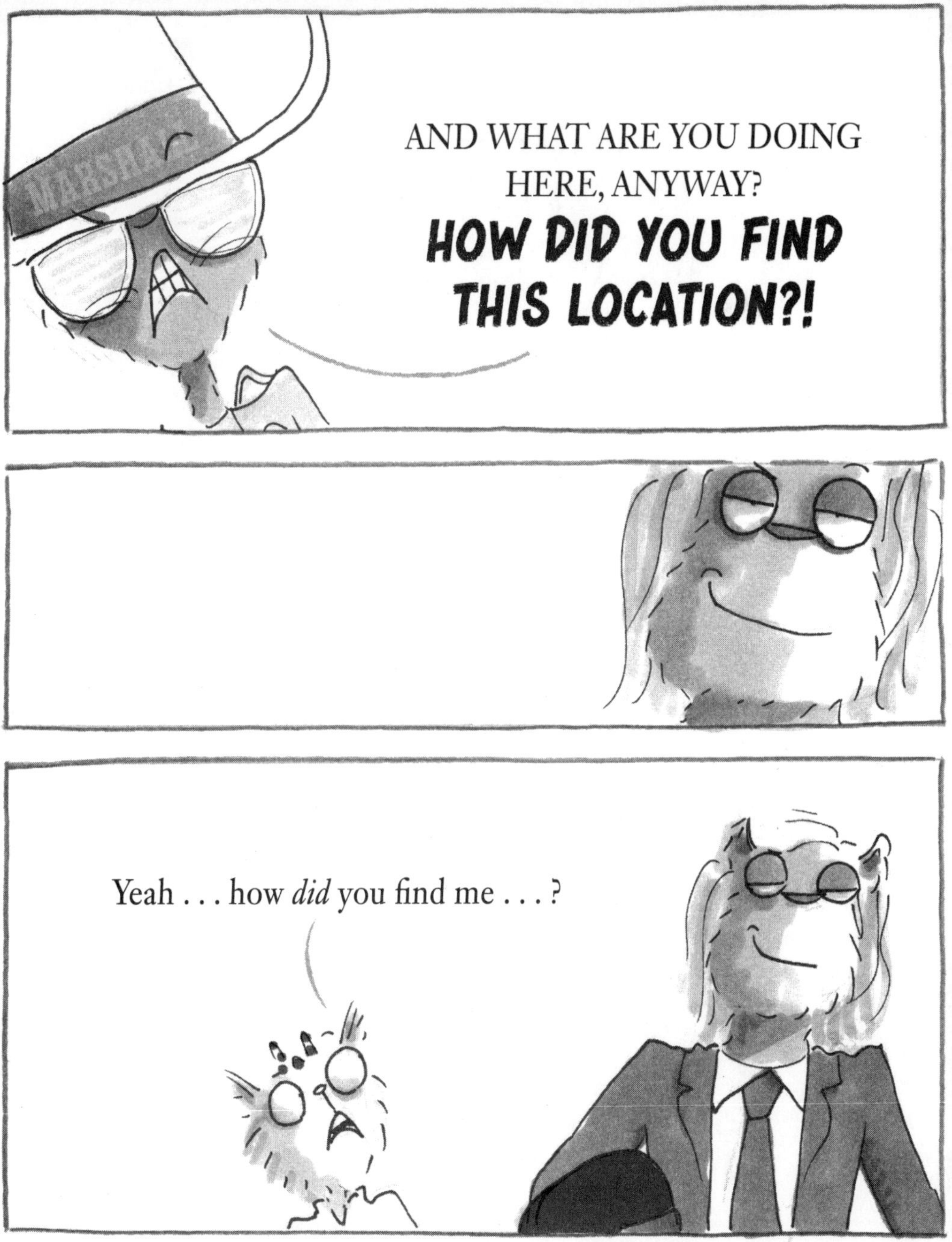
AND WHAT ARE YOU DOING HERE, ANYWAY?
HOW DID YOU FIND THIS LOCATION?!
Yeah . . . how *did* you find me . . . ?

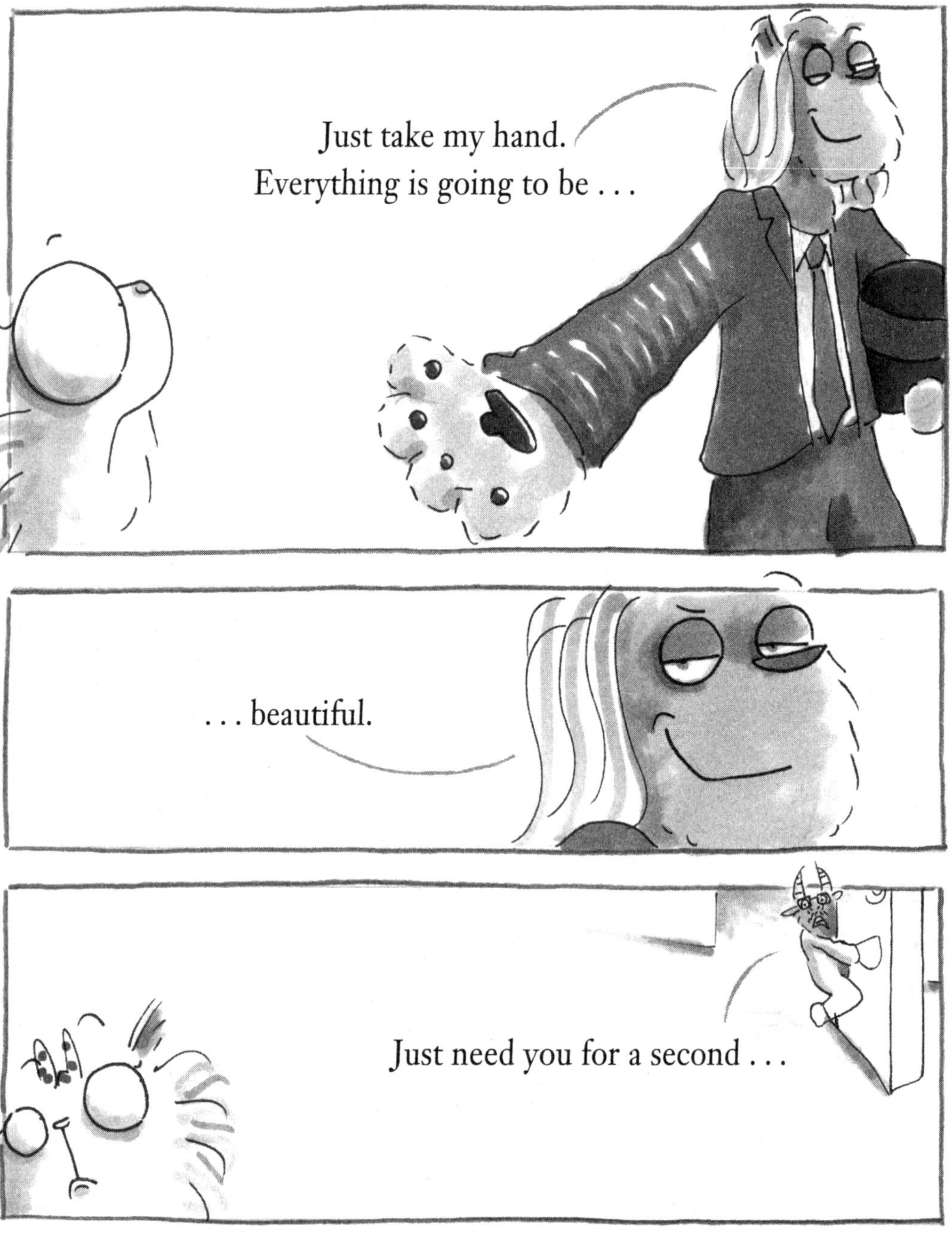
Just take my hand.
Everything is going to be . . .
. . . beautiful.
Just need you for a second . . .

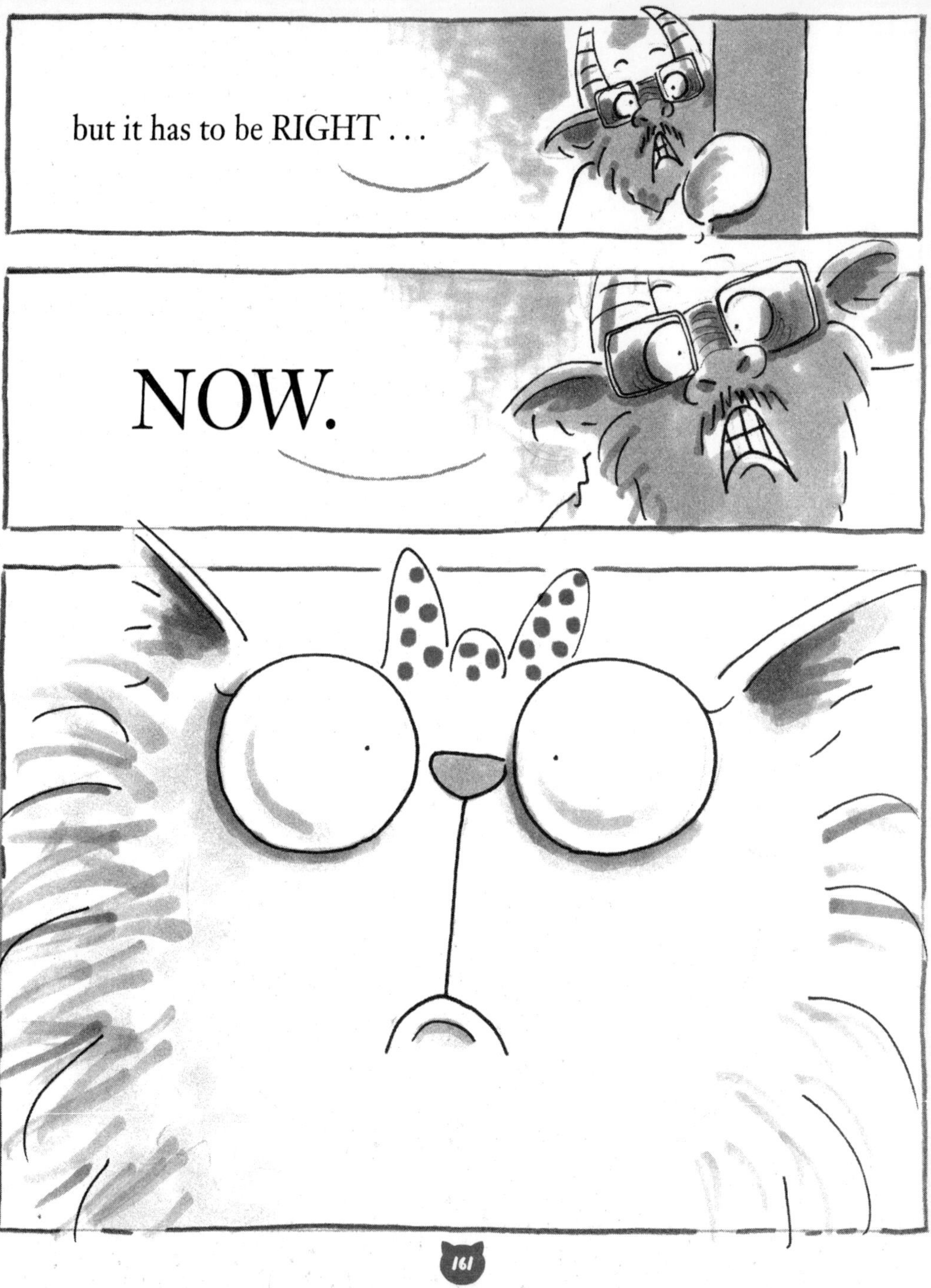
but it has to be RIGHT . . .
NOW.

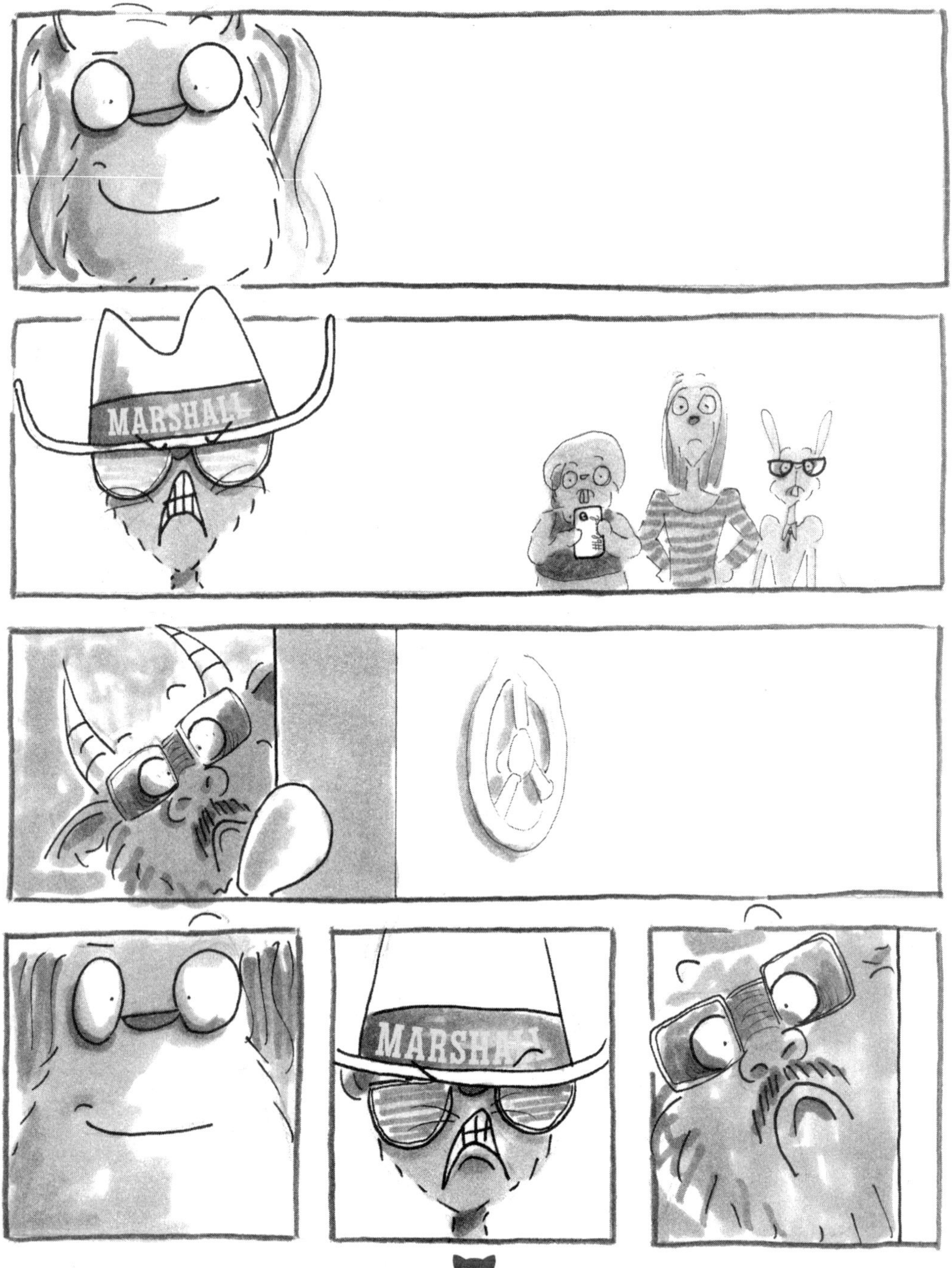
MARSHALL
MARSHALL

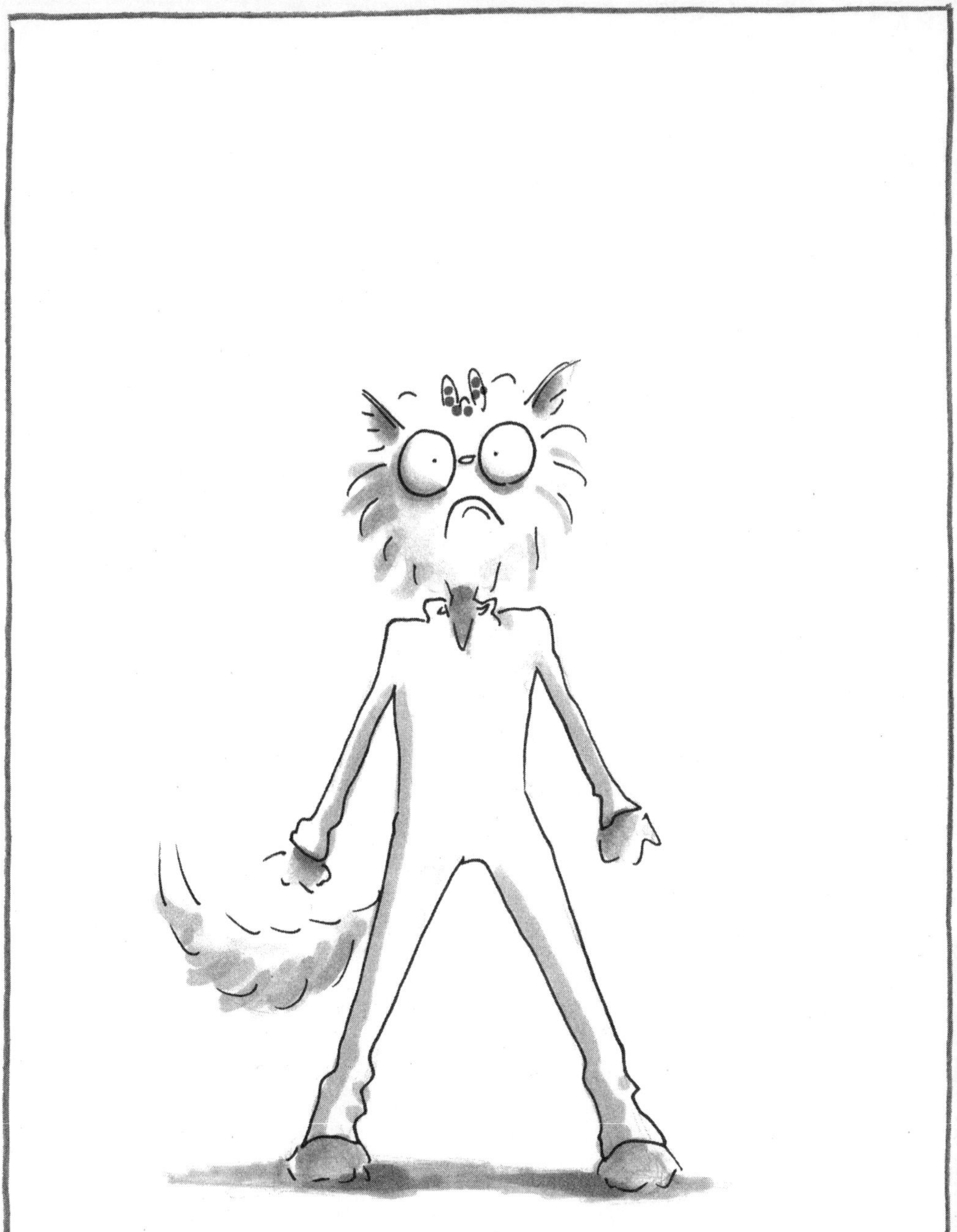

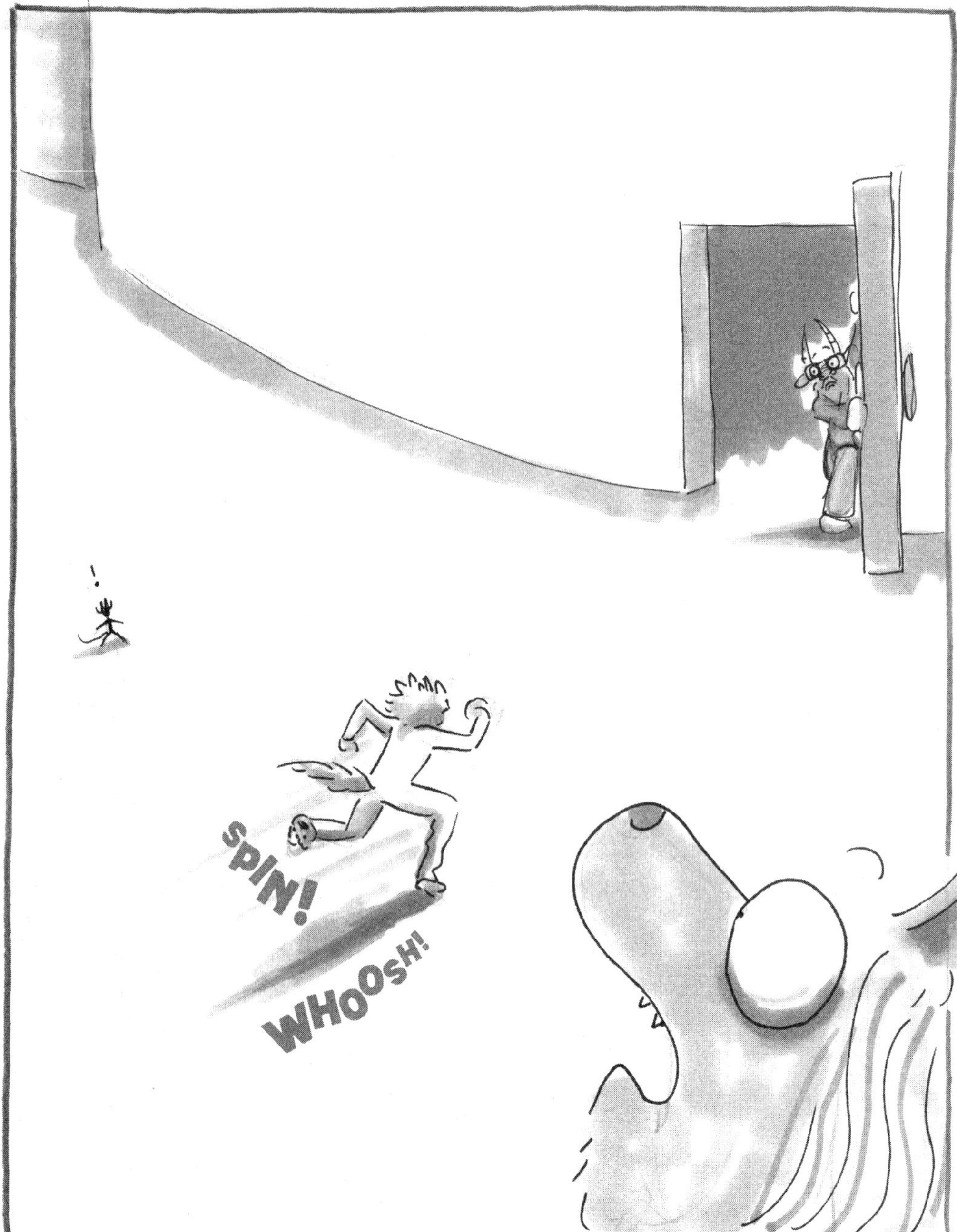
!
SPIN!
WHOOSH!

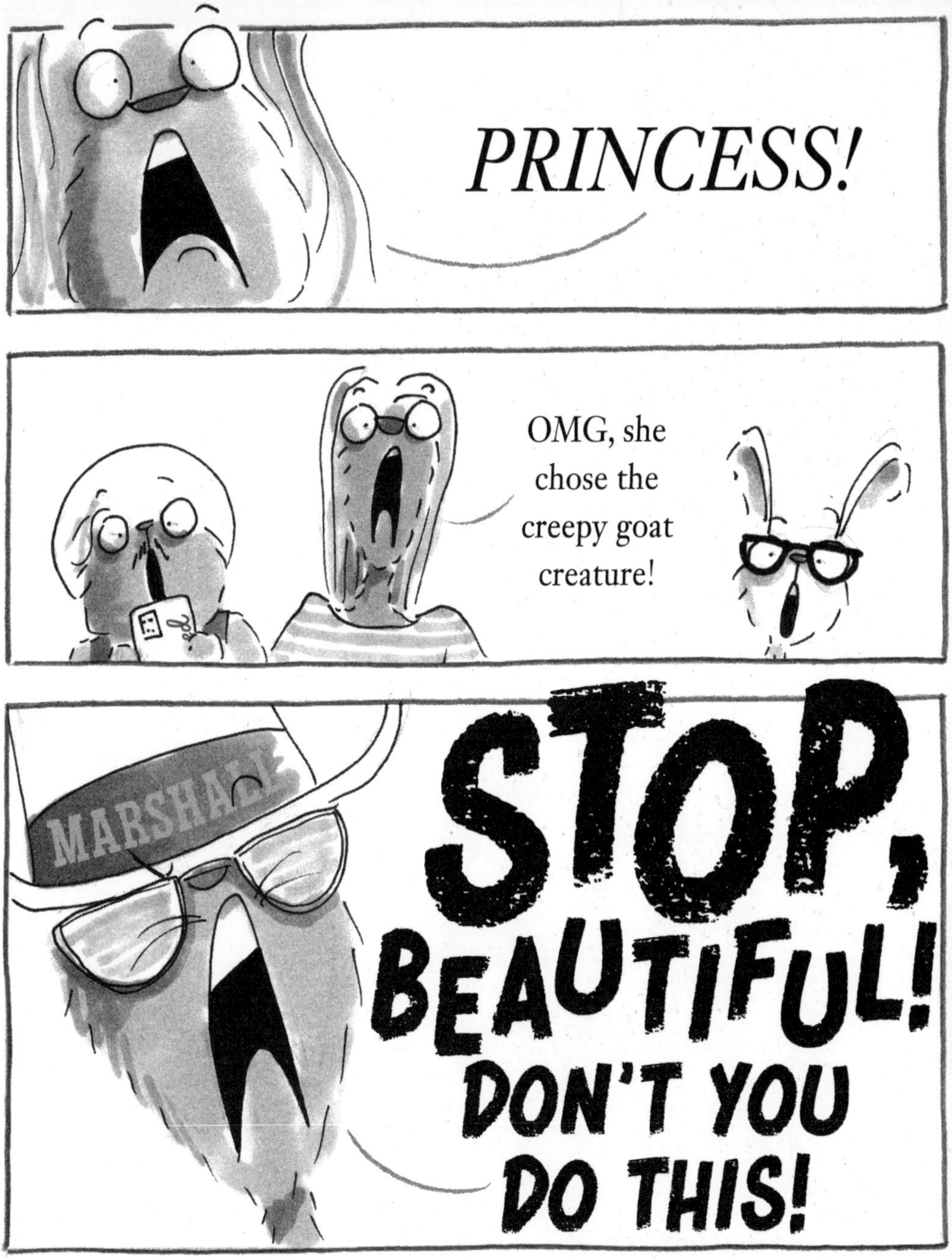
PRINCESS!
OMG, she chose the creepy goat creature!
MARSHALL
STOP, BEAUTIFUL! DON'T YOU DO THIS!

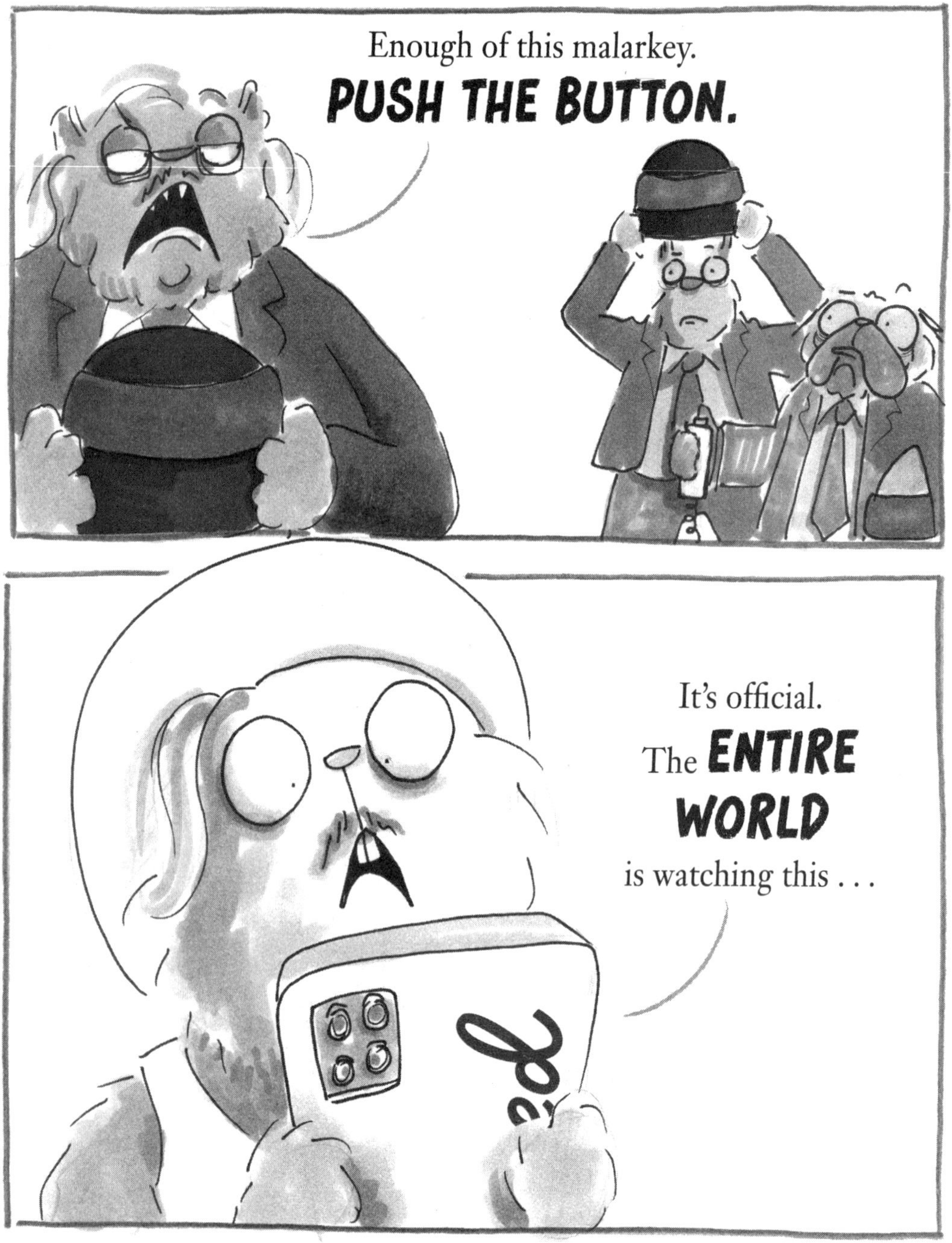
Enough of this malarkey.
PUSH THE BUTTON.
It's official.
The ENTIRE WORLD is watching this . . .

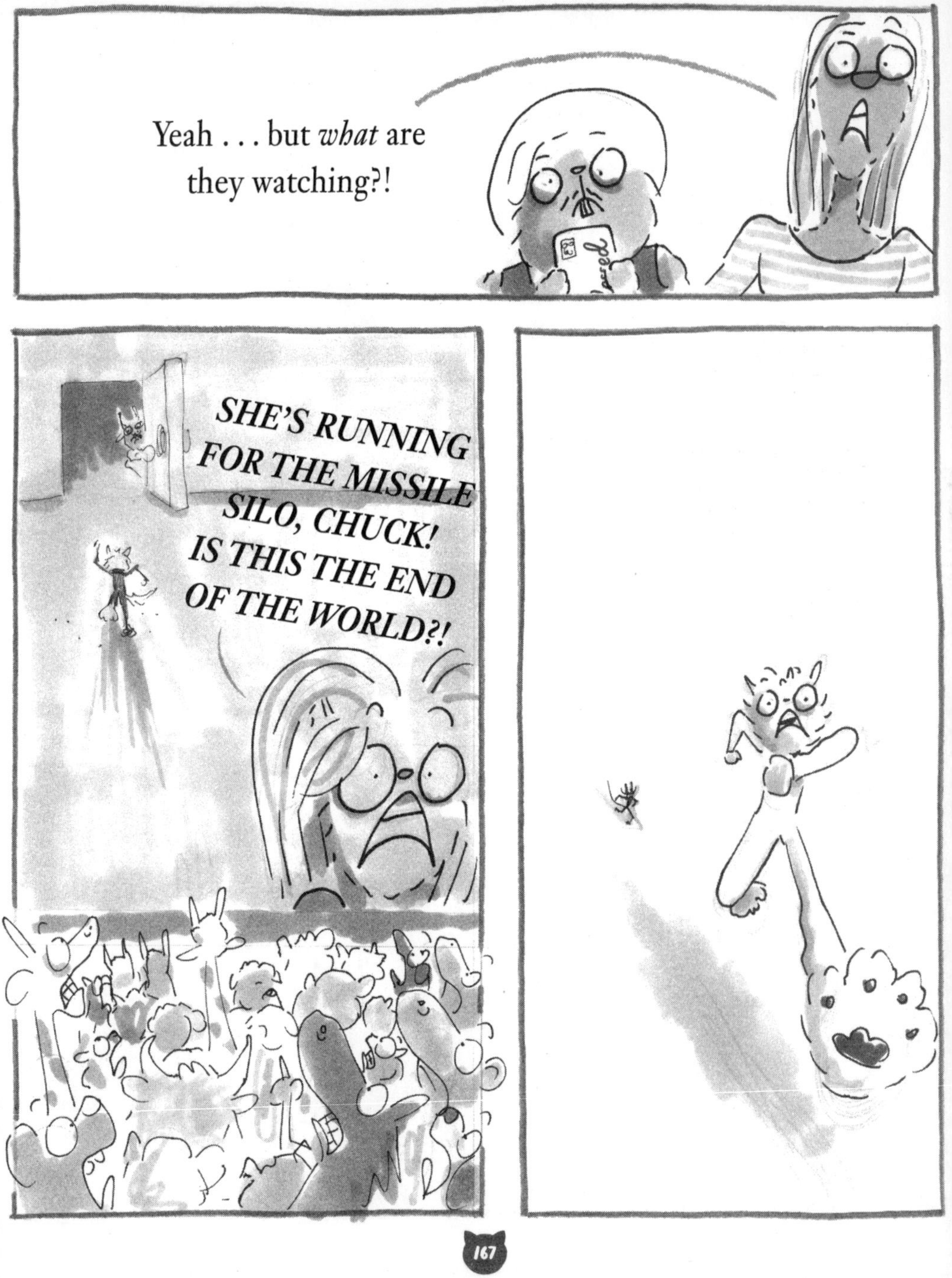
Yeah . . . but *what* are they watching?!
SHE'S RUNNING FOR THE MISSILE SILO, CHUCK! IS THIS THE END OF THE WORLD?!

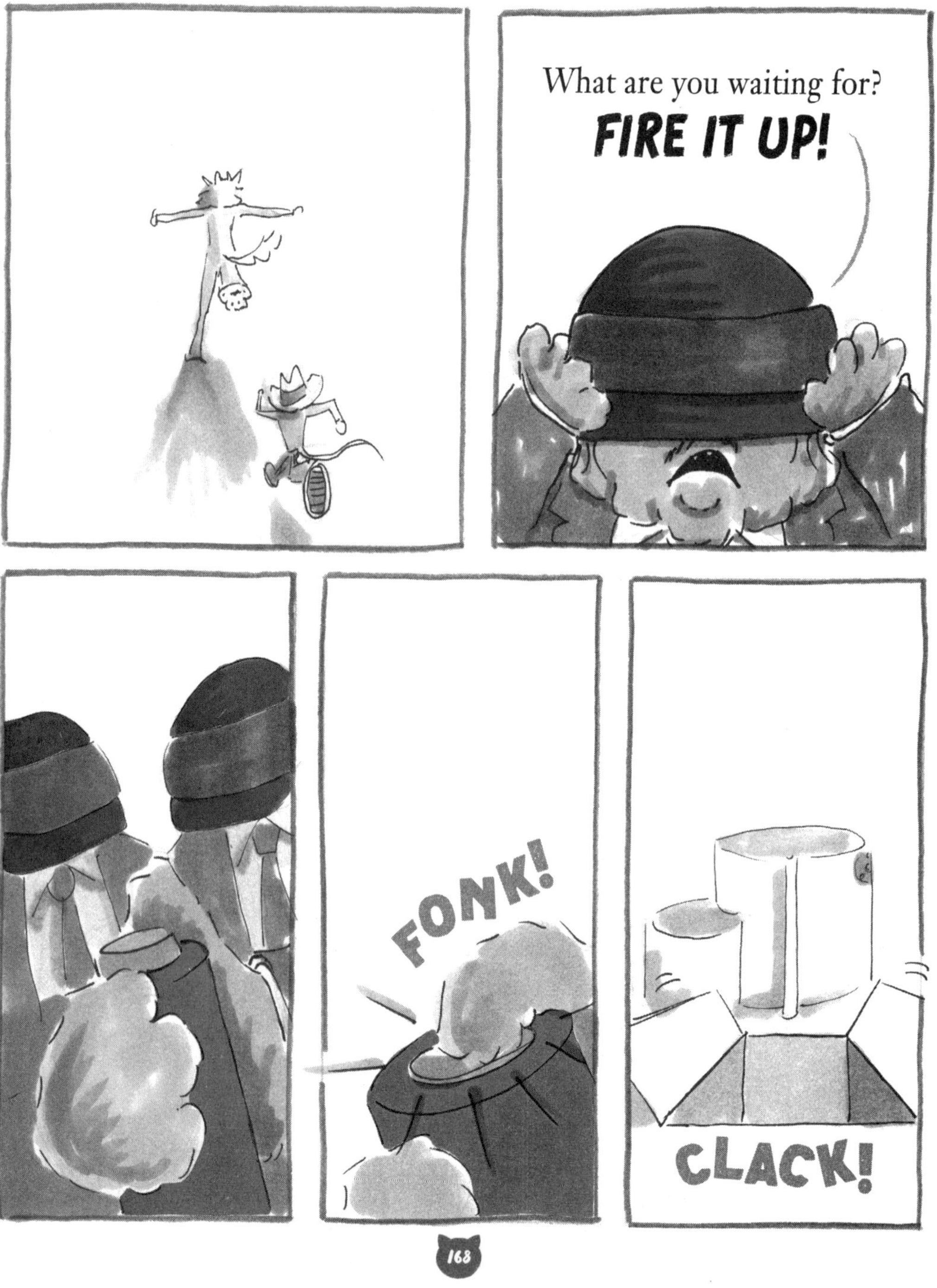
What are you waiting for?
FIRE IT UP!
FONK!
CLACK!

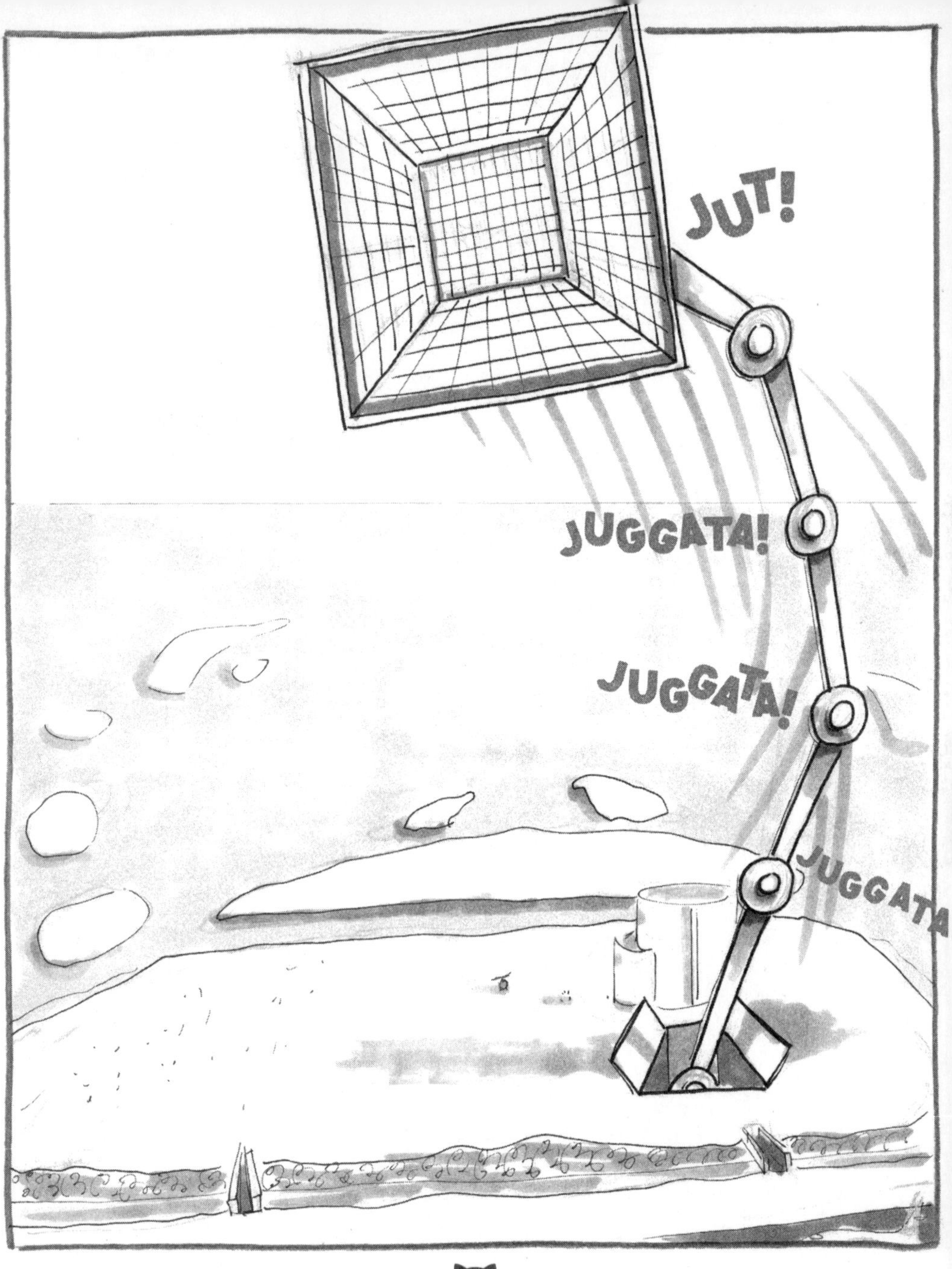
JUT!
JUGGATA!
JUGGATA!
JUGGATA

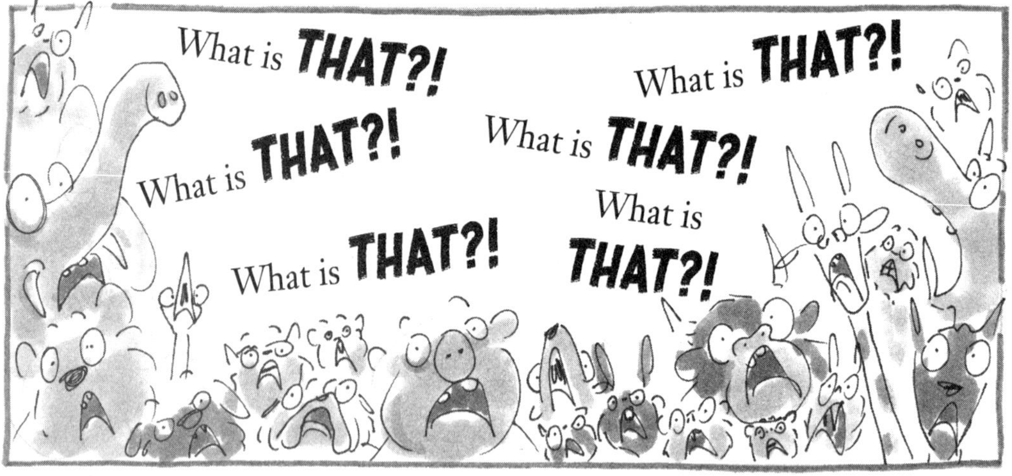
What is THAT?!
What is THAT?!
What is THAT?!
What is THAT?!
What is THAT?!
What is THAT?!

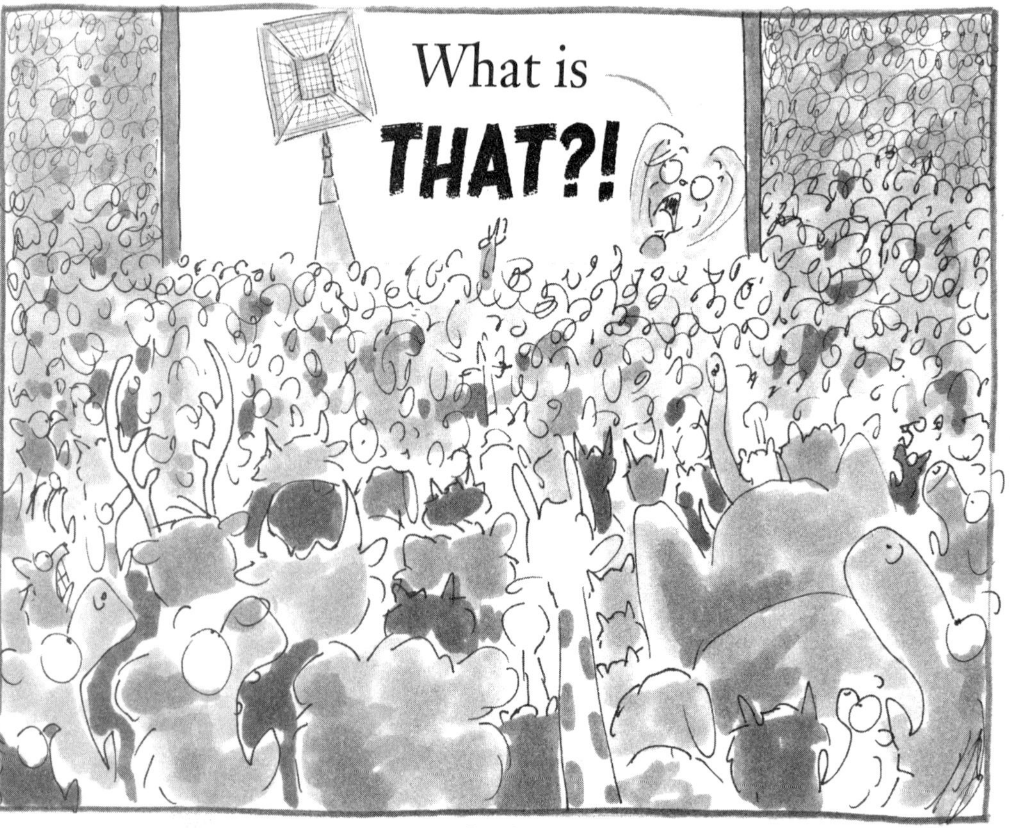
What is THAT?!

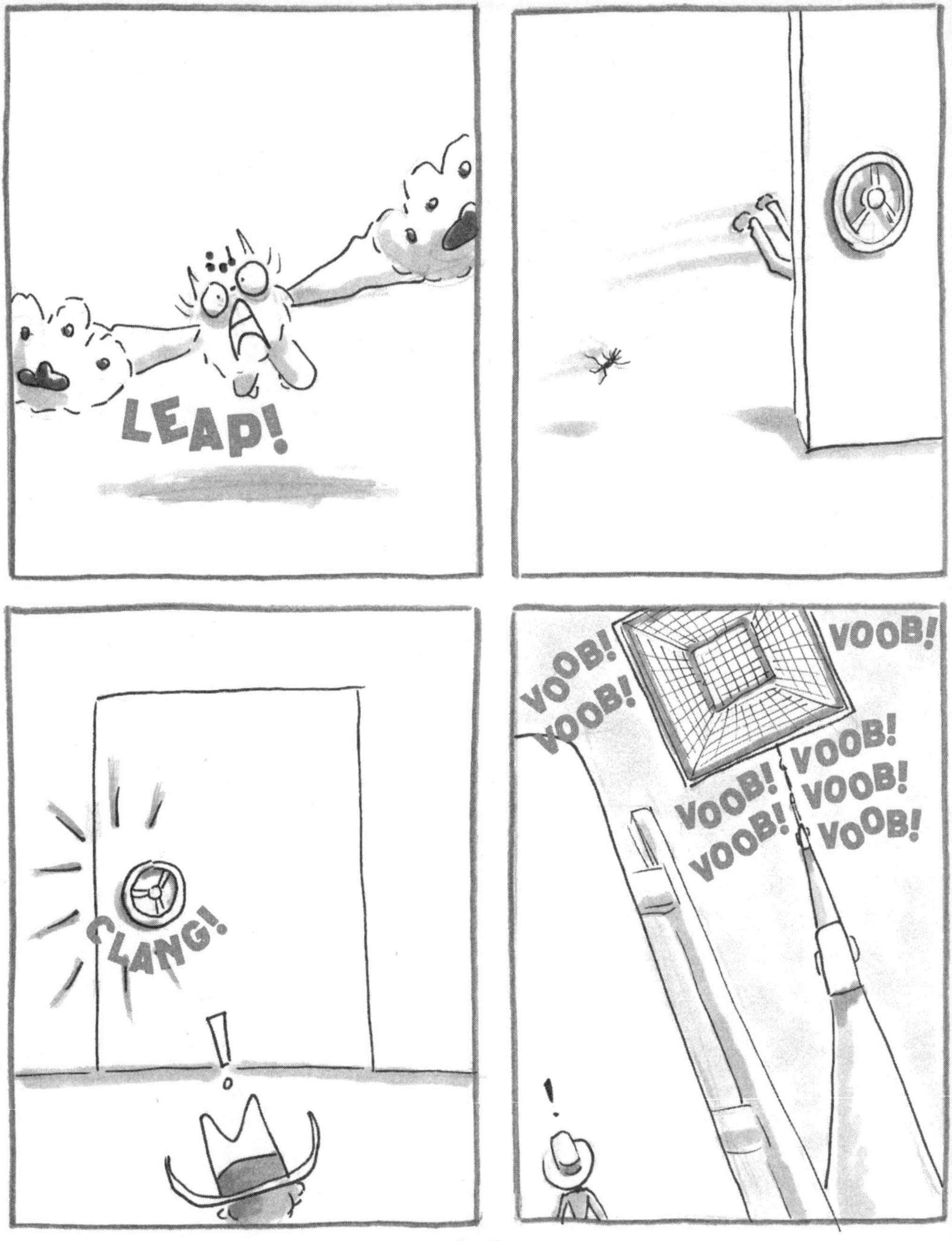
LEAP!
CLANG!
!
VOOB!
VOOB!
VOOB!
VOOB!
VOOB!
VOOB!
VOOB!
VOOB!
!

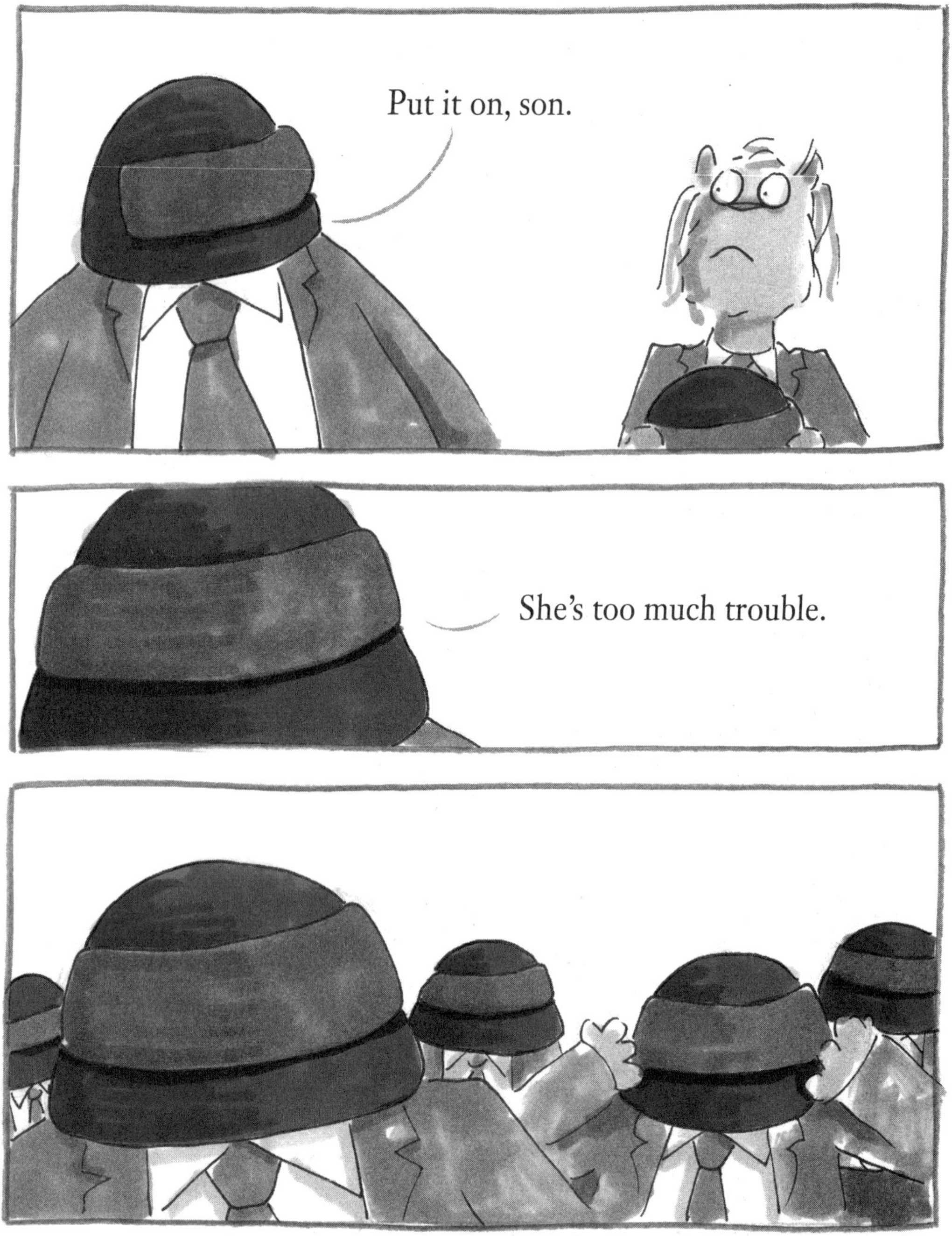
Put it on, son.
She's too much trouble.

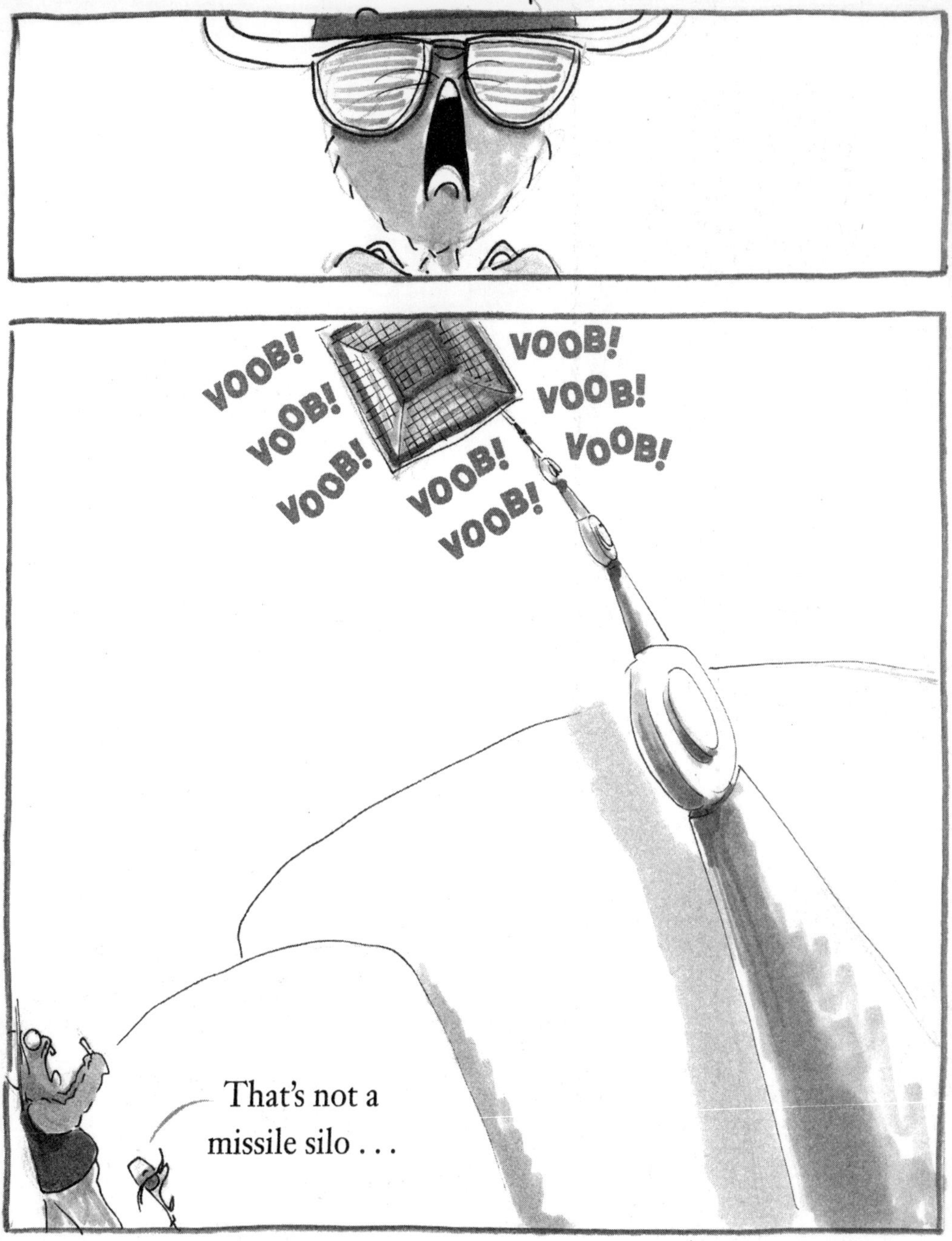
VOOB!
VOOB!
VOOB!
VOOB!
VOOB!
VOOB!
VOOB!
VOOB!
VOOB!
VOOB!
That's not a missile silo . . .

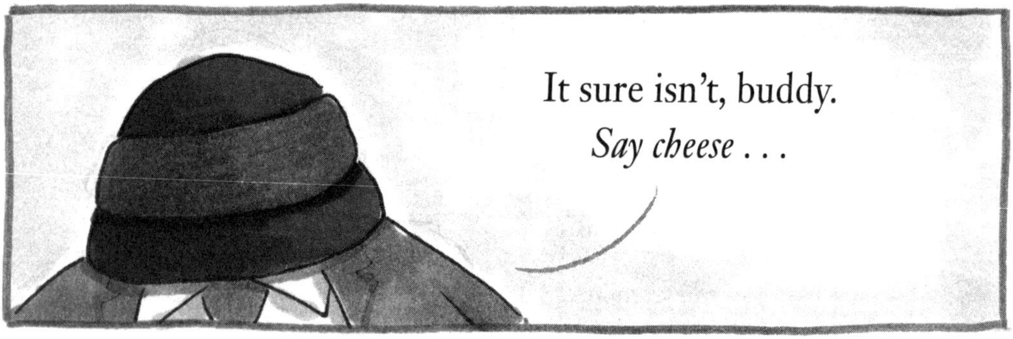
It sure isn't, buddy.
Say cheese . . .

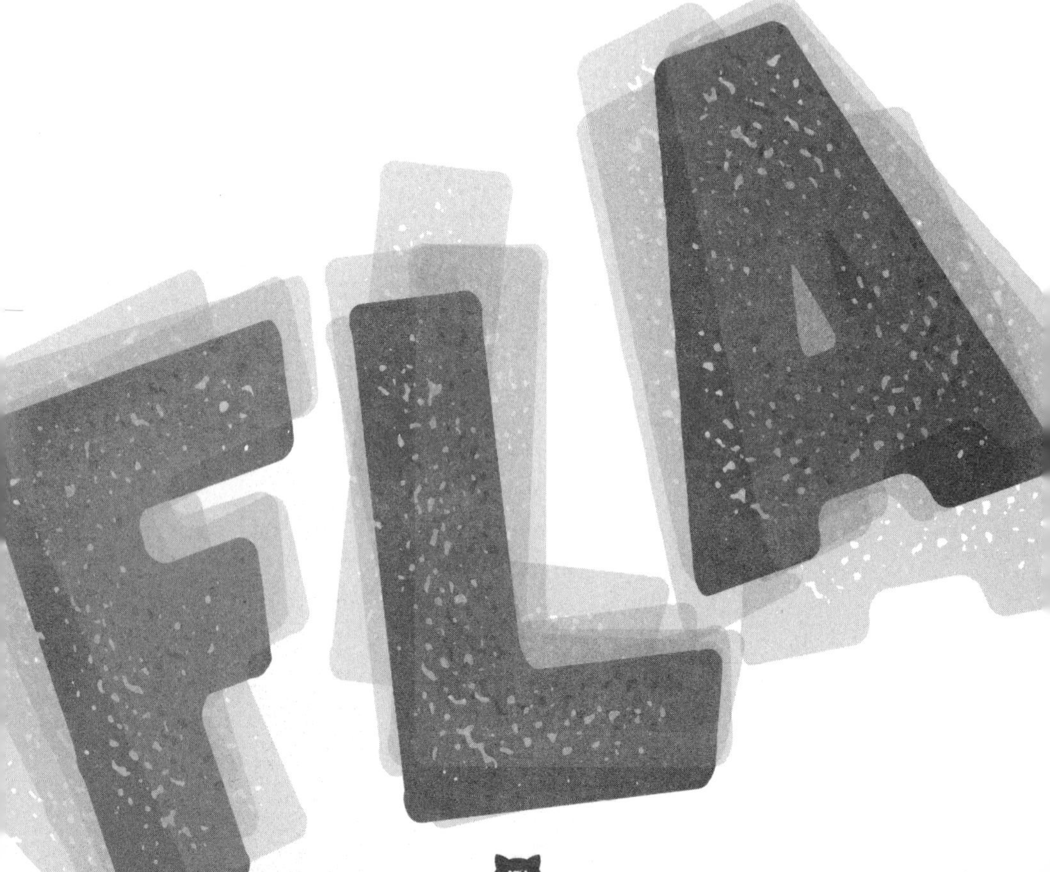
FLA

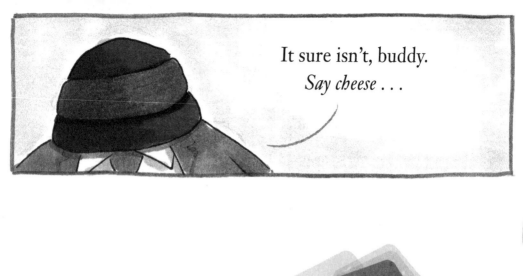

SH!

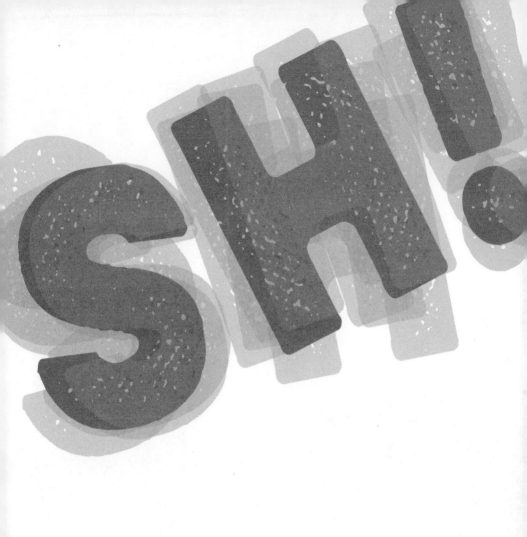

Nine

WHO OWNS THE INTERNET?

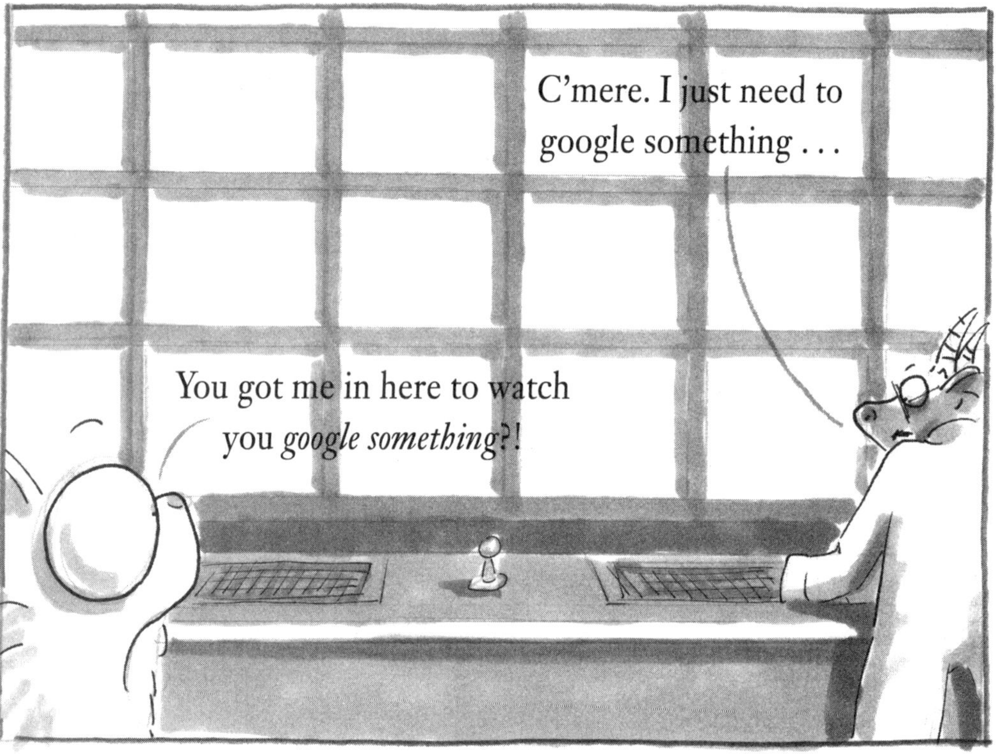
C'mere. I just need to google something . . .
You got me in here to watch you *google something*?!

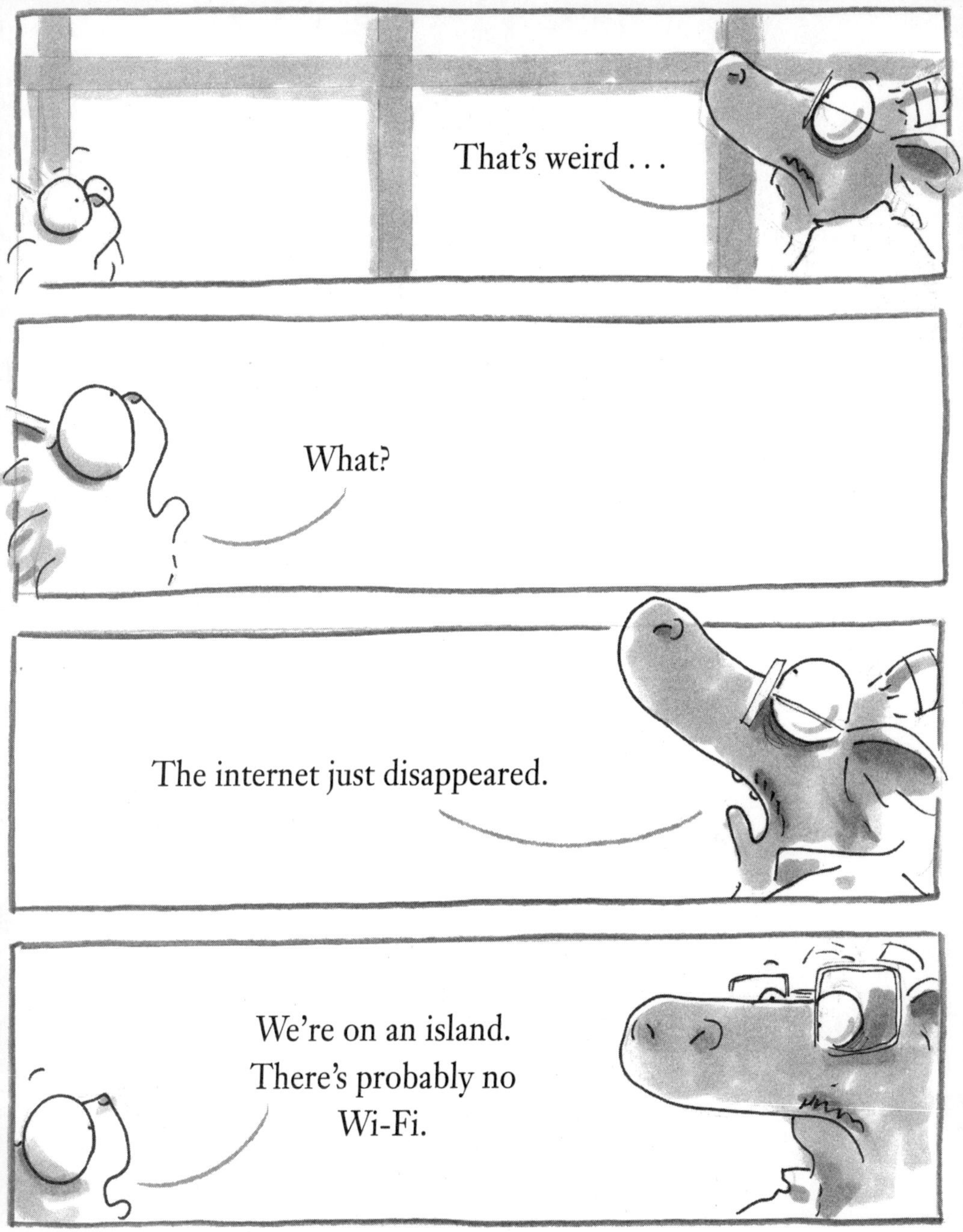
That's weird . . .
What?
The internet just disappeared.
We're on an island. There's probably no Wi-Fi.

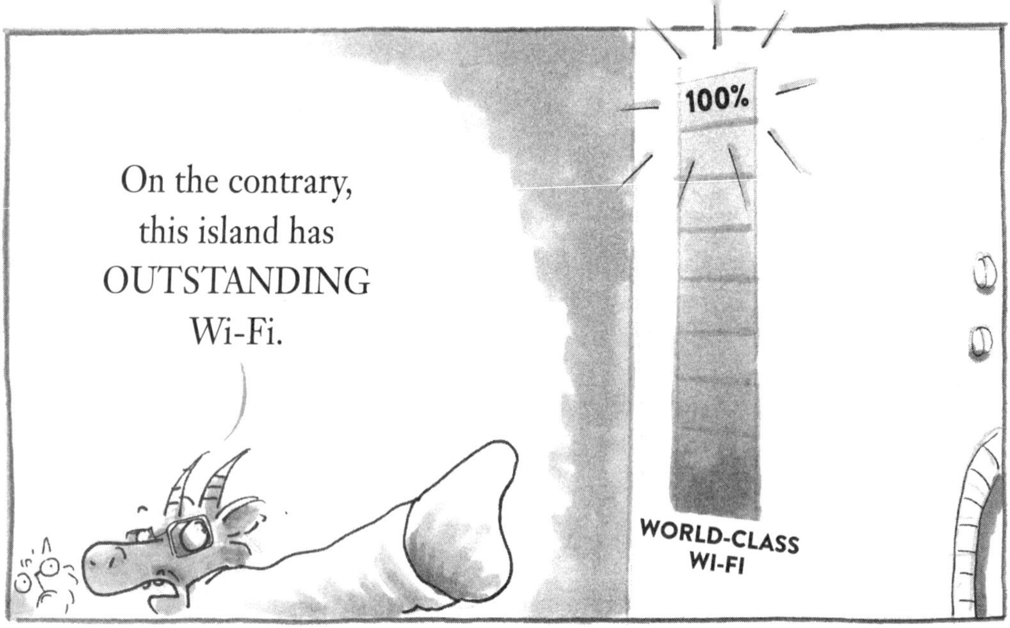
On the contrary, this island has OUTSTANDING Wi-Fi.
100%
WORLD-CLASS WI-FI

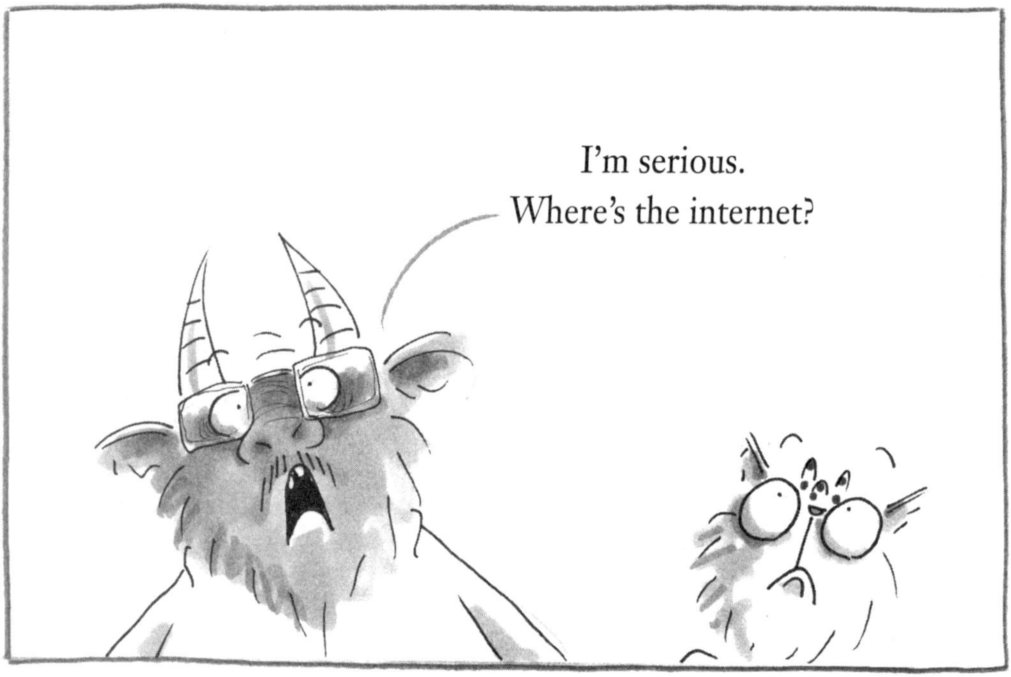
I'm serious. Where's the internet?

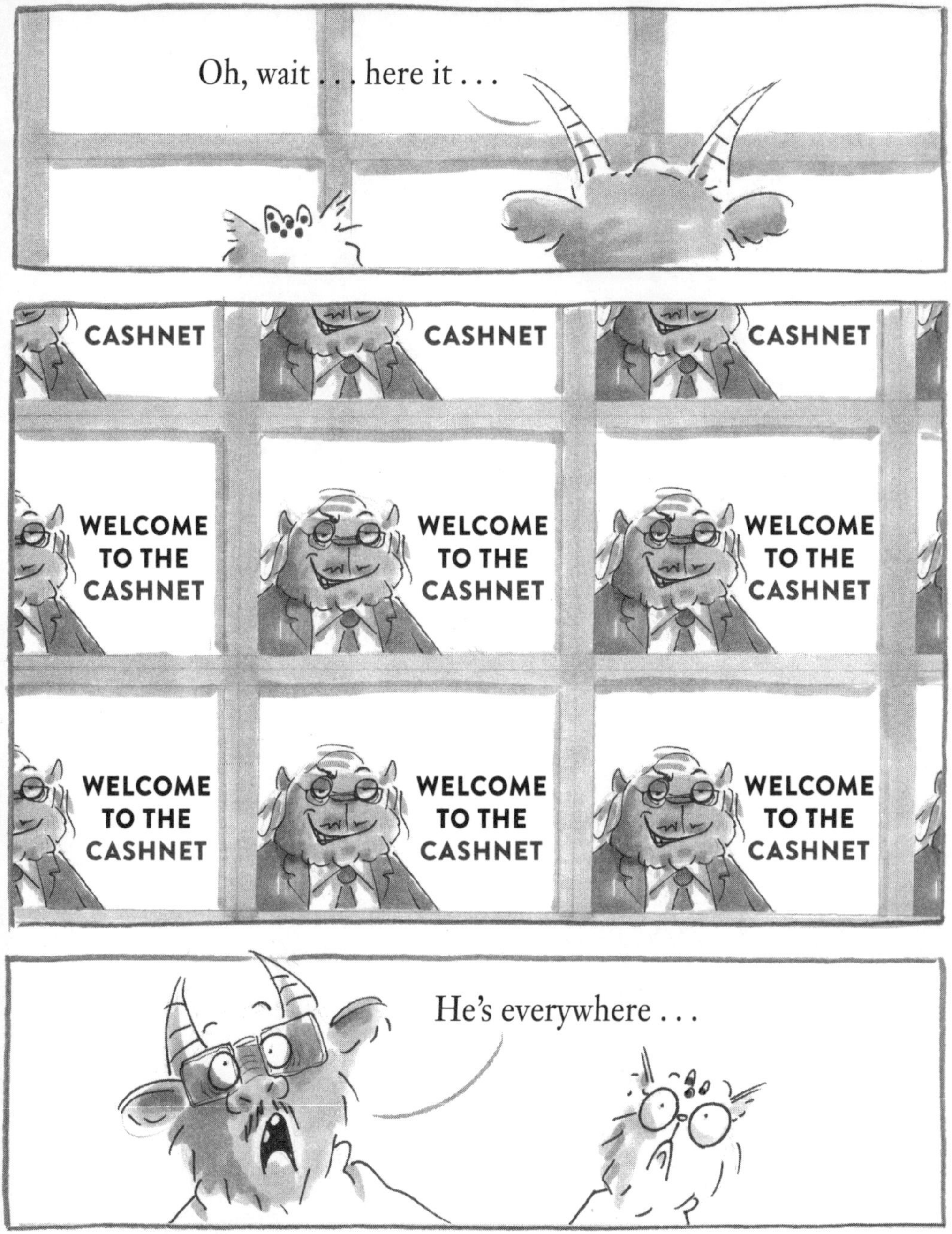
Oh, wait . . . here it . . .
CASHNET
CASHNET
CASHNET
WELCOME TO THE CASHNET
WELCOME TO THE CASHNET
WELCOME TO THE CASHNET
WELCOME TO THE CASHNET
WELCOME TO THE CASHNET
WELCOME TO THE CASHNET
He's everywhere . . .

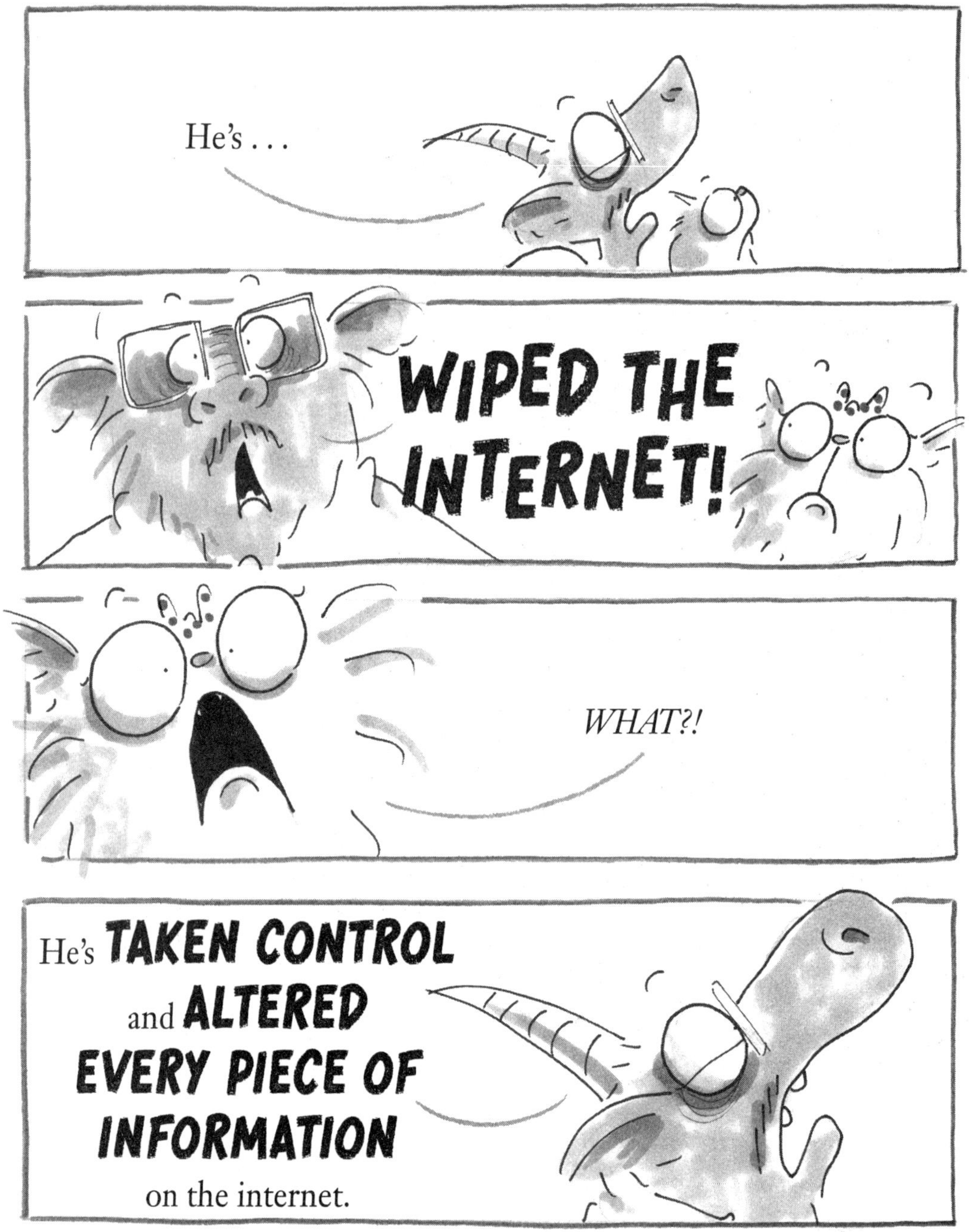

He's . . .
WIPED THE INTERNET!
WHAT?!
He's TAKEN CONTROL and ALTERED EVERY PIECE OF INFORMATION on the internet.

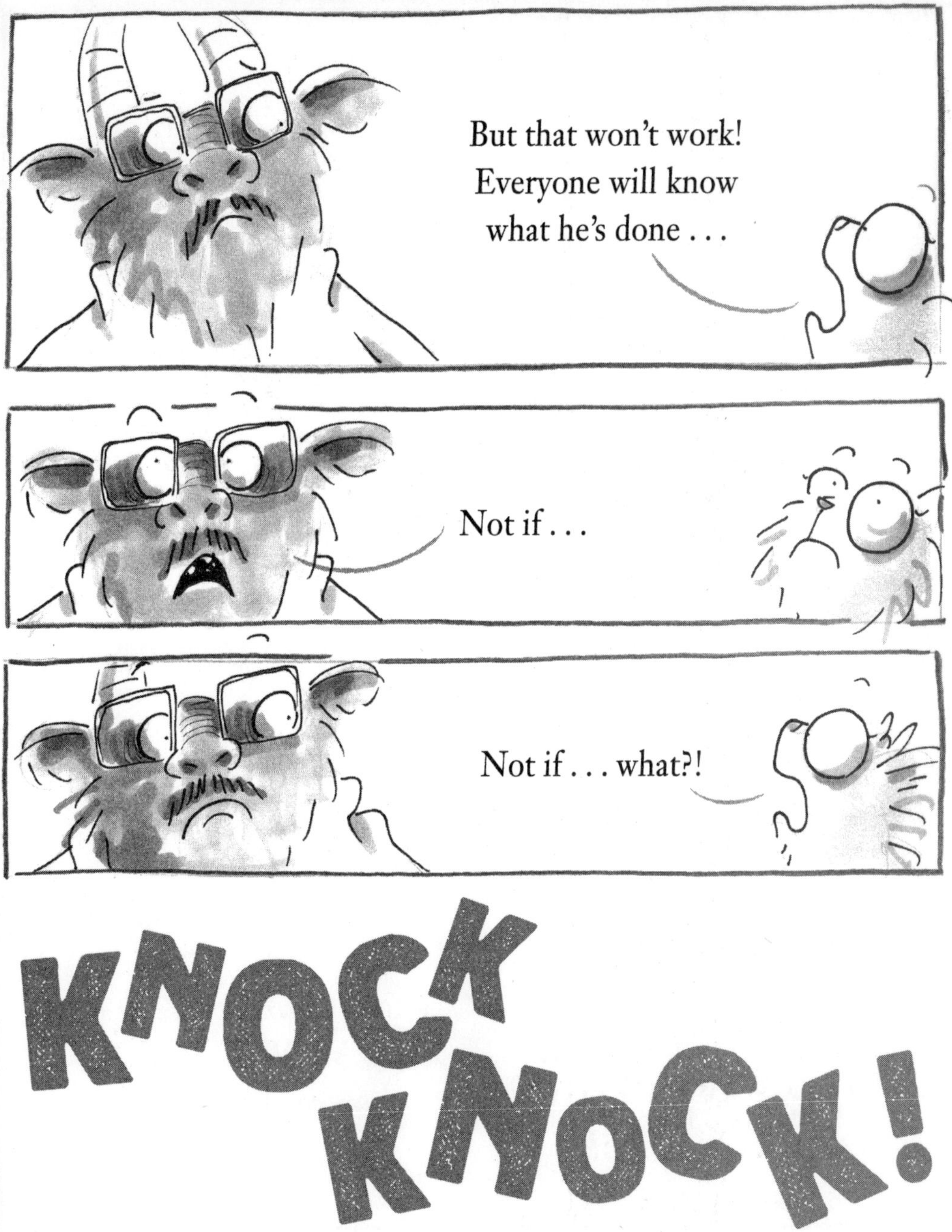
But that won't work! Everyone will know what he's done . . .
Not if . . .
Not if . . . what?!
KNOCK KNOCK!

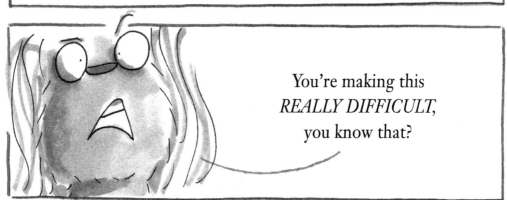

You're making this
REALLY DIFFICULT,
you know that?

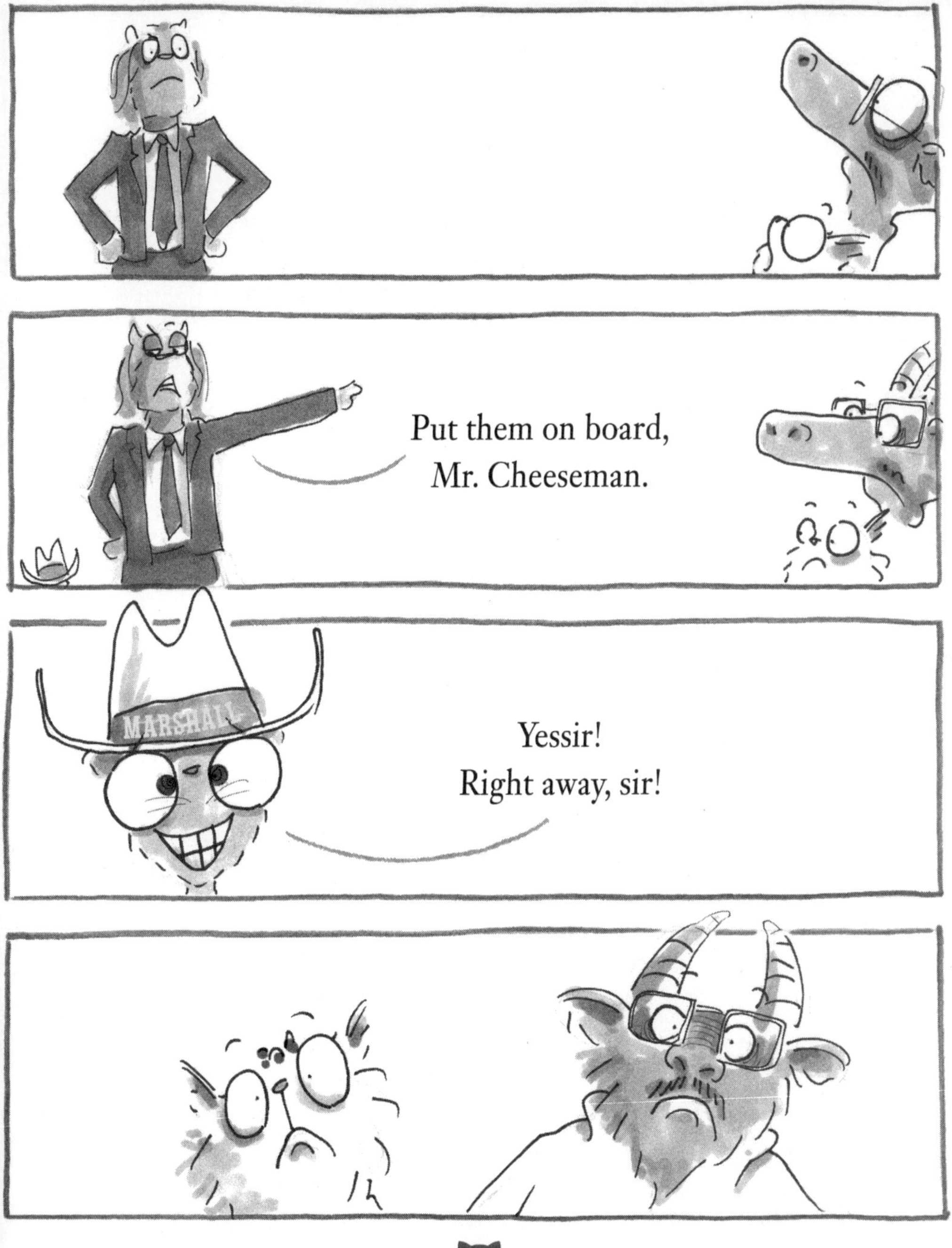
Put them on board, Mr. Cheeseman.
MARSHALL
Yessir! Right away, sir!

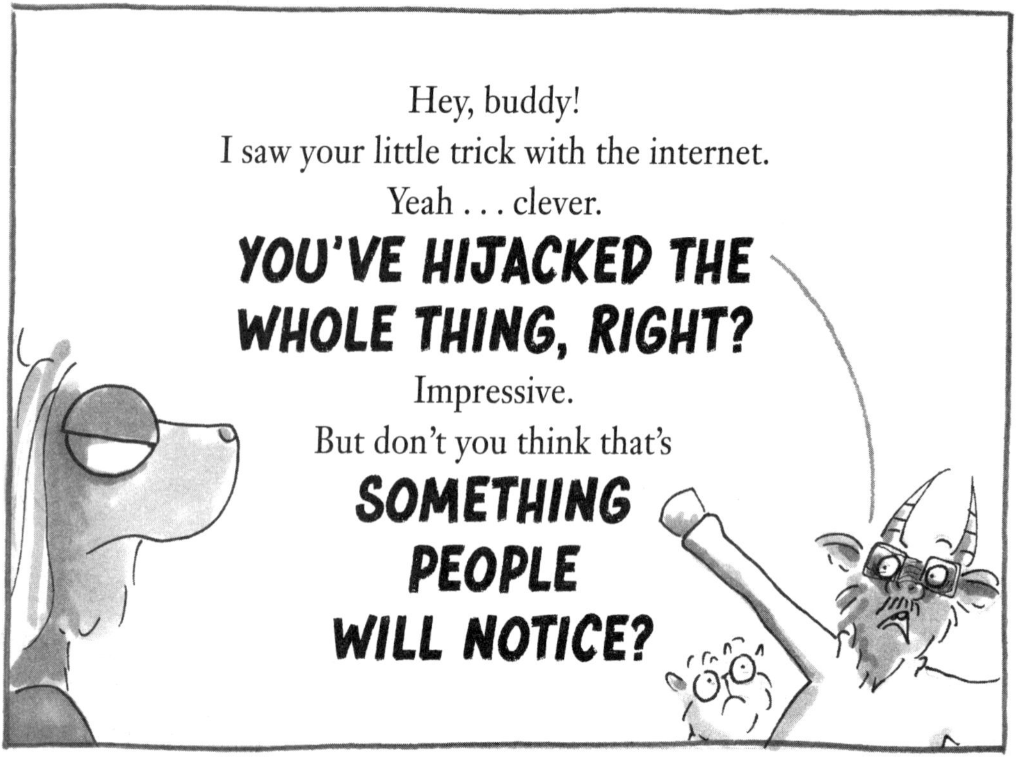
Hey, buddy!
I saw your little trick with the internet.
Yeah . . . clever.
YOU'VE HIJACKED THE WHOLE THING, RIGHT?
Impressive.
But don't you think that's SOMETHING PEOPLE WILL NOTICE?

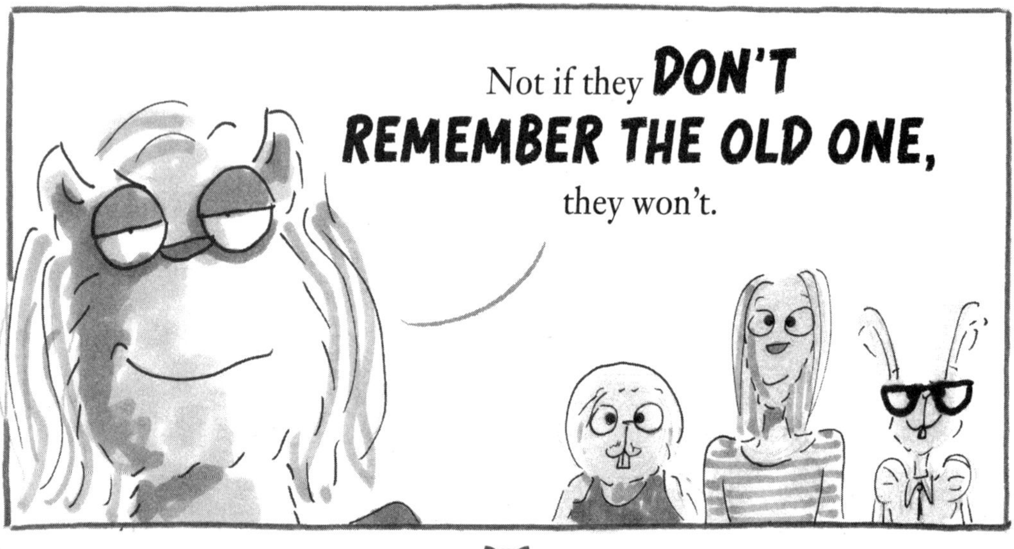
Not if they DON'T REMEMBER THE OLD ONE, they won't.

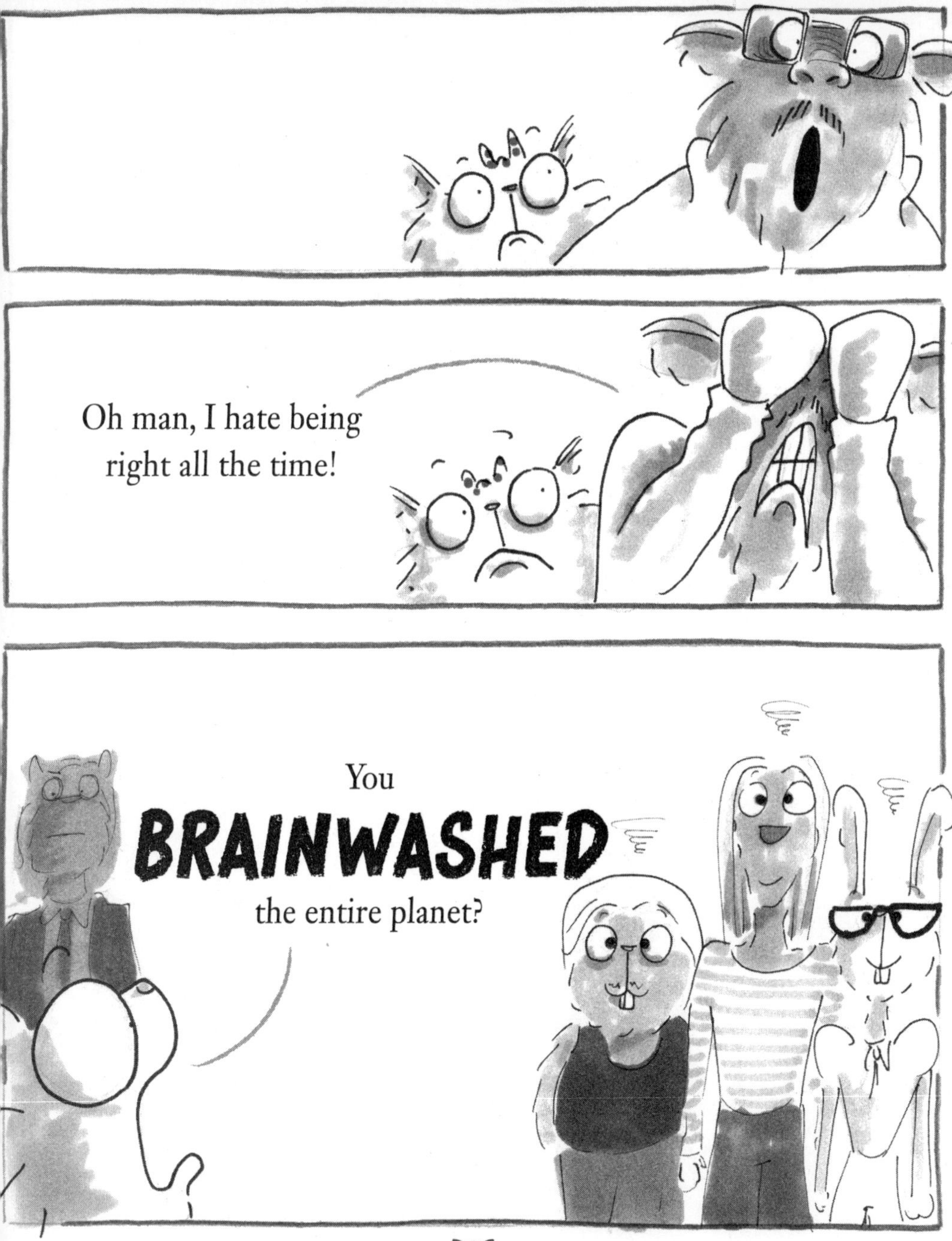
Oh man, I hate being right all the time!
You BRAINWASHED the entire planet?

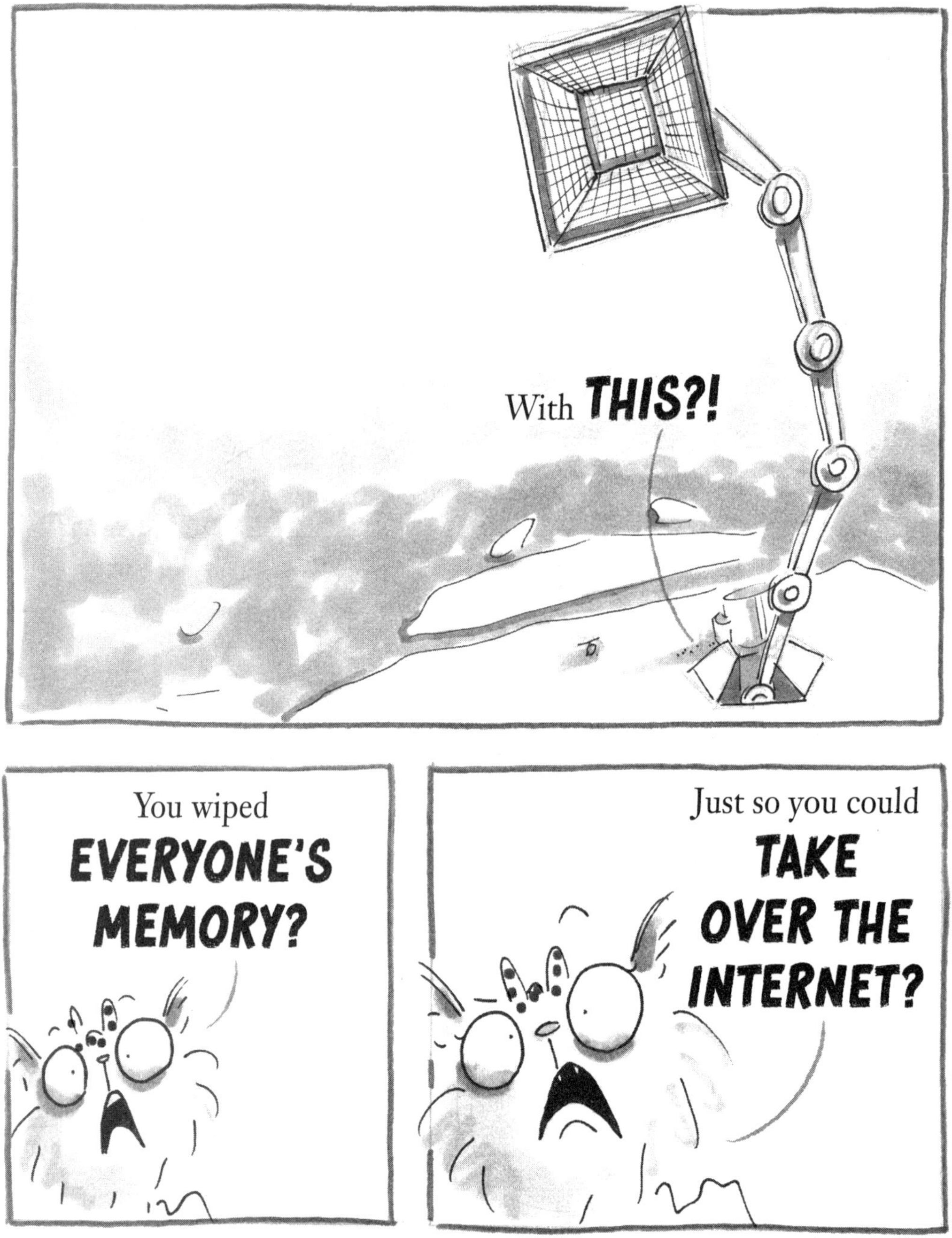
With THIS?!
You wiped EVERYONE'S MEMORY?
Just so you could TAKE OVER THE INTERNET?

Aw, there's more to it than that, darlin'.

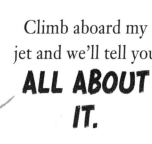 Climb aboard my jet and we'll tell you **ALL ABOUT IT.**

 I'm not going anywhere with you.

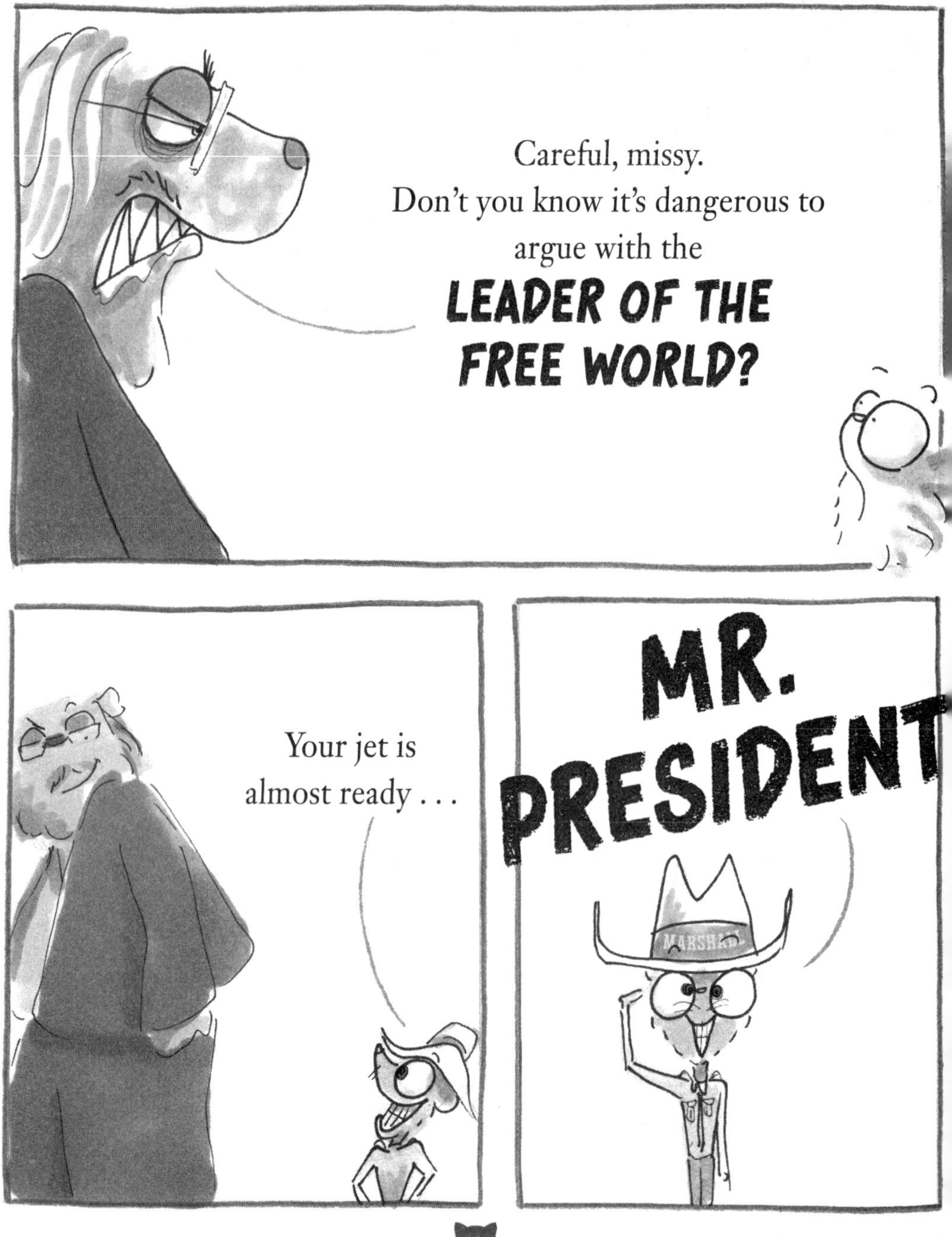
Careful, missy.
Don't you know it's dangerous to
argue with the
LEADER OF THE
FREE WORLD?
Your jet is
almost ready . . .
MR.
PRESIDENT
MARSHALL

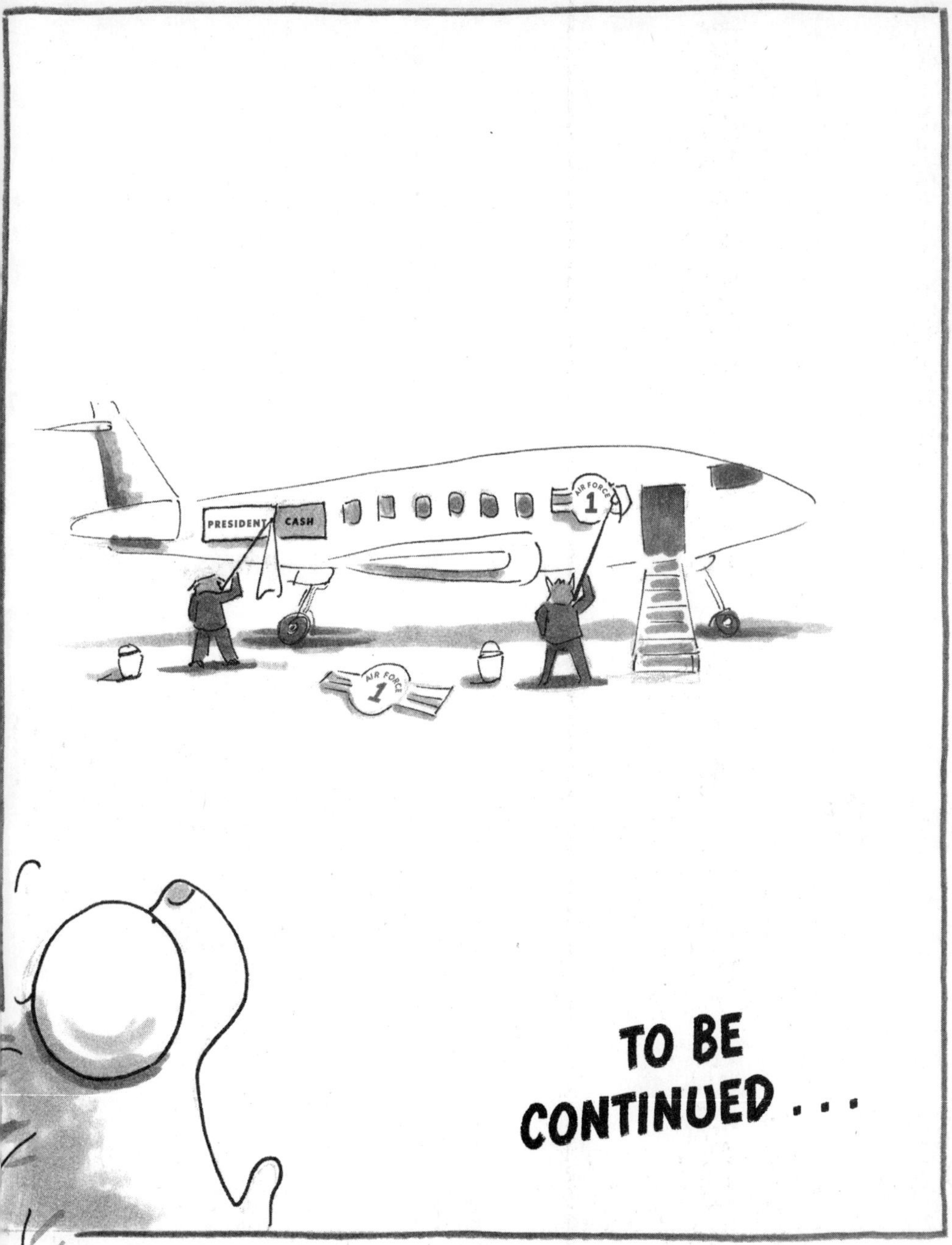
PRESIDENT
CASH
AIR FORCE 1
AIR FORCE 1
TO BE CONTINUED . . .

CAT on the RUN

BOOK #3

COMING SOON!